A SPY IN THE BLOOD

Paul Warner received a distinction for his Creative Writing MA at City, University of London. Long obsessed by espionage fiction, *A Spy in the Blood* is his debut spy thriller.

A SPY IN THE BLOOD

PAUL WARNER

ZAFFRE

First published in the UK in 2026 by
ZAFFRE
An imprint of Bonnier Books UK
5th Floor, HYLO, 105 Bunhill Row,
London, EC1Y 8LZ

Copyright © Paul Warner, 2026

All rights reserved.
No part of this publication may be reproduced,
stored or transmitted in any form or by any means, electronic,
mechanical, photocopying or otherwise, without the
prior written permission of the publisher.

The right of Paul Warner to be identified as Author of this
work has been asserted by him in accordance with the
Copyright, Designs and Patents Act, 1988.

This is a work of fiction. Names, places, events and
incidents are either the products of the author's
imagination or used fictitiously. Any resemblance to
actual persons, living or dead, or actual
events is purely coincidental.

A CIP catalogue record for this book is
available from the British Library.

Hardback ISBN: 978-1-78512-994-0
Trade paperback ISBN: 978-1-78512-996-4

Also available as an ebook and an audiobook

1 3 5 7 9 10 8 6 4 2

Typeset by IDSUK (Data Connection) Ltd
Printed and bound by CPI (UK) Ltd, Croydon CR0 4YY

The authorised representative in the EEA is
Bonnier Books UK (Ireland) Limited.
Registered office address: Block B, The Crescent Building
Northwood, Santry, Dublin 9
D09 C6X8, Ireland
compliance@bonnierbooks.ie
www.bonnierbooks.co.uk

*Dedicated to the memory of
Graham Stephen Warner*

*Skywatcher
Raconteur
Légion d'honneur*

Part One

London

1

A WELL-HONED SIXTH SENSE SPELLED OUT the danger, settled upon him like a faint key change in the night's atmosphere, and he jumped from his taxi as it ground to a standstill in the bleating traffic halfway across Vauxhall Bridge.

Mark Wolfe had always been a careful man.

Many wouldn't have noticed the over-guarded nature of his taxi driver, nor the steeled rear-view gaze that relayed the unmistakably battered aura of a spy, but this level of caution – some would say paranoia – had kept Mark alive on multiple occasions. Still, he might have buried his suspicion this time, even as the driver slid a furtive hand towards the glove compartment, had he not recalled his almost new BMW 5 Series refusing to start in the driveway that morning.

The taxi door slammed. It was a mild, early spring but he could still feel the Thames, as cold and melancholy as a foreign jail, and he strode through the swirling petrol fumes not caring how he'd just looked. He wasn't going to take any risks, and Pimlico station was close.

Mark crept his way towards the end of the bridge, streetlights alternatively stretching then shrinking his shadow beneath him, and shot a look back over his shoulder at the ziggurat-shaped SIS headquarters he'd just left, golden lights signposting its two central towers. The figure followed at a wary distance, his taxi orphaned in the left-hand lane, hazards flaring.

Instinct sped Mark through the tailback. A cyclist swerved to avoid him, and the second ring of its bell told Mark the taxi driver was mirroring this jaywalk.

To his right, steep steps led to the river walk and Mark almost threw himself down, but he'd celebrated more birthdays than the stranger following and didn't want to force a confrontation on a less populated, poorly lit path so turned onto Millbank at the traffic lights. The trees were budding and the Thames glittered in the lights cast from the south side as he stuck fast to the walls, habitually scanning the roads ahead, in case the man pursuing wasn't working alone.

Up ahead, silhouetted against churning waters, another figure rose from a bench.

With the rapid nonchalance of the professionally hunted, Mark strode across the street and up the stairs towards the classical portico housing Tate Britain's entrance foyer. He was surprised to find the wide lobby full of people queuing for the gallery's late-night Friday opening, and assumed the look of a man who owned the place, walking straight past the line and up to the main door. An attendant was about to berate him for breaking the queue when Mark flashed him a look layered with such superiority he could do nothing but nod and stand back, convinced to not do so would be more than his job was worth.

Mark clicked his way across the tiled floor, past signs for the Turner Collection, the Hockney exhibition, then barrelled on past the sculptures and down into an opening on the left, a smaller, darker room, the gold frames of the paintings serrated like postage stamps.

He waited behind a bronze ballerina of indeterminate quality, to get a good look at his shadow. The odds of a meaningful confrontation here, in a public place stuffed full of CCTV, were no lower than they would have been on Vauxhall Bridge, but he'd gained a foothold on the situation now he was the one – in a sense – controlling the hunt. Foreign powers had attempted to turn him before, kidnap him before, kill him before. But they hadn't succeeded yet.

He pretended to scrutinise the long-dead royals and Rubenesque nudes draped on chaises longues, while getting a good look at the art lovers around him. A few minutes passed, and still no sign of a follower. Several young couples entered, as London hip and well dressed as those visiting galleries ought to be, but no lone males.

Mark knew where he'd be.

If his pursuer had an ounce of espionage training, he'd station himself at the rear exit in a bid to second-guess his quarry. The question was: did Mark make his escape, or take the fight to his shadow?

Mark lifted a red rope and skipped through an empty room awaiting its rehang and hurried down a set of stairs. The rear Manton entrance, glass and steel against pale Victorian brick, was locked and dark, its cloakroom shuttered, gift shop abandoned for the night.

Footsteps on the stairs behind inspired his fingers to reach for a gun he hadn't carried in twenty-five years.

An alarmed-looking employee, reacting with concern to Mark's grim expression, told him, 'This part of the building's closed until tomorrow.' She looked fresh out of university, short hair matted across her forehead as though windblown, golden stud in her left nostril like an infected blackhead.

'I wonder if you might point me to a fire exit,' Mark said. 'I'm sorry, but I can't face all those crowds up there, not when I'm having one of my attacks.'

The girl stared at him, seemed to note the sweat on his face, then nodded in similar compliance to the attendant who'd let Mark through the entrance upstairs.

They crossed the Manton foyer as light sensors blinked on the bulbs above them, and through the studios normally out of bounds to the public. The walkie-talkie crackled at the employee's hip. She swept it up to her mouth. 'One minute,' she sighed. 'John Islip exit.' She turned to Mark. 'They're wondering where I am.' Her entire demeanour was apologetic, invisible.

The employee showed him into a small staff area, full of files, coats, a box of glossy pamphlets, then spent some time fiddling with the far door. Finally, it opened onto the road behind the gallery, Millbank Gardens lurking behind its canopy of gnarled trees and shrubs.

The taxi driver's outline was waiting for him, Glock pistol held casually at its side. From behind, Mark heard the young woman click the cylinder of a revolver into place.

'Nicely done,' Mark admitted, pinned between the two of them.

The taxi driver slipped through the doorway and closed it behind him. His eyes were as guarded and frosty as they'd been in the rear-view mirror, completely without triumph or hostility. A man obliged to carry out a job. He was, like the fake gallery steward, younger than Mark would have thought possible, his clothes black and well-fitting, revealing a gym-built musculature beneath. His hair was half an inch on both head and beard, reminding Mark of the flocked Action Man figures from his youth.

'What do you want?' Mark snapped. 'I'm not in the game anymore. Any secrets I have are older than you both.'

Mark took in the room. Coffee mugs were his only potential weapons and both doors were now shut. There was no window.

'We're not after secrets. We want you.'

'You won't get much ransom for a civil servant.'

'No one wants to kidnap you, Mr Wolfe. And you're *much more* than a civil servant.'

'If you say so.'

The taxi driver leaned against the wall, lowered his weapon. The young woman behind held her gun firm, all trace of her mousy deportment faded alongside Mark's freedom.

'We need you back in the game,' Action Man said.

Mark sighed in frustration. 'Why not just send an email? What's with the fake pick-up and funnelling me through this damn gallery? Was the thrill of the hunt supposed to make me nostalgic for my days in the field or something? The answer's *no*. I've told the Chief half a dozen times already, and the Foreign Secretary twice.'

'We're not MI6.'

Mark looked from one pale face to the other, the two pairs of eyes steady, sharp and emotionless.

'Who are you?'

The man gave the briefest of shrugs. 'You could say we're an independent problem solution service. And we pay a lot more than Her Majesty.'

'And you thought chasing me across the Thames and pointing guns in my face would persuade me to join your outfit?'

'The guns weren't intended to sell our ambitions to you. They were more for our protection.'

Mark showed no emotion as the second revolver was lowered. 'I'm flattered, but not interested.'

He was familiar with such groups, of course. Private military and security companies who provided significant 'operational support' to Britain's military overseas, in the killing zones of

Somalia or Iraq, Afghanistan or Yemen. The British government had been known to use such mercenaries in their fight against jihadi terrorism, to the tune of fifty million pounds each year. Despite its scale, the entire sector was shrouded in secrecy, demanding men trained in the dark arts of subterfuge and counterintelligence, men paid to watch from the shadows.

'Our organisation can make it worth your while.' It was the woman who spoke.

'I'm sure it can, but I don't work for the money, I never have. You've come to the wrong man.'

It had been a while since some group or other had tried this, but it wasn't a surprise they'd found him; nothing's watertight, and all information has its price.

'We could do with a man of your experience. Don't pretend you're not tempted, Mr Wolfe.' The woman again. 'You spend all day working at Vauxhall Cross for a pittance. We know your real value. *You* know your real value.'

Mark shook his head. 'It's still a no.' But she was right about him being curious. He considered himself past it, knew the world had moved on, but when strangers accosted him after work and offered him employment at the end of a gun he had questions.

'What's the name of your organisation?'

Action Man opened the door. The young woman joined him. Together, they stepped out into the night.

'At the risk of sounding wounded,' the man stated, 'you don't get to spurn us and then turn interviewer. But, if you're lucky, you'll hear from us again.'

The pair vanished.

He exited East Finchley station and marched the three streets to his house, senses on red alert. He counted one man sitting in a van, scrolling through his phone. Another on the corner, walking a pit bull. Usually, these strangers wouldn't have caused him to think twice, but tonight his own footsteps were laced, as it were, with menace.

There was an unfamiliar car in his drive, blocking in his BMW, and another in the resident parking space adjacent to their house that was usually empty at this time. A chill ran through Mark as a vague memory resurfaced.

His wife was hosting a dinner party.

He looked over his own car. Whoever tried to recruit him earlier had gone to elaborate lengths to bend his ear, putting his vehicle out of commission this morning by removing a seemingly insignificant fuse or using a remote technology too sophisticated for him to detect. No doubt he'd check the surveillance footage outside his house later to find nothing untoward. He tried his key in the ignition. Sure enough, it started normally.

Inside his home, two ten-year-old boys he didn't recognise were sitting in the hallway violating his Wi-Fi. He closed the door quietly behind him – a habit – and listened out for familiar voices. His wife, Alessia, was talking in English, so it was work colleagues she was entertaining, and the two scoundrels in the hall would be their sons. The colleagues were therefore younger than Alessia and himself by at least a decade and, if the volume of their voices was anything to go by, drunk already.

'Hello, Dad.'

He spun around to see a young woman standing at the bottom of the stairs. She was growing her hair out again, the length almost allowing for the reformation of her natural curls, and her skin, inherited wholesale from her Italian mother, had darkened to an enviable teak after several semesters spent in the Middle East and South Asia. She looked healthy and exercised, radiant with youth.

'Jody!' With all that had happened, he'd completely forgotten she was back for Easter.

She glided forwards and pecked him a chaste kiss on the cheek. She wasn't wearing make-up or perfume, never had, but her hair was still damp from a recent shower. 'Looks like Mum's throwing a party in my honour.'

This much was doubtless true. Alessia always liked to show off how functional they were in Jody's absence.

'You're late, *caro*,' Alessia cried good-naturedly at her husband, coming out of the kitchen followed by two younger women Mark didn't recognise. She kissed him on the cheek too. It was all part of her show; she seldom kissed him nowadays. 'Dinner's almost ready. You're just in time to set the table.'

Mark, still trying to dismiss the two handguns pointed at him less than an hour ago, did as he was bid.

'Mum says you're a spy,' the elder of the two boys stated.

One of the women, already flushed from the wine, waved her son into silence with flustering fingers.

'Dylan, I said nothing of the sort!' She turned to Mark. 'I'm sorry. I said you work in that Vauxhall building, you know. Dylan has a very active—'

'Do you have an exploding phone?' The boy's eyes were as wide as quails' eggs, though there was more than a trace of sarcasm in his tone. 'Does your pen squirt acid?'

These sorts of questions were an occasional occupational hazard. Mark's family and friends knew he worked at SIS headquarters, but little more than that. His nature was affable, friendly, sincere. He was the model civil servant, a man who seldom brought his stress home, despite being away for long periods of time, holed up in what they believed to be a murky office pod tapping meaningless numbers into spreadsheets with stiff index fingers.

Mark lowered his fork and looked the boy dead in the eye. 'I'll poison your carrots if you ask any more questions.'

Everyone except the boy laughed at the notion of this man with grey hair, a man who struggled to find the right TV remote buttons to pre-record *Question Time*, having anything to do with dead-dropping intel beneath clocks in train stations dressed as a rain-jacketed anachronism. Mark was good at assuaging suspicion, knew from experience that hiding in plain sight was the best cover. The mother cuffed her son round the head and pointed at the plate before him, but he didn't touch those carrots.

To change the subject, she told Jody, 'You're looking well.'

Jody nodded in thanks, unsure how she ought to respond to this anodyne remark.

It was an accurate observation though, and Mark had thought much the same thing. Jody had finally passed through her awkward early university years, when she'd returned home between semesters having lost what seemed an unhealthy amount of weight or experimented with her hair so much it was as if she'd determined to resemble somebody else. The close crop had upset her mother enough, but the red dye had nearly sent her over the edge. At one point Jody had taken to wearing poorly fitting gilets, headbands, and had stopped shaving her armpits, but she seemed to have swung back towards what her mother certainly considered traditional Western womanhood these days.

'We're very proud of her,' Alessia said. 'Three languages she speaks now.'

Jody smiled discreetly but it might as well have been an eyeroll. 'Five.'

'What's Oxford like?' the other colleague asked.

Jody made pleasant small talk about her course without saying anything, upholding the dinner party tradition, while her slowly inebriating interviewers nodded and eyed her with, unless Mark was mistaken, palpable envy.

'What made you study Arabic?' the first mother asked.

Had Mark even been introduced to these women? Though he could just about differentiate between Alessia's two colleagues physically – this one was forty and dressed as though she believed she were twenty years younger; the other was roughly the same age but wore the clothes of a devout Mormon – their personalities were impossible to tell apart.

'It's a beautiful language,' Jody said. 'I'm also learning the Persian—'

'She does really well in her tests,' Alessia interrupted. 'The second year of her course was spent in the Middle East and Asia. First in Abu Dhabi and then in ... Islamabad, wasn't it? A postcard would occasionally float back from her, when she remembered.'

'I did try to FaceTime you, but you could never turn the camera on, Mum.'

'But why Arabic?' the age-denying guest pressed. 'Wouldn't Mandarin be the better language for business these days?'

'Arabic's the fifth most commonly spoken language in the world,' Jody recited in a voice which gave away she'd had to justify her university choice more than once in the past. 'Middle Eastern contributions to global civilisation are huge and the natural resources available make job positions extremely sought after. If you speak the lingo and understand the culture, you stand head and shoulders above most.'

'An ambitious young woman,' the same, younger-dressed colleague patronised, angling the wine bottle towards Jody.

Jody's palm was lightning-fast over her empty glass. 'It's *haram*,' she joked.

'And any young, wealthy sheikhs on the horizon?' the other mother asked, pulling at her blouse cuff.

Though Jody remained silent in the five languages she knew, Mark understood human psychology well enough to read abject mortification in the faint flush at her neck.

The door slammed its rifle discharge.

Brandon breezed in, all six bastard handsome feet of him, and panthered towards the empty space he'd known would be there; with a flick of dark hair, Jody's little brother had arrived to steal everyone's attention.

Mark checked his watch. It was too early for Brandon to be home on a Friday night. This was a quick free lunch before he raced back out again. At the very least, his son would provide some controversy.

'Ladies,' Brandon said, 'and *gentlemen*.' He nodded at the two boys. 'I hope you've left me some wine.'

The boys giggled, already fans.

'You seen what Donald Trump's gone and sodding done now?' Brandon asked.

There followed a critical assessment of Trump's first hundred days in office, the travel ban, border wall plans and rolling back of Obama's gun control legislation. North Korea had just fired medium range ballistics into its eastern waters, in the direction of Japan, and Trump was baiting Kim Jong Un on Twitter. 'It's pathetic,' Brandon said between mouthfuls. Everyone nodded grimly. Politics was at the table. Ten minutes later, they all agreed leaving the EU was a stupid idea, except for one of the mums, who believed the NHS was going to benefit because it had said so on the side of a bus.

Brandon held court between mouthfuls. 'The world's at a nationalistic crisis point. Trump and Brexit are the manifestation of a new right-wing agenda. The West will be seen as racist, divided and weak. Trust me. Over the next few years we'll see all sorts of attacks on democracy, from within *and* without. There's something nasty in the air.'

His son spoke pragmatically about these issues. He was right – the fact that a private security company had chased him through the Tate two hours ago proved Brandon wasn't the only one concerned – but Mark didn't *like* the fact he was right. He remembered his own political awakening, at roughly Brandon's age, towards the end of *détente* and a refreezing of the Cold War. One moment the newspapers had seemed peaceable, if not boring: the Camp David Accords, diplomatic relations with China and nuclear rollbacks. And then, suddenly, it was all Soviets in Afghanistan, Iraq hostages and umbrella poisonings. Like his father before him, Brandon had become aware of the real world, and its surplus of news dismayed him.

'By the end of this decade, the deserts of the Middle East will be soaked with the blood of thousands of decapitated Western softies in orange boiler suits. Enjoy your humanitarian holidays in Syria, sister.'

'Brandon!' Alessia screamed.

His jibe landed, Brandon took a backseat to nebulous conversations about the weather and Alessia's plans to retire from her senior management position at the close of the following school year. Mark zoned out too – dinner parties were one long filibuster before bed at the best of times – and observed the boy who'd been asking him about spycraft attempting to watch a YouTube video on his mobile under the table, similarly bored.

In time, his mother noticed. 'Dylan. Not at the table!'

Mark stage-whispered, 'Hey, kid. Want me to take her out?' as he ran a suggestive finger across his throat.

The boy stared at Mark in horror before somehow finding the strength to shake his head.

Later, stood at his bedroom window, Mark tried to banish the unwanted images of the kind of Islamist executions his son had been describing with such disturbing relish; it was always his daughter's head he saw tumbling from blood-soaked shoulders.

But Brandon was right. There was something 'nasty' in the air. There always was.

His wife was asleep, full of wine and gnocchi, and her snoring was like the gentle sawing of lumber. He soundlessly crossed the room, turned out the light on her bedside table and returned to the window.

If you're lucky, you'll hear from us again.

Almost immediately, a figure peeled from behind a tree opposite their home, became a mere shadow against further shadows and then disappeared. A drunk. A late-night walker who'd stopped to relieve himself. A spectral figment of his own febrile imagination.

Mark checked his cricket bat was still beneath the bed, then pulled back the sheets.

2

'COULD YOU KILL AN UNARMED MAN?'

The interviewee locked eyes with MI6's Head of Recruitment and Asset Validation and set his expression to 'sincere'. His voice was cold, hungry. 'If my orders were to do so.'

Mark nodded noncommittally and slashed a pen mark through a box. The candidate was young, male and yet another Etonian.

He didn't *dislike* Etonians as such, but believing them an entitled bunch was hardly, he thought, a controversial take. His wariness of them was hard to explain, and hypocritical, considering he was paying a fortune for his own daughter to take part in the educational apartheid system. Clearly it was just his working-class roots showing, his own sense of inferiority colouring his feelings, because he outranked a fair few of the overprivileged old boys now. He found their breezy disconnect from reality hard to swallow at times; if a person's been promised superiority, then rewarded with it, of course they start to believe they deserve it. It was an attitude which made public schoolboys hard to trust. And therefore, perfect spies.

He peeled his way through the questions he knew so well, reciting from memory. He could predict the answers too. The young man opposite was, on paper, ideal, but it was Mark's job to find out why he wasn't. Like water ingress, he knew how to prise his way inside the most improbable chinks and track his way to the ruined plasterwork at the heart of man. The candidate had already passed several aptitude tests to get this far; however, the answers given now would go a long way towards identifying the mettle of this potential intelligence officer.

Mark stifled a yawn. University holidays were always busy times for MI6 applications, as starry-eyed students filed out into the big bad world to chase the lie of movie star glamour. It was the Thursday before Easter, a long weekend ahead. Outside the reinforced window, the sun was already below Battersea in the south-west.

'I wonder if you might go into a little detail,' Mark said, 'about how you'd deal with the pressures on your family life, should you be successful.' There was a lot of value placed on the answer to this one, but the candidate had done his homework and responded with textbook precision, selling his own attributes and revealing an intricate knowledge of the Secret Service's expectations.

Mark found himself nodding, almost against his better judgement. This kid smelt like a career politician, but he knew his stuff, his cute answers placed almost by algorithm. Whether his candidate wanted the world to be a better place, or simply needed to run from himself, wouldn't be a mystery for much longer.

Mark landed his final, killer question.

'Would you lay down your life for this country?'

The briefest of pauses from the unlined mouth, a stutter within clear blue eyes. 'It would ... depend upon what I ... Yes. *Absolutely.*'

Mark saw the candidate out of the meeting room.

He barely remembered his own recruitment, all those decades ago at Lambeth's Century House. Many in the Service had been doubtful about him at first – the Etonians, upon reflection – but that all changed fast. He'd proved himself, and then some. One thing he did remember was being asked if he'd die for his queen, and his response had been an instant, 'No.' It wasn't allegiance to a cause that earned you respect, it was the lack of hesitation, and that pause before the candidate's response had shown he was trying to give the answers Mark wanted to hear, not the answers his heart truly believed.

Mark Wolfe returned to his green leather-topped office desk, bought guiltlessly with taxpayers' money back in the day, and entered his interview feedback on the system. The decor in most of SIS headquarters was from its opening in the mid-nineties and, despite the non-offensive plainness and minimalism, its beige wood panelling looked dated now. Before he left, he swung past Jim's office to thank him for his week's efforts.

'Surprised you're still here, Jim.'

Jim Timbrell sleighted a file clumsily beneath a manila envelope. 'Oh. Yes, sir. I'll be here Saturday too, at this rate.'

Jim was twenty years younger than Mark but anyone would have guessed thirty. He was one of those pretty, tall career men that every vocation throws into positions of authority sooner rather than later and Mark had no doubt he'd make a sideways move shortly, given Mark wasn't planning on going anywhere. He appeared to be wearing his necktie in a Windsor knot instead of his favoured four-in-hand and Mark wondered if this was significant, his way of seniorising or readying himself for promotion.

'How was the interview?' Jim asked, palms resting protectively on his papers.

The older man shrugged. 'I doubt he'd deal with the burden, but he said the right things.'

'Putting him through to the next round?' Jim spoke as though it was a gameshow.

'Probably. Don't stay too late, will you? And don't even think about coming in on Saturday. I'll see you on Tuesday.'

The night was a degree milder than last week, and Mark elected to take a quick walk around the block, to enjoy the feel of walking streets he'd helped protect. Several times he checked for a tail but found nothing. Did he want them to try and accost him again? He was ashamed to admit he'd found the break from his daily routine exciting, though he recognised that taste of his old life had been far from accidentally deployed. Giving an addict a free sample was a common, though contemptible, business model.

But Mark had meant it when he'd said he wasn't interested in their offer. Even twenty years ago, he'd been past it. Now, he'd be nothing but a danger to himself, his once razor-sharp claws blunted by domesticity, an office job bookended by a tedious commute, a thousand Sundays spent trawling garden centres. There was a chance, a strong one, that they didn't really represent a private security company at all, but it made little difference to him. Mark Wolfe had spent a lifetime looking over his shoulder.

He arrived at the front of MI6's winged pyramid just in time to observe the lights dim in Jim's office and flare on in the meeting room.

He calculated the probability of Jim having an affair with somebody in the workplace and decided the odds were depressingly high.

The moment he found his wife at the stove, relaxed and humming in school holiday mode, that fleeting desire for excitement in the streets outside SIS headquarters turned to shame. Their little family was back together, briefly.

'Where are the kids?'

'Brandon's out. Jody's asleep.'

'Is she OK?'

'She wasn't feeling too well. I expect she's exhausted. She works too hard.'

The pair of them elected to eat in front of the television. The news was dominated by the bombing of Afghanistan. The United States had dropped the largest non-nuclear weapon in its arsenal, nicknamed the Mother of All Bombs, on the Nangarhar province in an attempt to destroy tunnel complexes used by Islamic State fighters. Donald Trump, in his overly long and phallic red necktie, was praising the US military, while Hamid Karzai, the former president of Afghanistan, was already accusing the States of using his country as a testing ground for 'inhuman' new weapons. The number of dead was still unknown, but what the reporting lacked in solid human casualties it made up for with war porn imagery of Lockheed bombers and long-range footage of smoke pouring from wounded mountains.

'This will set Brandon off,' Mark said.

'Probably.' Despite her family's appetite for arguing affairs of state at the dinner table, Alessia was stubbornly apolitical. When she voted, she took Mark's counsel and, before they met, she'd voted habitually, opting for the party she'd voted for the time before, a partisanship that was, Mark suspected, an aspect of an innate loyalty that beat at the centre of her, rather than laziness. In contrast, Mark always marched to the booth and voted for whichever backstabbers weren't currently in power, having seen first-hand how a government would come in and sweep everything to one side, gleefully breaking their election pledges. It was a knee-jerk political response that, in many ways, owed more to punk rock than common sense.

The slamming door heralded Brandon's return.

'Ask him where he goes,' Alessia whispered. 'He's out more than usual these days.'

Mark traced the noise of a nineteen year old wrestling with cutlery into the kitchen and was surprised to find his son in jacket and tie.

'Didn't know you owned a suit. You had an interview?'

Brandon carried his plate of fridge remains to the kitchen table. His brief, shocked glance told his father a lie was imminent. 'Er. Yeah.'

'Your mother will be pleased. What was it for?'

'Um. Computers.' A lame answer, but Mark didn't fight it. No doubt he'd been trying out a new look at the Bald-Faced Stag, affecting the pretence of success in order to get a date.

Alessia swung into the kitchen and asked Brandon for his reaction to the bombing, because she liked nothing better than to fan fires and stand back to admire the inferno.

Brandon's anti-Trump rant lasted until Jody appeared at the doorway.

'Feeling better?' Alessia asked.

'I've got it off my chest now,' Brandon replied.

'I was talking to your sister.'

Jody floated to the fridge and decanted herself a glass of orange juice. 'I think so.' Her brother threw his plates in the sink, blasted them with water, then left them for someone else to deal with.

'Lazy git,' Jody said.

'Feminazi.'

The pair disappeared to their respective rooms.

Mark and Alessia were left observing the weighty absence of their children.

Alessia didn't say anything, didn't need to. They'd had their fair share of 'Are we terrible parents?' conversations over the years and the silent, clairvoyant one that now ghosted between them followed familiar lines. Alessia was disappointed by how distant Jody was these days, but not as disappointed as she was in herself for believing it would be different this Easter. For that first welcome-home meal, Jody had made a token effort, but had quickly reverted to her old, insular self.

'She's fine,' Mark said.

'If you say so.'

Alessia had never understood Jody's island nature, why she wasn't a clone of her, why she was so condescending about those Italian traditions Alessia held dear. When Jody put Tabasco on *tagliatelle marinara* her mother didn't speak to her for twenty-four hours, and it was at moments such as these when Alessia labelled her 'Daddy's girl', but not as a term of endearment. His children's failings were frequently down to him; that had been made clear often enough.

'She told me she'll head back to Oxford on *Monday*,' Alessia said. 'I knew we should have gone to Santa Maria for *pasqua*.'

'She's a grown woman, with a life she's eager to get back to. It's not a reflection on our company.'

'If you say so.' Again, the undertones were unmistakable. Mark had been unavoidably absent for much of Jody's and Brandon's childhoods and this absenteeism had, in Alessia's mind, taught her children to play hard to get.

'Anyone coming over tonight?'

'So you can frighten small children by threatening to garotte their mothers? No, I don't think I'll be inviting anyone ever again.'

'Jolly good,' Mark said.

'Morning,' Maylis sang from behind her foyer-spanning desk at the Recruitment and Asset Validation entrance. Mark's secretary retained a strong trace of her French accent, existed somewhere in her late twenties, and often found herself in Mark's dreams, as an only vaguely platonic foil to a juvenile version of himself that left him feeling dirty for the rest of the day. Her hair was lush and brown and, now he thought about it, she resembled a younger version of his wife. Maylis was on a salary far short of his and yet was the de facto organiser of the department. He took the day's agenda from her and returned her full smile.

'How are you?' he asked. 'Have a nice break?'

'Not bad, thanks. You?'

'Moderately relaxing.'

'Did you have ... family down?' Her smile was somewhat strained as she busied herself amongst the diaries beside the telephone.

Mark considered himself an excellent reader of people, and Maylis was flustered. He briefly outlined his long weekend then left her to her work and, alone in his office, cast an eye over the day's tasks.

His department oversaw plenty of online applications, most of which they politely turned down, and Mark was kept busy that morning chairing the verbal reasoning tests and situational judgements which followed any satisfactory psychological profile. There were the usual wannabes, full of Hollywood spunk, who just wanted to blow apart dungeon doors and rescue ambassadors' daughters. Most of these hardballers, Mark knew, sorely lacked what it took to peer through hotel blinds for weeks on end, watching the same street for the slightest hint of an enemy target.

The afternoon was spent in a meeting with Finance, coordinating the advertising expenditure and allocating the budget for new software. It was even less exciting than it sounded on Maylis's jobs list.

At five thirty on the dot, his secretary rose from her desk and called a goodbye to her team. Mark had his door open and replied in kind, noting that Jim had left his office to offer his own farewell. A knowing look, so fleeting it might have been imagined, flickered across Maylis's face and was reciprocated in the eyes of Jim, who gave a momentary impression of a lover caught in the arms of another as he hurried back to his desk.

Mark's first thought was that they were conducting an affair, but that made no sense. He'd met Maylis's doe-eyed, arse-chinned fiancé on more than one occasion and the two of them were desperately in love. As he wrote up a report of the afternoon's meeting, Mark mulled the matter over, concluding their shared look must have concerned some minor business secret they were keeping from him. He finished his report, then put on his coat.

'Staying late again tonight?' he asked Jim from his doorway.

'Very probably, sir. Got a lot on.' His colleague barely looked up.

Mark recalled Thursday evening had been the same, added it to Jim's not-quite-concealment of a document and multiplied it by Maylis's unusual reluctance to talk to him. He smelt something akin to a coup.

'Oh damn,' Mark exclaimed. 'I forgot to ... Never mind. Guess I'll be here a little longer too. Need a coffee?'

Jim's eyes swam upwards from his computer. 'Uh. No ... thanks.'

Mark returned to his desk and pored through the department folders on the database, hunting for new documents, recently logged meetings or interviews. The system revealed no trace of uprising. Was he just being paranoid? It was possible, but if Jim now decided he was no longer going to stay late ...

Sure enough, five minutes later, Jim knocked on his door, feigning a yawn. 'I'm going to take it home with me after all, sir. Have a good one.'

Interesting.

Jim considered himself rumbled. Whatever rendezvous he'd been planning to stay late for had already been rearranged.

Mark watched him leave, then followed him out of the office, taking the subsequent lift down. Jim, by all accounts, had been a damn good case officer in his brief time in the field, but he'd never been a spy. Mark had every advantage over him.

He exited the lift just as Jim was passing through the door that led to the SIS car park and kept pace while Jim scurried to his sensible Mazda 3. When Jim fired up the engine, he hastened to his own vehicle to tail him along Albert Embankment, idling in second gear over Lambeth Bridge. All the way along Millbank towards Parliament Square, he maintained a respectable three-car distance.

He knew exactly where he was headed.

Jim parked on Whitehall Place as Mark drove past to dump his car on Northumberland Avenue before doubling back on foot. He shadowed him all the way up to the side door of The Clarence.

The Tin Belly Dining Room upstairs wasn't exactly an MI6 members' club, but it wasn't far off. Mark had been there with Jim on a few occasions, and quite liked the odd mix of Cabinet-styled booths and bright, eclectic modern artworks, a patterned floor that seemed designed to make your eyes cross. There was a chance the location was known to foreign intelligence, but then again so was the enormous eyesore they worked in, and the GCHQ office in Westminster before that.

Its location, on a street corner with exits on two sides, no shops or restaurants opposite, made it a hard building to observe.

Mark didn't dare walk in and order a drink in the bar beneath, having no idea if Jim's contact was already there or might enter at any moment. Those tricks of the trade – the seat in the far corner, a half-concealing broadsheet – wouldn't work here. He lingered for a moment at the cloistered rear of Admiralty House, but it didn't feel right, lurking in shadows within spitting distance of the Cabinet Office. It wouldn't do to be seen dawdling here.

He would have to use one of the two red phone boxes, which meant a limited view of the Clarence's Great Scotland Yard exit, the door Jim would probably use to leave, unless his contact required the main door for proximity to Charing Cross tube. He entered the nearest box, turned up his collar and faced away from The Clarence, setting up his mobile phone on the counter in front of him, angled so its camera provided a view of the dining rooms behind.

He called Alessia, making legitimate use of the phone box, to say he was going to be later home. 'Work business,' he declared. It hardly mattered he was missing dinner, now Jody was back in Oxford and their son was mysteriously out all hours. Yesterday evening, Jody's absence had been loud, and Brandon had rocked up at closing time in his new suit, projecting the image of CEO wealth, or whatever he thought he was doing. 'I know it's a strange number. My mobile's out of battery. I won't be much longer.'

Shapes moved in the upstairs windows. He used his thumb and forefinger to zoom his mobile's camera in on the Tin Belly frontage, but the shapes didn't resemble Jim. He prepared himself for the long game.

When it started to rain, he was grateful. There was no law against sheltering in a phone box and, since the downpour affected visibility, he felt safer turning to face the building without being recognised. The raindrops hallucinated against the glass, twisting the panes into kaleidoscopes of brake lights and weeping streetlamps.

An hour passed. The 453 double deckers swore up the street while the tourists dashed in plastic ponchos. Every time someone left The Clarence, he swivelled to get a better look, but it was never anybody he recognised.

Was Jim simply out on his own, relaxing after work? And yet ... This *was* where Jim went to talk shop. But did that mean anything? Had that chase through Tate Britain the week before last affected him more than he was letting himself admit? He would never have spied upon a trusted colleague normally, but the unthinkable notion had been seeded within that he was still in the game. The same sixth sense that made him bolt the taxi on Vauxhall Bridge also told him there was something odd about recent office behaviour, but was hiding in a phone box, his bones infected with damp, more likely to yield results than just coming out and asking Jim what was going on?

While Mark was torn between remaining in his hiding place and starting for his car, the front door of The Clarence opened and a man and a woman stepped out.

The woman flumped open an umbrella and the pair waved each other a platonic, professional goodbye before strolling in opposite directions, Jim round the corner and up the street to his Mazda, the woman towards Trafalgar Square and the slick, wet concrete that currently resembled an ice rink beneath the imposing Corinthian granite of Nelson's Column.

Mark stood still, but not to avoid drawing attention to himself. Despite all his years of training, he couldn't have forced his body to turn itself the other way if he'd tried. Shock had sapped him of all control.

Through the glass, he observed his daughter sweep on through the rain.

3

They'd lost Jody in Cherry Tree Wood when she was six. One moment she'd been marvelling at the squirrels springing from branch to branch, the next she was gone. Five minutes of sheer terror followed before he'd spotted her bouncing towards them from behind a tree. 'Did you see me coming, Daddy? Did you see me coming?' Mark had pretended he hadn't, but even pitted against his training, the whispering leaves underfoot and a fluorescent bright pink top, she'd done remarkably well. She'd been so proud. And the worst of it was – once he'd calmed down – so was he.

Had he known, deep down, as far back as that?

He banished the thought. To dwell on the memory rendered him complicit in her recruitment, when he – *head of goddamn Recruitment* – was the one who'd been left out of the process. It was unthinkable.

So, she'd been meeting Jim in secret to discuss the possibility of joining MI6, had she? Even pretending to skip back to Oxford early to throw her father off the scent.

It hadn't worked.

When Jim whisked into the department the following morning, briefcase in hand, his Italian cashmere coat already over his arm, Mark called him in.

'Morning, sir. Everything OK?' Jim sounded nervous, had already picked up on his superior's disquiet.

Mark studied his colleague carefully. How far through the induction was Jody? Was there any chance of talking her out of the process? Unlikely. Once Jody got her teeth into an idea there was nobody who could prise her from it.

'I need you to target and cultivate a young woman who could be very useful to us,' he told Jim.

'Oh, yes?'

'It's a delicate one, though. We'll need to keep it between ourselves.'

Jim pulled off his leather gloves, finger by finger. 'If you let me see the file, I'll ...'

'It's my daughter.'

Jim's eyes gave away his shock, suspicion. 'OK ...' He nodded in rapid overcompensation. 'Wow. I mean ... Organise what she needs, and I'll be available to—'

'I think you should handle it from the get-go.' The officiousness in Mark's voice didn't give away his emotion, but he found himself switching on the fan next to his desk, despite it being more than cool enough in the office already. The Post-its rippled on his monitor. 'Background checks will reveal she's my daughter so there's no point in me being coy about any of this to you, but few people need to know who she is. I can't, realistically, be present at any interviews, but I can trust my number two, can't I, Jim?' He smirked in what he hoped looked like genuine camaraderie.

'But ...'

'Yes?'

'She's *told you*, she *wants* to begin the recruitment process?'

Mark kept his eyes locked on Jim as his workmate averted his gaze. 'Not in so many words. Send in a cultivator. Approach her through the usual channels. I think you'll find her willing.'

Jim blew out his cheeks. 'Fine. Let me have whatever you can on her and I'll be happy to do the rest. I'm assuming she's ...'

'Yes?'

'Able.' This might or might not have been the word Jim was reaching for, but it hung pregnant with so many others. Trustworthy. Pathologic. Sacrificial.

'She's more than able.'

'Of course. It's just ... She'll have a hard job, living up to her father's reputation. And you must have conflicting opinions on the matter. This is *your daughter*, after all.'

Mark shrugged, then snatched the fan off in mild irritation. 'You'll do as I ask?'

'Naturally, if you're sure.' There was a creeping, faint humour in Jim's voice now. He was beginning to believe he'd got away with his deception, that he'd been handed a golden lifeline from his guilty conscience.

'What ... made you think she might be interested in our little game?'

'Oh, just things she's said lately. She's ideally positioned.' This was beyond question. There was secretive, and then there was Jody. Only recently, she'd startled him – a spy recognised as one of the best of his generation – at the foot of the stairs in his own home. She'd always been a ghost. Not only that, but she was highly intelligent, changed her appearance on a whim and had an extensive understanding of Middle Eastern culture. The fact that none of this had ever occurred to him before just showed how deep his denial ran.

'Does she speak any foreign languages?' Jim asked, as though he genuinely didn't already know everything about her.

'Five, I believe, including Arabic.'

'Right. Good.'

'We can discuss it in more detail later. I'll give you her address in Oxford. I won't take any more of your time for now, Jim. That'll be all.'

Jim left Mark's office in something resembling a fugue state.

Mark continued to stare at his still switched-off computer, the reflection of the clouds outside his window slowly dragging their purpled undersides across his monitor. He didn't feel any better for having falsely positioned himself in control.

If Jody knew about Mark's role within the Service, Jim would be in his office next door, right now, calling her to say her own father had just recommended her for intelligence work and the pair would realise they hadn't been subtle enough. Things would be awkward, but there was no way he was going to put himself through years of pretending not to know anything about this, to have them laughing behind his back at having got one over on him.

If, on the other hand, Jody didn't know Daddy oversaw MI6's recruitment, had Jim's deception – the running around after dark and hastily-rearranged meeting on Whitehall – merely been to protect Mark from the truth?

He stood and wandered to the window to watch the diseased, livid currents of the Thames.

Jody had always delighted in hide and seek. Growing up, she was never to be discovered in the same place twice and performed dangerous feats like pouring out half the freezing, filthy water from the garden butt and hiding inside until she heard everyone shouting for her in panicked, neighbourhood-alerting voices. The household had to introduce a 'Rule of Fifteen', banning the practice of remaining hidden for longer than a quarter of an hour.

He'd caught her once, creeping without footwear through the landing, and she'd looked mortified. Even once she graduated to womanhood, she was never caught in heels. But were these little habits innate or passed on? He had never knowingly pushed Jody towards the spy game, never groomed or suggested, and yet she'd walked barefoot, undetected, all the way to MI6.

He pressed his head against the office window, winced. Had his encouragement of such games helped build a spy? Some children inherited artistic tendencies or a susceptibility to melanoma. Jody was heiress to espionage intentions, which, by their very definition, at least explained how she'd managed to hide them.

The Houses of Parliament watched him back as he disinterred and re-pieced history.

He recalled how he'd allowed her to badger him into letting her take archery lessons instead of the horse riding or gymnastics classes her small group of friends had enrolled on, but it wasn't long before she gave them up, claiming boredom. The following spring, she'd signed up for taekwondo lessons after school and was the sole girl in the class. Her instructor told Mark she'd had a good chance of winning tournaments, but she bailed before she could be entered for them. Mark believed it was only right that parents financially cultivated their children's talents and, in this vein, when Jody expressed an interest in coding, he was more than happy to stump up the cash. At twelve, she built her own website. This was no pre-teen site where she gushed over boy bands, but was sober and instructional, with basic information on how to learn languages efficiently and navigate your way out of forests.

Then, one day, she took the site down. Having mastered an art, Jody moved on, as though uncomfortable at the thought of being recognised for her abilities.

Mark had never questioned this. Why would he? After all, he'd been the same.

He became aware of the day shifting behind him. The shadows across his desk pivoted in opposition to the sun, stabbing west then east while he ignored his growing hunger. The to-do list had lengthened with the shadows.

There was a knock on his door, breaking his reverie.

'Oh. Morning, Maylis.'

'Afternoon, sir.'

And that was when he realised he'd been sentried at the window for five hours.

In due course, Jim visited his office. Raising his head gifted Mark a headache.

'You OK in here?' Jim asked. 'Haven't seen you all day.'

'I'm fine. Busy, busy.'

'Want me to turn the light on?'

'Um. Yes, thank you.' It would be easy to tell him: *Shelve the plan. I don't want Jody involved in any of this.* With a superior's order, he could end it here and now. 'Jim ... Have you made any progress on what we discussed this morning?'

His colleague shuffled in the doorway.

'A little.'

'I was thinking ... Maybe I was a little hasty. Perhaps it would be wise if ...'

There was movement behind him, and Jody slipped into the office.

'With your permission, sir, I'll be off.' It wasn't a question. Jim backed out of the doorway and, shortly after, the department.

Silence reigned until they both heard the exterior door close.

'I knew you followed him,' Jody said. 'I saw your car on Northumberland Avenue.'

These were the territorial waters of his own office, and yet he'd never felt so ill-placed. 'I was in the phone box opposite The Clarence,' he stated for no reason.

She nodded, stopping short of claiming to have spotted him. 'Are you even slightly surprised?'

'Not at all. I'd always expected it.'

She prowled into his office and posed at its centre, beside the one photograph on his desk. Brandon was a few months old and Jody was – he wasn't sure – three? Four? The southern Italian sun was in their eyes and both mouths were twisted into winces that understudied genuine smiles. Mark didn't care for photos, or sentimentality in general, but his children were so young in the faded image they couldn't possibly be identified. Even here, within the fastidious security of SIS headquarters, and all these years clean, he wanted no tracebacks.

'You must have guessed when you found out I was thinking of learning Arabic.'

'Of course. You'd hardly pass for Russian, not the way you tan. Shouldn't you be in Oxford studying? It's an important last term.'

'I'm guaranteed a first. I'm ready.'

I'm ready. Despite all the praise of her professors, the thousands of pounds and air miles invested, those two words reduced her own hard work to little more than a lavish, mandatory exercise in stalling.

He thought of the hallmates she'd mentioned so sparingly in her freshman year. The Belgian girl who'd claimed lineage to the throne. The son of a Conservative MP with connections to a multinational pharmaceutical. Or had one of her lecturers persuaded her? A lot of Oxbridge types had links to the Service, and it would be all too easy to stuff an impressionable young head with dreams of duplicity. More than once, his nation's enemies had groomed a double agent right at the heart of MI6 in such a way.

She grinned, as though she knew what he was thinking. 'Don't worry. If someone had got to me, would I really be coming to you?'

'What's Jim told you so far?'

'Just preliminary stuff. I wanted to see if I could enrol without you knowing. I guess Jim wasn't very subtle.'

He wanted to explode at her – *This isn't a game, Jody! If anything happened to you, how could I live with myself?* – but found himself saying, 'Take a seat,' in the dry voice he reserved for line management meetings.

She did. He could almost feel the pride coming off her.

'If you're determined to go through with this, MI6 are going to rake over your entire life, and turn it upside down. A role in espionage requires an unflinching commitment to whatever state orders are given, and we need agents that follow rather than question. The Commonwealth secrets you'll be tasked with keeping will make you valuable to enemies, and potentially dangerous to people you know.' He knew the speech by heart.

'Are you trying to talk me out of this?'

He ignored the question. At this early stage in the process, it was all *about* dissuasion. 'These are things you must understand. No one will assume you're not compromised, just because you're my daughter. Once your interviews are officially underway, people will look upon you as a liability so don't expect favourable treatment just because you're related to someone in the building.' That was a lie. Jim would be favourable towards her. Assessment would be favourable. Training would be favourable. She was a shoo-in. 'Be prepared for various, shall we say, *brutal* scenarios to be explored. How would you deal with a traitor?

Can you condone the use of torture? Could you kill for Queen and country?'

He'd never told her – or anyone, for that matter – about his own successes or failures in the Service, but now wanted to. One perfect chance to put her off the scent. Those covert operations in Lebanon, Belfast, the imprisonments, the beatings, the escapes, the unparalleled adrenalin and fear of it all, the wanting out, out, out at any cost but knowing that, once in, you were tied to the organisation for life. Everything was incarcerated within him by the Official Secrets Act. Eras came and went, politicians changed, old spies blabbed luridly exaggerated memoirs about the Cold War, but the Service had so much more on you than you had on the Service. You would always be watching your back.

'I'll be fine,' she told him.

'In the interviews, of course. Might as well sign now. But ... afterwards.' He fiddled with the fan by his desk. 'How did you know about me?' He'd always made it clear he was a glorified accountant in the great scheme of things at MI6. A grey-suited office body.

'I'd always known.'

'No, you always suspected. How did you *know*?'

She let the silence speak for a time. *The same way you knew about me*, she seemed to mock. 'I picked up on things.'

Every cell in his being begged her not to go down the path he'd followed. A life spent birdwatching for Uncle was physically, mentally and morally suicidal. He'd seen what it did to the best of them.

'I remember you at the beach bar in Santa Maria,' he said, a tone of false victory creeping in. 'Having a coffee with that young man.'

'You've lost me, Dad.'

'You hadn't mentioned a single boy throughout high school, but you let that Italian peacock buy you a drink. Your mother had practically chosen a wedding dress, venue and order of service by the time you came back over. Do you remember?'

She clearly didn't.

'You told us his name, where he was staying, where he was going that evening, but you had no intention of meeting him. At the time, I assumed a straightforward narrative: you discovered he was a bore, a horny cliché of adolescence, and politely returned to the safety net of your family. But you'd been flexing yourself. Watching that early exercise in extracting information, *I knew.*'

Jody failed to suppress an arch smile. 'I see you've spent the day raking over my past.'

Mark reached for the fan again, snatched at the switch. 'Nothing of the sort. Too busy for that. I only remember because I'd never seen you so ... tactical before. Using your new femininity as a weapon.'

His daughter shrugged. 'It *is* a weapon.'

He regarded her with wonder. His father's instincts had always been, and always would be, to protect her, but his spymaster's intuitions were honed too. The thought of his daughter entering the Service was horrifying, but he also understood, as a professional spy of considerable acclaim himself, or at least what acclaim might reasonably be bestowed upon a shadow, that she was a perfect fit. She could pounce at you in Cherry Tree Wood in a bright pink jacket and hide in a water butt for over fifteen minutes.

'I'll have someone see you out. You can't walk back through SIS headquarters without clearance.' Mark reached for his desk phone. 'Are you coming home, or ...?'

'Oxford.'

He dialled for the floor security, arranged for her to be picked up.

'Jody . . . I want to explain something, before you go. In one of my training classes at Portsmouth, decades ago, I was sent on a mission to collect passport numbers from tourists. I managed to get seven in one night. I learned that people can be more trusting than you realise, but it taught me nothing about the reality of life as a spy. Differentiating the truth teller from the liar is another thing altogether; an enemy agent won't give you details, whereas a regular citizen probably will. Intel is useless unless you can trust the source. It's a hard game. The hardest game. After a while, you trust *nobody*. Everyone becomes Judas Iscariot in your eyes and the longer you play the game the greater the odds of it turning you into a suspicious, friendless martyr.'

She leaned forward. 'Once I've passed the training' – that supreme confidence; ninety per cent didn't – 'I'll be sent out on non-lethal missions, shadowing agents. But it will be a waste of time. Why? Because I've been shadowing an agent my whole life. You've used a false name at the corner shop for twenty years. On holiday, if someone makes pleasant conversation and asks you where you're from, you offer some silken remark and change the subject. The last thing you did before drawing my bedroom curtains at night was look both ways up and down the street. I know exactly what this job will turn me into.'

His chest tightened as the true reality of what he'd condemned her to rose towards his throat. In the old days, he would have washed the taste away with alcohol. By sharing his warpaint, Jody was in danger of summoning every ghost he'd previously exorcised.

Security knocked on his door and they both rose.

'Is this really what you want?' he asked, unable to keep the crack from his voice.

She smiled with a determination that terrified him.

'Yes, Dad. It is.'

He ended the day the way he'd begun it, sitting alone in his Vauxhall Cross office, eyeballing a dead computer and mourning his daughter's soul.

4

As head of recruitment and Asset Validation, he was aware of her progress throughout the summer. Every morning, he cruised down Grosvenor Road towards Albert Embankment in his BMW 5 Series to park in his designated space in the SIS car park while she, twice a week, came down from Oxford and climbed aboard the Victoria line to cross Vauxhall Bridge in pedestrian anonymity.

She passed the first round of aptitude tests with flying colours.

There was a UK intelligence history assessment that required a torturous cramming session. Endless medical evaluations. Encryption tests. Most failed, of course, but the potentials were earmarked early on, funnelled into cryptography, surveillance, or honest secretarial positions. It was when he came across her shooting range scores that he knew she wasn't going to settle for a job behind a computer. Those archery lessons had served their purpose; he hadn't seen such marks since his own days on the range. It would be a waste of talent to stick her in an office, and the knowledge of that made him both proud and sick to his stomach.

He never had to wait long before a new clutch of results came in. Intelligence gathering: excellent. Eidetic memory training: excellent. Self-defence; improvised weapons; hand-to-hand combat: excellent; excellent; excellent.

One afternoon, the westerly zephyrs carrying the promise of another hot night, Mark was at the filing cabinets, living the dream, when Maylis unhooked a thin coat she didn't need from the stand by the department door.

'You must be pleased,' she said.

His blank look prompted elucidation.

'You've not heard?'

He shook his head dismissively, pretending he kept the whole tedious matter at arm's length. He'd never discussed the way in which his own department tried to keep Jody's enrolment from him, nor his face-saving suggestion she be courted by the Service.

'She's bossing it.' Maylis grinned a faraway disbelief. 'Practically ready, they say.'

'Who's "they"?'

'Everybody.'

'Impossible,' Mark spat, before tempering the harshness of his words with, 'It would be folly to send her away so soon.'

Maylis nodded. 'I'm sure the Top Floor won't take undue risks with her. They've been here before with prodigies. I mean, she's a born spy and the daughter of the one and only Mark Wolfe. Her Majesty will save her for something important.'

She danced out.

Mark's day was ruined.

Father and daughter sat together on the bench Mark bought three summers ago, situated in a natural bower at the rear of the garden beneath an arch formed by two elms planted by some long-dead former homeowner. The spot allowed him to see who approached, with a direct view into the kitchen, where Alessia currently stacked the dishwasher. The kettle plumed, and Mark calculated they had about four minutes before his wife joined them with the tea.

'How's work?' he risked asking as the wind shook the leaves. A redwing hopped about the left elm.

'Intense,' she said. A rare admission, and one in contradiction to her body language. She looked healthy and in control, the rakishness of her early years of university gone, replaced by a sturdy femininity and clear-eyed purpose that shone from her like enlightenment. The brachioradiales of her forearms were as defined as blades.

'The training will get harder before it gets easier. The hardcore are pushed along an altogether *more challenging* route.'

'I'm doing parachute drops at Sandhurst for the next month. I expect that sort of thing was easier for you, straight out of the armed forces.'

He'd never hidden the fact of his army days but couldn't remember ever mentioning being recruited by the Service straight from the military. 'It's a long road out of apprenticeship,' he confided.

'Funny, isn't it? We're in the same business, the same building a lot of the time, and yet we can't speak about what we do.'

'They don't stop everyone from talking. They can't. Some spies I knew believed it was important to let someone they trusted in on where they were at all times, in case things got too hot.'

'And how many of them made it to pensionable age without being compromised by these "trusted" individuals?'

'None, actually.'

She was a true spy. He didn't even know where she was living right now. For both their sakes, the less he knew the better.

Part of him had hoped her new role as co-conspirator might bring the two of them closer, but in many ways it ensured they were further apart than ever, both bound by a commitment not to talk about their experiences, and it wouldn't be long now before she was off on her first mission, dropped into God knows where and left to fend for herself, leaving him to carry the burden of dishonesty to the dinner table on his own once more.

'I spent so long covering my own tracks,' he said, 'I never considered I'd be covering for two.'

'Not the first time you've been involved in non-official cover. Was counterintelligence your thing, back in the day?'

'Most of the time.'

In the kitchen, Alessia was loading the teapot and cups onto a tray.

He was beginning to regret this furtive talk. It wasn't uncommon for spies in training to be tasked with visiting someone and bringing back a specific piece of information, a motivation, a vulnerability. Maybe he was a test and her questions were nothing more than the acquisition of information from a source.

No. This overthinking was a hangover of his previous life, as much a habit as the casing of exits in unfamiliar restaurants. Even MI6 wouldn't be so crass as to make him her target, and he'd do her no favours by second-guessing her every intention. Soon she'd be in deep at Fort Monckton or some secret facility, learning to become a weapon of self-defence, an isolated field operative built to steal information and get out in time for last orders, and he was simply jealous.

'You were good, I hear.' She was looking at him with something approaching respect. 'In the field.'

'Not to sound too arrogant but, yes. There's probably a lot you could learn from me.'

'So why are you in recruitment and not training?'

He sighed. 'A good question ...'

Alessia was making her way across the lawn. The teacups chuckled on their saucers.

'... but one for another day.'

'What are you two discussing down here?'

'The begonias,' father and daughter chorused in union.

Mark met Jim in the Tin Belly above The Clarence. They sheltered in a dark wood booth, surrounded not by the usual establishment photographs of Churchill, Montgomery or Queen Victoria, but by a jazzy splurge of artworks that left Mark as cold as the ones he'd hurried past in the Tate. The phone box he'd lurked in sat opposite, an ever-watching reminder of the duplicity within him.

'Heard from her, sir?' Jim asked. His tie looked expensive, and he'd perfected his crisp Windsor.

Mark stirred his soup, shook his head.

Jody hadn't returned to SIS headquarters, or to family dinners on the occasional Sunday, for several months.

The daily grind, for Mark, had continued, but Jody's absence was a constant presence. Alessia was being updated regularly with subtle fictions. *Lovely here; Job going well; Early start today.* That sort of flimflam. She was always pleased to get a photo through, showing her daughter in generic pub gardens or unidentifiable beauty spots. The trick, always, was to not push the small, maintainable lies too far, and so Jody had found herself a position in the Red Cross, as far as her mother was aware, helping to organise training missions in preparation for disaster response, a role that justified her perceivably benevolent choice of bachelor degree as well as legitimising training sessions on military bases for long periods of time.

It pleased Mark that Alessia was in communication with Jody, but to find out what she was *really* up to he consulted her file, which felt both insurrectionist and second nature. Perhaps Jody suspected he was keeping tabs on her, which was why she didn't waste her time sending *him* bogus texts about emergency response missions. His training, and to a degree his very personality, normalised what she was doing, but he prayed she'd have an easier career than he'd had.

'Must be strange,' Jim said. 'The boot being on the other foot.'

'By the time I'd signed up to Six, both my parents were dead, and the rest of my so-called family were used to me disappearing for long periods "on business".' Mark had been the archetypal recruit. Few ties or loved ones. 'No one fretted about me.'

Jim looked him over, a heavy, searching examination. 'My cover as a runner was teaching English abroad, and the first thing I did in a new country was send my mum a postcard. She loved the fact I was a globetrotter. If I'd died in service, I knew the protocol was to tell my parents the truth. At times, I almost wished I'd get taken that way. Just so there was honesty.'

It went without saying they weren't supposed to be discussing these matters, detail-free as they were.

'She's pretending to be an aid worker,' Mark said.

'I didn't think that was ...'

'Neither did I.'

'Times are changing.'

The waitress, long reddish hair, mid-twenties, removed their empty starter bowls. They checked their conversation long enough for her to shuffle back to the kitchen.

'She'll be all right,' Jim said. 'You survived, didn't you?'

'Yes, but ... I was posing as characters who were, shall we say, mere extensions of myself. There was still a feeling that the British were honourable and ex-pats were treated warmly in several parts of the world.'

Jim put his glass to one side. 'You've lost me, sir.'

'My daughter's signed up to a life of secrecy in the Middle East and South Asia. She's a woman with olive skin, dark eyes, and a first in Arabic and Persian. She's going to be infiltrating terrorist cells for her entire service. A Middle Eastern terror group getting their hooks upon weapons of mass destruction has long been the West's biggest nightmare and MI6 will use her until her last breath, given the chance. We were pasty British boys, impersonating the odd dumb tourist when required, and our so-called notion of English fairness and what's "not cricket" looks pretty stupid in the era of al-Qaeda. Most of us made it home, but many didn't. And there were few women amongst us. Sexist times, perhaps, but we didn't put them in danger the way—'

'Mark. They won't send her out until she's ready.'

Mark relented. He didn't mention Jez Ronson, killed on his first mission after impersonating a marine biologist who'd claimed the Mediterranean was an ocean and ended up rotting under the Sicilian sun alongside the mafioso daughter he'd been hired to protect. Nor did he mention Pippa Beaumont, still green from training, whose Canadian accent slipped after four hours of wining and dining Libyan separatists and was found, two months after her last official report, tied in a storage tank with her legs gnawed to the knees by rats. Nor Samuel Jimenez, whose first and final foray into Cuba ended with a failed rescue following a report sent from an insecure phone. The agent dispatched to bring him in was harpooned through the throat as he boarded a vessel out of Havana and Samuel was keel-hauled over coral until his body broke apart like bread in a duck pond.

'She knows what she's getting into,' Jim said. 'She's a smart one. Not like some of the trainees we get, all piss and vinegar.'

'She's got plenty of piss and vinegar too, believe me.'

'No, she doesn't. She's the calmest, most cerebral candidate I've ever interviewed.'

'What does piss and vinegar mean again?'

Jim grinned. 'It means boisterous, rowdy, energetic.'

'Oh, right. She's not that.'

'My point is that she's one of the smartest, natural recruits I've met. She'll end up in some sticky situations, sure. But she'll come home after every single mission, wiser and more alive than before.'

'The more missions you're on, the lower your chance of coming home from the next. Continued survival simply eats away at those stats.'

'The average agents, not the good ones. I have a feeling she's going to be exceptional.' He called the waitress over. 'Louis XIII, please.' It was his tragic little joke; the cognac was Rémy Martin. Once she was gone, he asked, 'Is that why you retired from active duty? Because you felt you'd used up your luck?'

'There was no specific close call, but I realised I'd been one error away from death my whole career. Once, that had been exactly what drove me on, but the more I focused on the fact, the more I became obsessed with not making that mistake. I worried it would cloud my judgement. Does that make sense?'

'I think a lot come to that realisation sooner or later.'

'It's a shame, though.' Mark mused. 'A spy with forty years' experience would pass almost unnoticed. The enemies are looking for fresh-faced, risk-taking Etonians.'

'He'd struggle in combat situations.'

'Naturally, but he'd take better pains to avoid them. Once you're required to defend yourself, the mission's already gone tits up.'

Two cognacs arrived and Mark stared at his as though it were sentient.

'Shit,' Jim exclaimed. 'I only meant for me. I'll get you something else.'

'It doesn't matter.' Mark nodded the waitress on and slid the second glass of golden spirit across to his colleague, ice clinking. 'You have it.'

'I'm about to say something sexist and shocking,' Jim announced. 'Stand by your bed, sir. Women make better spies than men. Men are naturally reckless, whereas women evolve into more cautious, compartmentalising agents. I see it with my nephew and niece. Adrian dangles from trees at heights that would give me vertigo. Katy can't step in a puddle. Jody won't do anything stupid.'

'Stupid can be useful in our game. You can be in and out in a mindless second before anyone knows you've been there. You can't always wait for a risk-free moment. But she's not—'

'Full of piss and vinegar? Do you fret this much about all Her Majesty's agents?'

'You told me once you came to think of the spies you ran as your own children. You tell me. *Is* worrying normal?'

Jim sighed as though rumbled. 'You worry about their safety and the integrity of the mission that results from them being exposed.' The subtext was that the mission is always the priority. *We were expendable.* 'No one wants to lose an agent, but it does happen. I'd say Jody's odds are better than most, though.'

Jim was telling him what he wanted to hear, but no one was immune to a car bomb or a sniper's rifle across a crowded souk. Not even Jody. Not even his brown-eyed, beautiful daughter.

'If anything happens to her, it's my fault. That's the bottom line.'

The waitress brought them their meals. Mark smoothed the linen napkin across his thighs and watched Jim gulp his first drink down. Who the hell ordered brandy before a main course? There was something on his mind.

'What was it you wanted to tell me, Jim?'

Jim sat up straight, a little taken aback. Through the window, the London light came hard and clear. 'As it happens ... I'm moving on.'

'Figured you were. Taking me out for dinner isn't a customary habit of yours, and an important interview necessitated a new knotting of your tie. Where are you headed? Targeting? Intelligence testing?'

'Operational Management.'

Mark forced himself to show no emotion. 'Congratulations. I guess I'll be choosing your replacement soon.'

'I guess so, sir.'

Mark began the slow, intricate process of carving up his steak. It had always annoyed him when Jim threw in a needless 'sir'. Yes, he was his superior, but there was no need for such titles amongst team members. It probably wasn't meant in a sardonic way, but Mark interpreted it as such, especially now Jim was waltzing out the Recruitment door. 'You seem to always be one step ahead of me, when it comes to my daughter.'

'What do you mean?'

'You'll know where she's being posted long before I find out.' Mark put down his knife and reached across the table for the spare brandy glass, then stopped himself. 'Drink that quickly, before I'm tempted to.'

Jim, in full understanding, knocked back the drink.

Not too many weeks later, the British Secret Service's Head of Recruitment and Asset Validation was at his computer when a suspicious black pop-up took control of his screen, swallowing his spreadsheet on stationery outlay. He sat back, dumbfounded. This had never happened before.

In the centre of the box was a green icon not unlike the one he pressed when accepting a call on his mobile. Was this a virus? A hacking attempt?

Warily, he clicked on the icon.

Jody appeared.

She was lean and healthy, her long dark hair falling around her shoulders in new ringlets, a champion behind the eyes, so much confidence it scared him.

'How did you ...? To what do I owe this pleasure?'

He already knew. The break from protocol was too marked.

'Wasn't there a photo on your desk before?'

He glanced to his left, then back at the screen, waved his hand in front of it to ascertain where the webcam might have been. 'I didn't think it was appropriate once you ... you know.'

'I'm in,' she said, delivering the words with all the fanfare of a text message.

'Well done,' he heard himself say, affable, casual.

'And here to let you know I'll be away for a bit.'

'You want me to cover for you with your mother?'

'No need. I have it in hand. Emergency response. A training operation following in the footsteps of the Pakistan earthquake responders.'

He nodded. Pakistan. Not the worst location for a debutant, perhaps.

'How long do they estimate you'll be away?'

She shrugged.

'You know, I don't approve of this Red Cross cover. They're an NGO and should be exempt from our game, like religious figures.'

She smiled but said nothing. It was no doubt one cover out of several she'd be using, and it would be interesting to see if the locations she claimed to be sent to always matched those of international disasters.

'Do you remember your first mission?' she asked.

'It was probably very routine, and soon buried under the weight of everything that came later.' No specifics given, but not out of choice. He genuinely couldn't remember. If she'd asked him about Berlin, or Derry, or Montenegro, things would be different, but she took the cue she wasn't necessarily supposed to and didn't press any further.

'I would offer you a drink ...' He found himself pulling a bottle of scotch from the bottom drawer, its cap unbroken for a decade. Part of his unique coping mechanism, he kept alcohol within reach, but willpower guarded his lips from its taste; he could control whether he took the first drink, but after that he was alcohol's slave. He waved it, ridiculously, in front of the screen. '... but I guess it's still *haram*, and you're not actually here, so ... When are you off?'

'I'm already en route.'

'Oh, right.' Again, he failed to disguise the emotion in his voice, which cracked a second puberty.

'I better go. Wish me luck.'

Her image vanished.

Mark sought out the X at the corner of the black box that replaced her, then dragged up the recruitment folder on his monitor to check her file for the last time, knowing what he would find. Her status had indeed changed. No longer in training and therefore now inaccessible to his eyes, there was but one word honouring Jody's graduation:

CLASSIFIED.

5

'How long's she been gone now?' Alessia asked.
Forty-seven days. 'I'm not sure. Three weeks?' Brandon leaped onto the spare couch and grabbed the TV remote. 'I heard from her.' Television channels blinked into one another in a vicious collage of attention deficit.

'You did?' Alessia asked.

Mark feigned disinterest to the point it was as though he hadn't heard. A fellow perjurer on the payroll, he was masking what little knowledge he had of Jody's whereabouts with increasing guilt, especially when his wife was stressing, as now, over the lack of news from her.

'Yeah. I'm going out there and surprising her.'

'You what?' Mark turned to his son.

'That part of Kashmir is beautiful.'

'What do you mean "surprising her"?'

'She told me the village she's in.' The TV whipped its channels towards a region Mark didn't even know existed. Music videos. Teleshopping. American football. Mark had been vaguely interested in how much that antique telescope was worth, but doubted he'd ever locate his normal stations again.

'I don't think you can just turn up at a disaster zone,' he said.

'Course I can. There are still displaced people and internment camps and whatnot and I'm thinking of becoming a photojournalist.'

Excellent cover as far as espionage went, Mark considered, had Brandon been a complicated, calculated master assassin instead of a lumbering, attention-seeking womaniser.

'I can give you food to take her,' said Alessia.

Mark felt himself pale. He wasn't about to let Jody's cover be blown on her inaugural mission by her own brother. Why hadn't anyone seen this coming?

'Brandon, this is her first big job. I'm not sure she'd appreciate you turning up on her doorstep ...'

'I bet she's missing good, honest cooking,' his wife mused.

He put up his hand, as though to silence them both. 'I know you'd be discreet, Brandon.' *Hardly*. 'But these rescue missions have their own photographers attached to them. Contravening the Geneva Convention doesn't look good on a young photographer's CV. Don't get me wrong, I think it would be educational if you went, but ask her permission first. I think turning up unsolicited would be a mistake.'

And just like that, Brandon capitulated, his impetuousness doused.

Competent fieldwork was not dissimilar to being a magician and it was easy to fool the uninitiated with psychological sleight of hand.

In triumph, Mark took back the remote control.

The hotel room was dark and humid, his own sweat suffocating as he waited behind the locked door. A knife rested on his lap while he wiped and re-wiped his hands on his thin cotton trousers.

The moment the light went on, he'd strike. A fast stab, hand over mouth to stifle the scream.

This was a part of the job he'd never had to do before.

The mission was simple. Confirm the leak and then, if necessary, take out the operative. Well, he'd confirmed the leak.

And so, in a sweltering hotel room in Haiti, to keep his mind alert, he completed arithmetic, tried to remember the names of old schoolmates. Falling asleep was suicide. Occasionally, he'd stretch his legs out before him, pinching his shoulder to keep alert, listening to corridor sounds in the dark. Prostitutes used this hotel night and day, and he heard many come and go, doors sighing closed after them like the briefest expectorations of pleasure.

Finally, after what felt like two nights, feet stopped at the door.

Panic was a vice around his chest. He'd planned to make his move the moment the door closed behind his mole, but his mind fell blank as he scrambled through new possibilities. There hadn't echoed one set of feet down the threadbare corridor, but two.

From the gait and weight of the steps, he guessed both visitors to be men. He needed to quickly identify the one he wanted and then ... He'd probably have to kill the other too, to preserve his own identity.

The key was in the lock. It turned.

A thin hand reached out to flare low wattage above the three of them. Mark rose.

His knees cracked.

Too late, Mark realised his formative, bloody encounter in Port-au-Prince with two trained killers had been compromised by the fact he was a man of nearly sixty.

He burst awake with fear in his heart.

The house was silent, so he concluded Alessia and Brandon had gone out after he dozed off. Thinking about it, he did remember mention of buying ice cream. But he was uneasy. Something had woken him. Had that sound, innocuous or sinister, been them leaving or someone coming in?

In an instant, he was standing. His ears strained to listen for alien noises, footsteps over the dull thud of his heart.

His mind was always doing this, snatching him awake the moment he approached something like sleep. Yet another call-back to his previous occupation, when passing out might have let a quarry slip or allowed for his own capture. Benzedrine had been a help, deep undercover, but now he'd been prescribed the opposite kind of aid, suppressants that helped him black out the night. They didn't work. Not the way attempting to sit down with a newspaper after a large meal did.

There. Not a sound, but a presence.

It was an old hunch, and one he needed to act on. He slid from the sofa and grabbed the poker from the fire, hurrying as quietly as possible towards the conservatory side, listening for more information, watching the glass for reflections of motion. Had a would-be burglar seen his son and wife leave the house and assumed it was unoccupied? Was this, as promised, the return of the private security company, finally making harder inroads towards his recruitment?

He balled his hands. Killer's hands, once, now spotted and veined, tufts of hair sprouting from porous fingers. On light feet, he crept closer to the shadows of the conservatory, an easy escape outside if necessary. The slate tiles beneath his feet, cold in winter, warm in summer, radiated a smoky scent as though they remembered every log fire the neighbouring living room hosted.

And then he saw it, the reflected outline of a figure floating through the open lounge door, making its way towards him at the periphery of the room.

His old heart pulsed a new ache, but he knew he was in no danger.

'You'll have to try harder than that,' he called.

Jody's soft laugh puttered from the lounge.

'You've still got it, Dad,' she said, tripping lightly towards the conservatory. Mark had assumed a more casual position behind a chair, but he suspected that, if her training had been anything worth its salt, she'd pick up on the beads of sweat at his temples. He hid the poker against the back of the chair.

'You shouldn't be creeping around. At my age, a shock like that could finish me off. Aren't you supposed to be in Pakistan?'

'Mission complete. Decompression leave.' She didn't look as though she needed it.

'Brandon says he got a message from you. You know, he wanted to come out, surprise you. I had to talk him out of it. He's convinced he's a photographer now and your job will get him his first scoop. The cover won't work.'

'Then I'll have to educate him on the rules concerning photographing disaster zones.'

'I tried. But he's impetuous.'

'Exactly. He won't be a photographer this time next week. You know that.'

'Still, I'm not convinced the cover's bullet-proof.'

'This is as good as any. International emergency response operates under great secrecy too. They wouldn't tell someone who claims to be my brother where I really am, would they?'

'And what happens when you're sent to Saudi Arabia, for example, and there's been no earthquake or landslide or uprising in the area?'

'Mop-up operation. Crews are intermittently dispatched to follow up on where funds have gone and whether more aid is needed. Everywhere in that region has had an oil spill or earthquake or freak weather of some sort in the last five years.' It was good to see her smile. It had been so long. 'Dad, you need to trust me.'

There was the sound of a car in the driveway.

'I'll see you in five minutes.' Before he could question her, she'd made it to the conservatory door and twisted the key, slipping out into the garden.

'Ice cream!' Brandon called as the front door swung open.

Mark rubbed his hands together. 'Excellent.'

'You're in a better mood,' Alessia told him.

'I had a little sleep. Do you mind if I take mine outside?'

At the bottom of the garden, there was no sign of Jody. He hunted for footprints, scuff marks on the fence, decortication by shoe heel on the trunk of the elm, but nothing gave her exit away. And then the doorbell rang and Alessia screamed with delight when Jody surprised them all.

Mark watched the happy silhouettes through the window. Jody really was determined to do things her own, unconventional way. And she was right: he had to trust her.

It was becoming more and more obvious that the man hired to replace Jim was, in effect, hired to replace Mark himself. He was an Etonian (obviously), the right side of forty, and another former spy. He studied Mark's day-to-day routines as though a written examination might follow at any moment and worked longer hours than Mark, arriving half an hour before the cleaners and greeting everybody with the kind of forced bonhomie that natural office managers are hard-wired to perform. His name was Cecil, a sibilant, upper class designation for a truly sycophantic individual. Mark disliked him immensely and, though he worked hard not to show his mistrust of Cecil to his face, made a point of shovelling as much administrative shit towards his inbox as possible.

It wasn't just that he missed Jim, though Mark was surprised to find he did, or that Cecil's relative youth hammered home the fact the blues of Mark's eyes were blurring, the skin around them puffed into attaché cases by a lack of sleep. It was far simpler than that. A constant low-level anxiety, gnawing like toothache, told him his daughter was going to come home in a box draped with the Union Flag and this number-cruncher, this bureaucrat he'd been assigned without any say-so, undermined the very energy and commitment of true stars of the Service like Jody Wolfe.

Every few months, she went missing. Although she kept coming back, Mark knew there was a high chance, one day, she wouldn't. The rumours which filtered down to him from the top brass, the glowing reputation she was building for herself, filled him with a pride that couldn't fully negate the knowledge that a spy's reputation is also his or her kiss of death. An agent's work should never be recognised. To everyone, fathers included, that file should always read CLASSIFIED.

His spirits were lifted whenever she was back in the country, safe. And then, as abruptly as she'd reappeared – a doorbell; a cry of delight from Alessia – she would vanish back into mist and he'd force himself to grow used to her absences, as he'd once got used to the long departures of her university years. Jody's fourth, then fifth postings took her away. A year passed. A year when she would wisp back into his thoughts like candle smoke at random moments – changing gear at the Vauxhall Bridge Road traffic lights; at the shaving mirror – and it took all his strength not to succumb to the PTSD-inspired addictions of his past.

In the aftermath of his departure from MI6, he'd certainly been known to knock back more than he should have, to drown the ghosts. This was pure self-diagnosis, but it hadn't been hard to read the signals when he'd found himself, ten minutes after the alarm shrieked, standing in the shower holding a bottle of beer he couldn't remember opening. The return to MI6 after the job wilderness years had helped cure the shaking of alcoholism's fingertips, like the antivenom that contained a minute trace of the poison itself; by acknowledging his old masters, his new overlord – the bottle – had been beaten. He counted himself as one of the lucky ones. Many others wouldn't have made it out of that hotel room in Port-au-Prince, let alone the countless other missions over the course of his active duty, but the Service's after-care had failed him. However, when he crawled back to them as part of the Recruitment team, he was lauded as the perfect example of a field agent-survivor. MI6 was in him just as much as he was in MI6.

But now they had their hooks in his daughter too, and he was no longer sure the scales were as balanced as he'd once believed.

Returning from lunch, he found a piece of paper on his keyboard bearing a message declaring, T12 at 14.30.

Mark approached Maylis at her desk. 'Anyone visit us while I was out?'

'Not that I know of. Unless Cecil let someone in. Why?'

'No reason.' He'd definitely locked his office door.

At half two he walked out onto the roof space the note had mentioned. There were sixty separate terrace areas incorporated into the design of SIS headquarters and this was one of the more public. In the summer, it was full of civil servants eating lunch on picnic benches but, today, a week before Bonfire night, a cold east wind blew. Jody was waiting.

'What's the new guy's name?' she asked.

'Welcome back. It's been two months.' No reaction. 'His name is Cecil.'

'He looks a dick.'

'He is.'

There was no rule against speaking to his own daughter, just as there was no official rule on inter-service relationships of any kind, but he suspected this was the sort of meeting Cecil might report to the Top Floor. It was a gilt-edged sword, her growing reputation.

'Did he let you into my office?'

'I slipped past him at the filing cabinets. Maylis was on the phone.'

'Bloody hell. How did you evade the passkey?'

'It wasn't difficult.' He observed her register the thickness of the balustrade glass, sniper points nearby, the usual training stuff.

'You're off again soon, I suppose?' He knew, having the same espionage sickness in her veins as he did, she'd want to be. 'Be sure to show us plenty more of your boring, ill-lit photos of the local environment upon your return. It's stopped Brandon seeing you as a source of photo opportunities. I won't ask where you're going.'

Jody's look was conspiratorial, coolly vacant, and he understood the look at once.

She'd assumed he *knew* where she was being posted.

'I genuinely don't have a clue where they send you, you know.'

She brushed windblown hair from her face. 'Really?'

'I have no access to what our agents do after they've passed the first stages of recruitment. I could bend a few ears perhaps, but ...' He thought of Jim. No, he couldn't. 'I'm not the Spymaster General. The Red Cross cover is vague and frequently, I expect, doesn't match where you're really sent. Your first mission was close, in geographical terms, to your public cover, but there's less need for those precautions now your mother's come to terms with your ... supposedly philanthropic exercises.'

'Right.' She looked only slightly sheepish, as though she hadn't needed to visit, to ... Reassure?

There was silence for a time. It was obvious to Mark her next operation was going to be a big one.

'I quite liked knowing you had my back,' she joked. 'Would you prefer to know or not?'

He pretended to think about it, eyes on the slow planes unzipping the sky. 'On balance, information has always been my livelihood. Not knowing is death in this business.' He spoke as though he were still in the game.

Jody took a sheet of paper from her pocket and scribbled something, then folded it into a neat square and pressed it into his palm. It was her next destination, he knew – Tehran or Islamabad or Washington DC; a scrap of information that showed a degree of trust over and above service protocols, something he would later, privately, burn into black curls of memory. He was, to some degree, her insurance. Despite all the agents running her operations, monitoring, aiding, her father's hand wasn't too far away.

'If anything happens,' she said, 'there's an emergency number. Naturally, it connects straight to HQ, but Mum might find it reassuring.'

'And is this *my* reassurance?' He indicated the paper in his hand. No answer. 'This is a large operation, isn't it?'

The thinnest of smiles. 'Look after Mum,' she said, turning away.

He watched her go, then unfolded the paper.

Seconds later, he smashed it into a ball and flung it to the floor in exasperation, where the gathering wind spun it over the balustrade and into the uncaring London skies.

It was the last time she would ever be seen within SIS headquarters.

6

They came for him again, as he'd known they would.

Mark was taking a walk around his neighbourhood to shake off a restlessness caused by yet another of Alessia's dinner parties. Jody's continued absence had been brought home by repeated questions about her, most of which had blown in from the direction of one of his wife's colleagues who was casting around for dates for her dullard son from a previous marriage, so Mark made his excuses before the *limoncello* was passed around. Jody had been gone a month and, while he knew some missions were destined to last longer than others and told himself he'd grow used to the familial dissonance, the incompleteness, the anxiety was as horribly tangible as the glasses of wine everybody else wielded.

The shadowy figure was perched in a bus stop on the High Road.

As Mark approached, the man stood, the red and blue glow from the Phoenix Cinema revealing a closely shorn head and beard, winter hands thrust into fleeced pockets.

Mark recognised him in an instant. 'You took your time. Not driving a taxi anymore?'

The man cast a quick look around him. 'You're not the only ex-birdwatcher in London we've been working on, you know.'

'What made you think I'd be here?'

'You often follow this route when you disapprove of your dinner guests.'

Mark failed to keep the anger from his tone. 'Just how long have you been observing me?'

'It's on and off. Have you changed your mind yet? We've given you plenty of time to think about our offer.'

'I don't remember any offers. Only being chased around Millbank by two idiots with pistols.'

'The offer was more job satisfaction, more control, more money. And it still stands.'

Mark took a pace forward and was surprised when the younger man stepped back, arm flashing to his coat pocket. These people feared him. No wonder his accosting last time had got out of control.

'Wasn't I clear enough at our previous meeting?'

'You were perfectly clear, Mr Wolfe, but we wondered, now your situation has changed, whether you might have rethought the whole matter.' The man's eyes were ringed by shadow, resembling the sockets of a skull.

'My situation hasn't changed.' Mark looked about them. A man smoking a cigarette on the far side of the street. A woman in an idling car. A couple kissing in a shop doorway.

'That's not what we've heard.'

'I don't know what you mean.'

'You must be very proud,' the man said. 'Going off on mercy missions like Mother Teresa on behalf of the Liverpool Street Red Cross. Where was it last time? Turks and Caicos, wasn't it? Something to do with a typhoon, if I remember correctly.'

Mark didn't hesitate. In one fluid motion, he swung his arm and cracked the man across the jaw.

Being London, most people chose not to get involved in a confrontation between strangers and either crossed the street or passed by at speed. The younger man took a controlled step back but didn't fall. If the blow had hurt him – and, once upon a time, one of Mark's punches undoubtedly would have – he was able to absorb it with almost zen-like grace.

'You've got intel on me,' Mark spat. 'Point made. But I don't take threats lightly. Leave me alone.'

Mark turned and walked on.

'It's not a threat,' the man called after him. 'You could control this intel if you wanted.'

Mark stopped. Slowly, he stalked back.

'You know who I am and who I work for. I have access to information that would keep you awake for days. Why would I need your two-shilling outfit?'

The little fucker laughed. 'National Insurance numbers of Cambridge graduates? Online test scores by bored house husbands with delusions of grandeur? Give me a break.'

A bus roared past, and a puddle caught them both across the shins.

'So, you have people who know people,' Mark said. 'Very impressive. You clearly don't need me.'

Once again, he turned and walked.

About a minute later, he became aware of the young man ambling at his side.

'I've walked away twice and punched you once. This tenacity is going to become boring. Let me guess: whoever you're working for has made it clear they'll accept nothing less than my complete capitulation and you're scared of going back to them, once again, without me on side. I thought I'd made it clear to you last time. I can't be bought. I'm old and looking forward to retirement. You can stop spying on me now.'

'Where is she?' he asked.

Mark ignored him.

'Seriously. What's she told you about what she does?'

'This is sounding dangerously like the dinner party I just walked out on. You want me to wave some scant details at you the way I do my wife's guests? Fine. She helps to organise where supplies go – purification tablets, dried goods, whatever – and oversees where the fundraised money ends up. She trains the locals to help themselves after the aid workers have left. The end. Hope you enjoyed the soufflé.'

'But *where is she*? And what's she *really* doing?' the young man pressed.

'You know everything. *You tell me.*' Mark faced his stalker. 'We're grown adults. We don't need to play this witless parlour game. I see what you're doing, but there's no need. The less I know the better, believe me.'

'You don't believe that.'

'You know nothing about me.'

'I know first thing tomorrow morning you'll be tempted to run to the Chief and tell him you were approached by a man on the High Road. That there's a leak. That your daughter's compromised. But what will happen then? Will she be pulled out, her career strangled in its infancy? You know how these things operate, and you're too far into your own career to start climbing up towards the moral high ground now.' The man's hand went, again, to a jacket pocket. A business card, thick and lacquered, was produced. 'Take the card and think about it. I'm sorry if I've put you on edge, Mr Wolfe.'

'Are you after my help? Or are you investigating my daughter?'

'I think we can help *each other*. In the days, weeks, months to come, you'll begin to understand. The world's at a crossroads, and you were one of the best at what you did, so it goes without saying we'd benefit from your counsel, but we'd be useful to you too.' Something hard set in his eyes. Something that, despite the years spent fighting or fraternising with trained killers, chilled Mark to the marrow. 'For your country's sake – and your daughter's – consider our offer. I can't say any more.'

Mark took the card.

Mark sidled up to Jim the moment he saw him exit HQ on his lunch break.

Jim smiled, knowing this was no accident. 'Ah, Mr Wolfe. How are things going in my absence?'

'You know. So-so.'

Both knew better than to talk shop so close to the building, and eased into remarks upon the weather, the traffic, the latest debatable truths which had fallen from the mouth of the Prime Minister. Both were dressed in long black overcoats and leather gloves to fit in amongst the city bankers, January breath steaming from lungs like the last curlicues of dragon fire.

'Do you still walk around Vauxhall Pleasure Gardens in your lunch hour?' Mark asked.

'Half hour, these days, and not in this weather, no.'

'I was planning to, and I'd appreciate the company.'

And so they strolled to the park, bent against the wind in the same manner as the bare trees encircling them, the hulking spectre of the SIS building behind.

'How's my replacement?'

'He wears a bow tie.'

They fell into a long silence, breath fogging between them. 'Jody?' Jim asked.

It was often said, of military wives and widows, that life was so much harder for the ones left behind and Mark knew exactly what was meant by that now. Her absence was always at the back of him, lurking like a tumour. His daughter was not dead, not missing, not absent without leave, but a ghost nevertheless. When she failed to come home for Christmas, he knew she'd gone deep.

'We got a card from her. It satisfied her mother, but I suspect she wrote it before she left, for the Service to send on. From Tajikistan, apparently, although the postmark was too clean. Had it arrived a few days late, or been slightly battered, I might have believed it was genuine.' Mark delivered this guesswork with the smiling effrontery of one who knew he was, in this regard, addressing a superior.

'You know I can't—'

'I know.' The skies rolled grey above them. 'I feel I should apologise about my conduct at the Tin Belly. My constant brooding was ... unprofessional.'

'You were being human.'

'As I say, *unprofessional*.'

'She won't be there forever,' was the only bone Jim was willing to throw the sniffer dog.

'That's what I thought when they sent me to Belfast. I was there over a year.'

'I didn't know you were in Northern Ireland. They used your military service as a means of infiltration, I suppose.'

This felt like a deliberate overture on Jim's part to swerve the conversation away from Jody.

'Naturally. I was sent to watch a drug gang suspected of IRA involvement, so posed as a newly stationed English squaddie with ideas above his station who wanted a piece of drug money action. As the months wore on, it became obvious the gang's suspicions of me as an Ulster loyalist were keeping me at arm's length, so I exposed myself, deliberately getting caught attempting to steal a sample of unrefined cocaine on a factory visit. I was brought to the kingpin, who wasn't remotely the person MI6 had suspected, and was tortured with hot wire while they tried to find out which rival gang I worked for. They were completely unaware MI6 was trying to block the IRA's cashflow.'

Mark drew up his collar against the cold.

'Once I escaped, London wanted to put me on another mission, but I convinced them to keep me there. I hunted down several leaders, liquidated them and their security, and burned the whole operation to the ground three weeks before the ceasefire that accompanied Sinn Fein's re-admission to the peace talks preceding the Good Friday Agreement.'

Jim stopped so abruptly he might have stepped on a mine. 'Are you saying you caused so much damage the IRA were forced to enter legitimate politics?'

'I'm not claiming to have single-handedly brokered peace in Northern Ireland, no. But I played my part. Many of us did.'

Jim resumed his walk, polished shoes clicking on the path. 'I daresay the moral to this story is forthcoming?'

'Without information, a spy isn't a spy. He's furniture. I have no wish to be a spy any longer, and my latest mission – as a neutered father condemned to scraps of false intel – is the hardest yet, I'll be honest. *However*, if she's where the danger is, she's trusted to be there. I have faith in my daughter.'

'Very sensible attitude, Mark.'

'I think she's in Afghanistan. It's Tajikistan's most likely neighbour.'

Jim stopped again. This time, there was more than a hint of iron in his voice. 'I'm not going to compromise a mission by confirming that logic, Mark, no matter how charmingly you mention these musings. You've done a lot for the Service, but it doesn't owe you information. *Everyone* operates on a need-to-know basis. I don't know everything that goes on in the field, and if I told you what I knew you'd still know next to nothing. I might, *might*, tell someone in Recruitment details of a case, if I thought it had a bearing on the early retention of agents, but I certainly wouldn't tell the parent of an agent out there spying on behalf of our country. And you know that.'

'I'm just thinking aloud, Jim.'

'You understand the game better than anyone. I'd hazard even Jody doesn't know everything about her mission, so don't take it personally.'

'She knows whether or not she's tied to a chair in a basement, which is more than I do.'

'What were you expecting from me, Mark? If someone told you she'd missed her latest report, would *that* satisfy you?'

'I'm not the only one interested in her, Jim. I've been accosted twice now, by a private security company.'

He felt Jim side-eye him.

'Last week was their most recent approach. A young man tried again to convince me my recruitment was important for global politics, implied he knew about my daughter's role within the Service. I was mad at the time, but they don't know as much as they think they do. He couldn't confirm where she was. Said Turks and Caicos was her most recent job, but that was her cover three missions ago.'

'You think she's compromised?'

'Not necessarily. But I'd like them investigated.'

'Those guys are pests. Cambridge Analytica have caused us no end of trouble recently. Who did your friend say he represented?'

'He gave me a card.' Mark produced a white rectangle with the word TAJSS written in neon blue.

'This it?' Jim turned it over. 'No number? What are you supposed to do with this? What does that acronym even mean?'

'Beats me. The SS is "security services" or similar. Ever heard of them?'

'No, but they're keen to build, that's for sure. Want me to dig?'

'I think it would be best. Most indies have shiny websites and put their members up front and out there. This lot ... I don't know. They headhunt me and then don't even leave me a way to contact them. I don't get it.'

'You realise this digging is what they want you to do? You'd be better off throwing this in the bin.'

For your country's sake – and your daughter's – consider our offer. I can't say any more.

'Something tells me that would be unwise.'

Jim pulled himself up to his full height. 'That's why you've been asking me in such unsubtle terms where Jody is. You want to cross-check whether the intel from these guys is accurate. You're not actually *interested* in their offer, are you?'

Mark had spent years as a paid deceiver, but he couldn't look Jim in the eye. 'This isn't about me keeping tabs on Jody. This is about finding out what private agencies have on us. We might have sprung a leak and God only knows who they sell their information to.'

Jim nodded, seemingly appeased. 'It's not hard to find out basic facts about some of our missions, but ... You're right. I'll keep the card, if that's OK.'

Mark let him.

Jim was wrong, though. It wasn't easy finding out information about MI6's current missions. Not only was he locked out of Jody's computer file, but she'd mocked him with that piece of folded paper on the terrace. *Disneyland*, was all it had read.

He couldn't believe he'd been so stupid as to believe she'd really call on him as insurance. Big, strong, famous Daddy, who, if anything happened to her, would strap on his parachute, beat up the bad guys and carry her home. He was a fool clinging to a parental pipe dream the way other fathers fantasised about scoring a goal in the FA Cup final. Jody wasn't devoting her life to MI6 in the hope of being rescued from Islamic State like a glorified damsel in distress, and it was insulting and reductive to them both to even consider she might have done so.

They strolled back to headquarters without speaking.

'We should do this again,' Mark said.

Jim offered a thin smile and gave his former colleague's hand an extra, meaningful squeeze at reception before making his way to his new floor.

Jody was dead.

Bank transfers may have been dropping into her NatWest account, courtesy of the government, but his daughter – currently – did not exist, not as Jody Wolfe. Her cover was her life, her life her cover. Mark remembered what that existence was like and was simultaneously envious and fearful.

His daily grind now, dedicated to being a cog in the machine that created men and women as he used to be, was pale in comparison, and yet, as he'd grown into his semi-retirement, he'd become more comfortable with the warm bath that was life after active service. Like the sportsman who'd retired young due to mounting pressures on his body and slid into a soft tangent of management or punditry, his job reminded him *just enough* of what he used to do that dealing with relaxation and its attendant obligations – supermarket Sundays; soap opera omnibuses; mowing the lawn in his slippers – was possible. Most people he socialised with hadn't experienced death rearing at them from dark quarters of unmapped shanty towns, and he understood and respected that in much the same way Neil Armstrong probably had to accept sitting behind a desk was never going to be as stimulating as bouncing about on the moon.

There had been distractions, of course, in this mellow second life of his. For a start, he'd raised children. Other men collected stamps or played cricket or conducted steamy affairs with their secretaries; he'd forged a spook prodigy from a collection of subliminal tells and mistrustful DNA.

Jody's espionage gene wasn't his fault. Plenty of people watched spy films with car chases and perma-horny leads and dreamed of being secret agents, but they never acted upon those urges because the nurturing of spies was something more organic and ineradicable, a compulsion from deep inside like a sexuality you can't control.

She was born this way, he told himself. *I'm not to blame.*

His mind spun in circles on the matter. Day after day.

And it only got worse after he switched on the evening news and saw the devastating aftermath of the Kabul bombing.

Bloodstains on a dirt road. Men in khaki shouldering assault rifles. Women beneath hijabs staring at the camera with hard, weary suffering in piercing olive eyes.

'More than thirty people have been killed and over seventy injured in Afghanistan's capital by a series of suicide bombings and a shoot-out between Afghan forces and militants who stormed a government building. According to a ministry spokesperson, at least two hundred civilians were rescued during an eight-hour operation.' Two days ago, the newsreader casually added, a car bomb had killed twenty.

At that moment, Mark was certain Jody was in Kabul. Not only was Tajikistan nearby, a cover Jim had all but confirmed with his terse remonstration, but her latest mission was a large-scale one, and there was no larger-scale fuck-up right now than Afghanistan. Taliban and Islamic State fighters mounted almost daily attacks on Afghan forces, government workers and civilians, while every major political power circled like birds of prey for control of the country.

Mark scanned the panicked images of state troops bustling round the carcass of the bombed building for his daughter, hunted through the bodies covered by crimson-soaked sheets. In the face of Afghanistan's fury, what possible hope could Jody have? Any successful operations she might be involved in would still be as a pebble in that lake of rage, and even an MI6 operative's intuition for danger couldn't have saved her if she'd been in the middle of the bombing.

He snatched the television off, but the images lived in his mind all day.

'It's been months since we had contact,' Mark stated across the breakfast table the following morning. 'They gave us an emergency number in case of radio silence, and I think we should call.'

'I'd feel like I was interfering,' Alessia argued. 'She's busy.'

Mark knew Jody's runners would serve him what was now commonly referred to as 'fake news' but was curious about what they'd say. His wife, demonstrably, was less concerned than he was, believing their daughter to be engaged in little more than a Brownie summer camp.

'I read about a helicopter crash there yesterday.'

'What?' Her eyes bulged.

He sat beside her as she typed in the number.

'Hello, I'm ringing because my husband and I ... We haven't heard from our daughter for some time and were given this number to call in case of emergency.'

Mumbling from the end of the line.

'About ... Maybe seven weeks? Eight?'

'And the rest,' Mark added, leaning in to hear better. He'd always believed his hearing was fine but had started getting disgusted looks from other road users when he listened to Radio 4 with the windows down.

Alessia pored through her text messages, then detailed the date of the last exchange with Jody, went over where their daughter was supposedly posted and recited a seven-digit code they'd been given to 'speed up the chain of information'. There was a pause while someone passed the line over to a colleague working in contact with Jody's team. The crease between Alessia's brows lengthened. 'Yes. Wolfe. That's correct.' When instructed, she read out the security code again.

Mark indicated he wanted the phone passed to him.

'Hello? This is Mark Wolfe, Jody's father. Can you tell us *anything* about where she is, currently?'

There was an ostentatious and decisive pause. He listened for interference, strange clicks, ghosting, but these were the hangovers of a spy trained decades ago. Lines weren't physically spliced or rewired any longer; if there was another listener, they'd be thousands of miles away in silent, digital anonymity.

'Let me investigate this for you, sir.' Did the genuflecting 'sir' reveal they knew who he was? The man had clearly been thrown by the change of speaker. 'As far as I can tell, operations are continuing as expected. If you like, I can contact base?'

'Any idea when we might hear back?'

The voice was wary. 'The next twenty-four hours, all being well.'

It was evening when the phone purred again. All day, he'd been wondering what they'd come back with, how they'd delay the facts, but he wasn't expecting anything as lame as the lines they ended up feeding him.

'Mr Wolfe? I'm ringing on behalf of the International Red Cross. We have a message from your daughter. She apologises for not being in touch. Communication networks have been knocked out by storms in her area, but we got through on higher-frequency lines.'

He dug a little deeper. 'It satisfies things as far as I'm concerned but I think my wife might have some problems with this.' He adopted a conspiratorial tone. 'Am I to tell her power lines have been down for two months?'

There was a pause. 'I rather suspect she was busy before, and neglected to call you when she could have done. The communications outage is a recent issue.'

'And what should I say if our daughter fails to contact us in the next few weeks?'

Another pause, as though before a chess move. 'Perhaps, Mr Wolfe, you might want to consider informing your wife you've had contact with her. To put her mind at rest.'

'A very sensible suggestion.'

'And, depending on how long her silence needs maintaining, we'll engineer further strategies moving forward.'

'Thank you for your time.'

'Not at all.' The voice clicked out and Mark replaced the phone.

'Who was that?' his wife called from the bath. 'Was that about Jody?'

'Yes. Nothing to worry about. Power lines are down. Have been for a while. She'll call us using the base's back-up generator as soon as she's able.'

'Oh, that *is* a relief.'

'Isn't it? Great to know our little girl's safe and well.'

Grim-faced, he strode out into the garden to brood on his bench beneath the elms.

It was official. Compromised. Burned. Dead in the water. Something had gone wrong with his daughter's mission on a catastrophic scale.

7

SIS headquarters rose above the Thames, a flamboyant and tinselled carapace hiding in obvious eyesight of the entire world. What most of the world didn't know was the extraordinary security which lay beneath the conspicuous: triple-glazed windows made from twenty-five types of glass; hidden rooms; bunkers, moats and tunnels to Whitehall. Mark had often fantasised about how he'd react if there were an attempted terrorist takeover of the offices, if a bomb went off in Accounting. He knew his escape routes, an enemy's own likely exit. In many ways, he was better prepared for that eventuality than he was the telephone call he received the next morning.

It was a number from High Command. Only calls from the Top Floor failed to show any code.

The voice was female, to the point.

'Mr Wolfe?'

'Yes?'

'You are requested to attend a briefing. Room Delta November. Immediate.'

He knew better than to ask for more information. 'Right away.' He left his office and cursed his way to the lift.

Mark had been unable to concentrate on his work, watching words on his screen slide before him like so many ants on ice, and it hadn't helped that Cecil had returned from a week's leave and his over-officious urgency when it came to even the most mundane task was as exhausting as the fears Mark carried. He was not a man designed to wait. He needed to act.

But there was nothing he could do.

The news over the last month had seen increasing bloodshed in Afghanistan and, indeed, the night before had brought yet another Kabul bombing into his home. A squall of police sirens and blood running down stone steps had been more than enough to force him to snatch off the news and hurl the remote onto the opposite chair, much to Alessia's surprise, who'd been sitting in it.

The lift descended and Mark stepped out.

So enshrouded and idiosyncratic were the protocols of MI6, the Top Floor was in the secure, bomb-proof basement and Mark was immediately required to present his pass to an armed young man sitting within a glass box like a piece of votive taxidermy. He looked fierce, in that way most ex-military are once they find themselves deskbound. While his ID was checked, Mark tried to control his breathing.

'Room Delta November?' he asked. Mark knew none of the rooms down here had numbers and any appellations they were given changed on a regular basis.

The security man responded only by handing back Mark's pass and stabbing a buzzer. Seconds later, a woman dressed in fatigues appeared through an armoured door to Mark's left and announced, 'Follow me, please.'

The subterranean Top Floor was decorated very differently to the rest of the building. Whereas the area he worked in was representative of a traditional twenty-first-century office, with telephones ringing in Scandinavian-designed pods adorned with clearly marked health and safety regulations, the carpeted bunker floors had a more imperialistic appearance and looked more like luxury quarters than steerage. The dark wood-panelled walls hosted hundreds of portraits of admirals and realm defenders from days gone by, as though compensating for the lack of windows. Library-silent, chieftains buried themselves away behind multi-locked doors and anterooms that led to laboratories, workshops and computer suites.

The woman stopped in front of a thick metal door, identifiable only by the acronym CC.

'They're waiting for you in there,' she announced. 'Go straight in.'

But Mark found himself pausing before he did so. Despite his own ranking within MI6, he'd never been this far down, and he sorely didn't want to hear whatever he was about to be told.

This, as the initials on the door had indicated, was Command Centre.

His surveillance skills were on red alert as he stepped into a plush office bigger than he would have thought possible from the dimensions of the secretarial en suite behind him. Possibly some of the doors outside were false. The wall immediately to Mark's left was packed with leather-bound books, an armchair before it empty but for an iPad, charging. Set into the wall of books was a hefty plasma TV rolling silent news and, in the middle of the room, sat a sizeable conference table. The Chief of the Secret Intelligence Service, or 'C' for short, perched at one end, a greying, still handsome man of about fifty-five with a distinguished military and intelligence career behind him. He smelt of knighthood, the type of tall, composed individual who emitted innate, straight-backed leadership. There were two others with him, a man of about thirty-five whose body language suggested he was intimidated by the situation and a middle-aged woman with a baked-in nonchalant expression, both reposing in chairs opposite one another, flanking the Chief. The empty chair completing the four fringes of this democratic oval, opposite C, was left for Mark.

'Take a seat,' the Chief intoned, not kindly, not aggressively. Nothing about his voice betrayed what might come.

Mark floated towards the empty seat over soft, deep carpet, trying to maintain eye contact with all three of them, though the younger man's eyes immediately fell to the government-marked papers before him.

'I understand your daughter is currently engaged in an operation,' C said. Mark sensed this was no friendly preamble.

'That may well be correct, sir. I can't attest to the true nature of her brief.'

The Chief shot him an almost-respectful glance. 'It must be strange for you, your daughter following in your footsteps.'

'Not at all.' Mark tried to remember he was a man of considerable distinction within the Service himself, and kept his voice steady. 'If you knew my daughter as well as I do, you'd understand she was made for this sort of work.'

'It's not a concern, then?'

'I'd be concerned for my daughter whatever her career path – you can't turn off the worry for your children – but I can sleep at night knowing she's well trained, sir.'

The Chief nodded. It had come all the way to the top, then: the phone call to the helpline; the entreaty to Jim in the park; his idling desktop truancies. This was his official ticking-off over the matter, where he was ordered to keep his nose out and leave the professional field agent to fend for herself.

'This is Naomi Greaves, our Staff Chief.' C indicated the woman to Mark's right. 'And this is Adam Wellcome, our new head of South Asia Operations.'

'Good morning,' Mark said.

They both nodded noncommittally in return.

C passed over a decanter of water and Mark was aware of his near-steady fingers being watched as he poured himself a glass.

Once, there had been very little separating Mark from the Chief. They'd had remarkably similar careers up to about thirty. If anything, Mark's had been more successful. Mark was a head of department but, had he not spent those wilderness years chasing ways to forget the Service, it could well have been him in the Chief's chair. That gap in his CV led his MI6 paymasters to believe espionage wasn't as thick within his blood as it had once been and, by the time he'd gone through the vetting process again, worked his way up the ranks, he was deemed too old to train the recruits. But he could still spot the good ones, and Recruitment was where he stayed.

'Fill him in, Adam,' C ordered, but without taking his eyes off Mark.

Adam cleared his throat. 'For years, my department has handled agents we know will prove useful in strategic locations around South Asia.' His received-English voice instantly put Mark's back up. 'We've been building links with local forces and aiding them in their fight against various terrorist cells in the area. It's a long, desperate war but, alongside our cousins, we've taken out several terrorist heads in the last few years, though there are so many coming through the ranks it's no more than pruning. We're not just fighting terrorists: we're at war with ... an ideological infection.'

Mark looked around the table, waiting for more. It came, but not from Adam.

C took over, his voice low and measured. 'About two months ago, we began to suspect one of our agents had gone rogue in Afghanistan. The details are obviously need-to-know, but . . . Last night we lost four agents. Four. The rogue is still at large and there's an ongoing operation to bring them in.'

Mark fingered his glass. 'I appreciate you telling me this. Presumably my daughter's involved in this . . .?' Vocabulary died in his throat. Was this their way of telling him she'd been one of this rogue's victims?

'When did you last speak to your daughter, Mr Wolfe?' There was a faint trace of an Irish brogue to the woman's voice. It had a less accusatory edge compared to the others and her eyes even possessed a welcome degree of kindness.

'Um . . . I'm not sure. We received a Christmas card.'

'And she never indicated anything to you about her intentions over there?' Her palms opened in supplicatory enquiry.

'Why would she?'

C resumed the narrative. 'Our last communication with Jody was over a month ago. She's been underground since.'

The room seemed to shrink into a small dot of motion sickness.

'Are you trying to tell me you've lost her?' Mark refused to play the insubordinate and raise his voice – three of the most powerful members of the Service had summoned him to the bunker to lay this before him – but it took superhuman willpower to remain calm. 'That she's missing?' He knew the statistics. Deep cover was essential at times, but you made contact when you could. An agent who hadn't called anything in for over a month was highly unlikely to still be alive.

'It's worse than that, I'm afraid,' Adam coughed. 'Our intel points to her being the rogue.'

A weasel of a man named Dorian was waiting with Cecil when a shell-shocked Mark returned to the department. The weasel wore small glasses over a stubby beak of a nose and sat flicking through any piece of paper with Jody's name or number on it. Target practice scores. Theory results. Interview transcripts. Cecil, for once, looked nonplussed as he fetched the required paperwork for their unwelcome visitor.

'Had she always wanted to work for MI6?' Dorian asked, once Mark had shown him into his office. Snakes of rain hissed down the window.

'We never spoke about it. I didn't even know she knew I worked for Six.'

Dorian licked a finger and turned a page in the dossier, then looked up as though he'd been expecting more. 'And yet, you say, she initially went to elaborate lengths to hide her recruitment from you. How did she work out your role here?'

He paused. *Oh, I passed spycraft on in my genes.* 'I figured she just pieced it together.'

'There was no one who could have recruited her *before us?*'

'Isn't this all a little over the top? How do you know she hasn't gone deep or, worse, been captured? Shouldn't you be trying to find her?'

'We *are* trying to find her.'

'You won't find her hiding in our filing cabinets.'

'I should formally say that any reluctance to cooperate will result in disciplinary measures.'

Mark stopped himself before saying something he'd regret. 'My daughter is not a terrorist or double agent. She's clearly been compromised in the field and you're looking in the wrong place. Check the data for yourself: she was an excellent candidate. She passed our aptitude tests with high scores.'

'So it *says*.'

Mark tried to swallow his tongue.

Dorian picked up on the silence. 'Relax, Mr Wolfe. We're just checking every avenue. I'm sure there was a reason she was fast-tracked. I have it on good accounts she was an exceptional talent.'

'She was not "fast-tracked". She was a fast learner. That's not the same thing. She moved through the procedure quicker than most, it's true, but she didn't skimp on anything, as the records show. What the hell has happened to my daughter?'

Dorian shot him a look that was pure policeman. 'Did you ever have cause to wonder, at any point, during this process, why she was joining the Service?'

'Why did *you* join the Service? Why does anyone? We want to make the country we live in safer and, as a result, the world.'

'That's your answer. Not hers. There are many people who desire the exact opposite of those sentiments.'

'I can't give you her answer. For all I know, she's lying low in order to complete her mission without clumsy interference from short-sighted pencil pushers such as yourself.'

'I'll thank you not to insult me. We are following every lead in trying to work out where she is.'

'You're bloody lucky I'm only insulting you.'

'Agents have died,' Dorian said. His eyes were large behind his glasses. 'Missions have gone wrong over there. Too many. I understand you're upset by all of this, but I'm doing this by the book. And you must too, if you want to know what's happened to your daughter.'

Mark sighed. 'I assume you're grilling the head of operations over there as well as her own family?'

Dorian removed his glasses and pinched between his eyes in what seemed a well-practiced act of exasperation. 'Don't tell us how to do our jobs, please.'

'I have decades of service with this organisation. Decades. I was dodging bullets when you were learning how to wipe your arse and you insult me by implying my daughter has anything but unconditional love for our country. Look all you want, ask all the questions you must, but you won't find any dirt on her.'

Dorian said, 'We'll see,' with so much latent disbelief he clearly expected the opposite.

'Oh, get the *fuck out of here*, you useless politician. How dare you!'

Dorian blinked up at him. 'Are you throwing me out of your office?'

'Damn right. And if this glass weren't so bloody thick it would be through the window.'

Dorian smirked and rose. 'I shall be reporting to our superiors that you threatened me and deliberately refused to cooperate with the investigation.'

'And I'll be reporting that, less than half an hour after I found out from the station chief that my only daughter was lost in Afghanistan, a jobsworth who wouldn't know what field work looked like if it sat on his face accused my family of betraying the very organisation I've dedicated my life to.'

Mark did log a complaint, and so did Dorian.

An hour later, Mark was suspended from duties, pending further inquiries. Cecil was placed in temporary charge of Recruitment and Asset Validation.

Mark pulled up into his driveway to find an investigation team dressed like forensic scientists waiting for him. He knew his career was over.

He introduced himself, told them he was willing to cooperate, and they asked him to point out any safes or storage lockers before cleaning out most of his office and removing their evidence in thick cardboard boxes.

A mildly overweight investigator with a 1970s moustache – maybe they were back in fashion; what the hell did Mark know anymore? – asked him if Jody ever stayed on the premises.

'She sometimes sleeps here, but rarely.' Mark was already regretting his willingness to assist.

'Could you identify the bedroom she stays in when she does, please?'

Once Mark's cooperation was deemed over, and his mobile phone handed in, they asked him to leave his own home. He waited in his car while they searched without him, wondering if these investigators even knew who he was.

They did their job swiftly and thoroughly but were little more than state-paid robbers in his eyes, ones who reminded him of the aftermath of their burglary a few years ago, when officers picked through their home to make an inventory of the missing, leaving black fingerprinting dust on every surface. The burglary investigation hadn't been a regular follow-up, given the state secrets in Mark's possession, but MI6 soon decreed his belongings hadn't fallen into Chinese or Russian hands. The laptop stolen had been his wife's and the thief a junkie opportunist from Wood Green who was caught a day later attempting to rob a neighbour. The stolen items were never recovered but the lasting legacy was the invasion itself: coming home to an air of uncertainty every evening and wondering if a masked stranger was midway through ransacking their life. It was a disquietude that Mark had lived with for a long time but had been a new sensation to Alessia, and she hadn't liked being alone in the house for long periods after the experience. He prayed the investigators would be done before she got home.

What would he tell Alessia? Would the whole sorry tale come crashing down? All those years of subterfuge. If it did, she'd never forgive him. Or maybe she would, maybe she'd even be proud, were it not for the fact that their daughter was – Missing? Dead? A double agent? Better that than some hastily prepared MI6 cover story he'd have to live with for the rest of his life that claimed she'd tumbled into a ravine whilst trying to get supplies to orphans during a natural disaster.

What the hell had gone wrong in Afghanistan? If he hadn't been so rude to that desk-jockey they'd sent to investigate his department, he might have been in a better position to find out. MI6 were no good to him at arm's length, and yet his pride had lashed out and he'd done something he'd never done in all his years of loyal service. He'd questioned the information passed down by a superior.

By five o'clock, they were done. The last of the investigation team walked past his car, pretending he wasn't there.

A graveyard silence met him in the house. The air of intrusion.

They'd tried to put everything back as best they could, but it was obvious that pictures had been rehung hastily, their backs and innards searched. An escritoire in the corner of the living room had been carelessly ransacked, its papers checked, no doubt photographed. The sofa cushions had been unzipped, then replaced in a careless manner his wife would never condone. He set to work ordering the place before she came home.

His office was forlorn, despoiled, and he didn't have the heart to look it over properly. They'd spent all day going through his papers and the desk drawers had been turned inside out, possible secret spaces investigated. His computer was gone, so too his USBs and disks. Even he didn't know what was on half of them, but it was infinitely more likely to be dirty photos of his wife from yesteryear than proof of treason. He closed the door on his office and locked it behind him.

He stalked the steps to the silent upstairs, carpet rods lifted and returned to almost-original positions. Here, too, the pictures hanging in the hall were slightly off-centre. The loft ladder was out and he folded it away without bothering to inspect the attic space. He checked the bulbs in the lights for fresh bugs, the upstairs telephone, but MI6 wouldn't be so obvious, around him of all people.

That they had been so thorough in such a little amount of time was astonishing. Out of habit, he checked all the obvious alcoholic's hiding places in the bathroom and bedroom. The bedside drawers had obviously been pored through, the undersides of tables and desks checked, more pictures, ceiling fixtures. It smacked of a genuine search, as opposed to a routine, by-the-book follow-up. They'd told him about his daughter *before* they'd fallen upon his home, which he'd hoped meant the Top Floor still trusted him, but the investigators had arrived before he did, genuinely hoping to catch him with his trousers down.

He tried to distance himself from what had happened in his home, attempted to summon the spy's apathy which had served him in such good stead in the active days of his career, the cold-hearted professionalism that kept him alive, but such a detachment escaped him completely when he opened the door to his daughter's bedroom and saw what they'd done to it.

Kabul, it seemed, had come to North London. The walls were punched with holes where they'd searched for hidden spaces, the floorboards pulled up and probed underneath. The bed was against a wall, disassembled. All her books and notepads, what few she'd left, were missing. The stuffing was showing along the seam of a teddy bear. Her bedside lamp had been pulled apart and its metallic innards disembowelled on its table. A photograph album of school friends she hadn't seen in years was missing, as were many other objects he now couldn't place. Only their absence spoke to him. Sketchbooks from college, university admission letters, certificates, all would have been bagged up and taken off for clinical investigation under laboratory conditions.

That was when it hit him. MI6 made mistakes, sure, but this was a next-level post-mortem and the damage caused to her room was determined, a bedlam that evinced the utter disrespect for Jody that her own employers had. She'd passed from child to adult in these innocent four walls, from cot to double bed, via posters that helped her count and tell the time to the star charts and Klimt prints now ripped on the floor; golds and browns and yellows, mothers and children twisted in lifeless straight lines. What justified this destruction? This wasn't how the Service behaved when it visited leafy detached residences owned by well-off civil servants to make routine investigations. This was how it treated the bad guys.

What MI6 thought they were hunting for he had no idea, but his resolve vanished as he finally gave in to what he suspected would be rage but turned out to be long, body-shuddering tears of grief that dragged him down to the floor in the nature of a penitent and sent him prostrate at the doorway of his missing, enemy-of-the-state daughter.

8

THE MISSION IN ROME HAD kickstarted it all.

It was a simple job, retrieving a Ugandan scientist from the British embassy before his nation's secret police detected him, but matters had been complicated by a last-minute change of plan by the Italians and Mark found himself with two hours to kill, and no Ugandan scientist, so spent it at a local bar.

He could no longer remember the name of the place but it was one of those tourist traps, common in capital cities across Europe, which inexplicably pandered to visitors' nostalgia for all things Irish when abroad and hoped by festooning their establishment with posters of Guinness toucans and Van Morrison nobody would notice the inch missing from their pints and the sausages built from sawdust. A dark-haired, dark-eyed woman was sitting in the corner on her own, reading *La Repubblica* and enjoying what looked like vodka and orange. When she approached the bar, he made a point of speaking to her.

He pretended to be a tourist and asked her to identify some landmarks on his map, which she duly did, even though they were already marked. He offered to buy her a drink as thanks. She accepted.

They talked about travel and family and food – he kept it imprecise, as per his training – and it transpired she was in

Rome for a modelling shoot. She lived in Santa Maria, a beachside hamlet four hours' drive south, about which she waxed lyrical while shaking her ebony hair out of her face and sipping her drink through a straw. She had lips like a movie star.

'Your English is good,' he told her.

She downplayed this flattery with a roll of her *cioccolata* eyes, perhaps knowing that it wasn't true. While her English was undoubtedly better than his Italian, it lacked a certain fluency that rendered their conversation partly opaque. She occasionally guessed words based on their Latin origin, conjuring a beautiful nonsense.

It wasn't love at first sight. They were both barely thirty and, if he'd had more time in Italy's capital, he may well have bedded her and moved on. The fleetingness of their meeting captured him, the potential of unfinished business, and, as his hidden pager announced he needed to make his way to the embassy, he wavered in his career-long commitment to be an anonymous spectre. Against the instinctive caution hammered onto him like armour, he gave her his real phone number and name. None of the usual tells were obvious from her body language and he'd been the one moving on her. If she were a honey trap, he decided, Alessia was the best he'd ever seen.

He got the Ugandan across the border and returned to London.

A few days passed and Alessia hadn't called him so he took the initiative and rang to say how much he'd enjoyed her company and asked whether she fancied meeting when he was in Rome again the following week. When she informed him she wouldn't be around, he assumed a polite brush-off and relegated her to the back of his mind. After returning from an operation in Gibraltar concerning a Spanish people smuggler, he found a week-old message on his answerphone, saying she'd be in London for a few days. Due to the unreliability of his profession, he had missed the dates. By the time he was able to return the call, she was back sunning herself in Santa Maria. Had she been a sparrow, he considered, she would have engineered a date by now.

This sort of gradual not-quite-a-relationship continued for many months. He would receive postcards from her, and long letters in which she practised her English, each one a marked improvement on the one before on account of her evening classes. The paper always smelt of a perfume she'd purposefully sprayed nearby, a citrussy note in more ways than one. Her modelling, she told him, wasn't going well, the industry was full of creeps and perverts and she couldn't wait until they met again, so she could be reminded of what a real gentleman was. *When are you next in Rome, caro?*

He would respond with shorter, less informative letters, giving her the impression he was a junior civil servant with business interests in Italy's capital. Though his financial ventures weren't currently raking in much, he had his fingers, he took pains to tell her, in plenty of other pies. This was an idiom she took to heart and would often ask, 'How are your other pies?' at the close of most of her letters.

They met up for the occasional carnal weekend in Rome. Afterwards, they'd go their separate ways and resume a pen pal relationship, though he was guarded about putting too much of himself down on paper. He assumed she saw other men during this time, though never asked, and he certainly took other women. In those days, there was no guarantee he'd be alive at the season's end, so he lived while he could.

When he retired from active duty, the first thing he did was fly over to see her. Their relationship, in his eyes, only began the moment he'd left MI6, though he got the impression she'd considered their union concrete for some time. They spent two weeks swimming, dining, making love. When he returned to the UK, she came with him.

They were married soon after and had Jody the following year.

Mark's alcoholism followed.

Alessia knew he was struggling and chalked it down to the bankruptcy of his business investments, which he told her had been in silver, and his newfound role as a father. He threw himself into hedge fund work in the city and long hours, trying to hide himself in work, that day-long wait until a socially acceptable hour to start drinking, but it was unsustainable. The years of lies and the memories of the things he'd done, which he refused to share with the government shrink they'd tried to send, ate at him until he found himself, not in a hospital, not in rehab, but back at MI6's door.

'You are back with the civil service?' Alessia asked him one evening, bathing Jody in a tub of ducks and bubbles. 'Why? Was work in the city not going well?' The hedge fund work was making more money than thirty civil service jobs.

'It's what I want to do,' he shrugged, his eyes clear, his blood unintoxicated, and she couldn't argue with that.

This time around, he wasn't required to disappear unannounced to random parts of the world without a bye your leave and could easily maintain an honest pretence of the nine-to-five, but there was still a degree of white-lying to be told on occasion. He told her he was performing his old role in the new building on the south side of the river but that it was so monumentally boring it was barely worth discussing.

'The spy building?' she asked him. 'What if the Chinese attack you with a missile? What if terrorists drive a bus full of bombs into your office?'

He reassured her there was nowhere more Chinese-missile- or bus-full-of-bombs-proof in the entire continent and his spy-mingling career was only quietly goaded in private moments after that.

And then time began to pass at an alarming rate, as it does once you've had children, and he remained, in his head, forever in his early thirties while his children sprouted upwards at a rate of knots and his own body revealed itself to be significantly older until, one day, his children were adults and he and his wife resembled their respective parents. He didn't mind that; he'd meant the whole 'till death do us part' thing and Alessia was as beautiful to him now as she'd been that first time they'd met in Rome all those years ago.

And in all that time, she never found out the truth about what he really did for a living.

Not until the evening Mark fell off the wagon.

He'd managed to tidy up before Alessia came home. There was no amount of cleaning that could have repaired his study or Jody's bedroom but, suspended from duty, he knew there'd be time for him to at least try and do so, and to come up with a plausible explanation for the mess behind both locked doors.

The moment she walked in, she knew something was amiss.

'There is an odd smell.'

'Yes, I'm home early,' he tried to joke.

'Have you had somebody over?'

'Just Monica Bellucci, darling. Can I fix you a drink?'

She looked at him with the kind of suspicion you'd soon learn to fear if you'd lived with a southern Italian for your entire married life. 'Hmm,' was all she said, staring at the sofa cushions. Mark couldn't for the life of him see what it was she'd spotted that was so different, and he was the one with the espionage training.

After dinner, the doorbell tolled.

Ever hopeful, he rose from his chair and stole to the hallway, but the tall figure hovering behind frosted glass obviously didn't belong to their daughter.

'Jim,' Mark announced, loudly enough for his wife to hear. 'This is an unexpected pleasure.'

Mark ushered him inside, looked up the street, then snapped the door behind his ex-colleague. Jim was bundled towards Mark's study in a silence thick with collusion.

'Bloody hell,' Jim said, looking over the mess after the door was closed behind them.

Mark indicated the seat opposite his desk, then sat down himself. Neither seemed to know what to say until Jim finally offered, 'At least they left you the chairs.'

'What do you know?'

'I heard you'd been suspended.'

'That it?'

Jim shuffled in his seat and Mark watched his eyes take in the room. 'How are you doing?'

'Badly. Can I get you a drink?'

Jim checked his watch.

'Don't worry about it. It's aperitif hour.' Mark opened the bottom drawer and pulled out the unopened scotch MI6 had kindly left un-thieved. He found a glass and ripped open the plastic surrounding the bottle's cap. He filled the glass and handed it over. 'Knowing who to trust is part and parcel of what we've always done. I can't turn it off. It does make life very challenging at times. But I have to ask: are we on the same side, right now?'

Jim took the glass and eyeballed it with even more suspicion than Alessia had levelled at the sofa cushions. 'You understand the paranoia, then?'

'So you know what they're saying about Jody. I wondered.'

Jim placed his scotch glass on the desk, then grimaced as though he'd already drunk from it. He knew he'd been second-guessed. 'Yes,' he sighed. 'I do.'

'And what's Operations' position on the matter?'

'Personally, I haven't seen enough evidence to declare the Service's theory conclusive, but I'm sure there are good reasons for the investigation. Why does a teetotaller have a bottle of scotch in his desk drawer?'

Mark tried to remain as calm and affable as possible. 'To remind me of my strength. Care to share the evidence you *have* seen, or is this a social visit just to see me squirm?'

'I don't—'

'Do our superiors know you're here?'

'No one knows I'm here.'

'You think so? You honestly believe there isn't a car down the street with a man triangulating everything via my Wi-Fi? Or that the guys who cleaned me out didn't leave me dirtier than before?'

'I wasn't followed. And I'm not wearing a wire, if that's what you think.'

'Don't worry. I'm not asking you to take off your clothes.'

'You really *don't* trust anyone, do you?'

'What do you know about this mission of Jody's in Afghanistan?'

Jim looked down at his shoes for an uncomfortably long time, then said, 'I do have access to some classified information regarding your daughter, but not enough to make any difference for you.'

'No one has access to all the information. We're all just pieces of code, and put together we're scrambled. This whole game is institutionalised insanity and I've sleepwalked my own flesh and blood into it. Keep your bloody intelligence. Anything you tell me will only be what you're allowed to let me know, and therefore useless to me. Your fear, naturally, is that if you drip me some misinformation, I'll spill that knowledge at some point and our superiors will know where the leak came from. We're pawns in a game whose rules never change.'

'The rules did change, though, Mark. For you. You're no longer a secret agent. Out there, in the field, all the information you needed was available, remember? You played the game, got the intel you wanted and got out. It's far murkier on the other side, as the one being investigated.'

'They're not investigating me. They're investigating my daughter.'

Jim indicated the ruin of Mark's office. 'You think?'

'I'm too old for this, Jim. I wake up two or three times a night to piss and these days do so sitting down.' He indicated the scotch. 'Not drinking?'

'Trying to loosen my lips?'

Mark stared at the full glass sitting in front of Jim. It was rather generously poured. 'I keep wondering ... If she's even alive, has she got any idea the Service is under the impression she's gone rogue?'

Jim readjusted himself in his chair. 'If an agent fails to reply, we send people out to look, but if one plants a bomb and then disappears off the face of the Earth, well, the whole force of MI6 will rain down upon her. We'll find her faster if she's gone to the other side, if that's any consolation.'

'She planted a bomb?'

Jim took a deep breath, then picked up the glass. He seemed to think twice, then replaced it. 'She wasn't killed in the same explosion that took ... some of our guys.'

'She got herself captured, goddamn it.'

'You received a ransom note? Don't jump to conclusions.'

'What evidence is there for her turning over? It can't just be because she's disappeared.'

'Well, exactly. Look, I can't discuss the evidence with you because I don't have it, but the Top Floor doesn't run on guesswork. If they say they've uncovered proof that Jody's selling information, or killed our agents, or run, then we must take that as official. I'm sorry.'

'Why would she do that? It makes no sense.'

Jim leaned forward. 'How well do you know, really *know*, your daughter?'

'I know in my heart she's not a hostile.'

'I'm afraid that won't help the investigation. My wife knows in her heart that Jesus is watching over our dead dog. Think hard. Was there anything in Jody's behaviour that ever struck you as strange, anything that might be used to cast doubt against her?'

So, this was the *good cop* interview, was it? 'As I told the Service earlier, she passed through the recruitment process fair and square. *You saw to that.*'

Jim's shoulders noticeably drooped. 'I'm not here to exonerate myself. If I missed anything it was because ...'

'Because you trusted me.'

'Yes.'

'You *did* come here on behalf of Six.'

'I came here on *your* behalf. For you. I've been worried.'

'But you're not under investigation?'

'Of course I am. But I'm answering their questions and not threatening to throw people out of windows. Plus, Jody's not my daughter. That's the difference. Mark, if you doubted her intentions, even minutely, who would you remain loyal to? Your family? Or your country?'

'I wouldn't have allowed any of this if I'd even suspected for *a second* she was working for Russia, or whoever you think it is.'

'But you *didn't* suspect?'

'No.'

'And that, in the eyes of our superiors, is what makes you unreliable.'

'You think they've already made up their minds?'

Jim shrugged. 'They've brought the investigation all the way back to London. They must be pretty sure.'

Mark stared, exhausted, into the middle distance. 'What can I do?'

'Cooperate with the investigation. Help them as much as possible and you'll keep your job.'

'You're assuming I want it. This is how I'm treated? My daughter is *innocent*.'

'They don't think so. What you need to prove now is *your* innocence.'

Mark eyed his ex-colleague with undisguised suspicion. 'You can report back that I'll comply, but I'll never accept their verdict that Jody's been turned. And they won't find anything in the stuff they took today.' He indicated the glass again. 'Not tempted?'

'I'm driving. Just remembered.'

Mark reached for Jim's glass, knocked it back. It tasted miserable. He refilled it all the way to the brim as Jim watched him in genuine horror. 'What about you?' Mark asked. 'You believe Jody's done this ... *whatever* it is?'

'I hope for your sake the Service is wrong. But it's happened before. Agents turning rogue, I mean.'

Mark didn't appreciate the look of pretend sympathy which followed that oleaginous politician's answer.

'Happens all the time,' Mark hissed, bringing the glass back up to his lips. 'That's why they've pinned it on this case. Easiest damn solution.'

Jim sat back and picked at a mote of dust or hair on his right leg. He was rattled by Mark's drinking, Mark could tell, and, in this unnerved reaction, Mark had hit upon the only way he could pull rank over him. He raised the glass again.

'What will you tell your wife?' Jim asked.

'Nothing. That I'm working from home for a while.'

'About Jody?'

Mark closed his eyes and leaned back on his chair. The drink was already making it hard to confirm his own thoughts. 'I don't know.'

A weighty pause seemed to signal the end of the conversation, until Jim said, 'I've been investigating this TAJSS lot for you. You'll never guess what we've dug up.'

Mark snapped his eyes open. Outside, the shadow of the heather waved like the arms of drowning men. 'What?'

'Absolutely nothing.'

'Impossible. How could they target me and then vanish from the face of the Earth?'

'No one knows anything about them. What they stand for. Where they come from. We've identified no members. They have no history. No trace. They don't exist.'

'I can't believe that. They tracked me expertly. Had personal information on me. I have a feeling they suspected the death of Jody's mission long before the Service did.'

'Next time they approach, say you'll join them, won't you?' Jim laughed the false laugh of a Geiger counter. 'Maybe you can shed some light on who they are and what they're up to.'

Mark let his head fall. 'I might just do that. After all, as far as MI6 is concerned, I'm damaged goods.'

With the whisky bottle half-drained beside him, he sat under the elms and watched the sky in a stolen moment of relative peace. There were never many stars above polluted, hazy London, and his trees scratched and obtruded upon what view there was, but occasionally he glimpsed the Plough or Orion and it helped to put things in perspective. It was impossible, he always felt, not to be overwhelmed by the sense of inconsequentiality in the face of this mere fraction of infinity.

He liked to recall those early wish-upon-a-star nights in Alessia's hometown fishing village, when he would recline on her balcony and watch the sun-splattered sky in August, the zipping meteors that crisscrossed, the clear white smudge of Milky Way generations had wondered at and mapped, attempting to storify, to bring meaning to the terrifying, random enormity of a cosmos that couldn't care less. He liked, as the breeze from the sea made fiction the heat of the day, to imagine all those now dead who'd gazed up in wonder at those constellations, united beneath their cold brilliance.

They'd holidayed there, as a family, many times since that first time he'd visited her and had watched the village slowly become popular, noisier, more crowded. The dark, cicada-thrummed nights were no longer as dark, now lights had been threaded all the way along the *lungomare*, and the fire of those stars had been significantly dowsed, much like the passions he and Alessia felt for one another; not snuffed out, not super-novaed, just dimmed by the passing years.

He saw Jody's bedroom light come on and braced himself for the scream.

The anger didn't completely drop from her face, rather the confusion layered itself over the top of it.

'She's *where?*'

'In Kabul.'

'Why's she gone there?'

'Because that's where her mission's taken her.'

'I thought she was in Tajikistan.'

'No. Alessia, prepare yourself for ... I'm going to tell you something you were never supposed to know. I'm telling you now because ... Well, it's going to be hard to cover up why certain things are about to happen. I think it's best to get matters out in the open.'

'Have you been *drinking?* You're scaring me.' She looked exactly as frightened as she said she was, her forehead torn with concern.

Mark measured his words. 'Jody's not with the Red Cross. That was just cover. She's ... She's been working for the security services overseas. She's a spy.'

'Vaffanculo, Mark! Don't be ridiculous. I can smell the drink on you. What's happened to her bedroom? *Tell me!*'

'I know how it sounds, but it's true. I'm sorry.'

She stared at him for a long time. Maybe it was the sudden over-professionalism in his manner, but she seemed convinced. Her hand flew to her mouth as she rose, with the involuntary adrenalin of bad news, from the sofa.

'What's happened to her?'

He exhaled a long, painful sigh. 'I don't know. Something went wrong. She's missing.'

'How do you know this?'

He took a deep breath. *Because our entire life together has been a lie.* 'I was informed by the station chief at MI6. They ...' Should he start at the very beginning, with his recruitment or Jody's? How far back to go? To their very first meeting at that low-lit bar in Rome with the Guinness posters and Johnny Mathis spinning on the jukebox? 'I've been involved in the security services for some time now ...'

'You work in that building, I know that.'

He shook his head. 'A little more than that.' The words were like tar. He forced them out, one unnatural admission after the other. 'I haven't been completely honest with you for a while.' *A while.* 'I've been working in ... I've been involved in the spying game for most of my life.' He couldn't tell her he was in Recruitment, in case she blamed him. She would blame him anyway, of course, but he wanted to buy all the seconds he could. 'In fact, when we first met, I was ...'

'Why's she in Afghanistan?' The conversation had come full circle quick. He doubted she'd taken in anything he'd said since.

'A lot of personnel are in Afghanistan. It's a troubled country in a state of perpetual war. Our sources are pretty sure that Russia's supplying arms to the Taliban. China is the biggest trade partner of all its neighbours. The US foreign policy means ...'

'Why is *our daughter* in Afghanistan?' She didn't need the history lesson.

'She speaks the languages, or their mutually intelligible dialects. She can pass as Afghan. She knows the customs and has all the training and research at her disposal. She's a great operative by all accounts.'

'Afghanistan?' This really did seem to be her sticking point.

'She'd been on a few missions prior to this one. This looked like it was going to be a big one. I mean, she was picked for it because ... she's good. Really good. Take it from me.'

She swivelled round to meet his gaze, but her eyes were vague, shadowed. 'And you're ...'

'Used to be.'

Her mouth was a stuttering hole in the middle of her paling face. She hadn't suspected, even a little bit, throughout all the years they'd slept beside one another. A ridiculous phrase from her old letters stuck its barbs into his brain: *How are your other pies?*

Her voice was stronger, furious. 'Who did that to her room?'

'The security services have taken some of her belongings to look for clues as to her whereabouts. They didn't tidy up very well, I'm afraid.'

'What ...? When ... When did she ...?'

'Her last contact with our people was over a month ago.'

Alessia was staring out the window at the darkness. 'You made me ring the Red Cross. You told me she was in Tajikistan and then you said there'd been a power cut and she would call us in a few days. She never did. Why did you say that?'

'I don't know. I was buying time.'

Her hands gripped the hair at the back of her head. 'Is she dead?'

'MI6 don't think so. From what I've pieced together, they think she blew up an operations room over there, stole data and defected. Utter rubbish, of course. As her father, I'm not privy to a lot of information. It's been a nightmare, I'll be honest, not knowing ...'

'*How long* have you known?' she exploded. 'How long have you known our daughter was a ...?'

'I helped enrol her.'

She slapped him, hard. It took all his instincts not to block the blow. Alessia stared at him with red eyes then struck him again. The third one he did parry, grabbing her wrist.

'*Get off me!*' she shouted. '*Get off me!*'

That he hadn't anticipated how angry she'd be was now unfathomable. He'd actually believed he could explain this to her. He must've drunk more than he'd thought.

'*O, mio Dio,*' she wailed through her tears. 'How could you have kept this from me?'

'It's ... the nature of the job ...' Maybe in a few days, weeks, she'd understand the sacrifices he'd made, why he'd told her. 'They're investigating me, Alessia. They think I'm somehow part of this, even though I haven't been active for twenty-five years. They took my computer, my phone, everything. They'll probably interview you, too. I couldn't keep you in the dark any longer. I'm sorry. But I didn't lose our daughter, you must believe me. She came to us. She wanted to be a part of our nation's Secret Service. It was her ambition. Her dream.'

'So ... where ... is she?'

'Nobody knows.'

There was silence for a long time.

'Why are they investigating you?'

'It's a formality. I've worked, despite a gap of a few years, for MI6 all my career. I've been loyal and, though I say so myself, done excellent work. I've saved lives. Many lives. They've got nothing on me. And don't go thinking Jody's gone over to the other side. She hasn't. There's another explanation. There must be.'

She regarded him with deadened eyes. 'What other side?'

'China. Russia. Iran. Harry Potter's School of Wizardry. It doesn't matter. She's out there doing her job, deep undercover. New hair. New accent. New name. Doing her thing. She'll pop up in a few days' time with the solution to an issue of global importance, you wait and see ...'

She turned on him. 'Who are you? I don't know who you are.'

'Let's not be overdramatic.'

'*Really?* Apparently, I've been married to a spy for a quarter of a century and my daughter's a communist.'

'A communist? What are—?'

'Have you killed people?'

The question took him aback. 'Have I ...?'

'In this job of yours as a secret agent. Did you have to kill people?'

His pause was obviously enough for her to draw her own conclusions because she strode quickly, in a way that startled him, from the room. He listened to her footsteps gun their way up the stairs, along the hallway to their bedroom. A door slammed. Twice. Something smashed inside the closed room. And again. Then there was silence.

The next he knew, he was lurching awake on the sofa to a hungover dawn, the pain behind his eyes like all his years stacked up at once and the ghost of an already forgotten nightmare stretching his right hand towards an equally phantom holster. He could tell from the tone of the house, its silent attitude and sorry air, that his wife was long gone.

9

'Dad?'

Mark dragged his eyes off the goldfinch abseiling around the birdfeeder. There were a fair few of them in the garden this year. Word must have got around within the avian community about the quality of his sunflower seeds.

'Yes, Brandon?'

'Did we get broken into again?'

He surveyed his son, standing tall at the entrance to the conservatory in an indecently small T-shirt and a pair of shorts that would get him thrown out of any members' bar in the land. 'Are you off swimming?'

'The gym, Dad. I can't find my tablet. I thought I left it in the front room.'

'Maybe your mother borrowed it. She's missing too.'

'Aren't you supposed to be at work?'

'I'm working from home today.'

In fact, Mark had been prodigiously busy. He'd lodged another complaint with MI6 about the treatment he'd suffered and the ruinous state the investigating team had left his daughter's bedroom. He'd also bought himself another mobile from a disreputable stall on the high street and called his wife. She'd hung up the moment she heard his voice and, thereafter, must have blocked him because it was always unobtainable. He'd even fixed his sore head, by reaching for his old tried-and-tested hangover cure. Another drink. To dwell on the hangover, to suffer it, would have been to admit to his backslide, so was the only logical move.

'Brandon, what do you see when you look at me?'

His son paused, left hand hovering an earbud close to its intended destination. 'An old man asking a trick question.'

'When I look at you, I see someone with huge potential, but you miss the bigger picture. You know, real life's more than background muzak while you chat up barely clad girls at treadmills. Try again. What do you see when you look at me?'

Brandon shrugged. 'I see my father. I see someone who's ... tired. Works too hard.'

'That it? A pretty tragic résumé.'

'I don't understand what you're trying to get me to say.'

'Your sister saw me for who I really am. Why can't you?'

'O ... K ... I'm kind of concerned now. Are there bodies under the patio or something? What's going on?'

The doorbell tolled.

Brandon was quicker to answer it than usual, then immediately called for his father.

The lanky, plain-clothed individual waiting didn't need to open his mouth for Mark to recognise him for what *he* was; his very demeanour reeked of Secret Service. He was flanked by a woman who looked too juvenile to be working for SIS, though her eyes told him otherwise and he'd long ago got used to everybody being younger than they needed to be.

'Mr Wolfe? We'd like you to come with us, please. We have some questions.'

Brandon looked from face to face to face. 'What's the problem? Is this about the burglary?'

He knew the place. An office block MI6 often used for interrogation. White-walled, sixties-built, on Victoria Street in Camden. The two agents exited the car and Mark followed.

He was frisked at the door, confirmed clean.

The room they placed him in was bright but the windows revealed nothing except the brickwork of a small publisher's opposite. He sat in a hard chair beside a bare desk and waited alone, while the two escorts went to fetch whoever would be running the show. During the time it took for someone to appear, Mark had already calculated the likelihood of breaking the window with his chair and the poor odds of him surviving the drop to the concrete below. There was only one exit from the room, and it wasn't through the inch-thick glass of the two-way mirror behind him.

The door unbolted and a figure sighed in.

While Mark could remember exactly what this man had said the last time they'd met, the way he'd said it, the look behind his eyes that confirmed cowardice in the face of authority – a man he doubted would be willing to die for his service the way Mark had once sworn to – he couldn't for the life of him recall the posh bastard's name.

He told the man in charge of South Asia Operations, 'I'm sorry. I know we've been introduced, but I don't remember who you are.' It came across, as it had been intended, as insubordinate and petty.

'My name is Adam Wellcome, and I'm—'

'Yes, yes. I remember the rest of it. I'm surprised it's taken you twenty-four hours to apologise to my face.'

'May I ask what I'm supposed to be apologising for?' Adam sat down opposite.

'Let me think. How about sending a new recruit out without adequate back-up and then accusing her of defecting when everything goes to bollocks just to cover your own incompetence?'

Adam's voice was cold as winter glass. 'You don't know anything about the mission Jody was involved in.'

Mark crossed his arms. 'Enlighten me. I'm sure you weren't just sending agents in willy-nilly to chip away at the Middle East and South Asia one suicide bomber at a time, were you?'

A red blush rose at Adam's neck. 'You really think you have what it takes to *solve Afghanistan*? This is not your war. Times have changed.'

'So, what did you want me for, exactly? I deny, utterly, that my daughter is working for an enemy superpower. Pull out my fingernails if you want. That's not going to change.'

'We don't use aggressive interrogation techniques, as you well know.'

'If you believe that, you're a bigger fool than you look. What damning morsels have you dredged up after turning over my daughter's bedroom? An old Barbie? A work experience certificate?'

'Mr Wolfe. Please. I would appreciate it if you refrained from speaking to me in this patronising manner.' Uttered in the most patronising way Mark had ever heard. 'We're both professionals doing our jobs.'

'You might believe you are. My professionalism was suspended yesterday.'

'Surely you understand why, given the circumstances.'

It took all of Mark's strength to remain calm. 'I do not understand *the circumstances*.'

Adam shifted into interview mode. 'Has your daughter ever, to your knowledge, shown support for a foreign power?'

'No.'

'Sympathy for the plight of an occupied nation?'

'No.'

'Membership of Stop the War, 38 Degrees or any other leftist think tank?'

'Not that she ever mentioned, but she's got a head on her shoulders – at least she did the last time I saw her – and understands that not every act our government and allies commit is automatically the moral one.'

'Care to elaborate?'

'Not really.'

'During her years under your roof, did Jody ever make friends with anyone you'd consider to be, shall we say, subversive or counterculture?'

'No one's been swaying her mind. She has her own.'

'You can't be sure. Have you been with her twenty-four hours a day, all through higher education? All through her start at MI6?'

'Obviously not, but she's always been ... Resolute.'

'How long ago did her intention to join MI6 become apparent?'

Mark slumped in his chair. This wasn't going to be over any time soon. 'In retrospect, I suppose when she was choosing which university course to attend.'

'Interesting. Go on.'

'It must have been in her mind that she could pass as Middle Eastern or South Asian. She wanted to learn more languages and knew Arabic and Persian would be useful in this brave new world. She's always had a flair for languages. It helped growing up bilingual. I don't know how she found out what I do for a living. I certainly never told her. No one else in my family knows.' *Knew.*

'You think she chose Arabic because it would aid her entry into the Service?'

'Yes. Looking back, she'd always shown aptitude.'

'Elaborate, please. You think she'd always wanted to be a spy?'

'I suspect so. In a latent way. She was intuitive, good at spy games as a child. She was stealthy too. A natural. You know what I mean. You picked her for these operations, didn't you?'

Adam ignored the question. He'd probably had final clearance on the missions, but it was unlikely he hand-selected his operatives. 'Give me an example, off the top of your head, of this childhood "aptitude".'

Mark laughed, despite himself, as he looked out the window at the nothing view. He was in a position he'd never thought he'd be in, torn between helping his employer or protecting his own daughter. But, assuming her innocence, there was no way he could stitch her up. 'The incident with the snake stands out.'

'Go on.'

His sigh almost hurt. 'Some boy – I don't remember his name – had been calling Jody "Snake" ever since a primary school science lesson taught him certain reptiles come in both black and white morphs.'

'I don't understand.'

'The boy, no doubt, assumed the nickname was sophisticated, but … Look, Jody had come back from Santa Maria that summer particularly dark-skinned. The school had spoken to the boy about how such name calling, in this context, could be perceived as racist but Jody took offence. Long story short: the boy found a grass snake in his backpack.'

'I see. Jody put it there?'

'In all probability. I asked her about it, and she pretended it was the first time she'd heard of the matter, then just shrugged and said, "*Vinco*."'

Adam's eyes gave away his uncertainty.

'It's Italian for "I win". I wasn't convinced of her guilt at the time, to be honest with you. I was more annoyed at having to take the afternoon off work to discuss the ridiculous matter with the headmistress.'

'You worked a lot in those days?'

'Very long hours.'

'Did you see much of Jody?'

'She was often in bed when I got home during the week, but I spent my weekends with my family, when I could.'

Adam's eyes were as expressionless as a mannequin's. There was none of the bumbling, blushing novice in his demeanour now; Mark didn't threaten him the way C did, despite the fact Mark could, undoubtedly, reach forward and snap his neck if he so desired. His questions were delivered like a seasoned inspector, with no back-up, leading Mark to assume an army waited behind the mirrored glass. MI6 probably didn't consider Mark dangerous these days but, even so, they'd put this unthreatening weasel before him in a calculated attempt to disperse Mark's likely rage and cynicism, and it had empowered his interviewer tenfold.

'Did she have many friends?'

'Not really. Is there a reason you're talking about her in the past tense?'

'Many relationships, to your knowledge?'

'Of what nature?'

'Romantic or sexual.'

'What the hell does this have to do with anything?'

'Being in love is akin to idolisation. You'd be surprised how easily worship can manipulate a mind.'

'No, I wouldn't.'

'So? Many relationships with men over the years that you know about?'

'None to my knowledge. She never expressed much interest.'

'Was your daughter gay?'

'I suspected so, but she never came out to us.' He'd got Mark talking in the past tense too.

'Had she left the country before? Where did she go and for how long?'

Mark outlined their very safe, middle-class holidays when the children were young; Croatia, Paris, a lot of Italy, nowhere a hotbed of fundamentalism was brewing.

'And after she left the household? At university, perhaps?'

'She travelled throughout the Middle East and Asia during her studies. I believe part of her second year was spent in—'

'Abu Dhabi and Islamabad. We know. It's fair to say, is it not, that over the last – what – five years, she'd been in and out of South Asia and neighbouring territories over a dozen times?'

Mark blew out his cheeks in exasperation. 'That would be correct. And you know all this. The service investigated her thoroughly before she was added to the payroll. Of course she spent a lot of time over there. MI6 bought her services for precisely that reason.'

'True. We *believed* she was investigated thoroughly, but we've missed something.' He sounded rueful.

'My daughter hasn't gone rogue; I can assure you of that.'

Adam nodded his head. 'We're as surprised as you, Mr Wolfe, but, as you were informed at our meeting with C, there's a suggestion your daughter's the one who's—'

'"A suggestion". I want *hard facts*.'

'I'm afraid you're not in any position to have any. You were suspended yesterday.'

'Because of that arsehole lackey sent down to investigate my department. I shouldn't *be* suspended. I should be helping with this investigation.'

'Too personal for you. Your help would never be authorised.'

Mark leaned forward on his uncomfortable chair. 'You want to find Jody and take her in, but how are you going to do that? What tools do you need to find her? If I were you, I'd start with her father, the former spy. Six and I are after the same thing. We want my daughter back. Innocent or guilty, *we want her back*. I'll find her.'

Adam inspected his fingernails.

'If my daughter's innocent, that means there's an agent unaccounted for out there. You can't let her rot in Afghanistan.'

'"If" is a moot point now.'

Mark ignored him. 'And it would also mean the genuine double agent is still at large. If Jody's alive, she probably knows their identity.'

'This had all been considered but is no longer on the table. Is there not, in your mind, even the remotest possibility she might be the one who's set our boys up out there?'

'No chance. She's too good. If she were the rogue, there's no way you'd even suspect her.'

Adam chuckled. 'You hold your daughter in high regard.'

'And you should hold her in higher.'

'Or maybe she's pulled the wool over her old man's eyes. You wouldn't be the first to look foolish thanks to a daughter shinning down a drainpipe and disappearing after dark.' Adam paused, adjusted his shirt under the hot lights. 'For the record, I don't think you're in cahoots with her. I have the utmost respect for your years of service to our country, but I can't take your word as a father alone. You'll soon have to face the fact Jody isn't who you think she is. It's not pretty, I'm afraid, but there we have it.'

'Why are you so determined to pin this bombing on her?' Mark slammed a fist into the table. 'Fuck my suspension. I know enough already, and you've said yourself your investigation of me has turned up nothing. I'm clean. Show me this damned evidence. If I'm on her side, helping our enemies arm the Taliban, or whatever it is you think I'm doing, then I know this intelligence anyway. And if the evidence is as damning as you all seem to think, then showing me will simply put me in your camp. I don't see what reason our superiors could possibly have for keeping it from me any longer. Surely my service history counts for *something*.'

Adam watched Mark the way a hunter watches prey at the waterhole. 'Be careful what you wish for.'

He stood and departed the room.

Mark glimpsed two guards in tight-fitting black waiting at the exit. Their guns weren't exactly trained on him but he was in no doubt that, if he made a wrong move, those Glock 17s would be on him in milliseconds.

It occurred to him Adam had gone behind the glass to call a superior and Mark regarded the mirror with cold fascination. He'd lost weight and his beard had grown without his permission. His eyes were darkly ringed and his hair uncombed. He didn't remember having breakfast this morning.

It was a long time before Adam returned. When he did, he moved in yogic patience towards the interviewee, tall, his chin raised.

'You're to come with me.'

The Chief was behind his desk. The oval table had been cleared and the chairs taken out and placed facing the large screen, as though in preparation for a conference.

C nodded at Mark and Adam, his white dome of hair not even shaking a strand, then picked up his phone.

'They're here,' he told the phone, before gesturing to the chairs. 'Please take a seat. I hope you didn't have too much difficulty getting into the building, Mark?'

Mark winced at the use of his first name. Such forced geniality from the top of the food chain seldom indicated good news.

'I had an escort,' Mark said, referring to the armed guards who marched him through reception in lieu of his rescinded pass card.

As Adam and Mark took their seats, an unfamiliar woman entered from a door at the back and announced, 'Good afternoon, sir. Gentlemen.'

'Good afternoon, Galway.'

Mark assumed this new arrival was someone from Adam's team, and knew without question she'd got her hands dirty in the past. The way she carried herself was telling, the flint in the eyes, the strength in her forearms. She was mid-thirties and dark-haired, fierce, with a scar, two in fact, like crosshairs on her forehead, as though she'd been deliberately marked. The scars looked maybe two years old.

She nodded at Adam and then powered over to Mark and offered her hand. 'You must be Mr Wolfe. Heard a lot about you, sir. All good.' Mark took her hand, sufficiently emboldened by this praise. 'Sorry for what you're going through.'

Mark didn't say anything, waited.

'With your permission, sir?' she asked the Chief, taking her place in front of the screen.

Presumably there was a gracious nod from the desk behind them all, another rigid salute of white hair.

At the press of a remote control, a map of Kabul appeared on the screen and Galway indicated its midpoint with a laser pointer.

'On the thirteenth of November, your daughter was posted to a village in Bagrami, a thirty-minute drive from Kabul city.' Galway spoke only to Mark. 'She was posing as a Pashtun orphan from the Wardak Province, her parents victims of a landmine. She had the documents, or most of them – having everything in order would have raised suspicions in a country like Afghanistan, so there were necessary gaps, things lost in the flight from her home – and a well-prepared background ready, photographs of missing brothers and sisters in a tatty old purse. It didn't take her long to befriend the wrong – by which I mean the *right* – people. Soon she was in regular communication with known black-market arms traders, the same renegades who supply bombs to the terrorists. Government rogues. Criminals for hire. Members of the Golden Crescent.'

Mark nodded. 'And you were trying to ...'

'Ultimately, to smash the gun cartels that arm the Taliban and associated terrorist sympathisers.' Galway's voice was husky, as though permanently strained by shouting orders. 'We were hoping to pose as new buyers to find out for certain whether the Russians were arming these groups. Jody wasn't working alone, of course, on a mission of this magnitude. She was feeding information back to the gang we were setting up as false buyers.'

Mark nodded. It wasn't a dissimilar arrangement to the mission he was involved in many years ago in Belfast.

Galway flicked her laser pointer over a close-up of Kabul. 'On the twenty-eighth of January, Jody, or Fatima, as she was now known, contacted us to say she'd made contact with a seller in the Kunduz region.'

Mark picked up on the look that passed between Adam and Galway. He immediately asked, 'What kind of contact?'

'It was by the nature of a honey trap,' Galway said coolly.

'Right.' *My daughter has been paid by the British government to sleep with an Afghan terrorist arms supplier.* 'Right,' he said again, overdoing the casual.

'After that, things moved quickly.' The implication in her tone seemed to be that things had moved *too quickly*. She clicked her remote and the image changed to a large shack. 'She was in regular contact with Taliban members and sent us this image of what she purported to be a building where arms were stored. You can see the locks and the sentries outside. There was no doubt in our mind something important was being kept inside. It backs onto a large, fenced-off open space, as you can see. We tracked the location down to the Paghman district, which would be a good location for a base of this sort, with access to Wardak to the west, Lowgar to the east and its border with Pakistan. We thought, at this point, we ought to check it out with our friends.'

'Let me guess,' Mark interrupted. 'The Americans wanted to wipe the building off the face of the Earth.'

'They considered a strike, yes, until they discovered the building was nothing of the sort. No weapons, no bombs. Nothing.'

'She was fed misinformation.' Mark sat forward. 'They suspected her. That's a worry.'

'That's what we thought. Then, on the fifth of February we received another coded communication that claimed arms were in Dih Sabz.' Again, the pointer flicked. 'This happened a few times following this second tip-off, often more than once a week, always a different place. Never any arms when we checked. The weapons were being moved a lot, it seemed, and Jody was moving too, implying she was part of the carriage, and yet she could never give us precise locations. Then we received word that a terrorist strike was planned on

Karte Seh, a neighbourhood in Western Kabul, home of many of Afghanistan's Shia Hazara community, for the nineteenth of March.'

'I remember. But the attack wasn't in Karte Seh. It was in ...'

'Shahre Naow. Fifty people died. Three of our own men were injured.'

Mark scratched at the bristles growing on his chin. He refused to admit to himself that he was getting an adrenal thrill out of all of this. Sitting in the Command Centre bunker with C, being given a one-to-one debrief on the progress of an ongoing mission. That it concerned his daughter was uncomfortable, no doubt, but it was almost like being back in the field again after so many years of pedestrian, civilian existence.

'She was compromised,' he said.

'We thought so too, and we urged her to get out.' The X on her forehead caught the light and glowed as though wet. 'She refused to come in. Said she was definitely on to something and we had to continue to trust her. Claimed the terrorist atrocity was the work of as-yet-unknown separatists.'

'Perhaps it was.'

'I don't deny that Afghanistan has its fair share of angry young rebels who throw stones in several directions. We continued to follow her intel.'

Mark asked with apprehension, 'It happened again?'

'It kept happening. Not Bala Kohi as expected but Qala-e-Nazir. Not Sherpur but Dash-e-Barchi. All places with sizeable Hazara communities, though notably only Sunnis were killed.'

'At this point, the mission should have been to get her out,' Mark said.

'I agree. But then she fell quiet. We simply didn't know where she was. Until she popped up again with a list of names. Buyers.

Dealers. Terrorists. Government officials involved. You name it. It was the motherlode, and it all seemed to check out. She'd been working away for months on this. The deal was close to completion and our boys and girls were ready for the big trade. And then she went completely silent. The day got closer and closer. Our other sources confirmed the deal. It was due to happen on the third of April, then it was pushed back ... to the seventh.'

'Oh shit,' Mark said.

'That's right.' It was C who finally spoke. 'Amongst the victims of the Afshar bombing were four of our own. It made the news, but the deaths of our MI6 brothers didn't, for obvious reasons. There was no trade, just a trap. And still no noise from Jody.' He stood from his desk to wander to the board, his face grave. 'We dug into her intel. Most of the names she'd got to us were readily available to the Americans but there were a couple of extras designed to whet our appetites alongside more than a few false leads.'

Mark was silent. There was no doubt it looked bad.

'We were confused,' Galway admitted. 'Jody had shown too much competence to suddenly fuck up on such a major scale.'

'I agree,' Mark said. 'She was manoeuvred. She must have been.'

'If we'd been in the business of giving the benefit of the doubt then, yes, that would have been our conclusion too.'

'I still don't see how any of this is proof of her duplicity. I mean, yes, it looks dodgy, amateur even, but ...'

'There's more.'

The three of them exchanged conspiratorial looks and, as the room took on a darker edge, it finally dawned on Mark he hadn't been invited to the Top Floor to join with colleagues who trusted him as an equal. He'd been summoned to be served the damning evidence that put his daughter's rebellion beyond all reasonable doubt, to crush his hope once and for all.

With reluctance, Jody's father said, 'Let's hear it, then.'

Adam folded his arms and sank back into his chair. C took three steps away from the screen, as though retiring from a dangerous animal, and kept his eyes on Mark.

Galway spoke.

'We've had contact from Jody once since. Yesterday. It wasn't through the usual channels. She patched the following message to the head of station in Kabul on the emergency channel, who then sent it through to Adam. I should warn you: you may find it disturbing.'

She stood away from the screen too, as a dark box buzzed into an image. It was his daughter, sitting in front of a black canvas with Perso-Arabic script in white across it. She looked thin and tired, with determined eyes. Her hair was covered in a hijab and she wore a khaki military uniform.

Mark felt his stomach roil at the sight of her. Something about her demeanour looked otherworldly, unfamiliar. It was his daughter, but it wasn't his daughter.

'My name is Jody Wolfe,' she said, 'and I am saying this in sound mind and body. This is a message for my superiors in London. You cannot hope to win this fight. Your opponents are legion, their causes purer than yours, and there are many like me within your service. If you follow the intelligence of your agents, you risk further death and international embarrassment. May Allah have mercy on your souls.'

The screen went dark.

Inside, Mark was dying, but he hoped he spoke with clarity and strength. 'Has this been verified?'

'It's not a deepfake, if that's what you mean,' Galway said. 'Our analysts have been over it and it's certainly her. Our information points to their lack of technology first and foremost, and voice analysts and psychologists have been over the footage and she doesn't appear to have been coerced. She speaks confidently and, it seems, earnestly. She's calm and there are no signs of maltreatment. We have to assume the video, and her threat, is genuine, especially when coupled with the questionable tactical decisions she's made out there.'

'What does it say behind her?'

'It's Dari for "Agents of Allah", a rebel group now claiming responsibility for several bombings in Afghanistan, including the seventh of April massacre in Afshar.'

'Not a branch of the Taliban?'

'Highly unlikely. The Taliban, along with any al-Qaeda or Islamic State in Afghanistan, speak Pashto in the main. This is the first terrorist group we've come across that appears to be made up of Shia Muslims.'

'Any clues as to where this was filmed?' He was stalling now. He'd ask as many questions as it took to avoid accepting this evidence as truth.

'We're not sure. We're working on it.'

C reappeared in front of the screen. 'We have every reason to believe this video represents a genuine threat to our agents in the area. For all we know, your daughter – whom we now consider a confusion agent engaged in active measures against our country – has passed on information about a great deal of our operations and service people. We are taking this extremely seriously.'

'Are you pulling agents out?'

'As of now, our intentions are classified to you. I hope you understand.'

Mark looked to his right. Adam had stood. The meeting was at an end.

'So . . . you wanted to . . . gauge my reaction to this video? See if I confessed to being a part of this . . . plot? Just because she sounded resolute doesn't mean she meant what she said. It must be part of some bigger plan.'

'We showed you the truth. I'm sorry, Mark, but your daughter has turned. There really is no other interpretation. This has gone about as far from the plan as is possible.'

Mark looked at his hands, normally so still under pressure. There was a distinct shake to them now.

The Chief dismissed Adam and Galway with a curt, 'Thank you, both,' and they evaporated with military swiftness.

'You're still suspended, pending further investigations,' the Chief told Mark when the others were gone. 'I hope you understand. It won't affect your pension.'

'I don't give a shit about—'

C looked at him levelly beneath his solid fringe. 'I don't think you're an enemy agent, Mark. Your record is incredible. But can you think of any reason, any at all, why your daughter might be holed up in a cave with these murdering bastards?'

He stared over the Chief's shoulder at the now-black screen. To its right was a large oil painting of the Queen, painted in her Commonwealth pomp at the age of thirty or so, the crown on her head incorporating the lion and unicorn of the royal coat of arms, red, white and blue draped around her shoulders. Her Mona Lisa smile was half-concealed, but her patriotism never in doubt.

The adrenalin was gone now, leaving only defeat to contort his words into a hoarse, bitter whisper. 'Not off the top of my head, sir, no.'

10

MARK HUNKERED DOWN IN THE flowerbeds, weeding out his rage and pain.

Had his daughter really done this? Who had got to her? When? There was no childhood incident that stood out which necessitated this level of backstabbing; she was never abused, never wanted for anything, always delighted to see him whenever he came home before bedtime. And he always came home. These were the deceitful actions of a woman whose father had been killed by MI6, not one who'd devoted his life to the Service.

He pulled out some chickweed, some charlock, sprouts of common dandelion. They didn't know they were weeds, of course, and had every right to grow in the earth, but he tugged them from his land as though they were the very enemies that kept his daughter.

The goldfinch fluttered off into the branches of one of the two elms when it heard the approach of a car. Spending an entire life terrified of predators took its toll, as he knew full well. At the sound of a key in the door, his heart pulsed its familiarly cruel hope that it might be Jody, though in reality he knew she'd be nowhere near as unsubtle.

Mark looked over his lawn. He was wasting his time. These weeds, violently yanked from the earth, would simply claw their way back elsewhere. It wasn't therapeutic when his back ached this much.

Alessia's silhouette was pacing through the hallway.

In twenty-five years of marriage, they'd never had an argument like this one. Her temper had occasionally accused him of fictitious infidelity, the wrong approach to home decor, hiding whisky behind the cistern, but these were antique examples of minor altercations. There was nothing that compared to this, and now he had to drop a new truth bomb, should she give him the time of day: their daughter was not only a missing spy, but considered a killer of her own side, a terrorist.

He walked to the doorway. There was one positive way to greet her, at least.

'She's alive,' he said.

Alessia paused in the shade of the hall and her face showed her age in its sockets and shadows.

'She's . . .?'

He inched towards her. 'I saw a video of her. She's been in touch.'

'With you?'

'With the intelligence services. She's still out there, but she's OK. Completely unharmed.'

'*Oh, grazie mio Dio!*' Her body slumped in relief, but as he took a step towards her she backed away.

'Are you staying?' he asked.

'I haven't decided. Maybe . . . maybe it is *you* who should leave.' It wasn't spoken forcefully, but the notion took his heart and dug its fingernails in. His friends were few, his job had suspended him, his daughter had suggested betrayal on a nuclear level and now his wife was requesting he vacate his own home.

'I've nowhere to go,' he mumbled.

'There are hotels.'

'I've done my share of hotels.'

'During your life as a *secret agent*?'

She walked to the kitchen, pulled a wine bottle from the rack. Outside, the goldfinch was back.

'Alessia, I know you think you don't know me anymore—'

'I don't.'

'But you understand precisely who I am. I'm the same man you married. The man who left the Service when he met you, *because* he met you.'

She put the bottle down. It was an insignificant act but he still interpreted it as an opponent holstering a potential weapon. The fact he thought such a thing, he knew, meant he was *exactly* the same person he'd always been.

'Yet you still work for MI5.'

'MI6.'

'Whatever.'

'Look, it's all about to be sorted, I promise. I should never have told you any of this. I just ... want it back the way it used to be. Jody reported in. They're closing her investigation. It's over.' He told himself it was a white lie compared to the huge ones he wished he still carried within him. 'I mean, a few formalities need ironing out. She won't be back *tomorrow*, but her falling off the map has all been a big mistake. I'll ... I'll leave the Service if you want me to.'

She looked at him in what might have been wonder in the failing daylight, but was more than likely disgust.

'Seriously, I'll go in tomorrow and hand in my resignation. You and the kids mean far more to me than any job.'

She wasn't stupid. 'They're going to fire you, aren't they?'

'That's not ...'

'I want my daughter home, Mark. I want Jody home. I can't believe I've been lied to like this, for our *entire married life*.

What other lies have you been keeping from me? Other women?'

'What? No. No! Why does it always have to come back to—?'

'Is she really safe?'

'I saw her video yesterday. I honestly did.'

She flung her head back in despair. 'I don't know what to believe anymore.'

Looking at her now, face puffy from two nights of sleeplessness, goodness knows where, exhausted from the truth he'd exploded in her, he knew he should have kept the lie going. It hadn't hurt her to believe her daughter was involved in humanitarian relief missions.

'I broke a vow to you the moment we got married. I swore to be honest and I wasn't. I justified keeping a side of myself from you by telling myself everybody keeps secrets. Not blood and guts, but regular run-of-the-mill water-cooler fluff. You assumed I worked as a civil servant. It was fine like that. It worked. It worked for a long time. And then Jody joined the Service and threw everything into disarray. Suddenly, the secrets felt too much. And when she went AWOL, I struggled, I really did. These terrible things they were claiming about her at HQ . . . I couldn't keep them to myself. So I broke the other important vow in my life, the vow to my superiors. I wasn't thinking properly. I should have told you . . . something else. Because now I've lost everything.'

Her mouth twisted in the low light. 'We've both lost everything,' she hissed. 'Except now, I realise, I never had you.'

She strode back out of the kitchen, her footsteps heavy in the hallway. She was heading upstairs, probably to grab a suitcase, hers or his. He knew he was about to lose her for good.

'They think she's a traitor.'

She stopped. Her shadow had one hand on the banister. 'What?'

'Jody. They think she's a traitor. The video I saw ... She appeared in front of an "Agents of Allah" flag. A new terrorist organisation in Afghanistan. She's admitted to luring our agents to their deaths and feeding us misinformation. The service believes she's responsible for that Kabul bombing. She's on Interpol's most wanted list.'

'She ... What?'

He slid to the hall floor, his back against the wallpaper. 'She's an enemy of the state. A renegade. A terrorist.'

The silence grew heavy as the house darkened. The streetlights were blinking on as Alessia slumped onto the second step.

'I don't believe it.'

'Neither did I. *Do I*. But I saw the video myself and now don't know what to think.'

'She ... She must have been forced. She must have ...'

'She was confident, strong. Almost mocking. There was no gun pressed to her head off-camera.'

Alessia's throat swallowed in a panicked reflux. 'Why ...? Why would she ...?'

'I don't know.'

Outside, cars thrummed behind the conifers. A dog barked. He'd now exorcised the last of his secrets.

'You can't possibly believe it?' she asked.

'My heart doesn't. It never will. But the video is damning.'

'It's not her. It can't be.'

'See it from the Service's point of view. She's misled MI6 over and over. Defection on this scale takes planning, method, precision. She didn't act alone, of that there's little doubt – she has this *organisation* behind her – but every piece of intel she's sent us has been bogus.' He clenched his fists by his sides. 'You say you don't know *me* any longer, but who has our daughter become? How did this happen?'

The silence which met him echoed his own inability to ingest the news. 'What do we do?' she asked finally.

He looked at her hunched shadow. 'There's nothing we can do.'

'When she stood on a sea urchin in San Marco it was you who tweezered the spines out of her foot. When she drifted too far out in Lago, you swam to her and pulled her back in. You always know how to save her. You *always* know what to do.'

He felt the tears. Hot. Unwelcome. 'Not this time. She's chosen her own path.'

'Who knows about this?'

'I suspect the Top Floor all know. CIA will have been informed.'

'No ... I mean ... How public is this knowledge? How long until the neighbours hear?'

The fucking neighbours. 'These things don't leak unless we want them to.'

'You hear about spies on the news all the time. There was the ricin poisoning guy ...'

'Sometimes we release information if we need the Russians, for example, to know we're on to them. If MI6 wants something locked down, believe me, they lock it down. There's no value in telling the world one of our agents has caused the deaths of dozens of innocents. Betrayal isn't something we allow our enemies to hear about. Trust me, we don't advertise our failure.'

The video was all over the news the following day.

In the end, he'd volunteered to attempt sleep on the sofa again and she'd taken the marital bed. It'd seemed the sort of compromise their conversation in the darkening stairwell justified.

Mark was woken by the sound of the telephone. He ignored it.

He'd never considered himself to have been depressed, had always secretly chided those who let emotions overcome them. Depression was a weakness; feeble to suffer and doubly feeble to talk about. A cheapening construct of a pampered age. His drinking years were a repression of the trauma and stress he'd encountered on active service, but it had been a phase, and hardly a disease. Anyone would want to block out those memories, and if he could overcome his brutal past then goths on Universal Credit and banned YouTubers could bloody well drag themselves out of the mire and get on with it. It was an attitude, perhaps, of an older generation who refused to believe in spectrums of disorders or 'mindfulness'. But Mark Wolfe was depressed now. Bone-gnawingly, tooth-extractingly depressed. And so he let the telephone ring, the one in the hall that the Service had so graciously deigned not to confiscate from him.

In the end, Brandon stumbled down and snatched it up. There was a short, sweary exchange before he slammed the phone down and wandered off.

Shortly after, the doorbell tolled. Mark wrenched the curtain back and had just enough time to see a group of maybe five, six men milling outside the house before a flashbulb blinded him.

He bolted upstairs to the bedroom but his wife had already left.

To his surprise, she answered her mobile. 'I went to the shops. We were out of everything.' It was true; he hadn't exactly been houseproud in her absence.

'Don't come back. There are reporters outside. Go to Jennifer's.'

'What? Why are—?'

He scurried back into the front room and snatched on the television, scrolled through a few channels. It was the usual morning crap, chefs in bright studio kitchens, wittering simpletons mugging to the camera and cackling at innuendos. He buttoned his way to the news channels, slumped back down on the dishevelled sofa. There she was, in front of the Perso-Arabic font, her gaze unswerving. The room spun with the motion sickness of a thousand betrayals.

A news reader spoke to an expert standing outside SIS headquarters. News of the female agent who'd switched sides and was responsible for the central Kabul bombing, back in the news like some re-released blockbuster, was the leading item on every news broadcast. The scrolling banner at the bottom of the screen declared BRITISH DOUBLE-AGENT RESPONSIBLE FOR AFGHANISTAN BOMBING NAMED AS JODY WOLFE. Had news of this been building overnight, while he and his wife battled out their domestic problems? Beneath the panic, he allowed himself one small moment of congratulations. He'd been right to tell his wife before she found out this way.

The doorbell chimed again. He was trapped between the TV horror show and the salivating hordes outside.

He intercepted Brandon in the hall.

'Don't answer it,' he barked.

Through the door's glass, he counted even more misted photographers or journalists, his neighbours gnomic in their front gardens. He wondered if one of them had tipped off the press once they'd recognised his daughter in the video.

This was a cataclysmic failure of her anonymity. She was, at a stroke, the most famous spy on the planet and her new coterie of infidels had announced themselves to a global audience in a way a Hollywood agent could only dream of. The professional operative in him was curious. This was uncharted territory for MI6. How would they react?

He typed his daughter's name into his phone. DISGRACE TO THE UK, screamed the *Express*'s headline. The *Sun* had found some old university photos of her and went with SMOKING HOT SMOKING GUN. #thehijabspy, as she'd been monikered at sudden notice by the Twitterati, was trending at number one. Claiming responsibility for the Afshar massacre would have been bad enough, but the fact she was a beautiful young woman had turned the judging chorus apoplectic.

When the telephone rang, it was a reporter. He slammed it down, Brandon watching him in his underpants with the dazed, final reel-expression of a horror film lead.

It rang again.

The public school voice was unmistakable. 'Mark. It's Adam. I suppose you've seen the news. I don't need to tell you not to talk to anyone. We weren't responsible for this leak. The Agents of Allah released the video to damage and shame our country.'

The doorbell rang again. 'I've got half of London's press pissing in the shrubs in my front garden. What do we do?'

The next three words constituted the most terrifying sentence he'd ever heard a superior utter.

'I don't know.'

'At least get in touch with Communications. Get this lot off my lawn.'

An hour later, the police arrived and moved the journalists on. Mark received a promise that the image of him, gazing blearily through his lounge curtains, wouldn't be used in any newspapers. Nor the many shots of Brandon, sans trousers, running amok amongst the journalists, hurling cameras to the ground and locking the gobbiest of the bunch in sleeper holds.

'If you need water,' he heard her little voice chirp, 'look for birds and plants. That's where they'll be.'

His children, playing in the woods in Calabria, chasing the rivers and foraging in the bushes. Brandon was off, fighting imaginary baddies with sticks and dangling from tree limbs, trying to climb as high as possible, but Jody was busy utilising her survival skills, telling her parents everything she'd learned about surviving in the wild.

'Usually, blue and black berries are safe to eat. And if you need to purify water, drain it through a layer of gravel followed by a layer of sand followed by a layer of charcoal followed by a piece of cloth. Socks make good filters.'

It was astonishing, the information she squirrelled away. Mark had once taught her how to create enough heat to light a fire by bending a paperclip into an S shape and placing it on the contacts of a battery. She'd replied with the nugget that you can wrap a cigarette in a matchbook and light the cigarette to make a fuse.

And now she was mixing with bomb makers in Afghanistan.

What the hell had he created?

It was so clear now. He'd fostered in her an expectation of spycraft, flattering what he perceived to be natural abilities, instilling a reluctant obligation to follow him. Her skills were merely his own, projected onto his surrogate, and though he remembered those games she'd played he had forgotten his own involvement and encouragement of their initiation, his memories of her barefoot creeping drowned in inexactitude by alcohol. His firstborn child, a matter of months after he'd retired from active duty, was merely a placebo for his missions. Mark had been wrong about the lack of abuse in her want-for-nothing childhood. He was the obvious groomer all along.

Shadows fell upon the garden and he squeezed his eyes tight to banish the suspicion, now pacing what felt like his prison yard on yet another dark day without her. But maybe, he considered, she'd been lost years ago.

Was he buying that narrative too now? There seemed little option. She'd admitted her own actions in that video she'd patched to …

And there it was.

The sun burst from behind its cloud and it was all he could do not to throw himself onto the phone and hotline the Service, but he needed to think this through, dispassionately, carefully.

There was a message here, he was sure of it, a cry for help perhaps, and it had been not only ignored but taken at face value by the very men and women sworn to protect her.

He buried his face in his hands and searched every avenue of thought.

An hour passed. Two. That fragile, liminal space between truth and fiction pulsed with possibilities.

Finally, he rose and marched through the house and out towards his car. There was only one course of action.

He noticed the figure watching him from a parked van at the end of the street but, for once, didn't ascribe their intentions as the same ones that dogged his younger years in East Berlin, Czechoslovakia, Yugoslavia, or some other European land that no longer existed.

It turned out journalists were easier to shake off in traffic than spies.

11

'How did you know where I live?'

Mark ignored the question. He'd been part of the recruitment team who brought Adam on board, years ago, and his bear-trap memory retained the Mayfair street from his file. Adam's Etonian background wasn't unusual but the degree of his unbearable wealth was. Of course, Mark had had no idea whether he still lived there or which number he was at, so an afternoon in the square, watching the windows and doorways, had been in order. He'd discounted several houses as too showy for an MI6 suit. There'd be no open curtains, no bragging of lifestyle. Adam's would be a sparse, undecorated exterior. In the end, he recognised the car and left the protectorate of a plane tree to quarry Adam when he drove up at four o'clock. His Tesla was ostentatious, even amid the expensive company of the Service car park, and Mark had made a mental note of models and number plates over time.

'I need to talk to you. It's urgent.'

Adam glanced up and down the road. 'I demand to know how you found me!'

'I work for Six, for God's sake. Let me in.'

The ceilings were high and the place was cold. To Mark's dismay, the home was almost an extension of headquarters' above-bunker corridors: pale walls, clean lines, the odd sanctioned portrait from yesteryear in tidy, functional frames and almost completely devoid of personality. It was the home of a bachelor who was rarely there, or at least never the same room twice. It was too big for Adam by about five floors.

Mark was pulled inside.

'What do you want?' There was genuine curiosity in Adam's tone, if little warmth.

'I need your help.'

The expression said, 'Go on,' but the mouth didn't move.

'We have to work quickly. Jody isn't the lost cause you all think she is.'

Adam scanned the older man's face with barely disguised pity. 'You've been suspended, Mr Wolfe. We work in completely different departments. What makes you think I'm the right person to listen to your fatherly hunches?'

'I'm not operating on hunches. I'm operating on clear information that Jody has given us but no one has picked up on.'

Mark knew Adam was the weakest link in the chain of command right now, a man keen to make up for his own perceived failures in handling the mission, a failure that was written all the way through him. He'd heard it distinctly in his voice the first time he met him in the Chief's office, a quavering onslaught of over-compensation coupled with a furtive lack of eye contact. He couldn't rely on him but trusted him more than Jim right now, and banked on him being the only person fallible enough to help.

'I'm listening,' Adam said, trying hard to pretend he wasn't, standing well over six feet and using it to his advantage.

'Tell me again how Jody got that video to us.'

'You seem to be launching a one-man inquiry, Mr Wolfe.'

Mark repeated the question.

Adam sighed. 'It was sent to our Kabul head. We assumed at the time she was being monitored.'

'She *was* being monitored. Why would she send a video of that nature on a lesser-used channel if her intention was to try and ruin our operations in the area? Why bother with the secrecy? Especially when the plan was for the Agents of Allah to put it out in public anyway.'

'You've seen the video, and the footage of her bomb victims. What does it matter how she got it to us? The sentiment remains. She's gone to the other side and she's rubbing our faces in the fact.'

'She patched it through on the *emergency channel*, a scrambled line, thirty-six hours before it hit the media. It was her way of letting us know she needs our help, that this – most certainly – goes *way deeper* than it appears. By getting it to MI6 early, directly, she was buying us time.'

'For what?'

'I don't know.'

Adam stared at Mark. Finally, he nodded at his clothes. 'Why are you dressed like a farmer?'

Mark looked over his tatty jumper, trousers and wellington boots. 'I was weeding the garden.'

Reluctantly, Adam led Mark into his huge and characterless front room, the slatted light from his window illuminating a large etching of a man crossing a bridge at sunset by an artist Mark, with his minimal artistic proclivities, didn't recognise but suspected was worth a small fortune. There was something insipid about the image; it smacked of a third-rate attempt to conjure, too loudly, 'mysterious', something Adam so desperately wished he were.

'You've led South Asia matters for a few months now,' Mark said. 'You can fly me in under the radar.'

'I can't go above C's head. That's a court martial.'

'No one must know I'm there. It's the only way.'

'Why on earth would you want to go in alone?' Adam spluttered.

'Jody can't wait while action plans are being drawn up, committees convened. I need to act swiftly. Besides, I don't see what use I'm being here.'

'You'll get me worse than fired. And you know I'm not being overdramatic. Members of the Service have failed to return from "walking holidays" for far less than what you're suggesting.'

'The whole ethos of this Service is that nobody shares anything with anybody. It'll just be one more little secret you're keeping and will hardly make you sleep any worse. You mention this to C and he'll have men crawling all over the operation.'

'*What operation?* There's a pecking order, Mr Wolfe. The pawns are ordered to hide things from each other, by knights, by rooks, but they don't conspire amongst themselves to conceal strategy from the king. You talk as though you have a plan, other than jetting to Kabul and putting a magnifying glass to the dirt.'

'To me, that sounds like a plan. And, though I say so myself, it's how I always got results.'

'You were ...'

'Younger? Yes, I was. But no less driven. This is my daughter. I'm going over there, but I'm going to need your help.'

Adam shook his head. 'You'll get yourself killed.'

'It's likely. But I can't spend my remaining days wondering where she is, knowing her own service and father have failed her. And the fewer people that know I'm there, the better.'

'Speaking hypothetically, what makes you think you can trust me?'

'I *don't*. But if you throw me a few bones in Kabul, that'll be enough to start with. I just need her last known location, where that video came from. That's where I'll start. I couldn't glean that information in the bunker briefing.'

'Because it's classified. At this point, I'd be committing a crime by even telling you the name of her hairstylist.' Adam looked close to despair. 'Look, say I give you the information you want and don't take the matter higher. Your mission will still be DOA. I mean, it'll be obvious to everyone where you've gone. Your plan is to prove your daughter hasn't gone rogue by ... going rogue yourself? Madness. And you're asking me to cover for you?'

'I haven't waited in the park outside your house all day just to use your bathroom.'

'It seems to me I've got more to risk than you do, right now.'

'Any kidnapped daughters in Afghanistan, Adam? This happened on your watch, don't forget. With your help, I'll be able to bail you out. I don't see that you have anything to lose. Quite the opposite. We can both only gain from this.'

'Rather an optimistic statement for a man walking into the heart of darkness. We can, also, both lose *everything*.'

'I've lost everything already.'

'And why should I follow you down? There is absolutely nothing in this for me. If they ask what I know and I claim I know nothing, that's ...'

'Any intel you give me, I could conceivably have picked up myself. You won't even be following my progress there. Just *get me in*. I'll need decent cover, a black passport. I can't just rustle that up myself, considering the current investigation team following me around.'

Adam's eyes flicked to the window.

'Figure of speech. No one followed me. I made sure.' Mark had shaken off the van that had been tailing at the Bishops Avenue and Archway Road interchange. 'But I will need a few things from you. I could've stopped by your offices in Whitehall and brushed off my lockpicking skills, but it's imperative my legend doesn't light up the database like a forest fire when I pass through customs, and that's where you come in.'

'Your false ID will be traced back to me.'

'Possibly. Given time. But I'll have Jody by then. And maybe you'll even have been reinstated yourself.'

'Reinstated?'

'This house looks like you're barely here, and yet you arrived home at four in the afternoon. You're under investigation too, aren't you? As of today. Don't pretend we're not in the same boat. Look, if it all goes wrong, your hands are clean and I'm just another dead agent. However, if I blow this thing wide open, you get to claim it as your gig and the glory's all on you.'

Adam ghosted across the room then dropped down in an armchair. He steepled his fingers across his lips, locked his eyes on Mark's. The pause was a superior's pause, designed to let him know Adam Wellcome was nobody's bitch.

Mark knew his type well; a rudderless private schoolboy who'd followed orders his entire life and dreamed of a chance to show how he'd always known best, that the orders he'd been obeying were the reasons he hadn't been getting the results he craved. He'd met men like him many times. Guilty about Daddy's money. Backed into a corner by other people's success. You couldn't appeal to their morals or their pockets, but you could appeal to an innate sense of injustice. The Empire had never set on such men, and they waited for their chance to step out from under the weight of history, of their family name. They had been given every perk anyone could possibly want, but not the opportunity to rebel. If he'd read Adam correctly, he'd found a man whose ambition far outweighed his loyalism.

'Theoretically,' Adam said, 'what you ask is possible, but it cannot be achieved overnight. And it will cost.'

Mark narrowed his eyes, assented with a nod. Adam would not be preparing false documents on his own; he would need to call on at least one of his regular backstop forgers. 'Can you be certain that whoever you enlist to help with this silent operation will be one hundred per cent secure?'

Adam wore the death mask of defeat. 'One can never be certain of anything, Mark.'

Mark arrived home to find his son waiting for him on the stairs, fury standing his neck muscles out like rope.

Mark approached him with caution, relieved to see he'd put some trousers on. 'You all right?'

'She's a terrorist,' Brandon stated, his voice choked, ethereal.

'That's what's being said.' Mark didn't know how much of the story to commit to, how far down the line Brandon's knowledge stretched. His son had seen Jody's video on the news, and assaulted a fair few of the journalistic pests hovering outside, but had Alessia passed on information regarding Mark's own part in this nightmare? He didn't have the strength to go through the conversation again, though his son deserved the truth too. 'Brandon ... What have you heard?'

'I watched *the video*.' The implication was that the footage was as bad as things could possibly get. 'What's she playing at?'

He wished he could tell Brandon she was on a mission, playing a part, living a lie, but doing so might jeopardise the way he needed to handle his next few days, and so he merely nodded and said, 'That girl gets some silly notions sometimes,' as though she'd done nothing more outrageous than dye her hair.

Brandon stared at him in exasperation. 'She's joined the Taliban, Dad. I watched her on Sky gloating about blowing up infidels. Apparently, she's been a spy ever since she left university.'

'How's your mother?'

'She's fucking devastated, what do you think? I tried to talk to her about it but she just kept crying. The phone hasn't stopped ringing. I keep seeing strange men outside who drive away whenever I run out to challenge them.'

'Who?'

'Journalists, of course.' Brandon's eyes were ringed with fire.

'Could you describe any of them? Was one of them a man of about twenty-five, short hair, beard? Looks a bit like an Action Man toy?'

'What the hell are you talking about?'

'Never mind.' He'd have liked to get in touch with TAJSS right now, but they had a habit of popping up only when they wanted to. MI6 had drawn a blank with them and Jim had doubted their credentials as a serious concern, and yet any help that might come from beyond SIS HQ would be welcome right now.

'What can we do?' Brandon wailed.

It had never occurred to Mark that Brandon would be emotionally unequipped to deal with the betrayal the whole world was talking about. Of course it hadn't. Who was? Brandon had transformed, lately, into a headstrong, practical young man but Mark was seeing him once again as the baby of the family.

'Nothing. There's nothing we can do. She's made her choice.'

Brandon stood, made to rush past his father, and Mark's attempt to restrain him succeeded only in a first-hand lesson in how strong his son had become. The former secret agent was sent flying with one mistimed shoulder barge as though he were a coat from a hook.

'I'm going ... *I'm going to get her back!*' Brandon screamed.

'Don't be ridiculous, Brandon! You'll get yourself bloody killed.'

'*Someone* has to try something. We can't sit around doing nothing.'

Mark climbed back to his feet. 'What are you planning to do? Fly to Kabul and ask for a woman fitting her description? You wouldn't last an afternoon.' He was as good as parroting Adam now. 'Let the right people deal with this. Jetting off on an impulse won't solve anything and I don't want to lose both of you over there.'

'But... But...' Brandon was struggling not to cry now, the stuttering choke of masculine repression he'd employed ever since he was a boy and they'd told him *nonno* wasn't going to make it.

It was time to call for back-up.

Alessia taxied back from Jennifer's to comfort their son, and Mark made the decision to move into a hotel.

He hated himself for sidelining Brandon, but his priority right now had to be Jody, and so he sat by a desk lamp in a little room in Muswell Hill and read whatever he could get his hands on about the situation in Afghanistan as the shadows of the oaks and hornbeams of Highgate Wood stood to attention opposite. He read until he couldn't see through the tiredness, refusing to allow emotion to dominate him, knowing he had to remain in control, practical, fighting. This was just another mission. And certainly not the first time Jody had broken their Rule of Fifteen, no different to the Sunday they'd taken their eyes off her in the supermarket and she'd stashed herself amongst the clothing rails.

Mark scanned the sentried trees across the road. The waiting for Adam to organise things was killing him, and doubts crept into the space prised open by the absence of reason. MI6 may not be suspecting Mark the way they had a few days ago, but Adam was right: the moment he disappeared, they'd know exactly where he'd gone and he'd need to bring her home as quickly as possible, or they'd be hunting him too.

The meeting place was the British Museum, which Mark had chosen based on the raucous acoustics of the Norman Foster-designed main hall. He doubted Adam would be wearing a wire, but liked the idea of playing hard to get, just in case.

This was to be no brush contact, the quick handing over of passport and papers – there was still much to plan and discuss – yet Adam, when he turned up ten minutes late, was almost unrecognisable in beanie hat and sweatpants, hardly clothes that complemented his accent or mannerisms. Mark wondered how long it had been since Adam met an agent outside of the SIS building, but knew, through this absurd disguise, he was at least taking things seriously.

They sat at a café table beneath stolen totem poles and Adam winced at the cacophony of noise around them.

'Relax. There's anonymity in a crowd. You got anything for me?'

Adam nodded. 'I can supply you the necessary window dressing to get you in safely, and I'm setting you up with a contact over there, but after that I can't have anything to do with this.'

'I agree. Contacting anyone from Afghanistan is too risky.'

Adam took a surreptitious look over his shoulder, at the browsers of the giftshop in the aircraft hangar atrium, kids running around as their parents ate spoonfuls of dry cake. 'If Jody was feeding MI6 misinformation, and we're going with the assumption she wasn't doing so willingly, she might not exactly be trusted by whoever she's with. You'll need to be careful.'

'No shit, Sherlock.'

'On the other hand ... She wasn't a dangle in the traditional sense; we *did* send her in to act as a double agent and report back, whilst misinforming the enemy, but her blindsiding *us* has opened up too much confusion about what's been going on over there. She's owned up to killing our men through political and religious motivations and thrown her cover away. If her plan was to ingratiate herself with our enemy, then she's done so spectacularly.'

'You having second thoughts?'

'Naturally. What's in it for us? She's given every possible advantage to the enemy.'

Mark was distracted by the ridiculous hat Adam wore, the sales tag hanging close to his right eye. 'That's what it looks like, yes. Which is why it can't possibly be true.'

'You think she was close to being exposed and this was her only way of convincing the Agents of Allah? Committing murder on their behalf?'

'No.' Mark scanned habitual eyes behind Adam. 'Admitting to the murder doesn't mean she was responsible for it. There's something bigger at work behind all of this.'

'A mission of such global importance that it's been necessary to affect the pretence of a terrorist and deliberately ruin both our lives?' He blew at the hat's tag from the corner of his mouth.

'It chills me to believe that's the most acceptable option, trust me. But there's more going on than Six understands.'

'On that I'm inclined to believe you. How's your Pashto?'

'Non-existent.'

'Good. You're going in as a board member of a construction company with assets in the region. You're not required to know anything about the area, or the construction business. Most board members understand next to nothing about what's happening on the ground, trust me. They simply watch their stocks and shares with bated breath. I'm just getting you in. After that …'

'I know, I know. I'm on my own.'

'Best I can do.'

'I appreciate it.'

'Not that you'll be winging it from then on. My contact will assist you as well as he's able. Oh, I nearly forgot: Happy birthday!' Adam pulled out of his bag a large book-sized blue parcel, wrapped in gold tape and bound with an extravagant bow.

Mark took the parcel and forced a smile for the benefit of their neighbours. 'You remembered,' he deadpanned.

Shortly afterwards, he made his excuses and wandered to the bathroom with his parcel in his shoulder bag. Inside a cubicle, he tore off the wrapping and inspected the contents of his 'gift'. The passport was immaculately constructed and looked, for all the world, like the real deal. His name was now John Varta, CEO of various construction companies. There was a file of papers, detailing the various histories of these uniquely successful ventures, the facts of which he'd be required to cram before he left the country. There were a few other forms of ID, a driving licence, a medical card, some memberships of private clubs, the likes of which Mark wouldn't be seen dead near. It wasn't exhaustive cover, but the cobbler had done incredible work at a moment's notice and deserved the cash Mark had left him at a dead drop outside Victoria station two nights ago.

In a separate envelope, he found a one-way ticket to Hamid Karsai International Airport, leaving tomorrow evening, and the name of his contact in Kabul. FASSAD AL HALLAM was written in block letters on a piece of paper alongside a phone number and address.

Mark packed everything back into his shoulder bag and exited the bathroom into the noisy amphitheatre of the National Museum. He was grateful beyond all expectation and wasn't going to be shy about telling Adam as much. Seldom had he been so wrong about a character.

He re-entered the vast hall to find Adam gone, his woollen hat abandoned on the crumbed table.

Mark whispered his way back to his little hotel in Muswell Hill, as alone as he'd ever felt in his life. Tomorrow he'd be gone and there was a strong chance he'd already seen his wife and son for the last time.

It was too late to hit a gym and lose the belly or sign up for a stint of target practice; he would have to rely on the shadowy tricks of the trade he remembered from a previous life. As he'd mentioned to Jim what seemed years ago, an out-of-shape agent doesn't resemble an agent at all; no one would suspect a man of near-retirement age with a jittery heart and eyebrows so thick they blocked twenty per cent of every sky he gazed upon. But the killer was still in him, he was sure, and it pleased him that he'd be underestimated by the enemy. It was perhaps his only advantage in the game ahead.

He spread his new personality around him and memorised John Varta's employment history, his reasons for being in Kabul. He didn't dare research his corporate empire on the internet, knowing how easily that search would come back to him, so took what he read at face value. Mark pored over the lines of text, then tested himself on what he remembered. So began the process of ingesting the information that might save his life.

In the morning, he tested himself again and, when certain he'd memorised everything, burned the evidence and flushed it down the toilet. He parted his hair on the wrong side, refused the shaving razor and dressed in a suit he rarely wore. Behind sunglasses, he paid for the hotel room for another two weeks, then left, wishing there'd been someone besides the receptionist to bid goodbye to. He drove his car through Barnet and deep into Hertfordshire, parked on a quiet suburban road picked at random, then took public transport all the way to Heathrow carrying a pre-packed suitcase of his smartest, most CEO-quality clothes and hand luggage containing his fabricated identity papers. At some point, hopefully long after he'd landed in Kabul, MI6 would search his house again and his real passport would be found present and correct in his bedside drawer, although his missing clothes and a sizeable amount of withdrawn money would flag up his motives. There was no way of disappearing completely. If he'd learned anything from his years as a spy, it was that a scent is always left, but he hoped his suspension from the Service and the announcement he was leaving the family home after the drama of the previous week would buy him enough time.

He walked into the airport taller than he had in a long while. He was already John Varta. Instinct hurried beside him, looking for anyone who might be trailing, suspicious or out of place. There were plenty of suspects. Lone males people-watching from benches; security guards eyeballing turbaned passengers; airport cleaners in yellow jackets and glazed-eyed contemplation. He'd never know how close he'd come to being spotted by the plainclothes operative planted at the Costa but knew for a certainty the aggressively inconspicuous man sitting over a cappuccino was just such an agent. It took a spy to spot a spy.

He headed straight to the check-in desk for his moment of truth. It could all end here, if his cover were already known by the Service, or if Adam's man had rushed some part of the process.

Or deliberately set him up for entrapment.

A young woman squeezed into a blue uniform took the passport, regarded him with cursory approval after asking him to remove his sunglasses, then clacked at her keyboard with nails that looked particularly unsuited to the task. Mark forced himself to act unconcerned as he stared at the departure times. She clacked some more. A furrow deepened between her immaculately razored eyebrows.

'Bag on the conveyor, please.'

John Varta passed through customs with Mark Wolfe's usual problems. The metal pin in his right tibia, which a Latvian doctor had hammered into him after a parachute drop gone wrong just outside Riga thirty years ago, always set off the body scanners on the paranoid British side, where defences were routinely turned up to eleven. His leg had never set off a single machine in an Italian airport.

And then, after a blaring wait in an inhospitable departure lounge, cursing Adam for not utilising John Varta's fictitious wealth to book executive class, he was sailing through the clouds towards the most dangerous place on the planet, and whatever might be left of his daughter.

Part Two

Kabul

12

As the plane banked, Kabul appeared out of what seemed the only flat possibility for a hundred miles around, a low-rise congestion of houses and air pollution hidden within the rust-coloured Hindu Kush mountain range, stone honeycombs of half-built and half-destroyed dwellings on her steep flanks.

The airport in the centre of the dustbowl had been completely razed the decade before but the shining terminal Mark strolled through, with its huge advertising boards and arrival screens, wouldn't have looked out of place in Europe. Mark sought out a budget boutique inside the sparsely populated airport and bought a pakol hat and a green payraan overshirt he hoped would blend him in amongst locals. He knew it would be dangerous to leave the sterility of the airport before meeting his contact so awaited the arrival of the mysterious Fassad al Hallam from a café near the entrance and watched the backs of scurrying travellers over a rich coffee. The women, tiny and glamorous in their overdresses and head coverings, refused eye contact. He had been identified, he sensed, as an adversary, but the women's hostility wasn't his to bear for no reason; they were reacting to his naked gaze. It was rude of him to stare, a Westerner weighing up, sizing, ranking, judging. Instead, he turned his eyes towards the umber mountains, the haze of heat and sand dancing beneath the penetrating blue sky, and wondered which point of the compass his daughter was hiding at; if the wound that infected him would ever heal if he returned without her.

He became aware of approaching footsteps but didn't look up, instead keeping the figure in his peripheral vision until it hovered close enough to speak his new name.

'John Varta? *Aslam o alikum*. My name is Fassad al Hallam, but you can call me Frank.' It bore the hallmarks of an old joke, with its staid delivery and lack of effort to sell it in the dark eyes Mark turned to face. The man had not one ounce of fat on his body, was probably mid-thirties, with a large nose, light brown skin and black hair, cut shorter than most Afghans seemed to wear it. He had a hard, grim face Mark instantly mistrusted.

Mark rose to find Fassad standing close, invading what, from his Western perspective, he considered his own personal space.

'Pleased to meet you, Frank.' Mark stepped back and extended his hand, before wondering whether a handshake might be the wrong custom with which to greet a stranger here. 'It's hotter than London.'

'But the Hindu Kush has snow all year round.' Fassad took the hand, shook it loosely but quickly.

Recognition passwords over, Mark said, 'Please, call me John.'

Fassad ignored him. 'I have a driver outside. Let's go.' He began to amble towards the exit, leaving Mark to drag his own suitcase, which wasn't something that bothered him, though he suspected John Varta might have taken offence. He decided to let go of everything except that which lurked between the margins of the two men; he would be Mark in all but name, as far as possible. Until he found his daughter, and then John Varta could go to hell for all he cared.

'How's the family?' Fassad asked.

'Oh, you know . . .' Mark was thrown by the small talk. 'We have our ups and downs.' Fassad had obviously selected this question as the most inoffensive icebreaker, and revealed by having done so that he knew or cared little about Mark's reason for being here. 'Yours?'

'All healthy. Business good?'

'Moderately. I forgot to show you my papers.' Mark hurried a little to catch up with his contact.

'No need. I know who you are.' A false smile.

'Even so, I'd feel more comfortable if you saw my credentials.'

'Fine. In the car. If you like.'

'I'd like you to show me your papers too. I've grown distrustful in my field of work.' Mark put more effort into this one line of acting than in all his years of Recruitment interviews, though it was far from a specious remark. Seeing danger at every turn, he was like the hypochondriac quick to diagnose himself with something terminal.

They exited the airport and the warm day fell upon them. The very air told him Jody was close.

An old Toyota was waiting, white with black, dusty hubcaps, a man lurking in the driver's seat, the heavy shadow of another in the back.

Mark's instincts told him not to get in the car, but if these men were associated with Adam there was no problem; they just had an egregiously intimidating bedside manner. If, however, they represented opposing interests who'd intercepted a communication to meet a man going by the name of John Varta at Kabul airport then he was also onto something. A stranger in a strange land, he had no choice but to go with them.

The larger shadow in the back seat stepped out. Like the others, he was dressed in traditional Afghan clothing, his lungee turban hanging loose to the right side of his face. Mark couldn't tell if he was armed or not, though Fassad certainly had a piece at his hip.

'Put the bag in the back,' Fassad said, holding the boot open. Mark did so, then slipped into a rear seat, and the heavy shadow wedged himself in next to him.

Wordlessly, Fassad climbed into the passenger seat and the driver motored them away from Arrivals. Mark noticed several men in parked vehicles watching them from the parking lot.

'Where are we going?' he asked.

No one answered as they accelerated, too quickly.

He asked the question again.

Fassad swivelled in his seat and nodded to the man next to Mark, who reached under his overshirt without breaking his gaze from the Englishman and produced a local police force-issue Glock. Mark considered breaking the man's arm, but reason stopped him; he was out of shape, outnumbered, and in a locked moving vehicle. If he was destined to return to England in a shiny black body bag with a false name tied to a toe, then it wasn't going to be on the same bloody day as he'd arrived. Mark put up his hands.

The gun was upended and handed butt first to Mark.

'For you,' Fassad said.

The backseat heavy looked less dangerous up close. His teeth were as brown as his skin, his eyes haunted by tragedy or malnutrition. Mark snatched the gun, checked the safety was on, then released the butt and looked over the chamber. It was full. He stashed it in his payraan jacket and nodded his thanks.

He didn't need to ask his question a third time. They were headed to the safehouse.

From his window, Mark watched skinny children in rags kick a football against a wall. Every time the ball struck, fragments of plaster fell to the ground in little puffs. The sound of the game and the scramble of feet was somehow comforting, a link to a previous life when he watched much louder children playing *calcio* in the town squares of Santa Maria, their bodies just as brown and quick, their determination as equal. He longed for a Peroni or espresso, an existence as tranquil as his had once been. The irony in him spending those card-playing, *aperitivo* summers longing for danger and isolation wasn't lost on him.

The first thing he'd done upon arriving at the safehouse was take a nap. Tiredness was a killer, as the road signs were fond of pointing out, and his days of artificial stimulants in the field were over, thanks to his self-diagnosed angina and the associated after-effects of an old age paid for with hard drinking and perpetual stress. He rose from the bed and heard the rusty springs creak with him.

There was a knock on the door.

'Come in.'

Fassad's lithe frame slid into the bedsit. Something about the way he looked around almost seemed to belie a nostalgia, as though he'd often used this place himself, maybe for professional reasons, maybe not. Mark regretted being so quick to succumb to that bed's pull, no longer entirely trusting its sterility.

Mark placed his gun on the small table in the middle of the sparsely furnished room, then stared at the weapon as though seeing it for the first time. He must have slept with it in his hand. Before him was a functional kitchen, an oven, fridge and sink. The room was on the third floor and allowed a good view of persons of interest approaching from the north-west through the loquat trees. Before crashing to sleep, Mark had spotted the small groove on the windowsill, indicative of a steadying furrow for a sniper's rifle.

'Join me,' Mark said and Fassad pulled out a chair opposite.

'Mind if I smoke?' the Afghan asked.

'Be my guest.'

Mark watched as Fassad dug out a packet of Pine cigarettes and poked one into the corner of his thin mouth.

'I tried to visit you an hour or so ago but you were asleep, *Angraiz*.'

Mark refused to look sheepish. 'How much do you know about why I'm here?'

'I know your name's not John Varta. You've come to get your daughter back, like some Western crusader indoctrinated by too much revenge literature and bad cinema.'

'Am I to assume you think this mission is foolhardy?'

'I don't think you know half of what's going on out here and you're out of shape.'

'Well, fill me in. Where do I start?'

'I'm not sure you have carte blanche access to everything.'

'And you do?'

'Hardly, but, in any case, what I know isn't what you're interested in. I can tell you where the terrorist operatives work from – I mean, they're *everywhere*; the Taliban control this city – and I can tell you their future plans, who's working for them but pretends not to be, the Russian moles, the paymasters, the local politicians paid to look the other way, but the piece of information you want isn't something I can deliver. I don't know where she is.'

'But you know more than I do. You can guide me. You can put me in touch with—'

'Your daughter has disappeared, *Angraiz*. Pouf! If I don't know where she is, what hope does an old white guy have of infiltrating networks here? What odds does he have of lasting more than ten minutes after leaving this room? You want my answer? Next to zero. You can grow a beard and wear a headscarf and maybe make it a week, walking round the streets with a map, checking for footprints, but you can't speak to another soul without exposing yourself. You know what, you got me. Yes, this mission is "foolhardy".'

'Adam promised you'd help.'

'I didn't say I wouldn't help you, but I think Adam needs his head examining, letting you fly over here.'

'I might have bent his arm.'

'I bet you did. This CEO you're pretending to be, would he be staying in fancy digs like this?' Fassad swept his arms over the dingy room. 'The cover won't wash. I can book you into The Serena – it's a five-star hotel with pool, spa, all the mod cons – but your government isn't paying. Are you? How good is your cover, *Angraiz*? Your passport got you in, but will everything else hold up, or were you going to blag your way around one of the most dangerous cities on Earth with a half-cooked story? This is not the Maldives. *No one* is going to trust you.'

Mark watched a cockroach scuttle from under the cooker to the underside of a rotting sofa. 'The Serena sounds good to me. I don't care if I spend every penny I have.'

Fassad looked pained. This was one hell of an overtime gig for him.

'I can set up meetings with men who can get you arms, drugs, information, whatever angle you want to come at this from. But whether these guys buy who you are is another matter.' Mark felt Fassad's hostility, knew this hard-working agent was worried – with genuine reason – that a spoiled dad of two from North London, a spy from the analogue days, was going to blow everything he'd built wide open, exposing his underground network of agents and contacts for a girl Fassad either thought was already in a wooden box or genuinely believed to have defected. 'I'll do what I can to help you, but resources will be limited. I'm risking my neck for you every minute you're on Afghan soil.'

'I understand.'

Fassad sighed a sigh so hard Mark felt his own lungs contract. 'I don't think you do, *Angraiz*. If you did, you'd turn around and fly back straight away.'

'There's no one else who can find my daughter.'

'No offence, but there's no one else who believes she's worth finding.'

'If there's even an outside chance, then I owe it to her to—'

'And what if she's gone deep? Ask yourself that. Finding her could ruin everything that she's trying to accomplish.'

'You think that's what she's done?' He couldn't prevent his voice rise in pitch.

'No chance. I'm just trying to convince you to go home, *Angraiz*.'

'What is "Angraiz"?'

'Englishman. Would you rather I called you *Booda*? "Old man"?'

'If I discover she's still here, working, I'll back off. She knew the risks. If I find a body, or confirmation she really did go rogue ... My mission is over too.'

'The odds of you coming out of here with a good result are so stacked against you it's untrue. That's what Afghanistan is. Odds stacked against. Be prepared to lose big, that's all I'm saying.'

'I hear you.'

'I'll find you some connections and then ...'

'I'm on my own.'

'Not quite, but this is so off the record we're not even sitting here talking, do you understand? None of this is happening.'

Mark nodded. Fassad obviously owed a lot to Adam, and it was only his respect for the protocols of England's creaking Secret Service that explained even the slightest bit of civility towards Mark on his part. There was no plan. Mark had dropped himself inside no man's land and was prepared to fashion his shield as he strode towards the enemy trench. It didn't take a lifetime of handling spies to detect how flawed that strategy was.

'You'll need to familiarise yourself with the city, so I'll give you a tour. Once you're ordering room service from your jacuzzi, meeting you is going to be harder, so it's best to get a game plan up and running as soon as possible. Agreed?'

'Agreed.'

Fassad looked at him with tired hunter's eyes. It was like staring into the soul of a jackal. *'Inshallah.* I really hope you find her.' He didn't say 'but', yet the word rang throughout the room like a discharged rifle. 'There isn't anywhere on Earth harder to find a missing person. If she'd gone over to the Taliban, she'd be anywhere in the maze of tunnels outside the city, and that would make your search impossible enough. But she's joined a new terrorist outfit and we don't even know who their leader is, let alone where they operate from.'

'Still trying to put me on that plane home?'

Fassad extinguished his cigarette amongst a curling fury of smoke. 'Don't get me wrong, there are upsides to life in this part of the world – a man can have four wives, after all – but your life expectancy reduced dramatically the moment you put a foot on our land. You stand out like a cow with a white forehead, *Angraiz.*'

Mark regarded the hint of a smile on Fassad's gaunt face. 'So what's your story? How did you end up here, doing this?'

The Afghan rose from his chair. 'Let me know when you want to start.'

Fassad's personal drive-by tour of central Kabul lasted about five hours and took the form of an angry history lesson, but Mark made the effort to whistle appreciative noises wherever necessary.

'... the UN are inveigling their way into our provinces to take control of the poppy fields ... the Russians must be put out of sight of our untapped fossil fuels ... the Chinese have secured deals to reopen our copper and iron mines ...'

The sad truth was everybody wanted a piece of Afghanistan, whether it be her trade routes, oil, gas, textiles, drugs, gemstones or sugar. Nobody, according to Fassad, had her citizens' safety in mind.

Mark did his best to pay attention, but he couldn't help but be put off by the tone of the sightseeing tour and its attendant lecturing. Fassad was a proud Afghan and, despite Mark's mission pledges to Queen and country, he'd always found superabundant jingoism nauseating. All Mark saw through the car window was forlorn men who looked like they'd rather be anywhere else, women shuffling like tired chess pieces in bright blue burqas, pissed-off farmers astride pissed-off donkeys. These people were poor and starving. Of course, Fassad's pride came from a different place to Mark's own minor imperialisms; Fassad knew the struggle, knew innocents were losing limbs to landmines on roads outside the city, knew when wheat crops failed, whole families died, knew the slum settlements covering the slopes on the outskirts were full of illiterates and addicts and thieves, and he knew it was the fault of outsiders. Outsiders like Mark and the men he worked for.

'This country deserves better,' was the constant tagline, but it struck Mark that it was as much inhospitable geography as war that kept Afghanistan's inhabitants in penury. History had never been kind to landlocked countries with limited fresh water and extreme weather. It had been let down, for sure, by its litany of invaders. But life was never going to be easy here.

They glided past overloaded taxis on a perilous ring road of squawking, honking confusion outside the Adbul Rahman mosque.

'No one's taken any tests, *Angraiz*,' Fassad shouted, attempting to justify why the cars stuttered and bounced as though driven by children. 'When you add together the car bombings, jackings and the narrow mountain pass from Jalalabad, Kabul is probably the most dangerous place in the world to be behind the wheel of a car.'

Mark peered out the rear window, checking for tails.

'I don't think we're being followed,' he said.

Fassad continued to point out places of interest, giving a rundown on the kings or mullahs who commissioned their building, whether Sunni or Shia gathered inside, but Mark took little notice. He watched the women as they passed, looking for Jody's gait, her eyes through the burqa's gauze.

Fassad knew what he was doing. 'Looking for your daughter?'

'That's why I'm here. You'll need to put me in contact with the last person to speak to her. She was involved with people who sold weapons to Taliban forces.'

Fassad drove down a large poplar-lined street and past the university, new and white, its sign proudly bilingual. A few students were sitting outside in the spring heat but, despite the city's cramped, unsafe apartment blocks harbouring three million people, passers-by were in short supply. Residents didn't walk these streets unless they had good reason to.

'The last known person to hear from her,' Fassad said, 'would have been the person who received her emergency communication detailing her reasons for defecting. If she's anywhere, she'd have been spotted. Right now, she's the most famous spy on Earth.'

'Put me in touch with that last person. I need to start somewhere.'

'You have been put in touch with that person. That person is me.'

Mark snatched his eyes from the small crowds beginning to form around a makeshift market, the sellers dispensing their goods from cardboard squares upon the ground.

'You?'

'You'd underestimated my role in this part of the world, eh, *Angraiz*?'

At the sudden roar, Mark twisted. 'What was that?'

Fassad shrugged. 'An earthquake. They're common enough. That was Jody's cover, wasn't it? Emergency response worker? There'll be a power outage probably. Nothing to worry about. You'll get used to them, the longer you're here.'

'No, there's smoke.'

Now Fassad slowed, checked the still-shaking mirrors. 'You're right.'

About fifty feet back, people were running, a pursuant demon of grey pluming behind them. There was no fear that Mark could discern, just a reluctant obeying of protocol, a rehearsed dispersal from common danger. Amid the scurrying bodies and bouncing fruit, Mark saw a car on fire, its twisted bodywork reaching flaming fingers towards the retreating crowds.

'Car bomb?' Mark asked.

'Yes,' he said with the air of a man who hadn't seen anything remarkable.

Mark scanned the scene. There were horizontal figures in the road.

'Islamic State?' he asked.

'Your guess is as good as mine. There are four main powers trying to gain control of Kabul right now, three of whom use such tactics. It could be Islamic State. It could also very easily be the Taliban or al-Qaeda.'

Mark didn't ask whom the fourth power trying to control the region was. He knew full well that the US and their allies were supporting the official Afghan government, and he also knew, from the tone of Fassad's words, that he didn't approve. Fassad's allegiances were complicated, he could tell.

'Is this a Sunni or Shia area?'

Fassad took his eyes off the road long enough to snarl good-humouredly at him. 'You're learning.' He clearly felt his tour was having an effect on the cynical Westerner. 'It's somewhere between the two, so a hard one to call. The bomb's probably in protest about the two being allowed to mingle. Most parties agree on that much at least, that the two religions shouldn't break the same bread.'

'I thought both beliefs were represented in the Afghan government?'

'There are token Shia Muslims, yes, to try and keep the peace. Even this government doesn't bomb its own people.'

'What about the Agents of Allah? Where do they fit in?'

'They don't, *Angraiz*. I assume the European press are calling them a branch of the Taliban, since that's news-speak for "also terrorists". It's true that the Taliban aren't a single body and have different splinters, but the Agents of Allah have a very different philosophy.'

Fassad had swung the car into a circle and was now driving back towards the market, towards the smoke and commotion. In the distance, Mark could hear the approach of mourning sirens.

'What philosophy would that be?'

'They're mainly Hazara, kicking back at the Pashtuns. From their name, I'd guess they're after Sharia law, and have claimed responsibility for a number of suicide bombings, as you're more than aware, but I doubt they're after governmental power. They expect to influence change by their actions. Children raised in war, who've seen factions fighting amongst themselves forever, have grown into yet another angry bunch of murderous men.'

'And one woman,' muttered Mark.

Now they were a little closer, he could see what destruction had been wrought by the bomb. There were maybe four bodies that he could make out, face down in the dust, and a dozen more bent and bloodied. One victim staggered into their path as they attempted to pass the toxic-smelling ruin of the torn-open vehicle that had caused such mayhem. Fassad slowed down to let the man peer, unseeing, into the window, his blood a blindfold upon his shell-shocked face.

'Could this be their work?'

Fassad drove on. 'We'll know soon enough – someone always claims it – but they haven't used a car bomb yet, to my knowledge. Best we don't investigate. You don't want to get seen here.'

Mark noted Fassad's knuckles whitening on the steering wheel. He wasn't as calm as he was making out.

'They're all bastards, *Angraiz*,' he said eventually, as the smoke receded in the rear mirror. 'There is no ideology that justifies these constant attempts at widespread chaos. None. All any of them want is death.'

Fassad had seen these units come and go and was sickened by the lot of them, which was probably why he'd been an easy sign-up for MI6. Ultimately, these groups all had a common aim. They wanted the government overthrown and the US and UN out. The fighting wouldn't stop once the Western apostates were gone – it might even get far, far worse – but, for now, dreams of ethnic cleansing were secondary to the flushing-out of the bigger parasites. Which, right now, meant anyone who looked like Mark.

'An exciting climax to the tour,' Mark said. 'Thank you for that.'

'Oh, we're not finished yet, *Angraiz*. That was only half the city.'

The hotel room was too large, too bright. After dividing the room into quadrants, Mark systematically and meticulously swept it for hidden cameras and audio bugs. Everything plugged into an outlet had its reasons for being there and, though the appearance of what seemed to be two fire alarms aroused his suspicion, one turned out to be a carbon monoxide detector. The mirrors proved to all be one-way.

He was afforded a good view of the dusty city, the minarets of mosques protruding like hypodermic needles amid the mud-brown housing. Far away, the buildings built into the mountain were a mere sprinkling, some sticking to the summits, some settling halfway down like wayward scree; there seemed no order to their placement, no logical formation of community. He waited for the muffled call to prayer to die down – a sound that seemed to him both terrifying and peaceful, primal and numinous at the same time – and then immediately called room service.

'I need to change rooms,' he said.

'The room is not to your satisfaction, Mr Varta?' came the reply in impeccable English.

'The room is wonderful but I'm afraid the windows face south and, when the scirocco comes, it affects my asthma.'

'When the ...'

'The desert wind, you know, with the sand. It's what they call it in Italy. I don't know the local word for it.'

'The *sandstorm*?'

'That's right.'

'Those windows don't open, sir. And they face east.'

'OK, the truth is I don't like the view.'

'Sir, the view of the city?'

'I would rather see the mountains, if possible. I find nature more calming.'

'I'm afraid another room won't be free until tomorrow, sir.'

There were no surveillance devices in the room that he'd found, but old habits were hard to break. Did the Taliban even bug rooms? He doubted it very much.

'No, no. It's all right. Better the devil you know, eh?'

He waited for reception to hang up, listened in vain for further voices or disconnections, then replaced the bedside phone and gazed out over the city – what he could see of it through the pollution. He didn't really have asthma, but suspected he would soon.

Fairly confident the room was clean, he sat in a comfortable armchair by the large window and read up on a recent bomb attack at a wedding a few days before he landed. Like Fassad, he'd never understood why people spilled blood to prove a point. Everything he read – whether it concerned Taliban fighters crossing over to Islamic State, or terrorists from Chechnya and Central Asia joining the Caliphate – boiled down to one group of human beings condemning another as subhuman. Two rival teams unable to agree on who deserved the silverware and negotiating by blowing the legs off blameless children.

He stood, pressed his forehead against the glass and stared out across the, frankly, ugly city. She was somewhere down there. Fassad didn't share his optimism, and to be fair Jody could be anywhere in or beyond the mountains by now, but she would have known – wouldn't she? – in her heart that her father would come for her, and for that reason wouldn't have strayed too far, maybe even left clues for her discovery he alone would be able to translate ...

He strangled the fantasy before it wormed too deep.

Most of his ghosts had been drowned in the long, listing aftermath of his retirement from active service, but he'd always known the rest were only a hair trigger away and freefall felt very close right now. He needed to play the detective dispassionately. Separate himself, somehow, from his paternal feelings. It reassured him Fassad had been someone his daughter had contacted her 'emergency' information with. Their man in Kabul. It meant Adam had done his job and put him straight into the heart of the operation.

Before dropping him off at The Serena, Fassad had informed Mark he'd be in touch tomorrow, that a meeting would be arranged with an American who'd met Jody a few months ago. It might lead to something, but tomorrow suddenly felt a long way off. One thing was for sure, he wasn't going to find Jody sitting on his backside in this hotel room.

He made sure the Glock was cosy in its holster and let himself out of the suite.

The Taliban were waiting for him.

13

Mark hadn't spent a lifetime being suspicious for no reason. The man stood out like Fassad's proverbial 'cow with a white forehead', sitting in his dirty overshirt, the tail of a lungee turban wrapped across his withered face amid the five-star splendour of The Serena's reception foyer. He'd noticeably flinched when Mark came downstairs.

It occurred to Mark that he'd be dealing with blunt, unprofessional and – by the looks of things – hungry young men on this mission. He'd be required to get his hands dirty, naturally, but wouldn't be dealing with a high level of intelligence, in the espionage sense of the word.

The man's steady eyes followed Mark as he glided to reception in a suit he normally wore to his safe desk job in the MI6 building on Embankment. At the top of his game, Mark had been a conjurer in the field, misdirecting and manipulating to disorientate and disarm, and he now observed the man without letting him know he'd clocked him, using his peripheral vision and the mirrored edges of pigeonholes behind the reception desk.

'Any messages for me?' he asked.

A pause while the young receptionist made a peremptory pretence of hunting through his obviously empty box. 'No, sir,' he purred.

'Very well.'

Mark strode back to the lift. This hotel wasn't safe. That alone was more than enough information for now.

Behind him, he was aware of the watcher standing and prowling in his direction.

Was he seriously going to try something here, in public? Was Kabul as lawless as that?

Mark made a quick judgement call, stepped away from the lift currently ticking down from the fourth floor, and scurried back to reception. On his way, he made a point of bumping into his tail.

'Sorry,' he mumbled, taking the opportunity to get a better look at the man's face. Once upon a time, he might have felt confident enough to disarm him with that casual move but for now had to be content with ascertaining whether he was armed. There was the definite protrusion of steel in the holster beneath the armpit.

Mark strolled back to reception. The young man behind the desk gave him a plastic, effeminate smile.

'Sorry to bother you again. I was wondering if you could point me in the direction of the nearest pharmacy?'

'There small health clinical in Murad Khane. Would be OK?'

'Is this health centre within walking distance?'

He was winging it. All Mark wanted was to see where his tail went. He certainly didn't look like he had a room here, and yet nobody had called him out on his presence. In fact, there was nobody in the foyer who'd even dared make eye contact with the man. Everyone pretended they hadn't seen him.

Mark wound up his pointless conversation with the receptionist and went to sit on the sofa opposite, the one recently vacated by his watcher, and observed him dither for a moment before heading outside. He'd managed to throw him, but there was little benefit in Mark following; the man would either disappear into unsafe territory or wait outside, probably with others.

Mark hurried back up to his room to report back to Fassad about the encounter. It didn't sound like much, that a man dressed like a member of the Taliban and giving off the scent of a covert agent was in the foyer, but he wanted to run his physical identification past Fassad. He might be a known problem.

As soon as he was in his room, the rope slipped around his neck.

A heel kicked the door shut behind them.

Instinctively, Mark elbowed his assailant and attempted to throw him over his shoulder, keeping the feet in a firm stance, but he wasn't strong enough. The rope dug tighter into his windpipe.

Mark moved his hips perpendicular to his attacker's, the better to get his feet into play and, as he did so, took in a brief scan of the room to ensure there were no others present. They were alone. He threw his hands behind his head and grabbed at the base of the attacker's thumbs, the weakest part of the attack, but couldn't prise the forceful grip away. His attacker was far from the build of the slim character in the foyer, the agent who surely tipped off this one, and he tugged at the rope harder, almost lifting Mark off the ground.

He considered phrases that would disarm him, some nonsense which might prove he wasn't the intended victim. It was a technique that had worked before. In the cold Northern Irish night, he'd been jumped by an IRA informer and Mark had managed to overcome him with the simple phrase: 'Did Georgie send you?' His attacker, back then, had only loosened his grip by the tiniest fraction, but it was enough.

Thirty years later, he had no intel with which to bargain, no Pashto or Dari on his tongue, and no breath.

Mark estimated he had three seconds before the lack of oxygen through his carotid would render him unconscious and kicked viciously behind him into the man's right shin, then hurled his entire weight back into the brute, slamming them both against the wall. It had been his intention to wind his attacker, cause enough of a loosening of the rope to get a finger in, worm a little space between the rope and his neck. He succeeded, then let himself drop onto his knees. They both went down.

Immediately, Mark rolled to one side to face his opponent. His knees went up, hammering towards the groin of the body in front of him, his thumbs to the eyes, all the delicate spots. It was ugly, dirty brawling but he'd turned defence into offence in a matter of seconds.

His training was still there, coupled with an innate, primal will to survive.

He headbutted his assailant, breaking his nose, then disengaged and scrambled to his feet. It wasn't athletic, but he managed. Finally presented with the opportunity, he whipped out the gun he'd been given by Fassad's man on the way from the airport and levelled it at his attacker's dark eyes, lurking beneath a thickening canopy of blood.

'Who are you?' he gasped.

The man chewed his lip and stared hard at his would-be victim. It was obvious he didn't understand; there would be no information gleaned through mercy here. Mark had the upper hand, but the man was still stronger, younger, factors that would work in this opponent's favour were the situation to prolong itself. Killing the intruder was the best option, but one also fraught with unknowable dangers, not least the possible intervention of the Kabul police force.

The pause seemed to give the man hope, and he slumped up against the wall, the phantom of a lean smile showing. He was probably about twenty-five and dressed in a pale blue suit too big for him, as though trying to blend into this more Western of locations.

'Weapons,' Mark croaked, rubbing his throat, but the man looked blankly back at him.

A body search would most likely invite Mark to be overpowered. It was doubtful the man had waited with just a coil of rope on him, so Mark stepped backwards towards the bed, keeping his gaze on the intruder, whose obsidian eyes narrowed in dawning concern as he watched the older man pick up the pillow. Mark levelled the gun at him, placed the pillow over the barrel. No information of value would spill from those cracked lips, even if Mark dialled up the violence, which he was surely unable to do now the adrenalin subsided and that pain in his left side stabbed like a lodged blade.

There was a moment's pause, and then the man began to beg for his life. Mark knew he had him.

The man was still begging when Mark pressed the phone to his brown face.

For two or three minutes, Mark listened to the man speak Pashto to Fassad while he kept the muffled revolver on his would-be-victim. It was a bluff. The pillow would provide little silencing, since as much noise blasted from the cylinder as it did the barrel, and the pillow would provide, at best, the reduction of one or two decibels. It wouldn't prevent anyone running to the scene.

Hopefully, right now, Fassad was doing exactly that.

The phone was passed back to him. 'Want to give me a summary of what that was all about?'

Fassad's voice was breathless. 'I don't know how, but they know you're here.'

'Who does?'

'I'll fill you in when I get there. For now, shoot him.'

The phone went dead.

Fassad wasn't his superior, but this had sounded uncannily like an order. And Mark was as programmed to be suspicious of orders as he was trained to obey them.

He threw the phone to the bed and kept his gun on his enemy. Was there something darker or lighter, enervated or emboldened, in the eyes now? What had he said to Fassad that signed his own death certificate?

His phone beeped a dull *ping* and his eyes flashed to it, just for a moment.

The man leaped at him.

There was a spark of light and the gunshot cracked through the room. The man grabbed his chest just above his heart but kept on coming, succeeding in striking Mark in the face, purpling his vision as he fell.

Mark knew from grim experience how much longer men took to die than fiction suggested. There was no dropping in an instant, no pitching forward after a pithy remark. Unless it was a headshot, most men didn't even know they'd been shot at all, and simply kept going. And so it was that his would-be killer was raining blow upon blow on Mark's curled, foetal body. Mark didn't even dare take another aim, lest the maddened animal wrestle the gunpowder-scented gun off him.

Sure enough, the man began to weaken as his body understood the extent of its blood loss and Mark rolled out of harm's way, turned to face the dying Afghan, now grabbing at his wound and muttering in harsh, poetic Pashto. Last words that could never be understood, spat in blood. The white sheets of his hotel bed were a butcher's apron.

Finally, the man died, face down across the carpet.

When he closed his eyes, Mark could still bring to mind the musty, well-thumbed pages of that children's spying guidebook his mother had once given him for Christmas.

It focused heavily on secret codes and had whet his appetite for the game early on. He remembered spending most of his holiday preparing tramp signs and Cardan ciphers to while away the hours, cutting little grille holes out of a piece of paper to redact the majority of a text and render legible only certain words in a seemingly harmless story beneath. He used to write in his diary using transposition ciphers that were easy to crack before he fell in love with the Vigenère tableau and, upon his return to school, seriously neglected his homework to focus on its study. He was convinced he would become a cryptographer when he was older and probably would have become one had he not been beaten up a few weeks into the new term by Jonathan Johnson, a boy so ludicrously named it was little wonder he became a terrorising shit and assumed the far-catchier moniker of JJ. The boy was given a wide berth by everybody in town but young Mark was simply in the wrong town square at the wrong three o'clock. In the years to come, he would receive harsher pastings, but that was the first, and the mess of dirty hair and angry eyes that bore down on him before he was flung into the hedge stayed with him many a night as he lay wondering what he'd done to deserve his black eye and split lip. Perhaps inevitably, Mark's new obsession would become self-defence.

Since it was the early Seventies, he signed up for a martial arts class after school. Mark was small and feeble compared to the rest of his group, but what he lacked in strength he made up for in agility. He progressed to red belt in a matter of weeks and then dropped out. It had all begun to remind him of the cub scouts he'd fled from a few years before, the sterile church hall and the masters who touched you as you made your pledges, and he had no patience for the teenage members who thought they were Bruce Lee after five minutes of training but burst into tearful rage when they found themselves thrown to the floor. He wanted to train in jiu-jitsu but there'd been nowhere nearby that offered a course so his mother suggested judo, thinking it was similar, and he returned once again to his bedroom and his ciphers. He never got his revenge on Jonathan Johnson. He didn't need to: one February evening, the idiot trod on the live rail at Cranleigh station and died instantly. There was an afternoon-long school assembly about station safety during which the teachers all lied about what a model pupil JJ had been and Mark silently seethed that he hadn't had the opportunity to avenge himself personally.

Three months later, his mother died, and eleven-year-old Mark would forever fight the vengeful, all-powerful urge to view the rest of the planet as a potential four billion JJs. It was that long ago, the population was half what it is today.

Mark rose from the floor in his blood-splattered, low-lit Serena room and limped to the minibar on the far side. Water. Orange juice. Coca-Cola. After checking the seal of the bottle hadn't been tampered with, he poured himself an OJ and, cursing Sharia Law, made do with imagining the vodka.

He looked over the results of his first kill of the campaign. His field skills were returning, perhaps had never left, and yet, right now, he was overwhelmed by an almost infantile sense of being out of his depth. Was the water in these ice cubes even safe to drink? What were the punishments for buying bootleg hooch? He knew next to nothing about this country. He was a wildcat whose years of rich food had weakened his teeth and, truth be told, he was rattled. His hands shook. His heart ached. The drink was gone but he could still taste that man's blood in his mouth.

In many ways, being jumped in his hotel room was not only business as usual but a step in the right direction. His biggest lead was dead on his hotel room floor, but someone knew Mark was here, and had been shaken by his presence.

A knock on the door.

'Who is it?'

Explaining this to the hotel staff was going to be tricky. He wondered if he could blame a firearm that discharged by accident. Did many citizens own guns in Kabul?

'It's me.' The voice was urgent.

Mark teased open the door a fraction, to ascertain the corridor was clear behind his visitor, but saw that Fassad wasn't alone. He had with him a shorter man in white overalls holding onto a wide blue cleaning trolley. Mark bundled them both into the room and locked the door behind them.

'*Dogakh*,' Fassad said. It sounded rude.

'He didn't die easily,' Mark admitted.

Fassad stared at the body. Behind him, the wall exhibited a football-sized casserole of the man's innards, now running towards the carpet. The trolley wheels squeaked as the newcomer attempted to circumnavigate the bloodstains.

'He's a big man,' Fassad noted. 'You did well.'

'How did he find me? Who knows I'm here? What did he say to you on the phone?'

Fassad turned his eyes towards Mark, winced. '*Angraiz*, hang the "Do Not Disturb" sign on the door and then consider washing your face.'

The bathroom mirror showed him coated in his attacker's blood. It painted his hands and clothes, matted his hair, and he was taken back a lifetime to those first kills in Port-au-Prince when, afterwards, he'd scrubbed and scrubbed himself of two men's innards. He should have known. The job was no different, no matter the advancement of years. Hotel rooms had always been dangerous places for Mark Wolfe.

He exited, towelling his hair, to find the clean-up operation in full swing. The air conditioning was on high, to help dry the paint being applied to the wall his attacker's entrails once ran down. Fassad's helper, rolling emulsion up and down the wall in question, was small and round-faced, with epicanthic eyes, and he looked at Mark with wary hatred as the old spy slipped back into the room. The bed had been stripped and rolls of clear plastic were lying across it. Fassad was involved in a forensic search of the floor, dotted with foaming circles of carpet cleaner.

'Where's the body?' Mark asked.

Fassad nodded at the cleaning trolley.

'There was a man in reception. He was waiting for me but ... I managed to evade him. He must have tipped off the guy up here that I was returning to the room.'

'Could you positively identify him?'

'I remember him well. Can I help in here?'

'We're on it, *Angraiz*. How are you feeling now? Better?'

Mark indicated his neck, the red, raw necklace of pain encircling it. 'He tried his best.'

'I underestimated you.' It was all Fassad said on the matter, but Mark took some pride from it. The man he'd overcome was half his age, stronger, had the benefit of surprise. Years ago, as a professional assassin doing his job, he wouldn't have been pushed so close, but he wasn't going to admit that, nor the shaking hands he concealed in his pocket or the ache inside his left ribs. In the field, it often didn't matter if you only just made it out alive; what mattered was you did.

'Who's your friend?' Mark asked, nodding at the man with the paint roller.

'This is Yusuf, my right-hand man.'

Yusuf looked expectantly at Fassad, having heard his name. He grinned unconvincingly, revealing a couple of missing teeth and a face that was prematurely aged. He might only have been about twenty beneath that sun-roasted skin.

'He doesn't speak any English,' Fassad explained. 'But he's loyal.' Yusuf sounded more servant than employee.

'So, who the hell is the man in the trolley?'

It turned out there weren't too many safe spaces to talk in Kabul. The hotel room, now clean and bloodless but most definitely watched, wasn't one of those places.

Mark and Fassad sat together in the bullet-holed Chilhilsitoon gardens, Mark wearing his Afghan garb to blend in with the sporadic crowds.

'He was a Taliban informer,' Fassad explained. 'They watch everyone. There were Taliban at the airport, seeing who left, who arrived; that's why I met you with two locals, to prevent them intercepting you. They're everywhere. The Talib told me on the phone he'd seen you enter the hotel and was simply checking your suite out. A porter was letting him in any room he wanted, probably on pain of a beating. He claimed to be shocked to see you back so soon and attacked in self-defence. I don't think he knew who you really are, but it can't be discounted. It wasn't supposed to be a hit, if that's what you were wondering.'

'He had an accomplice.'

'That's worrying. He'd have been expecting news from his friend. It's likely they know he's dead by now.'

'I'm on the Taliban's radar straight away. Quite the fuck-up.'

'Did anybody besides Adam know you were coming out here?'

Mark thought back to Heathrow airport, the spy at the Costa, his own trailing paranoia. 'No.'

'You can't check out of that hotel until the room's dry, but you obviously can't stay there either. I'll ask Yusuf to bring your belongings back to the safehouse.'

'Thank you. You're doing far more for me than was arranged.'

'You underestimated the dangers of this city, *Angraiz*.'

'I did.'

'Anything else I can do for you?'

'I'll need the hotel watched. Also, the names of any known agents who worked with Jody out here. If she's infiltrated this Agents of Allah cabal, it means there's something afoot that she considers bigger than her life.' Mark watched Fassad carefully. 'I know you think she's probably dead or ...'

'It's not just that. This is a man's world. There are women involved in these terrorist cells but they do not lead, they do not strategise, they do not have access to any plans. She would not be trusted. Even aside from the fact she's a known former British agent. Take my word for it, if she is still with them, which I doubt very much, she is a trophy wife or a prisoner. They will not confide her with any responsibility.'

'Doesn't mean she hasn't gleaned intel along the way. Still no news on where the Agents of Allah are operating from?'

'Jody's final communication, the one she sent to the emergency line, was scrambled. It could have come from anywhere. And her group hasn't claimed an attack since Afshar. The bomb we saw at the market earlier was perpetrated by the Taliban, according to my sources.'

'Why's she made it so hard for us to trace her?' Mark mused.

Fassad didn't answer. To him, it was obvious why. If she wasn't dead, then she certainly didn't want to be found. Her face had been all over the news and she would have buried herself deeper as a result.

'I might have to start at the beginning,' Mark said. 'This suspected arms hut she sent a photo of, that was ...'

'Behsud, Wardak province.'

Mark kicked a stone across the dusty ground. 'I wonder if she really is on her own, or if she's getting help from another source.'

'What do you mean? Who?'

'That's what I need to discover. Who's this American you're trying to set me up with?'

Fassad slumped slightly. 'He's slippery. People don't linger long here. Those men Jody worked with, or spied on, have all gone to ground. The training bases pack themselves up and move across borders. The mountains are impenetrable, the cave networks vast. Men are killed in fighting every week. Those that survive vanish another day.'

'And this includes our American?'

'It looks like it. He goes by several names, but the Americans know him as William Stucker. I'd hoped to have set something up for you by now. I'm sorry I can't go any quicker, *Angraiz*.'

'Who is he? Where does he fit in?'

'He was a US cut-out in the past, a third party the local groups trusted, but ... He's either gone to one side or the other now, or he came to a dead end.'

'He put himself in the role of dangle between the US and the terrorists?'

Fassad nodded. 'He was facilitating the sale of arms.'

Mark sensed Fassad was leaving something out. This wasn't just Fassad's pride refusing to admit he was understaffed. 'He was Jody's initial contact here?'

'So it seems.'

'The other half of the honey trap?'

'I help to handle agents here. I'm not given all the details ...'

'Fine. I get the picture. They met, in the biblical sense.'

Fassad winced the corners of his eyes in sheepish understanding of this most Western of expressions. Mark wondered where he'd learned his impeccable English. 'Caution needs to be employed when speaking to the Americans. A word to a superior and you'll likely be sent straight back to London.'

'See what you can do about this William Stucker.' Mark stood.

'I will. You want to head back to the safehouse?'

'Not yet. I need to stretch my legs.'

'Unwise.'

'Someone tried to deep-six me. Trust me, that's a good sign.'

'It is?'

Mark regarded Fassad's concerned knot of forehead, attempted a reassuring smile. 'I'll be in touch,' he said, before leaving him on the bench and drifting off through the white-clothed visitors slowly traipsing the garden's well-tended hedges and pathways.

He stalked the busy, car-jammed roads. If it weren't for the advertisements in Pashto, and the snow-topped mountains ringing the city, occasionally glimpsed through gaps between seventies-looking apartment blocks, he would have sworn he was in southern Italy, but maybe that was just as far as his imagination let him travel. The eyes he passed on the streets of Kabul contained no malice and most residents weren't interested in him. Even when ordering a bowl of coloured rice, the young street chef didn't look him in the eye. Doubtless he was overcharged, but it was a good-natured swindle if he had been.

He found a low wall and ate his food, watching the strangely timeless city, a mix of cultures and eras. Down here, he decided, it was quite a beautiful place, full of mulberry and cherry trees, the scent of tobacco and cinnamon, and, as Fassad had frequently pointed out, undeserving of its larcenous history and violent underbelly, the rupturing of its soul by the Russians, the Taliban, and the Western so-called liberators. But life went on, vendors sold their wares, lovers loved, builders rebuilt, and the spies and children played their games.

He gazed about him, sizing up the neighbourhood, looking for anyone who might be watching from the shadow world.

He hadn't wanted Fassad to pick up on his suspicions, because he'd continue to need his local knowledge, but alarm bells were ringing. Granted, espionage and counterespionage made it hard to separate truth from paranoia, but suspicion had kept him alive into his afternoon nap years and those same, well-worn alarms were triggered now. They told him no Taliban member was going to try and snipe him as he walked the congested streets, that he was as unknown here as he was in Addis Ababa or Adelaide.

The bells rang louder as he made his way, pealing the certainty that he needed to be on his guard around Adam's valued connection.

Maybe it wasn't entirely bad news that his only contact in Afghanistan was also trying to have him killed.

It was at least a development.

14

Mark's taxi dropped him twenty miles from Wardak province, in the Paghman area from which Jody had originally sent photos of the alleged munitions deposit. Fassad had lied to his face yesterday and told him it had been in Behsud, and yet here it was, exactly as it had looked in the photographs he'd been shown in SIS headquarters.

He cased the area for guards, then, considering it unmanned, inched towards the hut. He trod as though learning to walk for the first time, wary about landmines, but the dry ground looked solid enough, with scant opportunity to conceal blast or fragmentation devices beneath its cracked surface.

The taxi driver hadn't spoken particularly eloquent English but Mark understood what he'd been trying to say: *Don't come here. Your blood is on my hands.* This was a poor, dangerous region, a Taliban stronghold where the government's special forces still fought underneath the shadow of mountains pockmarked by years of US airstrikes.

Those special forces were responsible for several bungled operations in this area, on top of the torturing and killing of village elders and civilians on the basis that they were Taliban insurgents. If government drones found large groups of people together, missiles were likely to follow, and the town was consequently abandoned, full of razed shacks. A gunfight waged in the distance, maybe a mile or two away. It was amazing how sound travelled over a deserted area, in the amplified dustbowl of the Afghan countryside.

The barn was empty, light splintering through beams and hanging dust in celestial threads as Mark poked around for papers, loose floorboards, the evidence of ammunition. He found plenty of the latter: shells and multiple patches of blood, as though left behind after a mass assassination. The level of dirt indicated this place had been abandoned for at least a month, but it was hard to quantify given the fine dust covering everything it touched in this area. At the time, the location of this storage facility was purported to have been genuine intel, but the weapons had moved on before MI6 could do anything about it – at least, that had been the story. Looking at the floor, there *was* evidence that heavy objects had been dragged around, though the scuffs could easily have been made by farming equipment as opposed to anti-tank missiles.

He left the hut and took a quick, disappointed recce. More deserted homes. Stray dogs. Card-playing tables left outside, their chairs pushed back as though recently forfeited.

Mark strode back to the road. For one terrible moment he thought the taxi driver had jilted him, but no driver in Afghanistan would leave a Westerner by the wayside; they represented too many Afghani dollars.

Mark climbed into the car.

'Find what you look for?' he was asked with distrust.

'No. There was nobody to ask.' Mark took out a photo of Jody he'd been carrying around inside his jacket since he landed – a smiling image taken over the summer between her third and final years at Oxford. The plan had been to retrace her steps, show the photo to locals, follow any leads that might have resulted from a positive identification. 'Don't suppose you've seen her, have you?'

'British spy. Very pretty.'

Mark pocketed the photo. This morning's journey hadn't exactly yielded the clues he'd been hoping for but it had at least proved that, had someone seen his daughter, they'd probably remember her. She was as much a celebrity here as she was back home.

'Why were all the houses abandoned? The Taliban?'

The driver seemed wary. Eventually, he replied. 'Everybody scared.'

They drove a few miles before passing a chain of people making their way along the road, heading out of town. They pulled mules overloaded with possessions, children on their backs, and tramped with a downcast solemnity that suggested they had little choice in the actions they took, tethered one to another in the manner of chain-gang prisoners. All of them had the same round-faced features as Fassad's helper from the day before.

'More displaced people?'

The driver grunted in incomprehension.

'Those families. They are leaving their homes too?'

'Yes. Hazaras. Many leave last two or three days, I notice.'

'Where are they going?'

The driver shrugged. 'Far from Kabul, *inshallah*.' He spat out the window.

Mark watched the landscape scroll past. Every now and again a man with an assault rifle watched them through fierce dark eyes from the roadside and Mark secretly prayed they wouldn't be flagged down.

He considered his options. He'd spent the previous night back at the safehouse, though there'd been no sign of Fassad.

Nevertheless, he'd slept with a chair jammed against the lock and his gun under the pillow.

Mark was brought back to the present when the driver, consulting what looked to be a pre-millennium mobile phone, swerved to avoid a goat and the car shuddered across the granulated road.

'Where I take you?' the driver asked with no sense of embarrassment, still typing a message into his prehistoric device.

'The American Embassy,' Mark said, closing his eyes to disregard the wayward driving.

The building was a large mustard-coloured cube on Bibi Mahru, the Stars and Stripes snapping ostentatiously in the wind. There were two M1 Abrams tanks outside in the plaza and five armed guards at the foot of the steps. Mark's white skin walked him without challenge as far as the glass front door. His clothes were glued to his back with sweat.

'Good morning, sir,' came the friendly but assertive brand of American military voice he'd come across many times throughout his life. 'May I ask the purpose of your visit today?'

'I have an appointment with Brigadier General Franklin Carney,' Mark told him.

'May I see your papers, please, sir?'

Mark produced John Varta's documentation and the security guard spent a thick slice of forever looking it over. Intimidation was something this man was qualified to do well. Eventually, he thrust the papers back and told Mark to report to reception, where he was patted down at gunpoint and his Glock sequestered. The same questions pertaining to the purpose of his visit were repeated, but with more smiling from the young woman seated behind glass.

The plan was a simple one, though he doubted it would pan out the way he hoped it might. There was no such man in this embassy by the name of Franklin Carney, but there was a good chance the second lieutenant at the door wouldn't have known exactly who was inside on any given day. Mark had said it with enough conviction to circumvent more questioning, but it wouldn't stand up to scrutiny now he found himself inside the building.

The woman, his daughter's age – they all seemed to be – relaxed her smile quickly.

'I don't know who I need to speak to,' Mark confessed in a low voice. 'I work for the British government and have information that needs to go to the highest possible level.'

She looked him up and down. There was no trace of the smile at all now. 'What's your name, sir?'

'That's classified.'

She lunged for the phone.

The room was not unlike the GP's office he used to avoid back in London, except for the American flags and paintings of dead presidents losing wall space to filing cabinets and out-of-date computers. The militaristic face staring back at him across the desk was Texas Hold 'Em unreadable.

'Let me get this straight,' the US Chargé d'Affaires drawled from beneath his not-inconsiderable moustache. 'You won't tell me your name or what you're doing in Afghanistan, but you want me to run a check on someone who might be of interest?'

'Correct.'

'Goddamn Brits. You just don't quit, do you?'

'No.'

'You do realise I'm not head of clandestine operations out here, don't you?'

'But you could put me in touch with whoever is.'

'Afraid I can't, old man. What I can do is take a name – this Fassad Whoever – and run some checks on him. You say he tried to assassinate you soon after you arrived here—'

'I *suspect* he tried to kill me yesterday.'

'—but we're still missing a lot of information from your side.'

'I don't know much more about him. He has a safehouse out in the Shakar Dara district. Look, I'm bona fide. It's just that my mission here isn't *one hundred per cent* endorsed by my people.'

'You took quite a risk coming to me, then.' The American slouched back in his chair, scratched his thinning hairline with a ballpoint.

'My only contact tried to kill me. He's also given me intel I know to be false.'

'And what do you expect to happen going forward? We don't know who you are.'

'I understand there's the matter of trust, of course, but I was hopeful any information I give could be returned in kind.'

'We may already consider this man Fassad to be of special interest.'

'In which case you'll have confirmed my suspicions, and hopefully my trustworthiness.'

'You misunderstand me. We may not have any use for your intelligence, or for yourself. You come here counting entirely upon goodwill.'

'That I do.'

The Chargé d'Affaires stared out into the fortified courtyard to the rear of the embassy, at the pomegranate tree not yet bearing fruit, the house sparrows and what looked, to Mark, like a white wagtail. He'd never viewed one of those from his conservatory back home. 'You claim to be acting alone. Could it be that your contact considers *you* the danger?'

'Undoubtedly.'

'Why are you here? In Kabul?'

'We'd need a two-way working relationship before I tell you that. There's too much at stake on my part. But I'm not looking to compromise your operations, don't worry.'

'For all I know, by walking in here, you already have.'

Mark wondered how close he was to being slung into a cell. He'd confessed nobody knew he was here, that he was working beyond the orders of his own government.

'If I tell you why I'm here, do I have your assurance that it goes no further?'

'No.'

'But I can rely on your help if my information proves to be accurate? This man tried to set me up in a hotel watched by the Taliban, and I can put you in contact with him, his men, his history. Everything.' Mark knew the way these Americans worked. Hearsay wasn't ever going to be good enough. They wanted absolutes.

'Are you offering to sell your own Secret Service down the river? Is that what you're offering?'

'I don't believe that's quite how I put it.'

'As good as. You need us more than we need you. Or else you wouldn't be here.'

'You drive a hard bargain.'

'There's no bargain being offered. Tell me who you are and there's a chance, a *chance*, that I'll take this further.'

Mark sat back and groaned inwardly. It was as much as he'd expected. The gamble was a huge one. He'd been here no time at all and already he was about to tell someone near the top of the food chain who he was. This man in his pressed suit and shiny oiled shoes was right: he needed the Americans more than they needed him, but he hoped he'd at least prodded this man's hunger for information.

'Have you heard of Jody Wolfe?'

'Of course. The hot double agent who slept her way into the tents of our enemy.'

'I'm her father.'

He coughed. 'Honourable girl.'

'And I've come to get her back.'

The American's face seemed to bulge with the effort of suppressing a laugh. 'Boy, are you out of your league, old timer. It's the British embassy you want. Although, I must warn you, I don't think—'

'Fuck's sake. I'm MI6. I'm working off the grid, and I doubt I have much time. The only contact I was given is compromised. There's a chance they don't *know* they're compromised, but they are. It needs looking into and I can't turn to my own people. I have no idea how deep this runs. I need . . .' He stopped himself. 'I would like to offer my services to the CIA.'

He realised, then, he should have started with that line.

The Chargé d'Affaires, not even the *ambassador* – little more than a pen pusher as far as Mark was concerned – studied him carelessly.

'I see,' the American said. 'Maybe I'll put you in touch with someone here. It might be in both our interests.' He started penning down some information. 'You've been in the game a while, have you?'

'Forever.'

'We'll need to run checks, of course. With that in mind, we will be requiring more details about you.' He smiled a set of teeth which looked as though they'd been coated with gloss paint. 'Just in case you're the subject of a British capture or kill order.'

It was one hour later when a man in an oversized suit and tie wandered into the embassy's holding room. Mark had been watching CNN the whole time and could lip-sync the headlines over the hum of the ceiling fan.

One hundred and sixty pounds of muscle sat down opposite and barked, simply, 'Go home.'

'Or, as I like to say, "Hello."'

'No offence, but you've been targeted once. You've risked your job. This is one of the most dangerous places on God's Earth. It's no time to be a hero.'

His real complaint wasn't any of the above, Mark knew. Yet another childless man was looking the Englishman up and down and seeing someone well past their prime. It didn't matter Mark was willing to move Heaven and Earth to find out what had happened to his renegade daughter, but the fact he was close to receiving a free bus pass rendered him a laughing stock.

Mark brushed this all aside. 'Let's assume I'm not going anywhere, that I'm going to remain here until I find out what happened to my daughter or die trying.'

'I understand your position. Now understand mine. I'm not going to risk men or information at the whim of a fool's errand.' The man still hadn't introduced himself to Mark, and he figured that was how it was going to stay. Men who didn't introduce themselves were, by and large, important people, at least in their own eyes.

'You don't have to risk anything. I just want some information about Fassad al Hallam. I want to know why he might be trying, in no uncertain terms, to put me off the scent. I'm not after anything more.'

The man blew out his cheeks and stared at the television. The president Brandon so hated was addressing a rally in the Deep South. 'Even if I do decide to listen to what you've got to say, you know we can't guarantee your protection.'

'Nowhere can. But I can look after myself. The man sent to kill me was thirty years younger than I am.' Mark didn't mention his heart had felt like a deflated balloon ever since the encounter.

'Where were you stationed, back in the day?'

'All over.' Mark, briefly, outlined some of his missions. 'You can trust me. If I were trying to double cross you, I wouldn't have walked in here under a white flag. Things may have changed since I was a paid operative in the field, but . . .'

'You're on your own. You're desperate.'

'We're all on our own. That's how it's always been. You're fighting a secret war. Fassad's fighting a secret war. My daughter's fighting one. The intelligence ties up somewhere along the conveyor.' Mark paused. 'I'm head of Recruitment and Asset Validation for MI6. My people will be looking for me before long.'

The man nodded abruptly. 'Of course they will. Where else would you have disappeared to?'

'I'm not asking you to harbour me, or lie to my superiors, but I was hoping we could move quickly. My daughter's damaged goods as far as London's concerned and they won't stomach any of this.'

'We're not prepared to support black ops either, but we do share some common objectives. Why don't we start with you telling me everything you've learned so far?'

'I've learned nothing. But I suspect a great deal.'

'This isn't exactly going to be two-way traffic, is it, Mr Wolfe?' An odd thing to say considering the man hadn't yet given Mark his name. 'Chicken feed doesn't buy you trust. You've just walked naked into our part of the world. You have to give me something. Now, you've identified a likely double agent working for MI6. If he has contact with any of my boys, they might be compromised too.'

'Exactly. Fassad mentioned a name to me yesterday. William Stucker.'

The American didn't openly react at mention of the name, but his pupils seemed to shrink back in their light blue irises, giving the illusion they just flashed a shade brighter.

'You've got balls, old man. I'll give you that. You've come in here determined to tear up any number of established operations just for a scrap of information about your daughter. Say this Fassad's clean. What then?'

'I've been doing this all my life. If something's not right, *I know*. Fassad's been stalling for time ever since I got off the plane.'

The American sat forward, the chair complaining beneath his bulk. 'I'd like to eliminate the chances of a leak at our end. I assume you contact this Fassad by phone. Yes? Good. Give me his number, and we'll monitor him.'

Mark read the man the contact details. On the TV, great rivers of flame raged across a dry Australian landscape.

'We're hardly going to plug any leaks immediately. I suggest you watch your own back in the meantime.'

'And if you happen to come up with anything regarding my daughter ...?'

'You'll hear from us.'

In the heavy silence, those four words chimed with an even heavier memory he couldn't quite place.

'So who can I say I spoke to if I need to follow any of this up?'

The answer was a vague shake of the head. 'That's need-to-know. This isn't going to be pretty if you're discovered by your people, and my nose is staying clean, understand?' The American narrowed his eyes. 'Have you not considered that things may simply be as they appear at face value, Mr Wolfe?'

'In what way?'

'Your daughter. Maybe she's a terrorist now?' He steepled his fingers.

Just in time, the memory snapped to attention. 'TAJSS,' Mark spat. That's what they'd told him. *You'll hear from us.*

'Say what?'

'This is a long shot, but I was approached by a private security company back in England by the name of TAJSS. I could certainly do with the services of such a group right now. Ever heard of them?'

'Of course.'

'You have? MI6 told me they were a non-starter.'

The American bellowed a short laugh that made the room shake. 'I bet they did. Your own people don't trust you an inch.'

The insult struck Mark like a scorpion's tail. Jim had told him the group were untraceable, nothing worth chasing. 'So who are they? Would they be of any use to me?'

'Hard to say, on both counts, but I doubt they'd have the resources at my disposal, for example, despite their presence in the area. They're not exactly big league.'

'Presence in the—'

'You really know nothing about them?'

'I don't even know what the acronym stands for.'

'It doesn't stand for anything. *Tajss* is Arabic for espionage or snoop. They have members everywhere, but no major scalps to their credit, as far as I know. Your lot doesn't deal with them. Neither do we. But a few intermediary groups and individuals treat them like cut-outs or guns-for-hire.'

'But they're here, in Afghanistan?'

'Of course. Who isn't? I expect your next question is going to be: Can I put you in touch with them?'

'Can you?'

'No. But I can dig a little deeper and see if they've been in the locality. Don't get your hopes up, though. Kabul's a ... *niche* market.'

Mark stared at the television without seeing what it was showing. The more he thought about it, the more convinced he became that TAJSS hadn't given up on him. The car he shook off on the way to Adam's Mayfair townhouse might not have contained a journalist at all. The watchers Brandon had told him were outside the house. Even the spy at the airport he'd been able to fool on account of a few props and a different gait.

There came a creak of relief from the overburdened chair opposite. The American had stood.

'No offence, but I think your limey ass has taken up quite enough of my time. What do you make of our city so far, Mr Wolfe? I expect it's changed a lot since you guys were running it.'

It was a hundred years since the British Empire controlled the territory, but Mark ignored the poor joke about his age and simply said, 'It's beautiful.'

The sarcastic smile was barely there. 'Ain't it goddamn just.'

The afternoon was a sticky but overcast one, the sky the colour of the *manti* dumplings sold in vast quantities by street food vendors. Mark roamed the swirling roads in his Afghan garb. It wouldn't hurt to play the role of John Varta for a bit and check out the richer parts of town, ask after potential American clients, make some noise about 'that pretty English spy'. It might pique someone's curiosity even if it didn't produce any leads, and right now that was better than nothing. Rumours and hearsay he would have to make do with.

He'd spent a long time trying to recall the details of Galway's briefing in the bunker. Jody had been posted to Kabul long before Christmas, pretending to be an orphan, and moved through the city fast. Even if Mark could remember the names of the places she'd visited, months had passed. He needed new intelligence, not the misinformation the British had been fed from day one.

He entered a coffee shop, every bit as echoing as its English equivalents. It was moderately busy with young people, slanted over laptops and chatting. Two thirds of the population were under twenty-five years of age, he recalled from Fassad's time-consuming tour. He ordered a coffee, flashed Jody's photo at the barista.

'She that spy!' the young man exclaimed, drawing looks from the entire café.

'Yes, thank you,' Mark replied, shuffling off to a table, suitably chastened. The photograph he was displaying bore more resemblance to the Jody shared by the media than the one from the video, in which she was darker, thinner, fiercer. All this time outdoors under the Afghan sun, even the winter one, would have turned her into – as that troubled primary schooler had called her – 'Snake'.

He drank his coffee and left.

It didn't take him long to realise he was being followed. When he turned off a street, the same three children stayed close behind.

He was on the outskirts of town, near the hotels such as The Serena, and these boys looked out of place in their dirty clothes and dazed expressions, the mouths of their broken shoes slapping against pavement. Despite his years of training, he knew he'd be unable to shake tenacious ten year olds off easily. It wasn't unheard of to recruit kids, especially in impoverished countries, but they were high risk and naturally unsubtle in their methods.

He resolved to ignore them, then misdirect them in a couple of miles. They weren't important, though they did confirm he was a going concern to someone, even if only as a potential mugging victim. Mark stopped under the rustling shade of a poplar and waited to see what the boys did next.

They paused too, sitting on the roadside and dealing out a pack of cards, clearly something they were instructed to do in such a situation.

Mark broke out one hundred Afghani from his wallet, a tremendous amount of money for a child, and strode towards the boys. One of them indicated the cash in their quarry's grasp and three pairs of hungry eyes zeroed in on his left hand.

He waved the money and reached into his payraan jacket. All three flinched as he flashed out the photo of his daughter. They passed it around with eager nods.

'Do you know her?' he asked.

They all nodded the same dumb shake that indicated nothing but an eagerness to please.

Mark palmed them the money and then turned and walked straight into the nearest hotel. He asked the receptionist for directions to a local mosque, then shuffled back out. The boys were already charging away across the street, to spend their money on much-needed food before telling their superiors the foreign agent had gone into the Hotel Excelsior, which would then be fruitlessly monitored.

Mark took a left, then a right. In time, satisfied he was no longer followed, he allowed his mind to wander.

Strolling into the American Embassy bordered on operational suicide, but he'd needed to make some noise. With no Pashto or safety net beneath him, dancing straight into Adam's 'heart of darkness' and digging for himself was his best option. There was little doubt in his mind that Fassad was a double agent but that didn't mean he should dismiss his intelligence out of hand; allegiances were hardly ever a fifty-fifty split and percentages could be prised wider when necessary. Fassad knew Mark knew nothing whatsoever, so why was he so determined for his partners to get rid of him? Clearly Mark was closer than he realised to some form of the truth. Had Jody, before she went incommunicado, got wind of Fassad's duplicitous nature too?

There was movement to Mark's left, a faint figure detaching itself from a shadow, and then an excruciating pain in his temple faceplanted him into the dust.

15

His head was a vice of migraine, the mother of all hangovers for a man who'd lived and ignored his fair share of them.

Two men wielding assault rifles loomed above, wrapped in the tumbledown, traditional clothes he'd come to associate with Taliban members in the area. His forehead was wet.

Mark couldn't believe he'd allowed them to close in on him on a quiet street. No crunch of footsteps. No shadows cast. No tingling spy sense. He was a vague spectre of his past self and had patently underestimated the training that went into fashioning these local warriors.

They yelled at him in tongues while he felt with inconspicuous hands for his concealed money belt and the handgun under his armpit, and was relieved to find them still in place. His head felt twice its size and he caressed the source of the pain with a hand that came away red with blood. Showing them the dripping fingers, they thrust their rifles back into his face, as though somehow insulted the infidel had dared to bleed.

One of the men grabbed him and hauled him to his feet. The street spun.

They were discussing him, he knew that much, debating the extent of his pallid skin, his sacrilegious lack of beard. Mark suspected they'd take a bribe but couldn't fathom the best way to reach into his payraan without alerting a trigger-happy suspicion. He looked from grim face to grim face in dizzy idiocy.

A cry from across the street disturbed them and Mark observed a third man loping nearer, dressed much the same, the face beneath the turban every bit as hard as the other two. He strode right up to Mark, muttered something to his comrades. They shrugged, replied at length and soon the three of them were sizing him up like slave traders at auction before marching Mark down the street, his feet scuffing at the pavement as they half-dragged him through the piercing daylight, his head throbbing with every step.

They stopped at an old Toyota pick-up and shoved him up into the back, where one of the attackers joined him. The newcomer slid into the driver's seat while the remaining man entered the passenger side and the engine coughed them into the road in a noxious gust of diesel.

They were heading out of the city.

Soon, the larger houses of whichever district Mark had wandered into were gone and the streets became mere dust roads, the yellow flesh of a village crumbling under the weight of its sun, derelict houses dotted here and there that looked to have been built before the writing of the Qur'an. Occasionally, Mark was aware of figures scurrying out of sight of the truck as it roared towards them, men lowering their gaze as they plumed past, as if willing themselves invisible.

They coasted up in front of a traffic light at a quiet crossroads, though the light hadn't been red, to allow for the resolution of an animated discussion between driver and passenger. They argued as much with their arms as they did their heated voices until, in a move Mark hadn't seen signposted, the driver whirled around and shot the Talib sitting in the back and then, a split-second later, put a bullet through the eye of his passenger. Blood burst against the side window of the pick-up.

The driver gently eased off the brake – incredibly, all of this had been performed without pushing the gear stick into neutral – and they continued up the road before taking a turn into the next field. They drove for another ten minutes or so, the dead man next to Mark bumping up and down with the turbulence of the landscape, a thin serpent of blood winding across the rusted cargo bed from his maroon-soaked tunic.

Eventually, the Toyota slowed by an abandoned farmhouse in the middle of dusty nowhere. The driver jumped out. He disappeared into the farm building only to re-emerge seconds later with a shovel in each hand.

'Here,' he said to Mark, handing him one of the spades.

Mark climbed down from the truck. The sun throbbed. A predatory flapping of wings swam down from above as his saviour opened the passenger door with the serenity of a pallbearer and the stranger's former ally tumbled out onto the dry ground.

Mark stared at the body. It was hardly the first corpse he'd seen and it probably wouldn't be the last but, since he'd always stacked every killing against the likelihood of his own death and found the odds increasing with each one, the sight of yet another dead man reminded him just how far his luck was being eroded. The spy within Mark regarded the corpse dispassionately, but the human wondered whether he'd been a family man. He banished the thoughts, lest they fester alongside all the memories of near-misses and other long nights of espionage gone sour.

'Least you could do is help me bury 'em. It's the religion. I'm not gonna leave here till they're under the ground.'

'You're American.'

The man squinted across the wavering heat at the English spy.

'If you say so.' He turned his mouth down at the corners. 'My father was a marine. My mother lived in Khaki Jabbar.'

Mark took a good look at his saviour's face for the first time. There was indeed something of mixed heritage about him, but years under the Kabul sun had darkened his skin to the point where it would be hard for most people to tell. Perhaps the jawline or shape of his face might have given an American parentage away, but the beard was long and black and his eyes were brown and lined. His shoulders were broad, his body obviously muscled under the clothing.

Mark cast a look over the landscape. It was flat and dry for miles, no cover anywhere save for the barn. A mazy run might buy him only a few feet before a bullet found him.

'Are you after a ransom or something?' Mark asked. 'I have money, if that's what you want.' He needed to know who to pretend to be: Mark the spy or John the businessman? The American voice had thrown him.

When the man next spoke, it was dry and humourless. 'You wanna spend money, you can pay to have my truck cleaned.' He looked over it, hanging his head at the sight of all the blood, then pulled down the rear door and grabbed the other body, hauled it onto the floor with a heavy thump that sent up a fat cloud of dust.

Mark tried to shake his confusion away but only succeeded in making the headache worse. 'Who are you? Why did you shoot these men?'

'Dig.'

They dragged the bodies twenty feet from the truck and began hacking their spades into the mud. It was like cement. Sweat was pouring from Mark after only a few minutes.

'Water?' The man was already walking back to the truck. He grabbed a canteen and handed it over.

'Thank you. Where is this place?'

'Somewhere I often find myself burying people.' His voice was curiously absent of regret.

'There nowhere with softer ground?'

'Not without eyes, no.'

They carried on digging. The marine's son made faster work of it than the Englishman, who soon apologised and sat down. 'I need to catch my breath.'

Mark watched him churn up the ground like a machine. He was no novice when it came to gravedigging.

'I haven't seen a single cloud in this sky yet. Does it ever rain?'

'It snows throughout winter, but it falls from a blue sky.'

'Are you going to tell me why you killed those men?'

'You ask a lot of questions, you know that?'

'I'm cautious. It's how I'm still alive.'

'Says the man who got jumped in Wasir Akbar Khan. You wouldn't be alive if I hadn't come along.'

'I was taking care of things.'

'Yeah, after your nap on the sidewalk, grandad.'

'You fired a Smith and Wesson. Is it the CIA I owe a debt of gratitude to, or did you get that off someone who's now under the dirt too?'

The man merely grinned in response.

'Can we at least be introduced?'

The man stopped digging and stood, silhouetted against the lowering sun. 'You can call me Bill, Mark.' And with that, Mark got the answer to two questions for the price of one.

'You know who I am?'

'I've been tailing you ever since you left the embassy. Out here, we don't do one-night stands with those who come to us for help.'

Mark picked up his spade and continued jacking at the hard earth. It was perhaps his way of saying thank you.

'You know you walked right into the part of town where a shitload of Taliban live, yeah?'

'I thought they lived in caves.'

Bill spat laughter. 'They don't live in caves, you moron! Not here at least. They might hide in 'em if they need to lie low, or meet in secret, but the size of the cave networks has been hugely exaggerated. The largest network at Tora Bora, 'parently, had a hospital, operation rooms, multiple generators to run the air conditioning, you name it. At least, that's what the Taliban claimed. But we bombed the fuck outta that place, so who knows if it was true or not? After the Ruskies rolled out, the Mujahideen revealed their true colours and the tribespeople moved into the city. By which I mean they turfed out anyone who was living in a nice big house, shot them in the street and then took their homes. You were wandering merrily through just such an area, my friend. Smart.'

They carried on in silence for a while. It was hard work and, in the end, Bill did most of the labour. After all, he was younger, fitter and, frankly, the one who'd shot them. Besides, Mark had hidden more than his own fair share of bodies over the years. The ground was solid and unforgiving and, when they were done, both were covered in dirt and sweat that ran in clean lines through the caked dust on their faces. Mark slumped, exhausted, and watched Bill as he said a few words at their graves and then patted down the earth.

'Will anyone look for them?'

Bill shrugged. 'Let me worry about that.'

They sat and watched the dying sun set fire to the sky.

Mark's new confidant said, 'Just one question: Why did you give my name to my boss?'

'You're William Stucker,' Mark rasped.

'The very same.'

'We have a lot to discuss. How much do you know about why I'm here?'

'The basics. I got the call to follow you before you'd even left the embassy. But I think danger kinda follows you around, so don't expect me to save your ass all the time.' He looked at him out of the tail of his eye, then announced, 'I'm hungry.' He stood, turned the truck's key in the ignition and music blasted out of the radio – Elvis Presley's 'A Mess of Blues'. There was an old well nearby that William had taken care to conceal, and he used its water to swab the back of his pick-up of blood. Mark helped.

It was dark by the time William decided their efforts would do.

They climbed back in the truck and William started the engine.

'You're a mole in the Taliban?'

'Not exactly.'

That seemed to be all the answer Mark was going to get.

'Forgive me,' William said. 'I gotta eat. I have low blood sugar and if I don't eat I get grouchy. I normally carry a bunch of candy bars in here but ... I ate 'em all.'

They drove in silence.

As they re-entered the city, William rummaged in his glove compartment and threw Mark a shemagh scarf. 'Cover your bald face and pretend to be asleep. Stay out of the light.'

A few minutes later, they swung up to a street vendor and William got out. A few words were spoken and then William was making his way back with what looked like two flatbreads or tacos.

'He gave 'em me for free,' he explained, proudly. 'Couldn't get rid of me fast enough. He was shittin' himself.'

'What is it?'

'Bolani.' He handed Mark's over. 'I hope you don't mind goin' veggie. I think it's safer not to eat the meat from some of these guys. I know how they treat their animals.'

Mark took it with a nod of thanks as William fired the engine again.

'Want me to take you to your safehouse?'

'I'm not sure I should be telling you where that is. No offence.'

'None taken. You told the Chief of Station it was in Shakar Dara.'

'So I did. Let's go.'

They parked four streets from the safehouse, in the dark where weak streetlights couldn't penetrate, and eyed the night. Like a faithful intelligence operative, William had reversed into his space; all the easier to drive away quickly in an emergency.

William said in a low voice, 'Play along with what Fassad tells you. I doubt he'll try anything again so soon but be wary. I can understand why he tried to rub you out, to be fair. You turn up in Afghanistan with no clearance. You ask 'im for operational secrets. You require protection. He doesn't need the damn hassle. But look, if he thinks you don't trust 'im, you'll really be in danger, so be convincing. Taking you out will have few consequences, as far as he's concerned. Men die here every day and no one bats an eyelid. Seriously. Terrible things happen in this city, and the world never hears about ninety-nine per cent of 'em.'

'Who do you think he works for?'

'Whoever's willing to pay 'im enough. There are big concerns about how the Ruskies are managing to stay one step ahead of our troops in Helmand, Wardak, here. The Taliban are being tipped off, that's for sure, and there's gotta be more than one person selling secrets. I've done business with Fassad before, and he struck me as a man with fingers in several pies.'

Mark smiled upon hearing the old expression Alessia had taken such a shine to.

'Fassad's been trying to convince me to go home from the moment I arrived.'

'I agree with him. This is no place for you, Boomer. If Fassad's a genuine person of interest, you owe it to the networks here to notify London.'

'I can't do that. Not yet. It's enough that you guys have got eyes on him.'

'He's not going to give himself away easy. People here have worked hard to build up their cover. He won't blow it open for nothin'.'

'You risked blowing yours open for me today. Thank you. Do you think what just happened was related to an attack in my hotel room yesterday? Did those men know who I am, or why I'm here?'

William shook his head. 'Opportunists. You stand out. But others will connect the dots fast. How many men would you say Fassad has working for him?'

'He was with two others when he picked me up at the airport. And there's a man called Yusuf who helped him clean up the hotel room. Looks vaguely Mongolian.'

'A Hazara?'

'I think so. Fassad probably has fewer contacts than he makes out. Unfortunately, his was the only name I managed to get before I came out here. He claims to be the one Jody got her last transmission to, and while I have no reason to doubt that, he's not exactly getting much done for me, given how much he's trying to convince me he's a big fish. He said he'd get in touch with you.'

William looked surprised. 'I've heard nothin' from 'im.'

'As I thought.'

The American tapped the steering wheel. 'Why me? I'm curious about why you namedropped me. That was what convinced the brass to hear your case, so to speak.'

'I was just pulling at loose threads. Fassad obviously knew you'd dealt with interested parties here in your time. I don't know. It *is* strange that he gave me a legit name, though. Anyway, I'm not here to investigate Fassad. I have my own mission.'

'You're really Jody's father, huh? She clearly got her looks from her mother.'

Mark ignored him. 'I was hoping you might know something about where she is.'

'Why would I?'

The embarrassment was suddenly so thick, Mark considered raising his voice. 'You weren't part of her original mission? The arms dealer she seduced?'

'Oh, that.' William ran his fingers through his black beard as a mobile phone buzzed on the dashboard. Its owner ignored it. 'Look, man. I help out a lot of people. Sometimes not always for the best of reasons. I'm William Stucker to some. I'm Hassan Fakih to others. I ghost my way around, trying to stay alive. What I can get back to the CIA, I do.'

'So you don't know anything about where Jody's mission might have taken her?'

'She ran off to join the circus. I'm sorry.'

'You haven't heard *anything*? You're in deep with the Taliban. They don't talk about this new terrorist group?'

'They spit on them. If the Taliban knew where the Agents of Allah were, they'd wipe 'em off the face of Afghanistan.'

'The Taliban are Sunni, right?'

'An extreme version. Their form of religion goes a little beyond the *hadj* and *namaz*. They support stoning to death for almost every possible crime. That ain't the Islam I was brought up with.' William looked at his watch. 'I have to leave. My people will be wondering where I am.'

'Will I see you again?' It was the sort of desperate question a spurned lover asks, and Mark was embarrassed to have asked it.

'No offence, but you've caused me enough problems.'

Mark's hand went to the door handle, but he didn't open it. 'You really have no suspicions about where these Agents of Allah operate from? Anything at all would be a help.'

'I know very little about 'em. A small band of Shia Muslims who've claimed a handful of atrocities. Save for the Afshar attack, most of 'em weren't much to write home about, at least not by Kabul standards.' William seemed to think for a while, his head bobbing. 'You might want to check out the Jabal Saraj district. The Taliban were using the caves nearby but gave up on the area some time ago, declaring the passes as too dangerous. It's not all that far from where I met her, and if Jody's still hoping to sniff round the arms bazaars of the Kapisa province she *might* be there. What was her original brief?'

'I don't know for certain. Engage the Taliban with gun sales then lure, identify and liquidate the main players, I guess. Jabal Saraj, you say?'

'Hey. That's where I'd try first.'

'Thanks.'

'No problem.'

Mark was halfway out of the pick-up. 'When you saw her ... How did she seem?'

William looked uncomfortable. 'How did she ...?'

'I mean, was she ...? Did she appear to have anything on her mind?'

'She was playing a role. So was I.'

This went unelaborated.

'Of course. Stupid question.'

'I don't know how long you're planning on hanging around, Mark, but if we ever meet again, I probably won't be William Stucker, OK? Just in case you try high-fiving Hassan Fakih the next time I find you wandering clueless through Wasir Akbar Khan.'

'Sure thing.'

'I mean it, man. Look over your shoulder. Good luck.'

He twisted the ignition key and drove off without turning on his lights.

Mark kept to the shadows on his way to the safehouse.

He was greeted by the comically patriarchal sight of Fassad waiting up for him, as though a curfew had been violated. The dining table was blanketed in steaming pans and the smell of cinnamon weaved throughout the room, completely drowning out the more familiar scent of damp.

Fassad relaxed once Mark passed the threshold and the Englishman noticed the Afghan's hand move subtly away from his concealed holster. '*Bismillah*! You have returned! I was worried, *Angraiz*. There is curry for you.'

Mark looked over the table, nodded in mute appreciation.

'You were not answering my calls. What happened to you? Your face ... What have you been doing for the last twenty-four hours?'

Mark paced towards the mirror, laughed at the sight of the dirt and blood.

'Making a nuisance of myself.'

'So I notice. Did anybody see you come here?'

'I was careful. This smells delicious.'

'Rice, kofta, lamb korai, naan. There is chai if you are thirsty and, if you eat it all up like a good boy, dessert is rosewater ice cream with crushed pistachios.'

Mark sat. 'I wasn't expecting room service.'

'I confess I did not make it. Yusuf is a marvellous cook. I'm sorry I started without you, *Angraiz*. I couldn't be sure when you would return. Or if.'

Mark was full in no time, having eaten the bolani not half an hour ago. Fassad didn't appear offended by his leaving untouched food on his plate.

'So ... Did your sightseeing yield much besides a bleeding face?'

Mark laid his knife down. 'I ran into a couple of Taliban. One of them tickled me with his Kalashnikov.'

'They let you go. What happened?'

'I paid them off.'

Fassad seemed to consider this. 'Hmm. It is not safe walking around. I am setting you up with people, I told you.'

'I know and I'm grateful, but I had to get out for myself. There are occasional arms bazaars near Jabal Saraj, I learned today. I was thinking of going there.'

Fassad wiped his mouth on a napkin. 'Jabal Saraj,' he repeated, as though mulling over something nasty. 'This, here, this is called a *safe*house. Right? Jabal Saraj: that is certain death for you.'

'Why do you say that?'

'Because, as of last year, when they kicked out the remaining Tajiks, that became a Taliban stronghold.'

'I was told the Agents of Allah might be there now.'

'The Agents of Allah are *not* the Taliban. I have already—'

'I know.' It was all Mark could do not to bang his fist on the table in despair. 'But, according to my source, the Taliban are no longer there and the Agents have taken over whatever inhospitable infrastructure remains. Fassad, with every day that passes my daughter is in greater and greater danger.'

Fassad poured himself a glass of water and asked, 'Where did you get this information about Jabal Saraj?'

'Someone I spoke to today.'

'They are misinformed.'

Mark watched Fassad's face carefully. 'Have you managed to set up this meeting with William Stucker yet?'

'Unfortunately, it seems he is unreachable at this moment in time.' Fassad waved a piece of naan as he spoke. 'Out of the country, perhaps.'

Mark let a moment pass.

'Have London asked after me at all?'

'Nothing. No one misses you, sorry to say.'

Mark hadn't even realised he'd taken the photograph of Jody out of his jacket until Fassad's voice broke his reverie.

'You haven't been showing this picture around, have you, *Angraiz*? A sure way to blow your cover. She is as famous as Jennifer Lopez.'

'Is Jennifer Lopez famous in Afghanistan?' Mark didn't know all that much about Afghanistan, and he knew even less about Jennifer Lopez, but was fairly sure everything about pop singers, especially the bouncy female kind, was *haram* here.

'Of course.' Fassad was almost defensive. '"Jenny from the Block". "If You Had My Love". And, of course, that *booty*.'

'All right, Fassad. Calm down.'

Fassad allowed himself a chuckle as his eyes glazed over. He was a lonely man.

'I may have a plan,' the Afghan announced.

'Yes?'

'But it is not, I think, a good plan. Who did you speak to that suggested Jabal Saraj? It is important.'

Mark speared a piece of meat and prepared to flex his thespian skills. 'One of the Taliban that accosted me spoke a little English. They hit me in the side of the head, wanted to know why I was wandering around somewhere called ... It's coming back to me. The Wasir Akbar Khan district.' Across the table, Fassad covered his face with his hands in disbelief. 'I said I was looking for the Agents of Allah because I wanted to bomb them to hell, that they'd killed a good friend of mine in their Afshar attack. I punched my heart, like this. They seemed to like me a little more after that, and they kept spitting whenever I mentioned the Agents of Allah. It was hard to understand them, and I don't think they fully understood me, but one of them said something like, "If I see them in the mountains outside Jabal Saraj, I'll bomb them myself." Then they took fifty thousand Afghani off me.'

Fassad scooped up curry with his naan, thrust it in his mouth. 'A member of the Taliban *said this*?'

'Cross my heart.'

'And then mentioned an arms bazaar?'

'Ah. That was something I found out after a little digging of my own.'

'In what way?'

'Well, if you must know: Google.'

Fassad, chewing, stood and wandered over to the shuttered window. He prised it open a crack and stared out into the night, lost in a dreamlike concentration.

'The mountains cover a large area. It would be like looking for a toothpick in a poppy field.' He released the shutter and wiped a hand across his mouth, tugged at an eyebrow. 'Yusuf knows that area better than me. There are, I believe, several passes through the gorges. You could go with him and see what you can find. But it could just as easily be suicide.'

Was that why Fassad was considering letting him go to the mountains, Mark wondered, because it would save him having to hire another goon to kill him?

'You wouldn't come?'

'As I say, Yusuf knows the—'

'Does Yusuf speak any English?'

Fassad conceded that he didn't.

He didn't trust Fassad, but Mark would need a guide who could not only go native but also translate. Yusuf alone was no good.

'I value your skills,' Mark said. 'If I went, I'd want you to come.'

At this, Fassad seemed to grow three inches. Pride, Mark knew, had led many men over the millennia to agree to terms that did not outwardly favour them.

'It is unsafe there, *Angraiz*.'

'I've been attacked two days running. It could hardly be less safe than this damn place. With you beside me, I'd feel a lot safer.'

Fassad turned, and as the light caught his eyes Mark thought he spied a twinkle in them. 'Perhaps it *might* be of benefit to breathe some mountain air.'

16

THEY WERE AMBUSHED ON THE second night.

The first day had been spent searching the desolate, crumbling town, its former glory now the humble ruins of a palace which had been destroyed by way of a parting gift during Russia's withdrawal three decades ago. The only businesses seemed to be cement and textile factories, while every other endeavour for miles around was back-breakingly agricultural. Dust blanketed the whole town, its residents trudging through long-forgotten streets with the energy of the wounded. At its outskirts, abandoned Soviet tanks slept like stray dogs in the sun while the remaining ends of a pedestrian bridge hung twice impotent at the crumbling banks of a dry river.

It seemed unlikely to Mark, with Bagram air base so close, that any terrorist groups would be operating from here, and he certainly didn't see anybody who resembled the kind of men who'd attacked him the day before, but the mountains loomed huge ahead, far larger than they'd been in central Kabul. Repeatedly, Mark was informed they may be almost on top of the Taliban and not even know it.

'Tread carefully,' Fassad said, as though he might in fact disturb their hive.

Mark kept his thoughts close to his chest and his eyes watchful. On little more than sketchy hearsay, Fassad, a supposedly trusted informant to the British government, had agreed to come to a forgotten place on Kabul's periphery and poke the hills with a stick. As Fassad attempted to make small talk with the locals – asked after a woman fitting Jody's description – they were met with a sombre chorus of shaking heads.

Their cover was simple. Yusuf was a guide from Kabul, Fassad his translator, and Mark the Western prospector, destined to leave empty-handed. And yet, in the late afternoon, they did appear to strike gold.

They spoke to an old woman wrapped in purple robes, one eye sealed shut and walking with a cane so thin she must have weighed next to nothing for it to support her weight. She claimed to have seen Mark's daughter with three or four men, strolling through the town two months previously. The woman jabbed her finger down the road, pointing out the direction she'd seen her go.

Fassad immediately tempered Mark's evident elation.

'This woman is no more credible as a witness than a camel, *Angraiz*,' he said, almost to her face. 'Do you not see her eye? It could have been any young woman she saw. It is also highly likely she just wants to make conversation to please us.'

'Ask her if she thinks anyone lives in the hills.'

Fassad put the question to her but was rebuffed in no uncertain terms. The likelihood of people dwelling in the mountains wasn't something she was remotely willing to discuss. She closed down the conversation and made her slow way down the dirt road, kicking up dust as though her shoes were on fire.

'That makes her evidence a little more compelling,' Fassad admitted as they watched her retreat. 'She wasn't so free with her tongue after all.'

They spoke to more locals, enquired after routes through the mountains, but, despite Fassad opening them up with humour, dissipating some of the suspicion they directed at Yusuf's Hazara features, they acquired little information of help. When Mark suggested a hotel, Fassad laughed as though taken by sudden fright.

'You see a Hilton round here? No, we go back to Kabul and return tomorrow. If they *are* here, it would be madness to risk the night.'

On the second day, they ventured into the lower mountains. Yusuf played the Sherpa and led the way, showing a natural aptitude for navigating the indistinct trails that ringed the overhanging crags, kicking away the scree from the paths as Mark and Fassad brought up the rear. Mark was the slower going of the three, but Fassad hung back with him, as though pretending he too was suffering from the increasing altitude. Once or twice, the path narrowed to mere inches and they had to traverse, with no climbing equipment, precipitous drops that would certainly have killed them had they fallen. Mark's natural inclinations told him they should turn back, and he would have suggested so had it not been clear others had been on the trail before. Multiple footprints were pressed like fossils in the powdery dirt sleeping upon the limestone.

Mark found it fascinating how little Fassad and Yusuf spoke, though when they did he got the impression Yusuf was anything but subservient or in debt to the other man. The intonation the Hazara used seemed almost condescending, as though he honestly believed Fassad worked for him and not the other way round, but there was without doubt affection and trust between the two men. Occasionally, Fassad would shoot Mark a humble look after a brief snatch of conversation with their softly spoken party leader, and the two of them would watch Yusuf as he surveyed the silent landscape, sniffed the air, strode forwards in panther-like caution. He had a map and compass on him, but Mark never saw him remove them from his bag. Out here, Yusuf was the premier espionage agent and they had no choice but to follow him.

Each man had his own canteen of water and Yusuf carried a backpack of food which they shared out every few hours, but Mark grew weary the higher they trekked. There was no evidence here of secret cave entrances, animal traps, doused fires. The footprints had petered out some time back, though Yusuf was convinced the trail they took was forged by man. It would be hard to get truly lost here, still at the foot of the range, but Mark felt sure the mountains were empty of all lives save their own. Even the vegetation had given up the ghost and the ground beneath them, so fertile a few miles back, was hard and unyielding. There was little above either, except for snow and the very real possibility of a rockslide.

Finally, the cold penetrating his bones and heart, Mark found himself sitting to gather his strength, and heard himself say aloud, 'I can't go on. There's nobody here.'

There followed a brief discussion between Yusuf and Fassad, then Fassad flopped down beside the older spy.

'*Angraiz*, Yusuf wants to go on alone for a bit. He says there is still a trail. It might not be the way most people come – I mean, it's doubtful there's a main entrance to a cave system here – but there has been activity in these mountains recently.'

Mark nodded. 'OK. We'll wait.'

Yusuf disappeared round a mountain bend, the endless ochre of the landscape scratching at the blue Afghan sky. A bird of prey circled them in wide, languid loops.

'Are you feeling all right, *Angraiz*?'

'I'm fine.'

They waited an hour. Fassad seemed to have picked up on the fact that Mark didn't want to speak. He might have put it down to Mark's exhaustion, or possibly regret that he'd convinced them all to come to this godforsaken place. Either way, Fassad was honourable enough not to mention it. Mark, for his part, was questioning the veracity of William's hunch about the area, and his own desperate yearning for intel that had forced him to value it so highly.

'How long did he tell you he'd be gone?'

Fassad consulted his cheap watch. 'He didn't.'

In time, the sun slipped behind the vast range and it grew colder still.

'How long until it gets dark?' Mark asked, though he could confidently guess the answer. Another bird of prey had joined the first and they swam a compact circle in the sky.

'Do you think you can remember the route back down?'

'I think so,' Mark said.

'Let's go, then.'

The way back was faster going and in almost no time they spied the town beneath them, grey and sparsely adorned with trees, telegraph poles planted unevenly along the main road. Dusk was settling.

'Should we wait?'

'He'll contact me with whatever he's found in time. We should go all the way down now. You remember some of those drops. When it's dark, we won't be able to see where we're putting our feet. The moon is merely a waxing crescent tonight.'

'Fassad, you speak better English than I do.'

'I probably read more.'

They crept down the steep mountainside, Fassad a couple of paces ahead.

'Is that your secret? A lot of English books?'

'I have many secrets, *Angraiz*, but, yes, I read everything. Dickens. Thomas. Christie. Conrad didn't speak English until his twenties, but he's regarded as one of the greatest writers of your language. Is it so strange that I use the tongue as well as a native?'

'Just curious.'

'I understand. In our line of work, trust is a valuable tool.' Fassad's voice became softer, as though he were relaxing into a decision. 'Twenty years ago, the Taliban were executing anyone who didn't go to Friday prayers, who supported the rights of women, who incited protest. Shamefully, I kept my head low. After the Twin Towers fell, your joint military operation rained hell upon us trying to remove the regime who harboured al-Qaeda and, shortly afterwards, Operation Enduring Freedom brought your countrymen to our very doors. I found myself torn. Invaders flushing out invaders. I wanted to fight everyone because I could trust no one. And then, humble teacher that I was, I met an Englishman on patrol near my school. We didn't see eye to eye on a lot of things, at first, but he convinced me to read the UN and Amnesty International reports concerning the human rights abuses which had been going on in this country under Taliban rule and I was sickened to my stomach. I hadn't realised the full extent of the horror being perpetrated on my people in the name of religion.'

'This Englishman,' Mark panted, 'he started running you?'

'You guessed it, *Angraiz*.'

They reached the foot of the mountain and limped on towards the town. It looked almost abandoned now, its factories closed, and very few lights shone in the darkness.

Fassad watched Mark massaging his chest. 'You sure you're all right?'

Mark ignored him, gazed up at the emerging heavens. Even now, before full dark, there were more stars above than he'd ever seen and he felt inspired to share too. 'That's Sirius,' he said, pointing upwards. 'When Jody was six, her maternal grandfather died and we told her he became a star. She used to stand on the balcony in Santa Maria and hunt for him, asking, "Which one is Nonno?" My wife said he was the brightest star in the sky, and whenever Jody found Sirius she'd declare, "There's Nonno!" and we'd all have to wave to him.'

Fassad squinted up at the sky full of the dead. 'Yusuf should have come back. Something's happened.'

'I'm sure he's all right. He seems to know his way around these parts.'

'That's what worries me.'

'You think I've got you involved in something you shouldn't be a part of, don't you?'

'I know you have, *Angraiz*.' Even within the gathering night, Mark could see every contour of his guilt. 'I work for MI6, but I'm known by many here.' The implication was that Mark was not only a massive risk to his cover, but to his income and life itself.

'No man can serve two masters.'

Again, the bible reference couldn't possibly be something Fassad had grown up with, but the idiom was clear. 'We both know that's not true in our business. How do you think I'd get information without my links to your "hostile" parties?'

'So what happens when your masters here find us? Do you turn me over?'

'I hope such a dilemma will not come to pass.'

'I'm stuck between my allies and my enemies with you, Fassad. It makes me uneasy. You told me the presence of your country's invaders left you feeling torn. *You're still torn, aren't you?*'

'Keep your voice low. Sound travels fast here.' His voice took on a genuinely wounded timbre. 'You do not trust me?'

'You said there was no response from William. Yet you never called him.'

Fassad swatted at a mosquito that drilled past his ear. He looked back, in the direction of the mountain they left Yusuf on, the range now one black mass against another. 'I tried every way I could to get in touch with William. He ignores me. You can't depend on that man to look after anyone but himself. I, on the other hand, am bending over backwards for you, *Angraiz*. We are here, looking for your daughter, are we not? On hearsay. On the mumblings of an old woman who claims to have seen her two months ago. On the word of a Talib you claim suggested to you that the Agents of Allah were—'

Very faint, and from some distance away, there travelled the unmistakable sound of a gun's safety being disengaged.

Instinct dropped Mark to the floor. He pulled Fassad down with him, his hand already snaking into his payraan for his Glock. Fassad reached for his own weapon.

'*Aoush!*' came a cry from the side of the road. The sound of assault weapons being loaded.

Mark didn't know where to aim. The men were well-hidden in the unlit umbra behind the road.

'Drop your weapon, *Angraiz*.' The voice was laden with bitterness. 'They have us surrounded.'

Fassad drew himself to his feet, threw his gun to the floor, empty hands high above him as the men approached from different directions. Mark calculated there were at least a dozen, their lungee turbans silhouetted against the faint lights of the town.

Mark pulled himself uneasily into a standing position. He wasn't overdoing it, either; a day of walking had melted his joints. Still, there was no reason not to pretend he was anything other than slow and crippled. It wouldn't hurt to let these semi-automatic-toting highwaymen underestimate him.

He dropped his gun on the ground, where it impacted with a dull thud in the dirt.

'I'll let you talk us out of this one,' Mark told Fassad.

Blindfolded, they found themselves frogmarched through the evening and bundled into the steel bowels of a waiting van. Mark listened out for anything that might aid him as they bounced along the road – running water; bird calls; suggestions of civilisation or farmland – but there was little save the buzz of the engine and urgent, gunfire Pashto from the front seats. As the van rose, he knew they were heading back into the Hindu Kush.

He wasn't sure how many others accompanied them, but he guessed from the to and fro of voices there were at least five. Some of the men, including himself, badly needed a wash. The air was rich with the cloying, soily musk of perspiration.

After maybe half an hour of slow driving, the acoustics of the engine abruptly changed and the outside noises were snuffed out. Shortly after, the van braked to a halt, the back doors slid open and Mark's blindfold was removed to reveal the barely lit darkness of a cave's mouth.

Mark took a good look at the man who let them out of the van, assessing his age, his weight, his likely left-or-right handedness, anything that might give him the edge should he be required to fight for his life. The blindfold had worked to his advantage, as his eyes now found this gloomy subterranean state almost enlightening, but as Fassad was yanked from the van and Mark glimpsed the mask of genuine fear stretched over his face he felt a storm in the pit of his stomach that told him he'd seldom been in as much danger as he was now.

Kalashnikovs trained upon them, they were paraded deeper into the cave.

After rounding a low bend, they passed into a larger tunnel lit by naked bulbs and sentried by two more rifle-wielding Afghans who allowed them to pass with heavy nods. Mark took note of the layout as best he could, the turns, hiding places and shadows. It wasn't long before the cave opened up and they took a chicane to the left and found themselves at a large metal door, where one of their captors stepped forward to strike its rusted surface three times in languid succession. The door swung open and they were ushered inside.

The room was a pastiche of palatial, with layers of carpets underfoot and a cheap glass chandelier hanging in the centre, powered by exposed wires running across the ceiling from a generator which hummed somewhere unseen. There was a lamplit desk in the middle of the room sporting a worn leather surface and an untidy arrangement of files and maps and old books. Conspicuously missing was any kind of computing, suggesting broadband was a rarity in the carved-out passageways of the mountain ranges. On threadbare sofas, two young ladies reclined in burqas before a large shisha pipe. Its smoke hung thick in the badly ventilated room.

A man rose from a dining table off to the right, the sparkling wine glasses and jugs adorning its surface in stark contradiction with the piety of his clothes, as much as the dry rock walls were at odds with the framed paintings of terrorist leaders skewered into them. Mark recognised most of the men in the paintings, one being Osama bin Laden, but he didn't know the man who, now upright, slowly walked towards them.

The man was brown-skinned beneath white clothes, his olive-green eyes glittering under the lights from the chandelier.

His hair had grown long, tucked up under a small knitted hat that was squatly cylindrical, like the round boxes that had once contained Mark's supermarket camembert. He was bearded in that tatty, patchy way so favoured by countercultural fighters over history but there was something undeniably messianic and attractive about him. The swagger of a Charles Manson or young Stalin. He was a leader, and it was evident in those piercing eyes, inherent in posture and aura.

He stopped before the newcomers and stared them over, paying particular attention to Mark, then turned to Fassad and spoke in a quick, lyrical stream of Pashto. Fassad stammered a response and the man's darkly browed eyes slid back to Mark.

'So,' the man said, 'you've come to spill your country's secrets?'

Mark risked a look at Fassad, who stood with a stoic look on his face but eyes that screamed for Mark to play along. It was obvious that Fassad, though he seemed to have more than a passing acquaintance with their host, was scared out of his mind. Suddenly, Mark doubted whether the hit in his hotel room had had anything to do with Fassad at all. The error about the location of the empty warehouse had likely been exactly that: a simple mistake. He recalled the buzzing phone in William's pick-up. Had Fassad genuinely been trying to set up a meeting, and William ghosted him? This level of fear wasn't something a man could fake.

Mark took a deep breath and bowed his head slightly, proffering respect. He decided to run with Fassad's hastily conjured plan. He had no other.

'I'm at your service.'

Mark attempted to meet his gaze but they weren't on a level. He may have been taller, in physical terms, but there was no hiding the fact Mark had no upper hand here, in spite of how righteously he may have uttered that one, sickening sentence.

'And what's in it for you?' A head cocked to one side. Shisha breath.

'Clemency,' Mark said, shrugging his shoulders. Something intercostal replied in agony. 'Protection from British reprisals. The usual.'

'And why should I believe you and not have you shot on the spot? What have you got for me that makes me believe I can trust you?'

'I'm no longer a young man. All I have is information and my word.'

The green eyes, two swimming abysses of madness, hovered closer. 'Tell me something that will spare your life.'

Mark's mind ran over what morsel of intelligence might allow him to continue the quest for his daughter without selling his country down the river. The names of dead operatives. Their past placements. As far as Vauxhall was concerned, as of now, they were right to bench him; Mark was in Kabul doing exactly what they feared he'd do, a rogue agent haemorrhaging their trade to terrorist organisations. If they got wind of this, the next bullet with his name on would be fired by his own people.

'I'm not going to pretend I don't have my reasons for being here. I do. But I have no allegiance to my government any longer. Whatever you want to know, about our operations here, the management of MI6: I'll do my best. All I ask is that, in return—'

'We don't kill you?' The green eyes pulsed, the possibility of unlimited leaks courtesy of this ex-British spy dilating his pupils, though Mark could only guess what had been in that shisha pipe. 'Start talking, old man.'

Mark did, unleashing a muddied list of intel that, fact-checked properly, wouldn't hold up, but sounded convincing at short range. He used real code names and operational details, to cover for the fact there wasn't much of substance. Fassad would have heard of these operations and been able to verify them, but he moved the geography of a few missions, swapped some agents' names, altered dates by one or two days.

And then he shut up. He wasn't going to blab so much that he wouldn't remember what he'd claimed when forced to go over all of this again.

The man looked him up and down, grinning without mirth, and used the tried and tested trick of silence to force further elucidation.

'If you have any information for me,' Mark said, 'I can pay you with as much intelligence in return as you wish.'

'And what sort of information are you after? Where to buy dentures in the mountains?'

'I'm looking for my daughter.'

Mark risked another look at Fassad, who held his gaze with some uncertainty, and saw a new mission ahead. While Fassad cosied up to his secondary paymasters, Mark would work his way through the Taliban until he found a man, or men, who even suspected where the Agents of Allah were holed up. It was Belfast all over again.

Something was shouted and the shisha-smoking women were escorted out through one of two portals at the back of the room. A fierce-looking guard remained at the tunnel's mouth, training his gun on Mark.

'I can vouch for this spy, *Amir al-Mu'minin*,' Fassad announced. 'He's one of the greatest agents the West has known.' He said this with a surprising outpouring of pride. Maybe he'd spent the last few days 'bending over backwards', as he saw it, to facilitate Mark's needs because he genuinely saw it as an honour to be working with him, despite his obvious misgivings and lack of resources.

Mark gazed at Fassad through sorrowful eyes. He'd been harsh on his contact here, but the Afghan had just committed a colossally amateur mistake:

By announcing his 'fame', he had surely seeded the notion of a valuable hostage.

'What's your name?' Mark was asked.

'John Varta.'

The name was mulled over, as though he recognised it. Jody wouldn't have been using Wolfe as an undercover, but the Afghan press certainly revealed her surname once she went full-on terrorist informer, and he was grateful Fassad hadn't let slip his real identity.

'Come and have a seat.' Mark's host indicated the sofa.

Mark moved with caution across the room, sat, while the green eyes looked down on him with an expression impossible to read.

'Can I interest you in a drink?'

Mark looked at what was on offer. He was desperately thirsty but didn't trust what this liquid might do to his insides.

'No, thank you.'

'So, my *friend* ...' The man's words had the sickly pall of stage-talk. 'This is a dirty game we're all playing. And you have vast experience. Between you and me, I can't trust any of these men that brought you to me. Fassad thinks I can't see through him, but I know he works for multiple people. He wears the hunted look of a hired man and no longer knows which boss to turn to. I expect him to double-cross me. The British, I understand, have worked with him for years, but at arm's length. A man in my position should be demanding complete loyalty and yet I am relying on people like this. Why?' Mark's host stared into space as Fassad looked warily around him. 'You are here, offering a more reliable service to me, Mr Varta, and yet you don't know who I am.'

It was true. 'I know what they call you,' Mark bluffed.

'Oh yes?'

'Of course. In Pashto I believe it means King.'

The man attempted to disguise a narrow smile, the first time his face had broken into any form of emotion. They were all the same. From parking attendants to Hitler, the raw fuel these little men required was adulation. He wouldn't even dig to verify its veracity. Praise was praise.

'You may refer to me as . . . Commander of the Faithful. And you are going to prove your loyalty to me.'

Mark hesitated. The tonality of the very room seemed to divebomb, as though the generator hummed a sinister, off-key pitch through the cave wall.

The so-called Commander of the Faithful turned his eyes to Fassad.

'You have served our cause for how long, Fassad al Hallam?' he asked.

'I . . . I don't recall, *Amir al-Mu'minin*.' He was standing to attention, inspected by the drill sergeant.

'And in that time, how valuable, would you say, your services have been to our operations?'

There was a ripple of concern in Fassad's throat. 'I helped facilitate the ambush in Surobi, Commander, resulting in the death of twenty-six infidels. I found you the men to oversee production at Musayi, increasing output by seventeen per cent. Thanks to me, distribution networks through Pakistan and into Iran and Turkey were—'

The Commander held up a hand to silence him, then swivelled eyes towards Mark, as though to say, '*That's* the kind of loyalty I command.' He reached behind his robe and pulled out a pistol, checked it was loaded, removed the safety, then held it out to Mark, butt first, the way parents insist young offspring pass over scissors. The men behind Fassad levelled their guns at the Englishman in perfect symbiosis with their master.

Mark hesitated, then reached out and took the gun. His hand was steady.

'Shoot him,' the Commander ordered, pointing at Fassad.

Mark watched Fassad's reaction. No longer was there the militaristic resolve, the thrust chest. There was only terror.

'*Angraiz . . .*' he mumbled.

The faces of the others bore expressions of faint amusement beneath the chandelier.

Mark looked from the gun – a 2005 Smith and Wesson easily found in these parts – to the guard at the door. He calculated his odds. The sitting position he'd been placed in had been designed to reduce his options. However, the obvious first target would be the Commander, and it was just possible he could shoot the guard at the far portal second, but he and Fassad would never leave the cave alive. Even if they somehow overpowered every single armed man in this room, there'd been guards stationed at regular intervals along the myriad dark tunnels they'd walked through.

Fassad's eyes were burning with panicked defiance as Mark raised the gun.

Still, Mark's hand was steady.

He lowered the weapon.

'No.' The word echoed round the cave. 'I'd rather not prove my loyalty to you by killing a man who has served you well. If anyone needs shooting, it's me.' He stood, moved towards Fassad and placed the gun inside the Afghan's limp, sweaty palm. 'Give the order, and I shall gladly lay down my life for you.'

Silence filled the cave, broken by the gale-force laughter of the Commander as he tried to square the logic of John Varta's suicidal fealty with the ruthlessness of his profession.

The Commander stepped forward. 'Give me the gun.'

'Certainly, *Amir al-Mu'minin*.' Fassad held out the weapon, never once taking his eyes off Mark. There was nothing in them, neither triumph nor concern. They were the dazed, out-of-body eyes of abattoir livestock.

The Commander snatched the gun out of his hands and fired it, once, into Fassad's heart. Mark heard himself cry out.

Fassad clutched at the entrance wound and stared up at Mark in agony, then collapsed.

Two guards ran forwards and picked up the dying man and carried him off into a black hole at the rear of the cavern. It took all Mark's strength not to throw himself at Fassad's killer, who walked forward and inspected the carpet where the body had fallen for bloodstains, then gave the gun's barrel a long, satisfied sniff, shivering in a minor ecstasy, before returning it to the sash behind his back and pouring himself something brown and misty. He didn't offer anything to Mark this time.

'I'm not interested in your intel, or your allegiance to whatever you think my cause is. You have brought me everything I need.'

Mark tried not to look too unnerved, but knew he'd fucked up. The smell of gun smoke hung in the air, charcoal and sulphur, like the *solfatara* of the Phlegraean Fields he'd smelt driving through Napoli in the forever-gone days.

'Stay here as my guest,' the Commander announced. 'I'm bored of your spy games. Fassad was my eyes and ears in your sordid little world, but he'd long outlived his usefulness. I'd always known he swung both ways, naturally, but I fear he swung a little too close to the British way of things. You slaughtered one of my men in your hotel, and I have now returned the favour.'

The Commander barked an order and his men pounced on Mark's arms, their fingernails sharp against his wrists.

'Would the British spy care to see his quarters?' the Commander asked. For an instant, it had sounded to Mark like, *Would the British spy care to see his daughter?*

The men hauled him roughly towards the tunnel at the rear.

17

MARK CRACKED OPEN CRUSTED EYES to survey the scene. Windowless room. Check. Zip-tied to a chair. Of course. A locked door. Yep.

He smiled to himself. Just like old times.

The bonds were easy to escape, day-one-of-spy-school easy, but if his captors walked in and found him waiting to assault them, he'd learn nothing. Then again, these people weren't treating him like a friend, and he'd gain nothing from playing the victim and allowing them to beat him up again.

He leaned back a little on the chair – his back exploded in pain – and lifted the front legs, slipped his zip-tied feet, one at a time, out from the chair legs, then brought his left foot up and slackened the lace on the shoe using what minimal movement the armrest ties allowed him. He pulled the lace almost completely out and threaded it through the zip-tie on his right wrist, then tied it back through the eyes on his other shoe. He began pedalling his feet as though he were astride an exercise bike and, ten seconds later, the plastic snapped and his right hand was free. He repeated the process with the other lace and the left wrist, sawing himself loose. He shook his bonds off, stood.

The room, if one could call it that, wasn't a patch on the 'lounge' he'd met the Commander in. There wasn't even one painting of a famous terrorist on the cave walls, and it was certainly lacking an abundance of other luxuries, such as running water and fresh air. If Mark needed to piss, he had to do so, presumably, into a corner.

He quietly moved the chair into the centre of the cell, climbed upon it and unscrewed the solitary light bulb. He waited until his eyes had attuned to the darkness and then brought a quick, hard foot down on the seat, splaying out the wooden legs with a horrible, giveaway crack. He bent down, the room spinning with what he hoped was only dehydration, and snatched up the leg that yielded what felt like the sharpest point. The only obvious place to await the return of his captors was behind the door and he moved swiftly into position.

He didn't have to wait long.

A few seconds later, indicating his cell was closely guarded, the key turned in the lock. Mark's body flooded with adrenalin as light from outside fingered through the opening door. For a moment, he was back in Port-au-Prince, waiting for the two men to either kill or be killed.

A hand flicked at the switch. It tried again.

Someone hissed a Pashtun swear word, then slammed the door back, flooding the room with light, revealing Mark's empty, broken chair and blocking Mark between the back of the door and the wall. Mark kicked the door back in return and heard the cry of surprise, then spun round the door and grabbed the man by the neck, pressing the sharp chair leg into his neck. The man didn't resist, and Mark walked him into the room.

The silhouette of another guard appeared at the door, then another. Then another. They all bore guns.

Mark released the first guard from his grip and awaited his punishment.

Three times a day, he supposed, a tray of whatever they thought passed for food was brought in by an unkind face behind an AK-47. Mark gagged it down his throat, left the tray by the door and then hobbled back to the opposite side to sweat out the wait for his next meal.

The room, perhaps thirty feet square, was lit once more by the single bulb, hanging a dull eye above him. They hadn't repaired his chair, but they had – graciously – given him a bucket to relieve himself in. It hadn't been emptied yet.

Mark assumed he'd been here two days, judging from the number of meals he'd been tossed, but the lack of a window made it impossible to tell. He may have slept in longer, fitful gulps than he realised.

He cast his mind back over the last few days, the mistakes he'd made.

Despite being the one thing he was famous for not doing, he'd trusted William. He'd taken his advice to come to Jabal Saraj without question, simply because he'd agreed with him that another man in close orbit with this cave-dwelling cabal was untrustworthy, neglecting to acknowledge that William himself was a satellite for the Taliban. William had killed two of Mark's attackers, gained his trust and, essentially, pulled rank over Fassad, and then sent him gift-wrapped to the Commander of the Faithful. Why? To get him out of the way? And now it turned out that Fassad had been right not to come, or fully trust William, and Mark had watched the only man who'd genuinely tried to help him shot to death before his eyes.

The door was cranked open, but the guard took his time entering, as though expecting to be jumped.

'You again?' Mark said. 'Am I not worthy of a visit from Herr Commandant himself?'

The man dropped the tray on the floor, slopping its contents to the rocky ground, then regarded him with half-closed eyes before taking a menacing step forward. His protuberant hyperplasia gave the impression he was morphing into the very rock he patrolled.

Mark indicated the walls around him. 'Pretty sure it's against the Geneva Convention to keep me in a place like this.'

The butt of the rifle was lifted and Mark raised his head to face the pain. His guard lowered the weapon in disgust.

'And an hour or so around the courtyard wouldn't go amiss either.'

The man slammed the door behind him. Mark sank back down on the floor.

That would be his last moment of human interaction for the day and he was already feeling bereft.

He fantasised about the sea. The personality of her tides, her glittering vastness.

In his mind, he waded out. The water was warm, salty, easy to float upon as the jagged vista of Santa Maria stretched behind him, his family waving on the sands. A riptide swam alongside him, teased him further and further out, until his children were tiny figurines upon the shore.

And then the sea floor disappeared and he trod water in his attempt to crawl back to them. He was dragged out, out, into deeper waters, the lancing cold a shoal of hungry piranhas tearing through his body. The sky fell and the seasons changed. His feet carved a useless ballet in the tangle of weeds trying to root him to the seabed in a disorientating, roaring rush of lung-bursting darkness.

Icy, he fell awake.

The cell echoed back his scream.

He lay there, staring at the dim wattage hanging above him. These people treated their dogs better than this, and they treated their dogs like shit.

By now, he guessed, word of his disappearance would be out back home. MI6 would be scrambling and trying to cover up the failed operation that didn't bag him long before he made a break for it. Questions would be asked, heads would roll, and they would do next to nothing. He was, and always had been, on his own. The British operation that sent out his daughter was now dead, thanks entirely to his first-born child's defection, and the Americans he'd met in Afghanistan had hardly taken him seriously. The odds of being rescued were on a par with him punching his way through the cave walls with his bare, arthritic fists.

His guard entered. Or maybe it was a different one; he only ever glimpsed him in the shadows as he pushed food into the light, and the clothes changed little from day to day. The Taliban shawl. The rifle slung prestigiously over the shoulder.

The food was dropped before him.

'You don't fancy emptying my bucket, I suppose? I hardly notice the smell anymore but ...'

The door was slammed and bolted.

Mark examined the food tray. It was metal, possibly galvanised steel. In a film it might have stopped a bullet, but in the real world, against a 7.62 calibre slug from an assault rifle, it would be as effective as cardboard. Still, it was his only weapon. That, and the so-called food. It would have to do.

They'd removed his watch, his belt, his wallet. He was entirely alone in the clothes he sat in. He stood and stretched, attempted an experimental lunge. The pain could have been worse, he supposed. He just wanted to land one good, true punch.

He began walking in circles around his prison to get his strength up, focus his mind. It did neither and he kept bumping into various gnarls of stone and stubbing his toes.

Mark found a ridge of ground the tray would wedge against and pasted some sticky rice underneath, to secure it. Even if the door didn't completely jam, the sudden jolt would still disorientate the guard, just for a second. But one second would be enough and the gun, proudly slung over its wearer's shoulder, would be his. Even a moment of freedom would be better than living another day like this, baser than an animal.

It was time to escape. All he had to do was remain alert.

Awoken by the metal grind of the lock, Mark scrambled to his feet in time to see the guard fling the door into the tray, which wedged itself underneath the door, as scripted, halting it firmly in its tracks. The guard looked momentarily surprised, then took a step back. Mark knew he'd lost a second of valuable time but was nonetheless surprised to find four semi-automatics aimed at him.

'Good morning,' the Commander of the Faithful said, almost cheerful, striding through his men. 'You're going on a trip today.'

Mark's wrists were bound with rope before he was bundled aggressively back down corridors he'd been escorted through days ago. He stumbled at gunpoint along uneven ground towards the mouth of the cave, daylight approaching with every laboured step.

His captors hauled a sack over his head and, his arms gripped, he was marched outside, where the sun boiled a pleasant relief after days of incarceration. For the sheer thrill of it, he attempted a good, hard stumble and was disappointed to find the arms on his didn't yield at all, kept him secure on his feet. The sacking smelt of hay and camphor and his scalp was already beginning to sweat.

Head pushed down, he was funnelled into the seat of a vehicle which started up quickly and puttered across the landscape alongside the impenetrable chatter of the men pressed into seats either side. Their scent was positively fragrant compared to his.

For roughly twenty minutes they drove, uphill, the car's engine struggling against the incline. He might have heard an occasional goat bleating on the slopes but the sound of his own breath was deafening and it was hard to make out much beyond the scrunch of stone under tyres.

Finally, they stopped, and he was hauled out and shuffled across ground he'd expected to be warmer. They were high in the mountains.

An eon passed as he was made to stand while voices droned around him. He tried his trick of falling once more, found himself successful in his aim, and there followed a brief panic as his hood was ripped off and he squinted against the high, harsh sunlight while forced to drink water. He took in a monumental view of mountains in every direction, some topped with snow, purpled by shadow and distance. There were about six men with him, five dressed in traditional Afghan garb, and one completely in black from head to toe. The Commander was nowhere to be seen.

Eventually, they seemed to agree on whatever it was they'd been so vociferously discussing and Mark was tugged to his feet, marched only a few yards, and dumped painfully on his knees. An orange, Guantanamo-inspired jumpsuit was dropped at his feet and he was forced to haul it on over his clothes at gunpoint.

Several men filmed him with their camera phones and one held an idiot board with English script scrawled across it in capital letters. The man in black stood to his side with a huge Khyber knife.

He'd suspected what was about to happen, but now there could be no other interpretation.

This was his execution.

Against his better judgement, panic drowned him. They'd untied him so he could wear the prisoner's jumpsuit, but he was outnumbered. Even if he could, by some miracle, struggle to his feet, he wouldn't make it to the car without being shot a hundred times.

The man standing over Mark began to drone in a forced, stentorian voice and the phone-wielders held steady. After a minute or so, they all huddled around to watch the footage, heads together like children, shielding the light from the screens. The general consensus seemed to be that another take was required and his black-suited companion drawled through the terrorist rhetoric again, then kicked Mark in the back.

He swayed forward, found himself struck again once he'd righted. Apparently, it was his cue to speak.

He ran his eyes over the idiot board in front of him, tried to drag something from his dry lips.

Another kick.

"'My name is . . .'" he squinted through the tyrannous sunlight, "'John Varta. I am a British . . . spy. I have come to Afghanistan under the mistaken belief that my . . . presence here, as an imperialist infidel, might tip the balance of power away from the will of Allah. If, by the third Sunday of this month, in three days, there has been no . . .'" What was that word? "'. . . declaration of policy change in the British media, and my Prime Minister has failed to give the withdrawal order, I will be killed in honour of the Almighty.'" There was more, but Mark took a long breath here and almost fainted with the effort of it.

Three days. He had three days in which to stare at the cave walls, nine trays of slop between now and his death, seventy-two hours of stale, unventilated air and the smell of his own faeces fermenting in a copper pot. Three days! He would not be meeting the halal butcher today.

He was kicked again and returned his eyes to the script. It was imperative he disclose his location, or at least his last known one. He had to risk it.

Mark read the line "We have more prisoners and will not hesitate to put them to the sword" as "'We have more prisoners in Jabal Saraj and will not hesitate to put them to the sword.'" It wasn't subtle but he banked on few, if any, of these six understanding the Commander's English scribbled on the boards.

The Taliban shared heavy looks as three, four seconds slowed to a nauseous eternity. Had they picked up on his ad lib?

Finally, the knife-wielder scowled across the mountaintop, lit himself a cigarette, then beckoned to review the footage. There followed a few minutes while they debated the merits of the video before Mark was bundled back into the car and re-hooded. He'd already seen the way the tyre tracks had been pointing, and he squirrelled this minor factoid away in his mind as the doors locked and the muzzle of a gun pricked his ribs. The car rolled them back downhill.

Mark spent the next three days in an out-of-body state, a forced headspace of tranquillity. There was little chance of escaping from his dark, fetid prison and his mind simply gave up trying to come up with plans for freedom. Whenever food was delivered, four armed guards covered the entrance, like the world's most paranoid concierge.

No, this was it. And he buried thoughts of his demise to the back of what was left of his mind after a week of near isolation.

This barely-Mark Wolfe creature refused to spend his final hours in fear. What use would grief, would mourning, do? It was hard, in that humid cell, to forget about his family, his past, his bodily discomfort, but he sought to find a zen-like place to embrace his death in silence. The three days felt like three thousand, and yet they were over in a heartbeat. He counted the meals, and when the ninth came he knew his end had arrived.

On the third day, his cell door opened.

Food was slung to the floor and the door slammed.

The next time the door creaked open, it was also a meal. And then the next.

If anything, a day's reprieve was an inconvenience to him, delaying the end of his mind's attempts to smash through his resolve. He had never known such torture as the one he'd endured in his head throughout this time. And it was now being prolonged. He knew he was close to breaking.

Finally, on the fourth day, he was visited by more guards than usual, guns slung over shoulders like anglers' rods. It was time.

Once again, the Commander strode from the blinding wattage of the outside space to enjoy his ceremonial goodbye.

'Today's the day, Mr Varta.'

'What happened?' Mark croaked. 'We're a day overdue.'

'We had some problems with the internet.'

Mark managed a weak smile.

'And the little matter of editing out your sad attempt to give your location away.'

'Ah. I see. How were your ratings?'

'It got the expected reaction.'

'You know that was all pointless. There's no chance in hell the UK government will tear up years of non-negotiation policy just to pay for my freedom.' Especially not for *his* freedom. The father of a known defector. 'Or was all of that just so, when you *do* kill me, it will show the world what big, strong boys you are?'

The Commander threw Mark's orange jumpsuit at his feet. 'Put this on.'

Mark stared at the suit. 'And what if I don't fancy being your movie star this time?'

'We can shoot your kneecaps off and film the video with you crying in pain, or you can go with some dignity.'

Mark shrugged the suit on over his clothing.

'There are worse ways to die than decapitation.' There was so much coldness in the Commander's piercing green eyes Mark shivered.

'There are?'

Were he facing the guillotine, the Commander might have a point, but Mark recalled the Khyber knife the man in black wielded four days ago. Large as it was, it would require as many hacks through his neck as a cub scout's penknife.

'They say the brain is alive for thirty seconds after the head comes off,' the Commander stated conversationally.

'Oh, good.'

'This is nothing personal.'

The Commander nodded and a man approached Mark with binds for his wrists. He was a step away when Mark stood wearily and headbutted him as hard as he could on the bridge of the nose. The man staggered back and, to Mark's disappointment, went for his gun instead of his shattered nose. Mark had no advantage left to lunge for, no live cover to hide behind. Several guns pointed at him, closed in like rustlers around a wild animal.

The Commander sounded disappointed. 'You do insist on making things tougher for yourself.'

The hood went on and he was practically sprinted out of the cave.

Once in the car, they began their slow climb up the Hindu Kush. For a while the grind of the gears was all Mark heard, but it became clear there was another vehicle in their party following. A cowbell tinkled faintly from far away. The acoustics of the wind, interrupted by thin trees.

The journey had, he estimated, another fifteen minutes, if they were headed to the same site as before. He wondered why he required the hood, if this was a one-way trip. Clearly, they expected him to fight his way out.

He mused on the possibility of veering their vehicle off a mountain with his hands tied, taking as many of these bastards with him as possible, but he was penned in by two guards, both of whom dug guns into his sides. And then, they were at the top; time had hastened as though fed through a projector at twice the speed. This, he reasoned, was what happened when one approached the very end of life.

A hand reached in and dragged him out as though he were nothing but a sack of luggage from a taxi's backseat. He couldn't steady himself and fell face first into the dirt.

The men laughed.

Someone ripped him to his feet by the collar. His hood was torn off and he blinked in the sudden light. Another man, in the periphery of Mark's vision, stalked back to the car and removed a rusted garden spade from the boot.

They led him to the spot he'd kneeled in four days ago as the wind whipped around the little group of men, making shawls and headscarves snap. There was no idiot board for Mark this time. His role today was purely non-verbal.

The hood being off inspired a welcome psychological change within Mark. He knew where his opponents were standing, which of them had the weapons, who he could take down with him. He turned to look into the eyes of the man due to sever the head from his body and wished he hadn't. It was like looking into the black eyes of a serpent.

The phones were raised, ready. The sunlight snickered off them like flashbulbs.

He was forced down, onto his knees.

Mark looked defiantly into the faces of the men, noting that, now their phones were up, their guns were down. But it was simply habit, he knew – much like the senses persevering after decapitation – that led him to pick up on this fact, the trace memories of his occupation, no more useful to him than the angle of the sun in the vast sky or the human shadows that seemed to rise above a rocky ridge thirty feet behind the Taliban.

The man in black placed the glinting knife at Mark's neck, held it there as though posing for a photo, and then Mark's world erupted in bloody confusion.

The first gunshot echoed a clap of thunder and threw his executioner back like a ragdoll. Mark assumed a headshot, since the man went down so fast there had hardly been enough time to even acknowledge the sound that ripped through the mountain range. The knife landed at his knees amongst a smattering of poppy-red beads of blood.

The shot was followed by a barrage of fire that made the men holding their phones dance like marionettes. And then their strings were cut.

Some of the Taliban returned fire as best they could, but they too were cut down, the bullets slugging into the bodies with wet thuds, men slumping to the dirt and spinning up twisting tendrils of dust. Mark looked in desperation for cover, but the nearest possibility was twenty yards away and the car that had driven him here was barely, despite what action films would have audiences believe, representative of adequate cover at all. An assault rifle would punch straight through that thing.

Shadows fanned out, firing as they stalked closer. The last two Taliban began charging back to the cars, shooting over their shoulders.

Mark did the only sensible thing and dropped to the ground. No one missed a man dressed from head to toe in orange in the middle of a gunfight.

The rearguard of the firing pair didn't last long and the Talib danced his way to the dust the way the others had, blood spraying from the exit wounds and casting nuclear shadows across the dirt. The last of them fled beyond the vehicles and found cover lower down the mountainside while Mark's rescue party, dressed in a soft brown khaki similar to the US military but with the skin tones of local militia, inched closer in two channels. There were six of them in a tight pincer, and another three approaching from the higher ground.

On the floor, bodies moaned. The figure at the vanguard of the trio fired bullets indiscriminately into the prostrate men, silencing them, and phones and guns, bullet clips and magazines were snatched off the dead. The man in black, collapsed beside Mark, still gazed serpent's eyes almost directly at the British spy, as though blaming him for his early departure from Earth, but Mark could see all the way through his missing forehead to the snow-capped mountains beyond.

There was a sudden renewal of gunfire and the near six men sprinted at the rocks in response to a volley of warning shots. One of them dropped, clutching his side, and scrambled to retrieve a gun that fell just out of reach.

A Kalashnikov was thrown over the rocks, clattering down the mountain to cries of alarm, and then the lone, defeated Talib rose, hands high above his head. Mark could tell, even with his own poor understanding of local dialects, that there was some internal debate amongst the newcomers about whether they should perforate him with bullets. Their comrade on the ground wasn't moving.

Mark's attention was returned to the smaller group approaching as a shadow landed across him. He tried to stand, but his legs didn't collect the command from his brain.

The figure bent down, its silhouette blocking the fierce sunlight, and plucked up the knife. In one quick movement, the ropes binding Mark's wrists were slashed through. A rough hand helped him to his feet.

Mark stood shakily and peered into the dark eyes.

'Thank you,' he heard himself say.

The figure tugged down his mask, as though he wanted to say something, but the expression beneath was another mask. The face was vaguely familiar.

'Who are you guys?'

The mask went back on. Mark received no answer.

In the end, the rescue party decided to take the Talib prisoner. It was necessary if they were to discover the location of his base, the men he was working with, their plans, and Mark felt no pity for him; he was sure he'd been one of the group who'd beaten him in his cell.

As he was dragged before Mark's rescuers, the Talib lunged at the nearest weapon in desperation and succeeded in wresting it off his capturer.

In that moment, the years fell from Mark, and he snatched the Khyber knife from his neighbour and flung it at his Taliban tormentor. A fast throw, he knew from experience, was more accurate than a slow one and, against all odds, the knife sailed twenty-five feet and embedded itself between ribs to the left of the sternum. His aim had always been true, but his eyes weren't what they were, nor his muscles. He had, in fact, been aiming for the neck.

The Talib flashed a look of surprise, displaying no outward sign of pain, then dropped the gun to fumble at the knife protruding from his body. He twisted it out as the wine-coloured blood saturated his payraan overshirt.

'*Yaast*...' He folded to the ground as though melting through his own clothes.

The militia regarded Mark with shock as he glared at the body on the ground. A foot either side and the victim would have been one of their own men.

Mark ignored their expressions as he massaged his shoulder – he'd definitely torn his rotator cuff doing that – and prayed they'd forgive him the silencing of their only prisoner. Some Dari was barked. Gallows laughter. These men knew the language of revenge; Mark had been a captive of the Taliban for days. He was owed that.

The man who'd cut his bonds looked him up and down, the way a doctor might survey for injuries, then turned his scrutiny to their fallen comrade as vultures wheeled in the silver-blue. Mark stared at the bodies, shielding his eyes from the punishing sun with an orange sleeve, and took a deep breath of fresh air, felt it fill his weary lungs, the intense creaking pain of it, before exhaling to a dozen shooting aches throughout his ribcage.

By some miracle, he was still alive.

Slowly, the group left the body, their sullen eyes downcast. Mark fell into line with them as they traipsed back to the rocks they'd lain in ambush behind, to collect equipment. He insisted upon helping with the digging of shallow graves, despite the pain it caused him.

When they were done, the men quickly bagged up what they needed and began to hurry down the other side of the mountain, where Mark spied a Hummer and a lime green VW camper van fitted with large off-road wheels sitting incongruously amongst the parched trees.

'We look as hippies, yes?' one of the men asked. There was no warmth in the voice, nor mirth in the thin smile.

'Not exactly. Thank you for saving my life.'

The man scratched at his wispy beard. 'We wait until knife is at your throat before shooting, to make sure Taliban all surprised, yes?' He spat a throaty smoker's cough.

The nine of them soon arrived at the two-vehicle convoy. More than a couple were checking watches.

'You late for something?' Mark asked his allocated translator.

'We have long drive, yes? And your execution was day late. My men are tired.'

Mark followed him into the camper van, the inside of which had been converted into a rudimentary minibus with broken or threadbare seats gaffer-taped in position, some of them pieces of repurposed garden furniture. One by one, he studied the sullen, bearded faces, then immediately understood why his first rescuer had seemed familiar upon pulling down his mask. He'd looked like Yusuf. In fact, now he regarded them properly, all these men had Hazara blood in their veins.

The Agents of Allah had found him.

18

Dusk was approaching, that hour of the day owned by rustling unseen creatures, and a stern wind rolled over the mountains from the Iranian deserts to sweep in a canopy of stars. As they bumped along in the little van, everything hurt. Death had been avoided for a time, but life would continue to be agonising.

Mark was seated near the front of the sweat-doused vehicle, presumably so everyone could keep an eye on him. His designated conversationalist sat behind, speaking Dari in a quiet, raspy voice that nonetheless commanded everyone's attention. When he stopped, Mark felt eyes swivel towards the back of his neck with narrowed exhaustion.

Eternity hung like a prisoner.

'You teach me throw knife, yes?' the man asked, miming the arc of the knife that killed the Talib.

'It was just dumb luck,' Mark replied.

'I do not believe, old man. I never see anything like that before.'

'If I was so skilled in combat, would I have allowed myself to get captured in the first place?'

Dark eyes refused to blink. The man's face contained the seeds of many emotions, but they were all uniquely negative and had warped and miseried his expression as a flame does to a candle. 'You British spy, yes? Or that what Taliban make you say?'

'I'm a businessman,' Mark stated. 'My name is John Varta and I own some crummy hotels out here. Those Taliban bastards think everyone with white skin's a spy.' But Mark sensed this man, on top of being someone he needed on his side, didn't believe a syllable of what he was saying, so cautiously changed tack. 'Look, I took a few knife-throwing classes when I was younger. Used to practise in my garden. The knife had a light handle, which always helps if you throw underhand, to keep the blade at the front, like an arrowhead.'

The man poked a cigarette into his cruelly slanted mouth and said something to the rest of the bus before swinging back round to Mark. 'Go on.'

'Most people will chuck a knife like this.' He demonstrated flinging a blade end over end. 'A spinning knife's not guaranteed to strike blade first. There's a seventy per cent chance it will hit hilt or side first and—'

'Wait. Wait.' The man turned and translated to the rapt audience. 'Carry on,' he said, when done. Mark was giving a knife-throwing lesson to a vanload of terrorists.

'It's a risky combat move. If it doesn't penetrate the body, you lose a valuable tool, and you gift the enemy a weapon to use against you. It's all about timing, and practice. Never use this option against a moving target.'

And so the lecture continued. They were rapt. Mark pictured himself leading a full-on training session in a few days' time, where all sorts of targets would be hit dead centre by pinpoint accurate throws in the manner of circus exhibitionists.

'So ... How did you find me?'

'We see the news, yes?'

'But why *rescue me*?'

'British spy. High value.'

'I told you, I'm not a …' Mark suspected these warriors considered their operation a success – they'd massacred many of their rivals in a matter of seconds – but they were still rolling home one man short. They'd sacrificed a lot to snatch him. Why? '… I suppose I do possess certain skills. What's your name?'

'You call me Abs.'

'Short for …?'

'Abs.'

Occasionally, Mark caught the furtive gaze of the man who'd cut his bonds, sitting at the back of the van, eavesdropping on the conversation. He blended in well enough, despite possessing, to Mark's trained eye, the bruised air of an undercover joe, but no MI6 agent would have done anything so clumsy as show his face straight off the bat the way he'd done.

'How did you know where to find me?'

Abs shrugged. 'Man from mountain know of place. Enough questions.'

Mark returned his eyes to the road, tried to sleep and recover some strength, but his mind was racing. If there *was* a spy – besides Jody – within the Agents of Allah, were they known to his daughter, or was he searching for her too? Things, as always in spyland, were thornier than they first appeared.

Jody was a known defector from the British, and yet the Agents of Allah had gone in all guns blazing to rescue an old MI6 agent from under the knife of the Taliban. If she'd been behind this rescue mission, even in part, then it was as good as giving up her cover.

Mark didn't believe in coincidences, and the Agents of Allah deciding to rescue him, independently of Jody, was an ugly one to swallow.

The van drove on into the night.

They stopped in a valley deep within the Hindu Kush. A river wound through vegetation which looked, from what Mark could see by the thin light of the moon's first quarter, sparse and flowerless. Torches burned outside rows of tents and a group of women sat around a fire, slowly stirring pots of bubbling food while undernourished dogs danced with children by the riverbanks. Mark was the oldest person, he guessed, by twenty years. Far away, in the black distance, silent mortar shells danced like lightning and he could just make out the fires of another nearby encampment or village.

He hung back while the women greeted their men upon return.

There was no sign of Jody.

One woman, heavily eyebrowed behind her veil, scanned the van and Hummer the way an apprehensive pet perches at a windowsill. Abs glided over and spoke to her. The eyes swept downwards, her shoulders shook and the mouth opened in a silent scream.

When she sprang for Mark, he was prepared but didn't fight her off. Fingernails scratched at him, once, and then the force of her grief overpowered her and she sank to the floor in sobs.

'Tell her I'm sorry,' Mark said before making his way down to the river.

He sat on its bank and watched the ripples beneath the lemon-slice moon. His training, so long ago now, had hardened into a way of life and he was surprised to feel empathy for the woman whose lover's life his had been traded for. Yes, it was the game he, and the man she grieved for, had chosen to play, but, much like Alessia, she hadn't necessarily opted for such a life.

And there, by the river in deepest Afghanistan, he felt something he had never felt on a mission before. He felt remorse.

Some while later, during which time he'd sunk his mind into the ebb of the river, a magical serpent glittering its journey towards an unseen sea, he heard footsteps treading a slow creep behind him, a little sound like droplets on dirt. Someone was trying not to be heard but doing a poor job of it.

He spun round to find a child's silhouette flinching away from his sudden movement. She placed a plate of food carefully on the ground then scarpered back to the camp.

Mark ate and watched the women hunched by the burning fire, their breath fogging red in the rapidly cooling air. There were fifteen tents in a crescent around the fire, all roughly the same size, bar one which was the length of an Olympic swimming pool and guarded by armed men, four of them. Could that be where Jody was? It would be impossible to investigate, given Abs or one of the other men always watched him. This place didn't share much in common with the prison he'd been in the night before but, despite the vaster vista and improved cuisine, he suspected similar conditions applied.

He heard the trees whisper, the hiss of the slow-moving current. A stray Kuchi that seemed to have been adopted by the nomads, large and brindle grey, its head high and tail low as though on red alert, took a shine to Mark on account of everyone else shooing him away from the cooking pots. Mark petted him until the halved moon curled behind a cloud. Then, taking advantage of the near-dark, slipped off his orange suit and eased himself into the river. He hadn't bathed for a week and his body was no doubt as dirty with dust and grime as it was bruises. He took a leisurely crawl to the far bank through the gentle current, the snowmelt pricking him numb, before swimming back again to find a torchlit trio of tooled-up mercenaries awaiting his naked body.

'Exercise, yes?' Abs asked.

Mark kept quiet. There wasn't anything he could have said right now that could have put him in a vague position of control.

'I think, maybe, you try swim away?'

'No. I was—'

The guns were levelled at him. 'Why you in Afghanistan?'

'I told you. I . . .'

Abs flashed up a hand. 'Taliban announce you as spy. You act like spy. I see information you *are* spy.' The coal eyes flashed. 'I do not trust spies. They creep through wilderness like stray dog, not loyal to any master. In this land of ruin, there many spies. Faithless, with faces of Janus, yes? Kabul is melting crucible of traitors. But sometimes stray dogs serve purpose. Like you, Mr Varta.'

Mark trod cold water, staring up at the silhouettes. His words shivered from him. 'Your English is . . . poetic. W-where did you study?'

Abs would not be diverted. 'This what I think: You sent to Kabul by foolish British government to investigate defection of Jody Wolfe. I am right, yes?'

Mark kept his eyes steady. 'Who?'

The response was a glare to his left. A torch was raised and lit a face.

'You two already meet, I think,' Abs said, indicating Yusuf.

Yusuf's wide eyes avoided Mark's.

'Thanks to him, we have idea of where Taliban base. His knowledge of mountain saved you, Mr Varta. Is fact. And lucky for you we found him. But there is much information about Taliban cave network we not know. You spend time inside. And you will tell us all you know, yes?'

Mark recalled the direction of those tyre tracks on the mountain, the barely audible sounds above the rasping engine as he was driven, hooded, to his place of execution. Given access to landscape images eight miles in a westerly direction of the spot the Agents intercepted him, there was a high probability he'd be able to pinpoint the cave's entrance.

The cold was intense now. 'And what if my . . . n-navigational skills are . . . n-not up to the . . . task?'

Abs shrugged, but it didn't disguise the unstable glare in his eyes. 'Then you no further use to us. And I consider that a disrespect, as mission to rescue you made with cost. Taliban occupied by – how I say? – *cinema* of your execution and not defend themselves properly, but not all my men come back alive.'

In the pause that followed, Yusuf gathered the strength to speak.

Abs translated. 'He ask if you know what happen to his Pashtun "master", Fassad, who I believe is MI6 informer, yes?' The smile on his face was controlled, but the voice was smug. Still, the eyes didn't appear to blink. 'He say you engaged him to look for woman. And still you deny your reason for being in Afghanistan?'

Mark grabbed the bank and attempted to pull himself up out of the water. Abs kicked at his arm.

'Not yet, Mr Varta.'

The Englishman gasped for air. 'F-Fassad was k-killed by someone c-calling themselves the C-commander of the Faithful. T-tell Yusuf he died an h-honourable death.'

This information was relayed to Yusuf in Dari and the little man digested the news in blank silence.

'He one of y-yours?' Mark stammered. 'P-part of your "c-crucible of t-traitors"?'

'He a Hazara brother. But not one of our fighters. Poor wretch we pick up on mountain who not aware of reckoning that is coming. Like many. You ask question a spy ask, Mr Varta.'

'You g-got me.'

'Then you help us, yes?'

'You l-leave me little choice. W-where is Jody Wolfe?'

'That not information I am wanting to give you.'

'W-why not?'

'My men bring you maps and satellite images and you tell us all you know about Taliban cave system. If you honour commitment to me then I consider to answer another of your enquiry, but there is much I not trust about you. You start now, while I make my men ready. Time is not to be lost.'

He laughed as Mark struggled, naked and gasping, from the water, then threw him a fresh set of clothes. The trio wandered back to the campfire and left him alone.

Still wet, Mark pulled on the too-small civilian clothes. The hatred spearing from the widow on the other side of the campfire told Mark the new threads he wore had, not so long ago, belonged to the comrade they'd left several feet under the hard ground.

The noise jerked him alert.

Even in his dreams, he was still poring over maps and compasses, blurry aerial photographs of crags and stone chimneys, and it came as some relief to find himself alone save for the dog panting in the darkness.

The campfire was dwindling and insects had bitten him half to death beneath his blanket. Fierce snoring grated its way across the night from one of the nearby tents.

There was the splash again, at a similar distance. The ripples were hard to make out, the water shimmering with the stars overhead, the Milky Way like a tearing of suns down the middle of the infinite canvas of space.

He sat up slowly, shivered and stared at the night on the other side of the bank.

Another splash.

He panthered into a crouch. Still nobody stirred in the campsite. He estimated it to be four in the morning. In his old life, back in London, he'd tended to wake at this hour.

From higher up the river he saw it. Four short flashes of light, followed by a pause, then a short flash followed by a longer one. Shorter flash. Pause. Final shorter flash. The whole message was repeated, but he didn't need it twice. He was already making his low, quiet way towards the source of the Morse code.

'Here' it had spelled.

His heart raced at the thought of seeing her.

Twenty yards or so from where the lights had come from, he parted foliage to spy another light, flickering idly through faraway branches.

Mark edged closer to find a candle burning in a clearing. It was skewered into the ground and close to guttering out. Like all predators, Mark was sensitive to gaze perception and he felt eyes upon him.

The candle fizzed its miniature death, the smell of sulphur dioxide swimming across the frigid night. A soft cough floated from behind and Mark spun round to face another wall of darkness. Slowly, one set of light feet approached.

'You?'

'Sorry to disappoint you, Mark.'

'You know who I am?'

The spy stepped forward, nowhere near as welcome a presence as the first time, when he'd slashed him free of his bonds on the mountain. 'And why you're here.'

Mark remained silent, sensing a trap. A wind whispered the grasses. He wondered how well their quiet voices might travel through the valley.

'It's OK. You can trust me.'

'I really doubt that. Does ... anyone else know I'm here?'

'If you're referring to Jody, then yes. Your mountaintop video was somewhat public.'

'She's ... She's alive. Thank God.' His legs felt liquid. 'Where is she?'

'She's safe, for now. But you have to leave. The Agents of Allah may look a motley bunch but they're some of the most ruthless human beings I've ever had the misfortune to infiltrate. There's a canoe moored a mile along the riverbank to the east. I can give you the names of contacts in Kabul who might even get you back to London without slitting your throat.'

'And what if I want to stay?' He shivered in the cold.

'You'll perish in this godforsaken place, your failure on your daughter's conscience for the rest of her life.'

'I'm not leaving without seeing her.'

In the dark, the sigh was like the storming of hightide. 'You must. Her cover is so deep her own government has officially turned its back on her.'

'I knew it! *I fucking knew it!*'

'Take the canoe. I'm handling things here. I was instrumental in saving you once but I can't guarantee to be able to do it again. It was a move that could easily have risked Jody. And matters are intensifying by the day. You must get out of here.'

'I'm not going anywhere.'

'As stubborn as I'd been led to believe.'

'You know nothing about me.'

'*Au contraire*. We know plenty.'

'MI6 can stuff their secrets and their duplicity. You'll have to take me down before you take me in.' Fury exploded from him. Vauxhall had officially disinherited Jody and even her father had been made to believe she'd been brainwashed. C had sat throughout his briefing in the bunker, watching Mark's face fall, *knowing* everything they'd said about Jody was bullshit. His house had been upturned, his marriage destroyed. And all for what?

Mark hated MI6 right then. Hated them with a passion he hadn't known he was capable of. Not only had they been recklessly disingenuous, but those suits in Command Centre were also short-sighted. They should have known her father would have caught a flight to Afghanistan to find out the truth.

If Mark had possessed something akin to a sheriff's badge, he'd have thrown it to the Afghan dirt without a moment's hesitation. This was his long-service reward, was it? In lieu of a golden clock for a lifetime of blotting out the suffering and destruction he'd witnessed, caused, received, he found himself decorated with the lonely tools of his former trade. Subterfuge and deceit. The only currency MI6 knew.

'Blame MI6 all you like,' the spy said, 'the fact remains you're out of your depth.'

'And you're not?'

'Possibly, but I'm not MI6.'

Mark didn't worry about hiding the confusion from his face; the darkness did that for him.

A long black silence reigned.

'You're ... TAJSS?'

Further silence from the man opposite confirmed the guess to be accurate.

'And so could you have been, but I'm not authorised to go into operational details. We saved you. You're welcome. Your daughter is alive. Now *get the hell out of here.*'

Mark locked fierce eyes with the shadow. 'Much as I'd love to take your word for it, I need proof my daughter's safe before I'm sent back to England by a private security service I didn't even know the name of until a month ago. No offence, but I don't trust anybody, except my daughter, and I'm willing to ignore the odd near-death experience in return for finding her alive and well. After all, the fact she's even in the spying game is my fault. There's something big brewing here, I know there is. The Agents of Allah leader said something about a "reckoning" that was coming. All night, they've had me poring over satellite images, trying to pinpoint the base I was being held at. What exactly are they planning?'

'Mark, stop. Just stop. I'm warning you. You must leave Afghanistan and you must leave *now*. This group have been waiting a long time for a moment like this, and now you've given them what they want they won't waste any time in—'

A cry came up from the camp and the man before him peeled away into the night.

Mark lowered himself and stalked back through the long grass as torches crisscrossed the night like switchblades and voices rustled by the riverbank. They were looking for him. Keeping the men to his right, he crawled up to the fire and slumped down in its corona before pretending to sleep. After a few minutes, the dog joined him.

The following morning, a dust storm tore through the camp. A great wall of grey powered and sluiced up the valley, battering the tents, curling out the last embers of the fire. For about fifteen minutes, the horizons disappeared in every suffocated direction and Mark lay on the ground with his hands cupped over his eyes as though playing one of Jody's infamous games of hide and seek.

But that was exactly what he *was* playing, of course, on the largest scale yet. His daughter may have broken their Rule of Fifteen, but with every hour that passed she was closer to being found. Not in a half-empty water butt she'd sacrificed her mother's lavender to upend, but two thousand feet above sea level in the desolate mountain ranges on the outskirts of Kabul, the sands and dirt roaring like fear itself between the vast rock formations on either side.

After what seemed hours, the winds moved on and the Hazara nomads climbed nonplussed from their flattened tents. To them the dust storm was merely a metaphor. Their itinerant lifestyle meant tents and tent owners came and went on a frequent basis.

Mark scanned the campsite. Storm-displaced belongings hung in the dry scrub by the river. Shallow tyre tracks had been wiped away, much like the sooty evidence of the fire. But Jody wasn't revealed bound and trussed in any pale square where a tent had once been pinned to the ground. Nature had uncovered far worse.

The largest of the tents had become detached from the earth on one side and the winds had rolled the huge canvas back, revealing to the world a long dark-green missile. It was the height of one man, the length of at least five, and markings on the side corresponded to the US military. The serial number, printed beneath an open panel at its tip, was too far away to read but the missile's shape looked similar to a traditional B61 device, only much, much longer.

The Agents of Allah scurried to reconceal their prized possession, but it was too late. It hadn't required the yellow and black radiation hazard symbol on its warhead to confirm to Mark they camped in the shadow of a not-inconsiderable weapon of mass destruction.

19

Behind Abs, the morning sun was hidden in the valley and its light was scattered, glittering through the sparse trees. The Afghan grasped the rolled map like a rapier.

'You sure?' Midnight-black eyes bored into Mark. 'This where is their base, yes?'

'I'm not one hundred per cent, but it's close to where I've marked.'

Abs nodded, the ghost of a smile playing across his cracked lips.

Around them, the men buzzed. Half the tents were being torn down and the boots of the vans stuffed with packs and food. The wives, again, were at the vast cooking pots. It was clear to Mark that the Agents of Allah were the male fighters of the group, the women simply appendages who fixed up their warriors' ripped, bloodstained clothing and mothered their children.

'Are we going somewhere?'

'Some of us return to Hazarajat. It is right.'

'And the rest?'

The mean mouth snarled. 'There other missions.'

Mark was aware of the TAJSS cleanskin watching Mark with undisguised disgust while keeping a poisoner's distance, and the woman who'd tried to tear his face off the night before spat on the ground every time Mark dared eye contact.

He risked it. 'I saw your bomb. Very impressive.'

Abs' expression didn't alter. 'Is not bomb. Not yet.'

'What does that mean?'

Abs was busy looking over the map, and didn't answer.

'My information is . . . satisfactory?' Mark asked. 'You'll tell me where Jody is?'

'Satisfactory, but is not confirmed.'

'Run it past Yusuf. He knows those mountains.'

In the aftermath of the sandstorm, Yusuf was to be found crouching by the dead fire, a lost expression on his prematurely aged face, and Mark wondered where fate would lead Fassad's right-hand man now, whether he'd be radicalised or set free. Yusuf didn't seem to fit in amongst this group any more than Mark did.

'You help us pack, yes?'

'I'm coming with you?'

'You find Taliban hole on map for us. You have use.' Abs laughed a wet cough. 'Is John Varta worried we shoot him like old horse? If we need knife thrower, you first choice. Also, you rich, yes?'

A large meal was prepared, sending the dog into pitiful whinnies of expectation. In the daylight, Mark saw that he wasn't brindle grey, but dirty white with patches of fur lost to disease. Prayers were said before they ate, cross-legged in the dust, and then the conversation became animated while Mark scanned the faces of the assembled, tried to gauge from their intonations the nature of the talk, though it was like listening to angry radio static. In this company, he was no kind of intelligence expert at all.

After the camp was tidied, the men said a heartfelt goodbye to their womenfolk and children before the wives hitched up their Hazaragi dresses in the swirling dirt and, with a final glare from the widow's murderous eyes, boarded two tatty trucks and a vintage Ford with its windows missing. Once they'd gone, the men threw their Kalashnikovs and ammo into the VW and Hummer and the ragtag band of terrorists climbed aboard, leaving behind a crew of armed heavies with the missile. As Mark boarded the bus, the dog's eyes bulged in concern, anticipating abandonment.

Not wanting to give the stray false hope, Mark didn't pet him farewell.

His route to the back of the van was blocked by Abs' hand across the narrow aisle. 'Next to me, yes?'

'We going anywhere interesting?'

Abs delivered a rare smile. 'There one member of group you not yet meet. You go to her now.'

They began their winding route among the passes, the sun a blowtorch on everything it surveyed. The dog ran, heartbroken, alongside them for about a mile before giving up to collapse alone in the shadowless dust.

Mark stared into the moving landscape and tried but failed to put the image of that huge warhead out of his mind, countered it with a painful heartswell of anticipation that he'd soon be seeing his daughter. He massaged his chest, encouraging a peaceful flow of blood through straining arteries, until he convinced himself he was better.

But he wasn't the only one on edge as they rolled closer to Taliban-controlled country.

At about midday, they stopped and Abs and Yusuf stepped out. Abs was determined, his jawline fierce, eyes sparkling black jewels. Yusuf resembled a man lobotomised.

No words were spoken.

As the bus restarted two men lighter, Mark's gaze automatically flicked towards the TAJSS agent sitting at the rear, who reciprocated his look with a slow, almost imperceptible nod as he idly balanced his upended combat knife upon an index finger.

Two hours later, the VW pulled up in a near-deserted village that looked, much like Jabul Saraj, as though it might once have been a focal point of industry. The rotten buildings were closed and derelict, the same pale colour as the dust that embraced everything. The grimy Hummer had led their way to this desolate place but was now nowhere to be seen.

Time passed at the speed of the stray dogs ambling in a pack of four along the broken pavement. They sniffed at the van, then traipsed off once the driver shooed them on. The eight Agents of Allah, and Mark, watched the pack round the end of the street in apprehensive silence.

Finally, a street ahead of them, a Toyota pick-up and a white van emerged and parked in the forecourt of an old mill. Mark rose in his seat to get a better look, wincing as his heart fought against the movement, but the vehicles were too far away to discern either number plate.

Two Agents, as good as unidentifiable beneath their shawls, slid out of the VW and stalked towards the newcomers' vehicles as the rest of the Agents drifted to the front windscreen to claim a better view. A shadow fell across Mark and a smartphone was pressed into his palm as the TAJSS spy crept forward with the others.

The news app was already open.

STILL NO NEWS OF MISSING BRITISH MAN IN HORROR VIDEO.

Mark flicked eyes towards the front of the VW, confirmed he was unobserved, then quickly scanned the rest of the article.

He'd been wondering how the press had reacted to a lack of follow-up footage of his promised execution. Government policy used to be that such things weren't even reported, to avoid providing fuel for the terrorists' machinery, but in the age of the internet this was impossible. There he was, in a still from the downloaded footage, blurry but recognisable in his orange suit. A rapid scan of the article confirmed that the mystery man in the video had been 'identified as businessman John Varta'.

Vauxhall must have scrambled like mad in the aftermath of the video being released, and the fact they were silencing all familial connection to his jihadist daughter was telling. It would be a stretch to say his mission was now endorsed by the Service, or that he'd been forgiven, but MI6 were hardly going to put his real name and reasons for being in Afghanistan out there. Far easier to corroborate the name he'd flown to Kabul under.

Mark casually pocketed the phone. Up ahead, the two Agents had almost reached the white van and the tense silence in their minibus was the false calm at the eye of a storm as they watched the driver's door of the pick-up swing open and a tall, broad-shouldered Talib in a headscarf slip out. Mark craned forward in his seat for a better view but the phalanx of anticipatory bodies at the VW's windscreen prevented it.

In the seat in front, a man with a light dusting of grey in his beard trained a pair of binoculars on the far-off meeting and, without thinking, Mark tapped him on the shoulder and indicated he wanted to borrow them. Perhaps forgetting it was the Englishman behind him, the man passed back the binoculars.

The prisms were misaligned and no one had thought to collimate the glasses, so the image Mark peered at through the eyepieces was a drunk and doubled one. He closed one eye and swept straight to the man who'd stepped out of the pick-up.

As he suspected, it was Hassan Fakih.

Otherwise known as William Stucker.

He watched as the driver of the white van sidled out and stood behind William, gun held upright, movie-poster style. A third Talib was standing a little farther away, beside the van's bonnet.

The engine thrummed beneath Mark, as though in readiness.

After a brief greeting, the two Agents were escorted to the rear of the van and, in a prime example of poor field espionage, they disappeared out of sight as the doors were opened. Mark knew William was bent, but assumed his double-jointedness only extended to small arms and drugs, the occasional role as bagman. What was being handed over here?

Three brief flashes blinked from a windowless frame in a destitute office block. Birds cracked to the sky in fright as the echo of the gunshots barked down the road.

In a scream of tyres, the van underneath Mark blasted forward.

Three gunshots. Three dealers. The Agents of Allah had prepared properly after all. Their VW van in the open had merely been the decoy.

But William's men weren't all down. Over the sound of the straining engine, came the ricochet of retaliatory gunfire.

The sound was met with another volley of shots from somewhere up in the buildings and, as a bullet confettied their windscreen, the driver pounded his foot on the brake. Mark cried out as his neck took the brunt of the jolt.

Ahead of them, the gunfight continued. Mark saw a figure crawling on the ground, another cowering behind the van. It might have been William but it was hard to make much out underneath the new wash of red he wore. One of the dealers made a break for it but was sniped before he got any distance at all and lay in the dirt, his insides puddling into the street.

The Agents of Allah in the VW began picking themselves up off one another, shaking out the ringing in their ears and squinting through the broken glass of their vehicle to ascertain the damage.

'You need to get this van out of the open!' Mark heard himself shout. 'We're sitting ducks!'

There was only one other in earshot who could understand him. The TAJSS man yelled at their driver, who restarted the stalled engine and tore them up a side road. The roar of their escape drew more bullets which thunked into the side of the van, instigating a scream from up front as one of the slugs sliced through thin steel to spear flesh.

The van spun a sharp right, then, out of sight, braked again. The injured member of the group ripped off half a sleeve and bound the tourniquet round his thigh, tied it tight with a controlled wince as the group began clattering off the van, one by one, guns raised.

And so Mark found himself crouch-walking, still wielding the binoculars, down a narrow alley towards the white van and pick-up truck from an alternative angle. He could discern the heavy breathing of the others alongside his own.

'We should be split up,' Mark whispered to the TAJSS spy. 'Tell these fools they need to spread out.'

As if they understood, two men peeled off through the garage area of an abandoned building, leaving four of them, plus the driver, who remained in the VW in case a fast exit was required.

Mark shuffled up to a crumbling wall and peered through a bullet hole to see the vehicles, the bodies in the road. There was no hint of movement from up in the windows, but none of them would stand a chance if they stepped out into the open.

'Your guys opened fire first. You fucked up,' Mark hissed to no one in particular.

The TAJSS spy's knuckles were white on the butt of his gun as he made his way to Mark's wall, and pretended to peer through a neighbouring hole.

'Agreed. We were supposed to take the pit and leave,' the spy muttered, sweat glistening on his forehead. 'If our sniper hadn't shot the Taliban in cold blood, we'd never have known their back-up was also hidden nearby.'

'What do you mean *pit*?'

The silence from the conflict zone was dense, pregnant.

'Do you mean a *plutonium* pit? Are you telling me there's a thermonuclear core sitting out in the open?'

Mark recalled the warhead beneath the hut, open at its tip, symbolically and suggestively ready to receive.

Open-mouthed, he eyed the TAJSS man. When was he going to make his move? Surely the plan wasn't just to hang around, making sure the Agents of Allah acquired the bomb part?

Or was that *precisely* the plan?

The other Agents had their heads cocked towards the scene of the carnage. This silence meant one of two things: either no one on the ground dared make a move due to the marksmen's hunger, or everyone had bled out.

One of the Agents, his face pocked like the piddock holes on British beaches, ducked to confer with the man next to him, and Mark took the opportunity to steal closer to the TAJSS spy, still squinting through the hole in the wall. 'That was William Stucker,' Mark whispered. 'But either the Americans don't know they have a loose cannon selling their munitions, or this is all a US sting that's gone very badly wrong. Which is it?'

'The former. That's American property sitting there, delivered by an American double, but he brought his own men.'

'What's the deal with them letting us have the plutonium? Is it defective in some way?'

Behind them, the Hazara terrorists appeared to have reached a decision. Mark took a step back from the spy.

The pockmarked man strode forwards, then reached out and indicated he wanted the TAJSS spy's Kalashnikov. With only a vague wince of hesitation, it was handed over. Mark watched as the gun was hurled over the wall, landing in the street with a clatter, discharging into the dirt for good measure. No gunfire followed. The pockmarked man nodded, apparently pleased.

In the leaden, expectant silence that followed, he addressed the TAJSS spy.

Mark didn't recognise a word being said but understood the look on the spy's face.

He was being asked to walk out into the killing zone and retrieve the merchandise.

There followed a tense retort from the undercover man. Still, the predatory silence in the forecourt of bodies behind the wall. The debate went on for some time, until the pockmarked man dropped the magazine from the grip of his handgun to check the chamber for live rounds, slammed it back, then jumped out from behind the wall and fired two shots into the blue air before diving back again to wait, back pressed to the wall. Still nothing.

This seemed to be the final reassurance needed. Everyone on the ground was dead.

The TAJSS spy walked out into the open, hiding his reluctance poorly, as the sound of his feet and a thin wind whispered through the broken windows to supply an eerie kind of incidental music.

Mark ignored the pockmarked man's handgun trained on his back as he observed the spy approach the white van, his shadow bolder than he was.

The gunshot echoed around the ghost town.

Through the bullet-holed wall, Mark watched the TAJSS man slump to the ground.

Panicked Dari flowed between the remaining Agents.

Mark swept the windows with the binoculars. The building's exterior wall was almost completely gone across the top few floors, leaving just the ragged cells of the rooms behind, but anywhere in those revealed nests would yield the best opportunity for a sniper, providing a clear view not only of the action in the forecourt below but of any comings and goings from the adjacent street. The marksman didn't stir, but Mark thought he could make out the muzzle of a rifle, projecting a few inches from the floor. From the steep angle of the barrel, pointing down, coupled with this nearness to the base of the room, he predicted the sniper was lying flat, close to the edge. Indeed, he glimpsed a face, reflected in broken glass, just for a second.

His heart flared once more, pinched and throbbed in glorious pain.

It was her.

The binoculars were snatched off him, the gun trained at his forehead. The Agents had just elected a new volunteer to grab the plutonium.

Mark stumbled out into the open, his hands raised.

If he were to be shot now, he prayed, please let it be a head-shot, one he would barely feel, even less know about. He couldn't have provided an easier target.

There was graveyard silence. Clearly, the sniper had no idea how to play this latest development, and he could only imagine what was going through her mind.

Up in the derelict building, he thought he saw a gun lowered.

It seemed to take an hour to cross the forecourt. He passed the gun that had been thrown over the wall, then the dead body of the TAJSS spy, eyes still open.

The first flash of doubt pierced his consciousness. Had Jody been the one to shoot the TAJSS agent? If so, had she known who he really was? Or was there another marksman, watching him right now through crosshairs as he made his slow way across the open space with his hands aloft? His weakened heart hammered inside his chest.

He arrived to find the rear doors of the bullet-holed van already open, an oversized silver briefcase sitting in its yawning cargo hold. He picked up the bounty, heavier than expected, and began his exposed walk back, cradling it as cautiously as a newborn.

Seizing their opportunity, a stalemate seemingly reached, the two Agents of Allah who'd crept farther on now charged into the clearing from the next street and hurried straight to the bodies of their fallen comrades, began dragging them and their all-important weaponry from the scene of their murder.

Now things could get tricky, Mark knew, if anyone showed nerves and discharged a bullet. He picked up his pace and staggered his way back to the VW under the weight of the briefcase. The other two, heaving the bodies face up, elbows under their armpits, brought up the rear, the heels of the dead scuffing four parallel grooves in the dirt.

The silence swimming around him was unbearable. His heart pounded, but he'd nearly reached cover.

Just a few more steps.

Too late, he sensed something in the air had changed. He'd neared the spreadeagled TAJSS spy when something made him glance to his right to see one of William's men, his eyes swollen wide by the endorphins of agony, reaching for his gun with his dying strength. Mark considered dropping the silver case, but in the split-second this terrible idea set hold, the black dot of the barrel had already hovered in front of the Afghan's forehead like a third eye as the shaky hand brought the gun to aim.

A gunshot rang through the dust and Mark's would-be killer arced a red spray of blood and whipped sideways with the impact, twisting heavily, permanently, to the ground.

Up in the building, he heard his daughter reload.

Mark stumbled over the splayed limbs of the dead at his feet, no longer sure whether the noise was his heartbeat or a hail of bullets as he charged headlong towards safety.

20

'**D**ad!'

The voice sheared through reality itself.

'Can you hear me? Dad?'

Eyes of deepest brown hung above. The shadow of a human form weaved, candle-like. His entire left side was aflame, and his heart felt inflated five times its size.

Something soft stroked his face. 'What the hell are you doing here?'

'You broke the Rule of Fifteen,' he heard himself mutter, before passing out again.

In all the dreams he'd had in which he'd found her, none had featured him stretched out in the back of a VW as terrorists sped them across mountain passes which jolted and bucked beneath him in heart-twisting agony.

He wanted so dearly to be deadpan, fatherly, affable, a mote of common-sense swirling in the sandstorm of pain he lay in, but the words, 'I knew you were still alive,' came out soaked with anguish for a world in which missions were so rarely completed with happy endings.

She lowered her gaze to disguise her own emotion, remaining, predictably perhaps, more professional on the job than he was. Her skin was so dark. Her eyes bore a tiredness that rivalled his own but didn't overflow the way his did.

'You shouldn't be here,' she whispered.

He was wounded by this quiet hostility but understood straight away. He was compromising her mission. The roar of the engine drowned what they were saying, though he assumed their driver couldn't understand, nor the man hovering behind her, the Agent with the grey dusting in his beard who'd unwittingly lent him the binoculars.

Where was she now? She kept floating away. Christ, his chest hurt.

'Jody? Where are you?' Sweating, he tried to look around but was alarmed to find he couldn't raise his head.

'I'm here, Dad.' The face swam back.

'I have questions.'

'Not now. Drink this.' Water spilled across his lips. 'There's some oxygen at the camp. Breathe deep for now.'

'MI6 told me you'd gone rogue.' His voice vibrated with the van's floor.

'I can't believe you came out here.'

'I had no choice.'

He may have been flat on his back, old and shaken, teary with relief, but his search was behind him now. Her mission, whatever it was, was in front. He experimented with a smile, but it wasn't returned.

'The TAJSS spy confirmed you were involved in deep cover. A bang-and-burn mission, I'd guess.'

'The . . .? You knew who he was? How *long* have you been out here?' She looked ten years older than when he'd last spoken to her in London, her eyes double that.

'I worked fast. I didn't know how much time I had. Where are the others?'

'Ahead of us.'

No doubt their precious plutonium was in the Hummer, which had quite obviously been parked some distance from the exchange point for just such a getaway. It was a safer vehicle, smoother, and the pit was valued higher than Mark. Jody would have volunteered to go with the Englishman, and the others wouldn't have complained; being a woman, they saw it as her role to nurse.

'I found you,' he said, his smile strengthening. 'I found you.'

'Rest, Dad.'

'You have the bomb. What now?' Mark knew better, after a lifetime of working for the Secret Service, than to ask questions, but he couldn't help himself. 'You're not with the Agents of Allah to prevent an acquisition of plutonium from going ahead. That much is obvious. Your role all along has been to facilitate it. Am I right? Your meetings with William prove that.'

Jody's jaw tightened and he barely recognised her. This steel was her mission face, and it suited her. Finally, her expression changed and he witnessed the bloom of her smile for the first time in a long while. It lit his soul like brandy used to in the old days.

'You're wasted in an office, Dad, you know that?'

The explosion slid him five feet across the floor.

Behind her, the sky was so intense it ate her away, reducing her form to that of a slim spectre. There was a vice of pressure where his heart ought to have been and his forehead was dressed in a torn piece of wet cloth. The world smelt charred.

His voice was still thick with painkillers.

'Oh God. You're slurring,' Jody said.

He concentrated on stilling his breathing. After a time, he tried again.

'I'm fine,' he said. Though the words slipped out as sharp as knives, he was relieved to hear clarity in them.

'You should be in a hospital,' she said. 'I'm sorry.'

He closed his eyes and focused on compartmentalising the pain, sucked down deep lungfuls of ashen air. Slowly, very slowly, he regained feeling in his limbs. The man with the grey in his beard bent over him and poured a foul-tasting liquid between his lips which Mark promptly spat over himself.

'What's that?' he croaked.

'Water with cayenne pepper,' Jody said. 'It's a traditional way to get blood around the body faster.'

'I'd rather have an aspirin.'

'You've had it all.'

The nausea had dissipated but the fear of another heart-stab kept him on his back, listening to his daughter's foreign voice as he reclined on a thin mattress in the shade and scowled at the ghetto field hospital consisting of only sky.

'Did you know about your heart before you came here?'

'I suspected. To be honest, it's got a lot worse lately.'

'I bet it has.'

That was a big one, though. His body was done warning him. The next protest from his heart would be fatal.

'Where are we?'

'Camp.'

Mark attempted to shuffle himself into a vague sitting position. He managed, but the look on his daughter's face told him it hadn't been smooth. Two men, the VW driver and the one who'd tried to force him to ingest cayenne pepper, hunched a little way ahead of them, as though over various maps and charts.

'You going to tell me what's going on now?'

'Just relax.'

'Not likely. Your pal William sent me to Jabal Saraj to die, to get rid of me. I want answers.'

'Don't worry about these things at the moment.'

'Was William with the Taliban or the US, or just out for himself?'

Jody watched the horizon for a time, then said, 'Look, I really don't want you stressed out.'

Mark set the cogs in motion and prepared for the mental machinery to fire. Gradually, he forgot about his heart. 'Your job ...' he watched his daughter's impassive face, alert to the signs of pride that would confirm his detective work, '... was to monitor the warhead exchange once you'd infiltrated the Agents. You liaised with William. No, you did more than that. You *bought* him. He was a US mole hiding in the Taliban and you were MI6 concealed in the Agents of Allah. But you both had the same aim, ultimately: to get this bomb here. That much is obvious. But why?'

'Dad ...'

'Who would stand to gain from a thermonuclear blast in northern Kabul? Who are you working against? Surely the Russians. Their interests here are well-documented. Being neighbours, the last thing they'd want is a return to the anarchy of the Nineties, but they also want the US and NATO out of here ...'

Jody had a hand across her eyes, a child's gesture of denial. *I'm not here*, it said. *The monsters can't see me because I can't see them.*

'Seriously, Dad. I'm not telling you. There are reasons why, not least the fact that you are *very sick*.'

'None of the nuclear powers move weaponry through this part of the world. Turkey, yes, but not Afghanistan. Pakistan has her own stockpile. That missile was American, at least its casing was. But the elements within could have come from all over ...'

'Dad ... please ...'

'The terrorists have been building it for a while. And William's been helping to supply the parts. My God. If the Agents of Allah – a Shia Muslim terror organisation – use a nuke on their Sunni enemies ... The Taliban cease to be a problem in the area. And that's good news for a *lot* of people.'

The hand fell from her eyes and she watched him steadily, a surgeon refusing to break her Hippocratic oath, and her silence only spurred him on.

'No. It's worse than that, isn't it? No foreign power would ever trust a terrorist organisation such as this one, especially after your threats to the British government. That bomb, sold piecemeal by rogue agents to your terrorist friends, has ... *something* installed, undetected, into its software. The moment that plutonium's connected, it'll blow, blasting the Agents *and* the Taliban from Kabul. And it will look, to the world, as though the terrorists stole it from the US and then didn't have the nous to use it properly. This "accidental triggering" will remove many countries' problems in the area in one fell swoop. It's ... unconscionable. Monstrous. Who's behind this, Jody? Who wanted the bomb here?'

Jody's eyes narrowed as she watched her father stack the pieces together.

'Presumably you had to ensure William sold dud plutonium, or some vital weakness, to prevent the bomb from arming properly,' Mark continued. '*That's* why you're in Afghanistan. You helped facilitate getting bomb parts, but not the bomb parts anyone thought the Agents were getting. You've been plotting *against* a foreign power and, if this gets out, the British government is at war with ... Who? Tehran? Moscow? Beijing? *Washington*? That's why you couldn't let anyone know. Even me. I'm right, aren't I?'

Jody's disbelief was palpable. Her fingers had torn the dry earth where she sat.

'Jody …? It's the only explanation that makes sense. I'm right, aren't I?'

Slowly, a tear fell from her, and brought the first drop of moisture that wasn't blood to this dry landscape in a long time.

'So, what's the matter? Job done. You both did it. You and William. England calling.'

He was grinning. Despite all that had happened, the thrill of the hunt was everything. By way of experiment, he clenched and unclenched his fists. There was less pain now.

'Have you examined the merchandise we took? Was William able to build a weakness in, before he was killed? I mean, for all you know, someone knew what he was up to and set him up, used that handover to deliberately shoot him during the crossfire.'

Jody shook her head, still avoiding his eyes. 'I haven't, no.'

'Why not?'

'Well, for a start, it was stolen.'

'It was …?' He remembered now. The explosion. Shooting five feet across the floor of the VW.

'We suffered a roadside attack as we entered Parwan province.'

Mark knew it wasn't uncommon for the Taliban to fire missiles at passing vehicles on the Salang Pass, simply to practise their range.

'The VW has always been our attempt to look inconspicuous to both the Taliban and government forces. The SUV, up ahead, was being used to transport the chemical element. They ambushed it. We were far enough behind to look like regular traffic. They let us go.'

There was something overwhelmingly sad about her, as though she'd seen too much, done too much.

'I'm sorry so many men have died,' Mark said, 'but the Agents not having the plutonium is *good news*, isn't it? They're not going to leave half of Kabul under a radioactive cloud for the next fifty years now, either on purpose or accidentally. Hundreds of thousands of lives have been saved. A lucky strike, I'd say.'

Jody tugged at her hair. 'Look around you.'

Mark hauled himself onto his knees, his clothes sticking with sweat, and took in the view.

There were charred puddles all around where tents had been set on fire. Everything looked as though a terrible black wind had slapped it sideways.

'They came while we were gone. We didn't leave enough men to defend.'

Mark understood who that lonesome tear had been for. It was hard for field operatives to remain distant from those they worked amongst, especially when infiltrating entire communities. On missions such as hers you play the part too well, and she'd invested a lot of mental energy in building up her portfolio of lies. She'd lived her other reality for so long it had become close to her true one.

The two men left alive weren't gathered over a map, as he'd first thought, but were sunk to their knees in desperate prayer.

'They took everything. What they didn't take they burned to the ground. No one was left alive.' Her eyes rested on a series of small mounds of freshly dug earth.

Mark turned to where he thought the largest tent had once stood. There was nothing but a gutted tangling of black metal sticks. 'So ... The Taliban have ...'

'The warhead. *And* the core.'

Mark felt the black hole of his heart, where the supernova had left its deep ache behind his ribs. 'If they go ahead and put that plutonium inside the bomb ... Will it go off?'

'If the plutonium survived the roadside ambush intact ... It could do. And, even if it doesn't ...'

On unsteady legs, he stood, finished her sentence. '... the Taliban now have a *massive* nuclear device.'

'Going somewhere, Dad?'

'We have to intercept, disable and destroy that bomb.'

Somehow, she managed to laugh. 'You're going nowhere.'

'I've got this far. I'm not going to—'

'Don't argue with me, Dad. I didn't bloody ask you to come here. I didn't *want* you here. You were a good agent in your day and you may still have a brilliant tactical mind but you've let emotion cloud your judgement. Look at you. Can you even hold a gun right now? You're in no position to do anything. This will literally kill you.'

The sun re-emerged and Mark shuffled back into the shade.

'I'm fine.'

'I don't want my father to die *because of me*.'

'I chose to come here.'

'You should've trusted me.'

He raised his head, charting the angle of the sun. In the end, he decided to pretend not to have heard anything she'd said.

'We're not going to be able to charge into the Taliban stronghold on our own. It's time to bring others into this.'

Jody watched him as he patted down his pockets.

'What are you doing?'

'That TAJSS agent gave me his phone.'

She shot him a look of petrified defiance. 'You are *not* calling anyone in on this, Dad. I forbid it. I went rogue. That was the deal. Anything I tell MI6 would be instantly distrusted and dismissed.'

His pockets contained nothing but lint. The phone was long lost. 'You being damaged goods has nothing to do with this. The Taliban have stolen a bomb, for Christ's sake!'

She pulled the hair at her temples, furious. 'No! This has to be done underground. This mission was *always* bigger than me. It's not about being "damaged goods". The British are counter-responding to an operation they aren't even supposed to *know* is happening. Trust me. We ring this in, we'll have bullets in the back of our skulls the moment we give away our location. This information is too hot.'

Mark felt the hairs rise all over his body. The world had changed since he was an operative. The black and white Cold War era looked like a disagreement between parish councillors in comparison. Putin's Russia. Trump's America. Ayatollahs with nukes. Sanity was off the table. 'Which of Britain's valuable, morally bankrupt trading partners is behind this, Jody? Tell me.'

'Dad, you ought to calm down.'

She was right. The anger within him was its own nuclear bomb, a red button he needed, desperately, to step away from.

'There are good reasons I'm not telling you everything. OK? It's my job to prevent Armageddon from happening. And I nearly have, with the help of William and TAJSS. But I must see this through to its conclusion. OK? Me. This is my mission. Not yours.'

'Unconscionable. Horrible. Every country will deny they got their hands dirty and fake news will rule. Victory at any cost. Welcome to the new blunt trauma of international politics.' It was sickening that a war-torn country like this one was considered so disposable, that its sectarian problems were deemed solvable with one unaccountable holocaust. 'Who's planned this goddamn atrocity?'

'Dad, you're not listening to me. This is my—'

'Do you even know how to get to that cave? Because that's where they'll have taken the missile.'

'I'll find it. I'll—'

He watched a flicker of uncertainty pass across her green-brown eyes.

'You *need* me. Don't give me any nonsense to the contrary. You can't get to the damn Taliban base without me.'

'Dad ...'

'I'm involved now. Yes, I'm half-dead, but you get me back to that mountaintop and I'll find my way. I can do that. You need me as much as I need you to get out of here.' He nodded towards the two men, now clearing scattered and singed belongings from the dry floor. 'Can we rely on these two to help?'

She dropped her shoulders, watched the men a while with a faraway expression. 'Their urge for revenge is strong, I know that much.'

'Good.' He began limping towards the two remaining Agents of Allah. 'There isn't much time.'

Later that day, the sun already diving for the horizon, they were back at his place of intended execution. Some graves had been opened and bodies exhumed. Many different blood types stained the sun-baked ground.

'They came to investigate what happened,' Mark said.

'Of course.'

'We arrived from that direction.' Breathless, he pointed to the downwards incline the cars took.

'There are still tracks. We might be able to follow them.'

Mark sat beside her in the VW's passenger seat and closed his eyes as Jody spoke to her men in urgent, musical Dari, explaining, no doubt, that Mark was recreating his previous visit here, listening out for memories of sounds. He suspected the men didn't know much about why they were headed back to Talibanville; perhaps they thought of the trip as a simple revenge grab. Kill as many Taliban as possible. Die in the process. *Inshallah.* They looked up for the challenge.

'Stop the van,' Mark said.

Jody did so. They waited.

'I heard bells,' he remembered.

'Mountain farmers,' Jody explained. 'They put bells round their goats' necks to make it easier to locate them. How far from the base did you hear them?'

'About ten minutes. But it wasn't as steep as this.' He pointed down a hillside sporting faint tyre tracks. 'Down there. There was a hard right about one hundred metres down, so we'll be looking to turn left. After that, I suggest we ditch the van and proceed on foot. Less chance of anyone hearing us.'

'I agree.' Jody relayed the information to the two men in the back.

They found the turn and parked the VW.

'They'll see it.'

'Tomorrow at the earliest,' Mark said. 'It will be all over by then.'

They crunched on without talking. The sun was low but blasted them with heat.

'How do you feel?' she asked him.

His heart felt like half an orange being ground through a juicer. 'Absolutely fine,' he said. 'I think I'm cured.'

'Fuck's sake, Dad.'

They walked for twenty minutes. Mark suddenly stopped. What few weeds and flowers that grew beneath their feet had been crushed by tyres. The winds had removed recent tracks but there was a rudimentary path, eaten into the rock by at least several dozen car journeys along this route.

'We're on the right track,' he declared.

Another half mile followed, all of it in a back-breaking crouch, lest the four of them be seen from the cave entrance somewhere to their left. Mark suggested resting behind the shade of a crag.

'This is it,' he announced.

They all sat, sweating, and watched for activity. From this vantage, there was nothing to suggest what they were looking at was anything other than a particularly unimpressive series of minor mountains underneath a cloudless heaven. The entrance was either expertly concealed or didn't exist.

'What's that? Jody asked.

It sounded like an engine.

'Take cover.'

It was a long time before they saw it. The car drove cautiously up to the base of the mountain ahead of them, its wheels leaving two perpendicular clouds of dust in its wake, and stopped next to the rock wall, discharging a Talib who disappeared out of sight for several minutes. Then the car rolled forwards and too vanished from view, as though swallowed by the rock face itself.

'Where did he go?' Mark asked.

Jody shrugged. 'Beats me. These caves rely on natural camouflage or man-made structures designed to resemble their surroundings. We'll have to get closer.'

Mark fought to get his breath back. The others were doing a commendable job of ignoring his laboured wheezing as he scanned the nearby peaks for watchers.

'If the bomb goes off in there,' Mark mused aloud, 'how much damage is it going to do? Say, compared to other attacks on the Taliban? The States dropped the Mother of All Bombs on a cave network nearby, didn't they?'

'That was a large yield, not a nuke. It was nothing like the size of this one. The damage would be ... Huge.'

'The cave wouldn't just sort of *soak it up*?'

'From here, we'd be obliterated by the blast. Thirty miles away, we'd be crushed by the kind of earthquake news stories cover for weeks and – along with a large proportion of the five million residents of Kabul – blinded by a release of radiation that would turn this part of the world into the new Chernobyl. No, the cave would not *soak it up, Dad.*'

'I was just wondering.'

'"Dad"?' the minibus driver asked, looking between the two English speakers with a deep-carved frown.

'What can we expect from these two?' he asked. 'Where do their specialities lie? I need to know the talents of the men I'm putting my life in the hands of. Are they good at close range combat? Can they speak Pashto or only Dari? Do they—?'

'They're useless.'

'Pardon?'

'Abdul operates the radios and drives our bus. Massad used to be a sheep herder and now cooks a passable curry.'

'But ... They were with us when we faced William's men. They survived.'

'These men aren't soldiers. The training they've had amounts to knowing which end of a gun to hold and which to aim at an enemy. But they know who the enemy *is*, don't worry.'

Mark, ignoring the fact she was talking to him like a superior, turned back to the mountains and mused aloud about the possibility of CCTV.

'How big is it in there?' Jody asked.

'It's a labyrinth. Even if we can get inside, there's no guarantee we'll head the right way. They have every advantage. They know the paths, the hiding places, the dark corners. The bomb could be anywhere. And the guards will recognise me.' Mark looked to the sky for a moment, mused to himself. 'Maybe you could go down there and, you know, use your ... feminine wiles?'

Inside her glower lurked a heated steel core. 'I'm sorry? Is this nineteen seventy? I go down there in my bra and knickers and, while the men are ogling, you punch them all out and wear their clothes? Was that your plan?'

Mark's mouth moved but no words came out.

'Seriously. It was, wasn't it? You know the world's moved on, Dad. Why shouldn't Abdul go down there with his bits out? I think that would get much the same reaction as me.'

'I didn't mean ...'

'This is why you haven't been in the field for over two decades, Dad.'

'*You're* the reason I haven't been in the field for over two decades!'

She looked at him in quiet rage, stood.

'Where are you going?'

She'd already begun her descent towards the base, her two Agents of Allah warriors close behind. Over her shoulder, she hissed, 'I'm not waiting around all day.'

'What are you going to do? Stroll up and ring a doorbell?'

'Do you have a better plan? We won't be able to follow that car's tyre tracks once the light fades.'

He rose from his crouch and made his way towards them. The incline of the slope was steep and scree crumbled under his footsteps, leaking a miniature rockfall.

'We can't use our guns,' he said, wheezing. 'It will alert the lot of them.'

'Obviously.'

'And, another thing. I hope this doesn't sound too alarmist, but ...'

'What?' She didn't stop her careful descent.

'You don't happen to know how to disarm a nuclear missile, do you? Because I'm out of practice, I'll be honest.'

'The TAJSS man – his name was Basir – was an armament expert. His role here was to oversee and secure the merchandise William and I obtained, to render it safe. I know you won't approve that MI6 are outsourcing talent, but that's how things are these days. I'll just have to do my best without him. I have a basic idea of how to disarm it.'

'Do you think, in layman's terms, you should tell me how to do it? In case ...'

'Yeah, sure, open the shroud, disconnect the warhead from the deployment module, destroy the module and isolate the plutonium pit and the explosives in the primary. That's the easy part. Inside the secondary, you'll find highly enriched uranium and fusion fuel which can only be made safe by separating—'

'OK. Fine. I'll just guard your back.'

They'd almost reached the bottom of the incline when Jody recommended they shelter from view behind the last piece of cover before the exposed trek up to the cave.

'This is it. No going back. If we get through that entrance, wherever it is, what will we find?'

Mark explained, as best he could, the network as he remembered it: the guards behind the door; the long, darkly lit passageway humming with artificial light; the overly elaborate and Western-influenced main hall with its drinks' cabinet, shisha-supping concubines and portraits of Taliban leaders. His daughter watched him with sad eyes.

'What?'

'How's Mum?'

'She ... she was shocked by your defection. I didn't believe it for a moment.'

Jody bit her lip and nodded, blinked herself back to professionalism. 'You know, if something does happen to me here, this is how I wanted it to come to an end. Honestly. I need you to know that. I'm sorry for what I said about not wanting you here. I couldn't imagine a better way to see this out.'

He hastily rejected her unusual moment of sentimentality. 'We're not done yet. The way I see it, the men on the other side of the entrance can be taken out easily, without—'

From behind him, a fast hand smothered his mouth. There was the recognisably sweet taste of ether, accompanied by a forearm jabbing back into his carotid, as the image of his daughter's solemn face swam into shards, like scattered diamonds.

21

THE COOLING WORLD SNAPPED HIM alert. Above, grey and umber rock formations seemed to stretch all the way to the towering sky itself and, even now, in late spring, snow dusted the loftiest mountain-land, thin pennants of snow trailing their way like comets' tails from peak to peak in winds that never eased.

His hand went straight to his heart, to check it still beat, then he risked a look over the rock they'd left him behind. Nothing stirred.

Judging from the length of the shadows, he'd been out for anything between half an hour and an hour. The choke to render him unconscious had been reinforced with a crude local chloroform and its nausea lingered a sickly deceit.

She hadn't wanted him to be a part of this. He'd brought her here and she'd unceremoniously disabled and discarded him. Jody would no doubt claim she did it to save his life, and he couldn't really argue she hadn't, temporarily, but after everything he'd been through this felt like the most painful betrayal yet.

He had no weapon, no back-up.

In one furious headrush, he stood and scrambled his way from his place of safety towards the silent cave, its dark entrance now revealed against the mountainside.

They'd left the mock door up, and he found it to be a rudimentary corrugated affair that simply lifted and curled on castors along the cave's ceiling. On the floor were two dead Taliban guards, their necks broken. He wondered which of the so-called 'useless' members of the Agents of Allah had performed the neck-breaking, or whether both deaths were attributable to his daughter.

Out of instinct, he frisked the bodies for any weapons Jody may have missed but found nothing.

The car they'd seen drive into the cave mouth was waiting with its hood raised in the entrance. Its fuel line had been cut, as had those connecting to the battery, which had a bullet punched through it for good measure. Mark peered past it into the cavern's gloom, then stepped fully inside.

Inside, the cave was cool and smelt familiarly musty, its high humidity level accounting for the smell of mould, but he was convinced the hot musk of blood could also be tasted in the air. And something else. Hydrogen sulphide, normal in closed caves with low oxygen levels but not something he recalled smelling the last time he was here.

He waited until his eyes had adjusted and then stumbled forwards into the darkness. The lights having been shut down was bad news. The Taliban would know the cave system so much better than his daughter and the power being down potentially indicated they'd become aware of intruders.

Mark fumbled for the wall and dragged his fingertips along in the manner of a blind man, taking care to place his feet softly on the uneven floor. His eyes were still refocusing, and he thought he saw faint bluish light ahead and crept towards it, heart jackhammering, lungs gulping deep breaths through the abiding sulphurous scent.

They'd been right to leave him there. Was he even going to be able to defend himself in a fight if the situation arose?

He didn't care. If he thought about being knocked unconscious and left behind that rock, his blood boiled. He'd never been stood down from a mission in his life and he was buggered if he'd allow his eldest child to pull rank over him.

As he stole closer, he saw how the light originated from a tunnel set off to the right, a screen from a laptop or computer shining a pale cyan glimmer in a room empty of everything except a desk and chair. He investigated the computer, but it showed only a lock screen in worming Perso-Arabic. This was where the entry guards spent their time, caretakers awaiting a doorbell.

He shuffled along, the subtle acoustics around him altering as the passage widened, and soon the blue glow was far behind.

The first body tripped him over.

He went down heavily. In the aftermath of his fall, he waited with faltering breath for anything that told him he might have been heard. Satisfied he'd got away with it, he heaved himself into a sitting position and felt around him.

The body still retained its heat. He was relieved to feel a beard, then patted down the rest of the body but discovered no weapons. The corpse was dressed like a Taliban fighter, so not Abdul or Massad, and he'd been stabbed. Mark had a vision of the three of them before him, scampering along the darkly lit passage, clamping hands over their victims' mouths to silence the cries as the knives fell. He wondered how many other bodies he'd walked obliviously past.

The second body didn't trip him. It grabbed his ankle.

There was no strength in the arm and Mark easily disentangled himself. From the sounds the man was making, someone had cut his throat and he was still bleeding out, moments from the end. By the time Mark had resolved to break his neck, he'd already expired.

Sticking to the wall, he quickened his pace towards the belly of the cave.

The silence was broken. Muffled cries from some chamber ahead, the sound of hand-to-hand combat, a shout, shots, then nothing but echoes fluttering down the limestone walls as brittle as bats' wings.

The Taliban knew they were here now. Their element of surprise had lasted them a fair time but, up ahead, they were fighting for their lives.

He pushed on, groping against the darkness. The sounds of fighting subsided and Mark found himself straining to listen for clues as to which direction to head, the cave walls rebounding his own breathing back at him.

It was a game of hide and seek, that's all this was. Jody would pop out at any moment and declare herself the winner and he could go home.

The lights blinked on and Mark flinched from them, blinded by the wattage. Was the invasion over?

He ran on, faster now. If someone appeared at the far end of the tunnel, he'd be a dead man; the creases and folds of the cave wall provided scant cover.

Ahead of him, the tunnel veered left. Heart pinching, he hugged the wall and peered around the turn. Another tunnel, decorated by a further body on the ground. Mark hurried over, patted it down like the ones before. Again, no gun, but he found a knife concealed on the right calf, missed by those who searched before him and indicating the victim was left-handed. He helped himself.

Luck rather than memory brought him to the Commander of the Faithful's lounge. This time, the pretence of hospitality had been replaced by utter carnage. Two men, who must have been taking cover behind the desk, were sprawled in their own blood, which mingled with the blood of two more who'd been waiting behind the door. A fifth had fallen face first over the desk. Another had been shot at the entrance. All were Taliban.

Mark stood amid the aftermath of the massacre and heard himself sigh. His little girl, along with two others, had crept in here with the guards' guns and, in a brief stand-off, killed a lot of human beings. The proud, framed faces of terrorist leaders watched him dispassionately from the rock walls.

He tore a gun from the nearest corpse and slung it over his shoulder.

Bloody footsteps tramped from the red pool beside the table all the way to an exit on the left, and Mark tracked the footprints until they faded to invisibility on the hard cave floor. Drops of blood succeeded them, and he took up this version of Ariadne's string, unsure whom he was following through stone tunnels that stretched away from him like the grainy imagery at the end of a colonoscope.

The trail of blood soon became impossible to see, and his heart raced faster than his feet. The humidity was in his bones now, which ached in protest, and his mind – dehydrated, tired and still suffering the ether headache – conjured whispers that chased him down the tunnels. Surreality sang him past dark rooms that might have once been his cell with the solitary lightbulb and the bucket of excrement, and he stopped to peer in a few chambers, in case he saw himself sleeping there, dreaming a lucid dream in which he stalked these very corridors.

There was someone ahead.

He saw him, just a glimpse, as he rounded a bend. A figure dressed in the casual fatigues of a Taliban fighter, gun pointed ahead of him in a hunter's stance, was a brief silhouette before disappearing as though imagined. Mark ducked and scurried to catch up with the ghost before it disappeared down another tunnel and, at the next bend, Mark saw him again, shuffling with the slow, lopsided tread of a wounded animal.

It was the Commander of the Faithful.

Mark waited until he was out of sight, then hurried after, levelling his stolen weapon. Only now did he realise the rifle was bolt action and not automatic; loading the weapon would not be a silent matter, so creeping up on the Commander was the only option. The knife felt significantly heavier in his hand, now he knew he'd have to use it.

He reached a fork in the passageway, two dark mouths, and inspected the floor to check which way his quarry might have gone, but the rock revealed no clues, nor could he hear footsteps any longer.

Dad.

Spinning, he found no one. Just haunted whispers through the swirling acoustics of the caves.

Choosing the second tunnel, he ran, the cave ceiling brushing against his hair as the passage pressed in around him. He could reach out either arm and touch both cave walls as he scurried, bent like a broken limb, his knees aching with the burden as the cave constricted. By the time he was reduced to desperately crawling forwards on his elbows, it was as though he burrowed straight into hell.

Dad.

Behind the whispers lurked a faint hum and memories of training camp – his old drill sergeant barking him onwards as the skin flayed off his elbows layer by painful layer. His military discipline, as it so often had, powered him through, the thought of ten minutes shining each toecap, the early morning runs, the chin-ups in the rain. Then, in an instant, he fell through space and dropped a foot to the floor as the dark tunnel came to an abrupt end.

Dad. Dad. Dad.

He was in a thrumming, wide room which appeared to contain nothing but a large, noisy cargo crate fitted with blinking lights. It was an old generator, but clearly adequate for the power needs of the cavernous network. They could have been near an underground river, he supposed, since this looked to use hydroelectric power, but it was more likely one of several portables that housed a couple of hundred litres of water. On the floor was a large quantity of sawdust, footprints scoured into it beneath the crank handle.

He limped towards a door to the left and found that it opened, letting in a thin mist of light. Cautiously, he slipped through. He was in an old kitchen, now nothing more than bare cupboards and calcifying water marks in steel sinks and, passing through, a further door led him into a large meeting room, with corralled chairs and tables facing a whiteboard on which was scrawled a map, bound with strategic arrows. Olives and powder-dry breadsticks still lay in little trays on the tables.

Mark stared at the map, trying to work out its black-markered geography. Finally, it hit him. It was the map of the Agents of Allah's camp by the river, including the location of the missile. This inconspicuous and grubby room was where the Taliban had planned their siege, their massacre of unexpecting and poorly defended Hazara.

His hand was on the door handle when a hard-won caution made him stop.

Mark turned out the light and took five paces back, waited.

A faint shadow moved within a thin lozenge of light beneath the door as Mark backed behind the whiteboard.

The door opened and the injured Commander staggered forwards as though drunk.

When the Commander fumbled for the light switch, Mark took the opportunity to throw his decoy: a board marker pen. As it landed in the far corner, the man turned sluggishly towards the noise and Mark cranked the bullet in the chamber, stepped out from his cover and shot him in the chest.

His opponent had enough time to realise what had happened and let off a bullet of his own, but it was snatched and wayward and Mark had already hit the deck.

The Commander slumped to the ground.

This is nothing personal.

Once he'd convinced himself the Commander hadn't the strength to rearm and fire back, Mark climbed to his feet. The Commander's dazed expression slowly changed to one of recognition, his fingers curling uselessly in the vague direction of his weapon.

'You ...' he gasped.

The Commander's breathing was shallow and evenly punctuated, his pupils wide with a narcotic's influence.

Mark sniffed the air, caught again the fading scent of the hydrogen sulphide.

The entire cave had been pumped full of poison.

That explained why the Taliban had been so easily overcome, Mark's own hallucinatory progress through the tunnels. They'd all been drugged.

'Where's the warhead being kept?' Mark demanded, but the Commander was already dead, the look on his face one of enviable peace.

Mark snatched up his gun and slipped it over his other shoulder, making sure he checked its loading mechanism this time, then carried on through the network of darkness until he found himself at the bottom of a steep set of crude stairs carved into rock. Two dead men were sprawled halfway down them. He recognised them instantly.

One was Massah, former sheep herder, the white flecks in his beard now red, and the other was Abdul, the Agents of Allah's bus driver. Both had been shot in the back of the head from close range.

Executed.

The floor reeled beneath him.

It was his health rather than his espionage skills which trod Mark slowly up the stairs and, panting, sweating, he found himself at a large steel door at the top.

The door had a pin tumbler mechanism and he set to work manipulating the lock with the knife, then placed the blade between the door and the jamb's striker plate. The door popped open and he stepped through.

Inside, the bunker was a curious mix of modern office and ancient mosque. Two arabesque portals led from the entrance foyer, carpets layering the floor. Above an open safe wedged full of grenades, ammo clips and belts, a low ceiling fan spun at a despondent speed, nevertheless circulating an air fresher than that outside the bunker and he gulped down as much of it as he could. He had arrived at the Taliban strongroom, their version of Command Centre. Few Westerners had ever set eyes on such a place.

Mark's brain screamed at him to get out of there. His sixth sense had served him well all these years, but he wilfully ignored it now.

He followed an arrhythmic clicking, and a hurried whispering of unintelligible conversation, into a large antechamber, two vast metal doors at the rear sporting large C-shaped handles wrapped with a thick chain, as if to keep an army out.

Inside was the missile, sleek and green and deadly. Standing in front of its open front panel were two figures.

One was Abs. The other was his daughter.

The first to turn was Jody, and her face imperceptibly changed expression when she saw him. There was something steadfast about her appearance, triumphant too. Nevertheless, an enemy unseen haunted her. Mark knew the look. It was the face of a person who'd won at terrible cost. Many find out too late there's been one kill too many, and the life of a spy, perhaps, wasn't so different to that of a terrorist; theirs was a game that required belief in a higher justice as well as blind obedience to flawed men, and the two didn't always sit perfectly with one another. She bore another expression, beneath the fatigue, and it closely resembled regret. He remembered it well, because he hadn't seen it very often: it was the face she wore when she got caught.

She stroked the panel closed. At her hip was what looked like a large old-fashioned mobile phone.

'Jody?'

Abs twisted to meet the voice, unholstering a pistol.

'This is that old fucker I was telling you about, *habibti*.' He strode towards Mark.

Jody put up her hand. 'Don't shoot him.'

'He's outlived his usefulness,' Abs sneered. All traces of his fake accent and ropey syntax fell away; he sounded as English as Mark.

Mark struggled for something to say, failed. Behind the pair, the idle death machine seemed to emanate its own black silence.

'What's the British interest here, really?' Abs asked. 'I've never understood. You just follow the Americans around, hoping for the crumbs from their table. You'll never convince the ayatollahs to divvy you up any land or oil, but you still believe your foreign policy of blundering immaturity gives you the moral high ground.'

'I'm not here on behalf of my government.' Mark made a show of lowering his left gun, pretending to abandon it while preparing for the possibility of firing from his stronger right-hand side. 'I came to get my daughter back.'

Abs looked at them both then, slowly, began to laugh. 'This is your *dad*?'

'Why did you follow me?' Her eyes misted with the glaucoma of tears.

Mark was programmed to be moved by his daughter's grief, but he couldn't summon it now. After everything that had happened, it felt like an act. Things had escalated beyond his comprehension.

'Sorry, Dad. You backed the wrong horse, after all.'

She removed the black box at her hip. It wasn't a phone.

It was a detonator.

22

There comes a time, early in every human life, when a choice must be made.

The choice is as unconscious as it is universal. A sleepless young mind fathoms the magnitudes of its own mortality beneath cracks in the bedroom ceiling, cries out for reason and finds none. In panic, his or her embryonic brain pictures, figuratively, two doors. One leads to ignorance – a simple refusal to even think about a world beyond our primitive, primate understanding, or the seeking of comfort from contingent chaos in one of humankind's many religions – and the second door leads to madness. Unfiltered, fuck-it-all, bag-of-cats madness. The vast majority of children, hinged there before the two options following their first huge dalliance with cognisance, choose self-saving sanity, and slip through the door marked 'Ignorance'. After all, it's easier to block it out, to build walls that look like the face of God. But, for just a moment, fragile minds have already glimpsed what's on the other side of the second door, and that spark of burning insanity remains dormant within the soul, waiting for a trigger. A death. A transcendent work of art. An injustice. And then the fear rears itself again with a preternatural force bearing the potential to shatter cosy domestic life in all directions.

To outsiders, those who'd been unaware of his battles with the bottle, Mark had survived the crises of his life with ease.

His twenties had seen enough death and moral ambiguity to last him a lifetime. But by the time he'd hit middle age, he'd slipped securely into middle England ignorance. The German car in the driveway. The Hong Kong-owned bank account. The South Asian indoctrination of his daughter. And yet there'd always, *always* been one arm stretching out to grasp the door handle to 'Madness'.

And here he was, sweating underneath the lower Hindu Kush, his daughter wielding a nuclear detonator, the crimson blood of her enemies staining both sleeves up to the elbows. He felt the vertigo of insanity and knew he'd never find peace again.

'I'm working with the Agents of Allah,' she told him. 'Always have been.'

Mark took a step back, as though from the announcement's fallout. 'I don't understand, Jody.' Surely Abs was holding her hostage. This was her plan, a further misdirection. It had to be. '*Why?* Why sell me the false flag about a foreign power wanting to nuke half of Kabul?'

'You came up with that storyline, Dad. Remember? I simply didn't deny it.' There was the rasp of pity in the voice. She wrapped black tape around the device in her hand, twisted flat a silver hoop that stuck out of its end. 'After a while, I went along with your fantasy. It seemed the best way to keep you onside.'

'You ... You led me to believe you were working for the British government.'

'What else would you have believed? I didn't need you on my scent.'

A banging in his head grew louder, seemed to vibrate throughout the entire cave. It sounded like a hundred blacksmiths' hammers on an anvil, workmen breaking apart an entire city.

'You *had* been turned. How long have you two been . . .? No. Don't tell me. Oxford. How did the Service miss him when they went through your history?'

Jody reached for a coil of wiring Abs held out. For a second, she held a terrorist in one hand and a nuclear bomb in the other. 'Abs was expelled halfway through my second year for . . . dissidence. We kept in touch.' An understatement. The way she met Abs' eyes betrayed a love he hadn't seen in her face since . . . Ever. Out of nowhere, he recalled the flush that burned her neck at the dinner table when Alessia's friends quizzed her about romantic interests at university.

He rounded on the terrorist leader. 'So, you rocked up at the Taliban door with information about the Agents of Allah's bomb and camp location and they just *let you in*?'

'William had already introduced me at a few merch handovers. They couldn't resist hearing me out.'

'And the Taliban thought they were using *you* for information, seeing you as a dumb Hazara mole within a new terrorist outfit, but you knew exactly how to get to them. That was your map I saw, drawn on the whiteboard in the Taliban's planning room. And here we are, beneath the mountain you're going to turn into a fucking volcano and use to kill millions. You're mad. If you wanted to get rid of the Taliban, why position yourselves on top of the bomb? Did something go wrong with it that needed fixing?'

'Never heard of suicide bombers, old man?' Abs' voice was calm and unhurried. The pistol was directed between Mark's eyes. 'Drop your guns.'

Mark shrugged them off his shoulders and they clattered to the floor.

He stared at his daughter, so dark against the white walls. She'd played him like a fool, convincingly forbidden him from calling SIS headquarters for back-up. What had she said to him in the burnt-out camp? *You still have a brilliant tactical mind, but you've let emotion cloud your judgement.* She wasn't wrong.

He tried to speak but there was only pain.

'Thanks for showing me how to find the cave, Dad. I admit I was a little curious, to ...' Her voice tapered into self-censorship.

'To see the "legendary Mark Wolfe in the field"? You wanted to humiliate me.'

'No, not at all. It's kinder like this. Sitting on top of the blast, we'll be vaporised. No radiation poisoning, no painful lingering death ...'

'This isn't a game, Jody!'

'Isn't it? *You've* treated it like one. You weren't even that pleased to have found me. All you cared about were operational secrets of "the mission". Well, *this* is the mission, Dad! Here we are. About to ascend.'

He'd never known her. Never known his own daughter. The stupid old man had to play the spy one last time, and completely ignored the fact that Jody wasn't coming all the way here to disarm a bomb, but to prime one.

MI6 had been right to worry when she followed in his footsteps all those months ago. They'd been right to question her loyalty. They'd been right to try and pull her out, take her down.

They'd been right.

'I came to rescue you,' he said, pointlessly.

'You came to rescue yourself. Congratulations. It's still in you. You haven't forgotten how to follow trails or pull a trigger for little England. You made it to the end of the line.' There was both coldness and defeat in her tone. 'Ironic, really. You were never there for me, growing up. Always so involved in your own work, and now you've tracked me across the world to die by my side, for *my* cause. I emulated you. I worshipped you. But I got ... nothing. I was a lot older when I found out who you really were, but I always hated what you stood for. I *was* turned. You're right. I guess you could say *you* turned me.'

His mouth opened, closed in mute agony. Finally, he rediscovered words. 'We found nothing on you. They turned our house upside down. How could you do this to us? What about all the innocent people in Kabul? This is senseless.' He looked from one face to the other and saw vacant extremism and nothing else, the brainwashed stares of the pious. 'Jody, these caves will ...'

'Be radioactive for fifty years,' she finished. 'The Sunni infidel in Kabul will never recover from this. Never.' Her eyes gleamed with inner glory.

'This is wrong,' Mark cried. 'This isn't you. I came all this way to prove you *weren't* this person. And yet you let me lead you to the cave, to *fucking die!*'

'You led yourself here.' She returned her gaze to the objects in her hands, then carefully placed the detonator atop a stool and began snipping at the end of the thin cable with wire strippers. 'The Agents rescued you from the Taliban execution. TAJSS had an escape route planned for you that *you rejected*. We gave you medical attention after your heart gave out, and you *still* insisted on escorting me here and then following me inside! This is on you, Dad. This is *all* on you. MI6 *told you* I'd defected. You never listen to *anyone*.'

Even Abs regarded her emotion with concern.

'I couldn't leave you, Jody ...'

'You were supposed to think I was—'

'Killed on a mission and mourn you for the rest of my life? Was that what I was supposed to think? You've betrayed *everyone*.'

'I haven't betrayed the people that truly need me.' Another devoted flick of her eyes towards Abs. 'The Hazara have been "disappeared" for decades. Yet another genocide the world ignores. These beautiful people have been routinely discriminated against—'

'Spare me the fucking history lesson!'

The banging in his head grew metallic, closer.

'What *is* that noise?'

Abs nodded at the far bulkhead doors. 'The remaining Taliban are trying to get in through the main bunker entrance. Don't worry; the doors will hold. The men are very weak now.'

'You drugged them all,' Mark said. 'Using the generator's air conditioning to pump hydrogen sulphide through the cave, you eased Jody's route through.' Involuntarily, Mark took another long pull of fresher air. 'Their gunshots didn't turn it into a fireball, so you'd been filling the cave system with a low level for hours. The effects have been slow acting. We're relatively safe in here, but that was risky. Jody and the others might have succumbed.'

'They'd have lived long enough.' He took the wire cutters off Jody with his free hand and watched her pinch the silvery ends into the underside of the detonator. 'The poison was another acquisition from our friend William, as was the amyl nitrite antidote I took before my visit to the generator.'

Taliban swarming behind the metal door. Abs armed with a handgun. His daughter clutching the detonator. *Odds stacked against.*

Mark had to keep them talking.

'Why did William sell parts to your organisation, and not the Taliban directly? Why not just send a compromised bomb to your Sunni enemies in the first place?'

'It's the old Trojan horse problem,' Abs said. 'An American selling US parts to the Taliban would have looked suspicious. They'd never have gone for that. But the Taliban had no such qualms about stealing it off the Agents of Allah. Especially after we'd mounted an attack on them the day before.'

Mark groaned in primal failure. He turned to his daughter. 'That's why you sniped William at the exchange. It was the last segment of the bomb you needed. Death guarantees silence. I think you shot Basir too. The man from TAJSS was on to you, wasn't he?'

'I'm sure he was.'

'He told me you were legit, just to get me out of here, but he was planning to take you down as soon as the plutonium was out of William's clutches. He knew what you were planning.' Mark could barely bring himself to vocalise his next, most unpleasant, thought. 'The Agents of Allah saved me from the Taliban, but only to use me. You weren't *saving your father*.'

'I *did* save your life, remember? When you were wading through the bodies and dust to retrieve that plutonium ... You should have gone home like Basir warned you.'

'You're sick. You allowed the Taliban to steal the warhead, and raze your own camp?'

'The camp was practically empty, Dad. Most of the Hazara community have already gone back to Hazarajat.'

Mark recalled the dispossessed Hazara walking in sad single file by the side of the road, making their exodus out of Kabul. He'd assumed they'd been persecuted to the point where they had no choice except to leave, but they *knew*. Word had got around their communities that a retaliatory uprising against their Pashtun oppressors was being planned. Was *that* why poor Yusuf had vanished in the mountains? Like so many others, had he been on his way home, fearing what was to come?

'Jody. Countless people will be unable to live in this city the moment you press that button. You'll kill, mutilate or displace millions of innocents.'

'We'll *sacrifice* millions,' Abs said. 'Sunnis in the northern provinces will be obliterated. The fallout will stretch way beyond the plains of Dih Sabz. The Americans in Bagram will be dust. We'll maim a city to save a country.'

Incredibly, the zombielike banging on the farther bunker doors was still going, underlaid by a faint chorus of angry voices.

'What happened to the two we came with, Jody? You murdered them, didn't you, once they'd outlived their use? And the victims of the roadside mortar attack that got the plutonium here? And all the others?'

Her eyes were glazed as she clicked a panel into place on the back of the detonator. 'Merely pilgrims that made this all possible. The rest are in the hills of Hazarajat, awaiting our glorious victory. I shall provide that triumph in the name of Allah.'

He wanted to leap forward and slap her, and he'd never struck her in his life.

Mark returned his attention to Abs. 'You were helped here by Yusuf. Where's he? Executed too?'

'Press the button,' Abs told Jody. 'We are prepared. *Man asheghe shoma hastam.*'

She turned to her university flame. Was there a flicker of doubt there?

Mark didn't give up. 'There are sixty thousand Taliban in Afghanistan. You'll kill but a fraction of them. And what will the Taliban in Helmand, in Herat, in Zabul, do? They'll retaliate with everything they've got. Your poor, downtrodden Hazara won't stand a chance then.'

'They will rise,' Abs said, his dark, soulless eyes wide with the promise of jihad. 'Press it, *habibti.*'

'Wait!' Mark scrambled desperately for words to keep them all breathing. 'I love you, Jody. I don't know what's happened to turn you, but ... I'll try and understand. We can work this out. You don't have to do this. I'm sorry I let you down. I'm sorry I wasn't there. *Don't do this. Please.*'

A faint whimper dragged itself from Jody's throat, but it was overpowered by the seismic roar of the steel bulkhead cracking open, a rent in the very fabric of Jody's piety as angry, slurred voices poured through the wound. The Taliban appeared to have clawed the doors from their hinges, but the vast steel sheets still held, the tight chain wrapping them fast, for now.

When Jody and Abs twisted towards the noise, Mark reached back for the knife and tossed it – employing the signature underarm move Abs had once been so impressed by – through Abs' right eye. As Jody screamed, Mark raced over and forced Abs' gun arm down, disarming him easily. Abs clawed at his face, crying out in agony as the livid Taliban roared ever louder.

Mark stared down his daughter, who brandished the detonator above her head as though about to drive all her force into activating it.

Abs slumped to the ground. Mark raised Abs' pistol towards Jody.

'You wouldn't,' she taunted.

'I can't let you do this.'

'Too late.'

He fired.

Jody's thumb plunged towards a red button no longer there. Mark's shot had exploded the controller into a disparate jigsaw of skittering plastic, wiring and mashed battery.

She glared at him with raw, unmistakeable hatred as, behind her, the Taliban voices grew fiercer than their owners, whose narcotised, somnolent shapes lurched behind the thin gap between the bulkhead doors, hands reaching through to unknot the chain that kept them prisoner. Mark sprayed a bullet in their direction. The hands withdrew.

'We have to get out of here,' Mark urged. 'There'll be dozens through any moment.'

Keeping her in his sights, he rapidly checked the chamber of his purloined gun. A single bullet left. She appeared unarmed, but his abandoned rifles lay between them.

'The detonator's destroyed, Jody. You can't fight the remaining Taliban on your own.'

She turned her back on him and approached the warhead.

'What are you doing?'

Jody flipped the panel up.

Mark's understanding of fissile material wasn't as advanced as his daughter's, but he knew one thing: it wasn't the impact or explosion involved in a missile strike that triggered the plutonium, it was a pre-programmed detonation of a TNT cap around the pit. Mere brute force wouldn't set it off – in the Sixties, a nuke fell from a plane in Palamares, Spain, and it simply left a small dent on the runway in its wake – but tampering might leak radiation; in short, they were still standing feet from a potential dirty bomb. Worse than that, his destruction of the detonator had only bought Kabul a few seconds of time if she still could still use the primed warhead to blow them all into the next world manually.

'Jody!' he barked, in his most forceful father's voice.

She twisted to face him, leering in absent-minded triumph, her arm outstretched, index finger resting on a seemingly inconspicuous dial. In the background, a Talib was squeezing himself through the thin gap between the doors. Another wriggling through at his feet. Abs' body twitched on the floor.

One bullet. One choice. One split second.

He could fire through the warhead, with the aim of ruining the integrity of its design, taking a guess about where the important components were stored, or … he could shoot the jihadist whose hand, even now, was cranking a switch towards her within the bomb's open panel. One thing was absolute: Jody Wolfe wasn't going to be talked out of her cataclysmic plan.

It seemed to happen in slow motion. A decisive twist within the open panel on the warhead; figures swarming behind the straining bulkhead doors like vengeful spirits awaiting a cursed soul; his finger on the cold trigger of a gun which felt leaden and obscene. He was pointing a weapon at his baby.

And still that terrible look of triumph upon her face.

'Bye, Dad.'

He heard the crack of the gun as it recoiled. At the exact same moment, he saw the bullet punch into flesh and fabric.

Her whole body shuddered with the impact and slumped back against the missile, wobbling its length along the stanchions as her hands scrambled for purchase on the smooth steel. Collapsed, consumed by an agonised expression of disbelief, she struggled to raise herself, seemed confused she couldn't command her body to do so, then fell sideways as though drunk.

The gunshot must have sent the Taliban back to cover, for Mark saw no sign of them behind the doors as he leaped the few feet towards her body, blood already pooling around her, flowing from her exit wound and starting its serpentine creep from the left corner of her mouth as she stared at him unblinking, a look of childlike surprise paling her face into a lost, distant impassivity he'd seen many times before. She wore the common blankness of approaching death, the body's last surging, adrenalized fight against pain and the oncoming dark. He took her face in his hands and howled.

At the sound, a distant spark widened her misted pupils and she seemed to focus upon him, but whether she heard him as he apologised – over and over in a teary, clotted voice he didn't recognise – he couldn't tell.

He wasn't even sure what he was saying. He didn't want his last words to her to be incoherent, and yet he was crying something about the doors to madness and ignorance, how he'd never close the former. You have killed me, he was telling her. You have killed me.

Her pulse was faint, and it was fading.

He hooked his forearms under her armpits and dragged her up into his embrace, then attempted a parody of a slow dance towards the bunker door behind them. He wouldn't leave her body at the mercy of those animals. His only priority was to get her out of this cave and, staggering under her weight, hauled her with him, awkwardly sidestepping the body of Abs, now still, whose remaining eye stared sightless with neither illumination nor intelligence.

Mark dropped to one knee and allowed his daughter's body to flop into his open arms, *La Pietà*-style, and then wheezed his way onto both feet and staggered forwards with her. It was a miscalculation, for she was heavier in such a carry, and he managed three tumbled steps before his legs gave way and they both sprawled together to the cave floor.

And yet, he'd known he'd never be able to get her out of the cave. That had been the major catalyst for his split-second decision, after all. She couldn't have fended off every one of the cave dwellers, and leaving her maimed would have bestowed her a fate worse than death.

He'd had to kill her. To save a city of millions. To *save her*.

It had seemed so straightforward. And yet the hand with which he'd shot her at close range had been far from a steady one; as he'd watched the bullet thud and blossom just above the heart, he'd wondered if he'd missed that beating target on purpose.

It didn't matter now. The bullet had done its damage.

Mark fell back from the body as the Taliban rattled and rattled the doors. There were dozens of tunnels between this hell and a comparative freedom and, even if he selected, by some miracle, the correct routes, the journey might still be miles. His own heart simply couldn't carry her.

A whisper from the floor. Jody's brittle voice was the muttered kiss of autumn leaves, and he leaned down to gain a clearer understanding.

It sounded Italian. Her mother's language, a voice from their shared past, from Santa Maria holidays full of sunshine and promise. He must have misheard.

It sounded like 'Vinco'.

I win.

It chilled him to think she'd been playing a game all this time, as though this was merely part of some greater strategy of which he still basked in ignorance, but a roar came up from the Taliban and he was forced to consider the deadly here and now.

The chain slithered from between its handles and clattered to the floor as the huge doors cracked apart.

The Taliban were through.

As their guns raised, Mark attempted to drag her once more, but she felt heavier somehow. A dead weight.

A bullet ripped just beyond his left temple and then ricocheted past his right.

Within seconds, it was as though he stood at the centre of a malfunctioning fireworks display. A sharp pain in his left shoulder jolted through his entire body. From his right thigh, he felt a chunk of flesh tear itself loose.

He let her go.

Bullets clanged and chinked into the missile's casing as he threw himself back down the steps and clawed his way into the claustrophobic tunnel, the ghost of a nuclear explosion at his back.

Eventually, the tunnel widened but he remained on his knees. He had nothing left. The remnants of the poison in the air would find him, and so would the Taliban survivors, who'd re-imprison, torture or kill him for kicks, and never know he'd saved their miserable, troglodyte lives. Somehow, beyond spent, he found the will to keep crawling, hoping the labyrinth would remember him, guide him out. He blotted the pain, the way he'd always done. Superiors needed notifying and reports had to be sent. His only goal was to see starlight.

Rat-like scuffling in the tunnels behind him. They were giving chase.

Instinct pushed him onwards, nothing more; he couldn't go on, and yet on he went. A left, a right, trying to retrace his route past lifeless bodies scattered like the statuary of a fallen dynasty, scurrying with his hand over his heart, to keep it from exploding out of his chest, pretending he might soothe it into ruder health.

He tripped, fell. Stood. Fell again.

On his knees, he crawled at a speed little faster than lying still. These tunnels all looked the same, yet he had the terrible feeling he'd taken a wrong turn somewhere and found himself, without thought or future, slumping defeated to the rocky ground. His legs wouldn't let him continue, not a foot more. He'd die here with her.

He should have let her nuke the cave. Thousands, possibly millions would have been atomised, himself included, but he wouldn't have had to live with what he'd done.

Through the pain, an unpleasant thought burrowed in behind enemy lines: Her terrorist boyfriend was dead, their plan defeated, and yet she had still claimed a victory. Why?

He'd had no choice. To have not fired would have meant risking apocalypse. If he'd done anything other than fatally wound her, Jody would have found a way to reprime that device. It had been his trigger finger against hers . . .

Bye, Dad.

His mouth opened in a silent scream. *No. No. No.* Banish that thought. It couldn't be. Reach for the door marked 'Ignorance'.

But it was too late, the truth within her final word – *Vinco* – was dawning.

And now the scream was no longer a soundless one.

Once hoarse, Mark sensed faint footsteps and raised a heavy head to spy the silhouette of a man loping with murderous intent towards him. Behind the lumbering spectre, further shapes gathered as voices swelled in the near distance, tumbling and amplifying an incandescent rage throughout the mountain-bored warrens.

Even before the shadow swung its ancient rifle off its shoulder, Mark's vision was fading as his world oscillated in a dizzying violence of exhaustion and grief and blackening defeat.

He had reached the end of his fight. The dark was coming. Madness's final cure.

23

He watched the dry sunlight sharking through white curtains. It seemed solid, this sunlight, as it burgled the ward, a tangible wall of bright, blistering luminosity, the kind that would melt a vampire to instantaneous ash or torch an entire library should someone slant a magnifying glass within its swirling radiation. London light had nothing like the quality of this, with her bruised skies and damp artillery of impatient clouds. This was a languid, defiant sunlight, for a languid, defiant land.

The rushing quiet and antiseptic smell of the military hospital was as unfamiliar to Mark as peace of mind, but it was that light which challenged him the most. It exposed him, interrogated him, left him with no shadows in which his guilt might safely hide.

From his bed, invaded by tubes and his bloodied bandages still wet, he explained everything – almost everything – to the same hundred and sixty pounds of barking US muscle he'd spoken to at the embassy. Mark was deemed worthy of his name now: Lieutenant General Curtis Ray, three stars glinting on his considerable shoulder.

His listener shook his head in impatient disbelief. It was a familiar gesture from their brief conversation at the embassy all those infinities ago, but this time Mark wasn't giving him 'chicken feed'. He'd upended the entire coop. Curtis ran his hand through what was left of his hair.

'Let me get this straight,' he said. 'Your daughter – self-elected kamikaze on behalf of the Agents of Allah – was in cahoots with William Stucker to set up the theft of a nuclear device – piecemeal, over several months – and it's now in the hands of the Taliban.'

Mark forced the words out in an emotionless monotone. 'That's about the size of it.'

'And their plan was to nuke the cave, to take out the Pashtun "infidels"? *Jeez-us*, William was our mole in the Taliban. He was supposed to be bent, but not *that* bent. Your daughter must have really turned his head.' His voice trailed off.

Mark waited until he felt strong enough to reply. 'He made himself easy to buy, plus you had a leak the size of the Panama Canal. If such hot material was changing hands, William can't have been working alone.'

'Those exchanges happen more often than you'd think. We need as many groups as possible to defend themselves against the Taliban. William negotiated plenty of those merch trades.'

'He should never have been trusted.' It was himself Mark was scolding. He tried to sit up and felt as though he tore his entire left side.

'Don't try and move. You're lucky to be alive. This Abs person, the leader of the group: what do you know about him?'

Mark stabbed the morphine button. The IV wasn't ready to release yet. He grunted in irritation.

'Did he receive an education in the UK?'

Mark nodded. 'I expect he was part of a Hazara diaspora, probably from a wealthy background.'

'Rich enough to afford a thermonuclear warhead? That's beyond the paygrade of most Afghans. Did you find out how the Agents of Allah financed their operations?'

Mark shook his head. 'How do the Taliban do it?'

'Heroin. There aren't many poppy fields in the Hazarajat region, traditionally, but we'll investigate.' He spoke fast, aware there was little time to lose. 'When we talked at the embassy, you'd just survived an assassination at your hotel. You thought it was masterminded by ... I don't remember his name.'

'Fassad al Hallam. I was wrong about him. In fact, I'm inclined to believe he was one of the only honest men round here.' If the American took this as a slight, he didn't flinch over it. 'He identified my attacker as a member of the Taliban. Fassad was killed in cold blood by someone calling himself the Commander of the Faithful, who admitted to the attempted hit on me.'

'That's a title Taliban leaders call themselves. Getting rid of him would be a major achievement.'

'Job done. You're welcome.'

'You know, you haven't done badly for a man off the clock.'

Mark swore. He'd been told he'd be in this hospital for weeks, and was still too ill for the bypass surgery. 'I only came to find my daughter. I wish I hadn't.'

Curtis swallowed what little empathy he appeared to possess. 'How far are we from those caves?'

'Firmly within the fallout radius.'

'And how powerful is this goddamn nuke?'

Mark sighed and hurt himself in doing so. 'Several megatons, judging from its size. How the hell was it so easy for Stucker to steal the parts necessary to assemble a fucking *nuclear weapon*?'

The Lieutenant General stood. 'A full inquiry will be launched. For now, don't die on us. We need you. This operation is far from being tidied up. On the contrary: you're telling me I need to send men into a secret Taliban cave system to retrieve a stolen nuclear warhead. That sounds to me like the most complicated, dangerous mission anyone has ever overseen in Afghanistan. So, thanks a bunch for that.'

Something unspoken held the American by the bedside. The silence thickened.

'Your daughter ...' He squinted down at the broken body in the bed. 'Is she ...? Did they get her, the Taliban?'

Mark met the iron gaze. Through the ward, white noise couldn't drown the frantic beeping of vital signs.

'Yes. Yes, they did.'

The pressures Mark put his body under, both physically and mentally, while under the auspices of Her Majesty's Government, should have been enough to send most people six feet under the cold clay not even halfway through the length of a likewise career. He'd looked death in the face more times than an undertaker and distrusted hospitals simply because he knew the nurses who mended him were little more than gaolers to a richly deserved afterlife. Hell had long been waiting for him.

And he was well and truly in its flames now.

It was a vague relief to see the devil's disciple strolling through the ward armed with a serious expression that declared an official visit from Vauxhall's Top Floor.

'Well, look what the cat coughed up,' Jim called.

Normally, when Mark moved some part of his anatomy these days, no matter how minor, something ached, but he got away with a thin smile.

'We had quite a shock when you called in, Mark. Even before you popped up on prime time in that flattering orange jumpsuit, it was obvious where you'd gone.'

Mark didn't feel this needed elucidation.

'We didn't know whether to be worried or relieved when that second video failed to materialise.'

Mark tried to stress the words he thought made him sound normal, human. 'The press named me Varta and not Wolfe. MI6 keeping my true identity hidden probably saved my life.'

'We weren't going to drop you in it, even though no one trusted what you were up to. As for other matters, London's quite pleased.'

Mark tried to read his old friend's expression. Jim's attempt to be upbeat wasn't working and his words were dispensed with, it seemed, great effort, as though shouldering the full weight of the elephant in the room. He hadn't mentioned Jody, nor Mark's report on her death due to Taliban crossfire, and Mark was curious how long he'd hold out for before doing so.

'How, exactly, is London pleased, Jim?'

'You wandered into Yankie territory and showed them how to boss a job. At least that's how the Top Floor's playing it. Their bomb. Their salesman. But you went in and exposed the whole thing in a fortnight.'

'The president, pro tempore of the Senate, described the ensuing tidying-up operation as "the biggest political stink of the post-Cold War". I wouldn't describe the job as "bossed".'

'Admittedly, everyone's a little uneasy about the fallout. No pun intended. Vauxhall's crediting the Taliban with enough sense not to shit in their own backyard, but the minute they attempt to hijack a B-52, we'll know their intentions are to use that warhead. Military planes in a thirty-mile radius have been grounded for that reason, but an evacuation order hasn't been given. Me being here is proof of that.' He sounded understandably rueful. 'From what I can tell, they're scrambling troops everywhere, dialling it all up to eleven. You caused quite a kerfuffle. Not bad for an old guy with a desk job.'

'Why did they send you? Is Adam Wellcome no longer Head of South Asia?'

Jim took a seat by the bed. 'It would appear he's fallen out of favour.'

'He's a damn hero.' Mark judged the tone of the silence, then pressed home. 'How much of this did you know, Jim? When you came to my house to warn me, how sure were you that Jody had gone over?'

Jim suddenly found the view outside the window worth investigating and his voice cracked like a teenage boy's. 'As sure as everyone. Except you. I tried to convince you TAJSS weren't a going concern, because not only was I attempting to discourage you from blundering into Afghanistan, I knew there was a TAJSS operative, hired by MI6, actively investigating Jody over here.'

'They'd been sniffing around her for ages. I'm willing to bet they suspected her long before Six did, hence their interest in me throughout her recruitment and beyond. I've been a bloody fool.'

'Yes, but if you hadn't come out here, this whole place would be a radioactive crater with an Agents of Allah flag stuck upright at its centre.' Jim kept his voice in a gruff whisper the nurses at the central station couldn't discern. Mark wouldn't be the first spook they'd had to put back together, and he wouldn't be the last, but no one needed to know there was the possibility of a nuclear bomb exploding underneath them. 'Your daughter was on to that TAJSS agent, let's not forget. He may have known what was going on before you worked it out, but he couldn't stop her. *You* did.'

Mark flinched at Jim's brutal choice of words. *Yes, he had stopped her.*

'You should've seen her eyes, Jim. She was gone. There was just this crazed and angry ... I don't know. I don't understand what happened to her. I know she spent a long time in this part of the world, preparing for her career in intelligence. After she left university, I found all her textbooks on the Soviet-Afghan War, the arming of the Mujahideen, the Bin Laden stakeout, but it never occurred to me she was on the other side of the fence. Why would it? I thought I knew her better than anybody. Turns out I just projected my fantasy of her onto her, and she comprehensively rejected it. In fact, she downright resented me for it. How could I have got it all so badly wrong? All this time, there was poison inside her. A poison that convinced her the Agents of Allah made a better family than the one I provided. She turned on me. She turned on all of us.'

'Don't blame yourself.'

'Have we investigated this Abs who befriended her at Oxford? Not to put too fine a point on it, but *you* were the one in charge of running background checks on Jody.'

Jim dropped his head. 'I ... *was* aware of him, to tell the truth. Grandson of Sultan Ghulam Ramazam, who fled with his family to Europe from Kabul in the Seventies, just before the Soviet invasion. He seemed clean, Mark. Maybe he was ... *too* clean. That itself should've been a clue. Oxford said nothing about any radicalisation, but ...'

'What?'

'I didn't exactly deep dive. She was your daughter. I trusted you, so I trusted her.'

Mark attempted another grin, but this one did hurt. 'It's not your fault.'

'London needs a full report, urgently.'

'Am I allowed my quadruple heart bypass surgery first?'

'Not saying it won't be successful, but they recommend doing the surgery afterwards.'

'You really should've been a comedian, Jim.'

'You went inside a Taliban cave and came out alive. There can't be many of us who can say that. Your intel is going to be invaluable. Truth be told, London's a little jealous the US knows more than we do right now, especially since this concerns our agent. She may be your daughter, but she was also a government operative. There'll be approximately ten thousand inquiries, our own *and* jointly with the US, given it was their dubious strategy of arming resistance groups that made most of this chaos possible. How William was getting hold of plutonium they may never tell us, but the resentment of the US presence here was always a ticking time bomb. Leaks were running deeper than anyone thought.'

'Twice.'

'Pardon?'

'I went inside a Taliban cave and came out alive, *twice*. I'll file a report, don't worry.'

'I knew we could rely on you. Make no mistake, you've more than done your part already. The retrieval operation is for others to worry about, but you know the caves. The world needs you, Mark.'

'You sound like you still write ads for Recruitment.'

'The US won't dare an airstrike, which means men on the ground going in. I know you're recuperating, and there are surgeries to come, but are you up for strategy meetings at your bedside? Generals flapping maps at you and whatnot? Because you'd better be. The Americans will go in hard.' He looked Mark's chest over. 'They put stents in my uncle last year, two of them. You'll be right as rain in no time.'

Mark lacked the energy to tell him his upcoming surgery was considerably more invasive, and Jim, mistaking his silence for concern, patted him on the arm the way one might a sickly child.

'Don't worry,' Jim said. 'This may be a Third World country with a life expectancy of forty-four, but I gather they have the best surgeons in the world. In Kabul, they have to be.'

An intangible quiet swam through the ward.

'There's something else, isn't there?' Mark said.

Jim locked his eyes firmly on the floor. 'This is delicate but ... The plan is for MI6 to officially designate Jody as a triple agent, that she helped get intelligence back to us regarding the theft of a weapon by the Taliban. Once the mission is successful, she'll be lauded.'

Mark watched the light play across the Hindu Kush outside the window.

'The Top Floor knows your part in this. Rest assured. You're the real hero here, Mark, but ... MI6 don't need her stain on the Service any longer so they're giving her a martyr's death, and the official line will be that she died in the line of duty ...'

'I get it.'

'She doesn't deserve this, but MI6 is desperate to restore the international community's faith in it. For your part in the operation, you'll be compensated. I daresay the New Year's Honours List will have your name on it in some capacity. Your daughter's deceit will never be known, officially, and you must admit this will be a great comfort to her mother, if not—'

'God damn it, I said *I get it.*'

The nurses at the workstation spun to observe the commotion at the bedside of the patient they'd been told to wrap in cotton wool, whom the US Chargé d'Affaires was visiting every day and the Lieutenant General had sent flowers to.

Mark lowered his voice. 'Of course London was going to respond this way. I understand perfectly how it works, Jim. You don't need to sugar-coat things for me. I've been in the game a long time. Has anyone ... informed my wife?'

'She knows you're alive, but she still doesn't know the ... *whereabouts* of your daughter.' There was a monumentally heavy pause. 'You haven't spoken to her.'

It was Mark's turn to avoid eye contact. It was true. He hadn't felt a phone call to Alessia would have been welcome. Notwithstanding the fact he'd left the country after revealing their entire life together had been a lie, there was the not insignificant matter of him being wholly responsible for the death of their only daughter.

'I'll break the news,' Mark said. 'It would be better from me.'

'No one's insisting you do that. We just need your blessing, that's all, to push ahead with this story. Leave it to me.'

'And Brandon? He doesn't deserve to find out his sister's dead by opening a news app.'

'I'm on it.' Jim stood to leave, then looked down at his broken friend. 'No one believes the decisions Jody made are a reflection on you, trust me. You've always gone way above and beyond what's expected of you. Your country owes you a huge debt.'

Mark sank further into the bed but was still unable to make himself invisible. 'What I've done for my country is irrelevant. I sold my daughter's soul to the devil, and I wasn't even aware I was doing so.'

'In time, you won't feel that way.'

'Won't I?' Beyond exhausted, Mark prepared to put voice to his greatest fear, the one which had been clawing through his head every second he'd been left alone, hunted him as he tried to sleep through the ticking and beeping of the insomniac ward. 'Jim, do you know much about nuclear warheads?'

'A little. Why?'

'Can they be ... detonated by hand? I mean, is there a switch on, say, a panel somewhere? How complex is the fusing system?'

'You're worried about the Taliban setting it off – we all are – but arming one is complicated; there are multiple mechanisms, all backed and interlocked with systems that make tampering almost impossible to those who don't know what they're doing.'

'But if someone *did* know what they were doing, would she be able to detonate it by hand?'

'She?'

'Whoever.'

'I'm not sure, Mark. I don't think so. There's no red button on the side of a nuke that someone can press to liquefy a city, if that's what you mean.'

A shrill beeping intensified.

'Mark ...? Are you OK?'

'Thanks for visiting.'

Mark could feel Jim's concerned eyes upon him for a time, and then the footsteps clicked across the ward and swished their owner out through the doors at the far end.

Alone, the terror settled back upon him. The light bled brighter through those curtains.

Bye, Dad.

Those words hadn't been a threat; merely a farewell.

Jody had accepted, at the end, what he'd needed to do, even if he never would.

And her finger on some sort of detonation lever was simply a bluff; she'd goaded him into taking the fatal shot, and her final curse upon him was the sure knowledge that his actions would haunt him forever. That was the true meaning behind her dying 'I win'. She'd always been a girl who refused to be slighted, who would do anything, anything, to avoid losing, and so, having found her plans thwarted, the least she could do was hide the most venomous snake she could in his backpack.

Footsteps returned twofold. Jim had dragged a nurse along with him.

The high-pitched beeping had evidently come from Mark's own heart monitor and a sedative was rapidly syringed into the IV drip on the back of his hand.

For some while, Mark drifted, Jim never leaving his bedside, even when the Americans came – broad-shouldered jocks in fatigues; Ivy League suits promoted to federal positions – and his former colleague handled most of the conversational heavy lifting on Mark's behalf.

The warhead was to be taken via military force – officially, no one save the National Security Councils of the US and UK knew there was a warhead in the Taliban's possession, so negotiation wasn't an option – but Mark's knowledge of the cave layout was essential for success and they quizzed him ragged as he squinted over maps, propped up in starched sheets.

The briefing was only considered over when Mark threw up blood into a kidney bowl.

'There's one thing, I haven't asked you,' Jim said as the Americans filed out with their heist plans.

Mark braced himself for the questions about his daughter's final moments and last words, prepared his soul for the exorcism. Maybe it would help, getting it off his chest.

'Yes, Jim?'

Jim nodded to the far end of the ward, to the brown-skinned man hooked up to mechanical ventilation, his eyes as closed as they'd been when he first entered.

'Who's the guy in the other bed?'

The shadow had reached through the dark and grabbed him. Powerless to resist, barely conscious, Mark found himself dragged through tunnels, a black ceiling scrolling above.

Mark explained to Jim how the difference in visibility between the inside of the cave and the sky itself had been so negligible he hadn't realised he'd been hauled all the way outside until he'd felt himself being scraped over rough, dry plants, at which point he'd tried to disentangle himself from the panting shadow and stand. This had proved difficult, and he found himself steered by the arm up the hillside as though he were blind.

Upon reaching the refuge of the wide rock Mark had previously been knocked out behind, Mark's unlikely rescuer had revealed himself to be Yusuf, holding his wounded stomach, the lower third of his payraan soaked black. Mark encouraged him to lift his shirt at the side so he could inspect the injury but, even in the dark, could tell it was an exit wound; the bullet had pierced him in the back and the resultant blood loss was substantial. He convinced Yusuf to keep his hand pressed tight over the torn flesh, but, in truth, didn't know if it would make any difference.

Yusuf and Abs, Mark clarified, had left the VW to find the cave network together. Perhaps Yusuf had taken a bullet in the siege. Perhaps Abs had shot him once he was no longer useful. It hardly mattered.

Mark had tended Yusuf's wounds as best he could before Yusuf delved into a pocket to produce a phone with a trembling hand. Mark took the mobile, rested his hand on the Hazara's shoulder then let Yusuf fall into the resulting crook of his body, where the younger man passed out, cradled in Mark's embrace. Knowing neither would survive the cold night unless he found help, Mark had gently pushed Yusuf's weight off him and shaken the phone through the air, hunting for a signal. There wasn't any. The number he'd had to ring, to call in the operation with the duty officer, was burned into his memory like his home address, but he'd need to limp undetected through the dark to find the abandoned van, and knew he was beyond that simple act.

Nevertheless, as he'd done throughout his entire life, when he couldn't go any farther, he forced himself to rally, and rose on shaking legs. Suddenly, remaining alive seemed more critical than before, as much for Yusuf's sake as for international security, and, one foot at a time, he climbed the mountain.

Six long hours it took him to find the van, trekking through the freezing, claustrophobic night. A night of wild animal eyes and burning hunger. A night in which, as a Jennifer Lopez fan had once explained to his *Angraiz*, even a minor fall could be fatal. A night through which he kept going, deeper and deeper into the lonely mountains, his lame body begging him to sink to the ground and embrace his future as food for vultures. A night when he finally found the VW and followed the stars back towards the cave mouth to scoop Yusuf up and prop his half-frozen form in the passenger seat. A night in which, on the outskirts of Kabul, the van's tank almost empty, the phone's battery showing four per cent and the tears freezing in his eyeballs, he'd found reception at last.

Contact was made, a signal traced, and a medevac helicopter from Bagram air base came screaming out of the pink dawn.

Yusuf's eyes opened.

Mark was sitting beside him; the artificial sleep of propofol had finally given him cause to rest after his surgery and the physiotherapists were recommending little walks around the ward so he often sat with the Hazara, to check on his recovery. They had no language in common, but Yusuf's dark brown eyes recognised Mark instantly and reciprocated the pained smile.

The nurses checked his vitals and took his readings, fussed up his pillow and made him comfortable. Normally, of course, a native wouldn't have ended up in an American military hospital but Mark, weak and near death, had threatened to break people's arms if they didn't admit him.

There was a television in the ward, permanently broadcasting an American news station, one of the less right-leaning, shouty ones, though it still sounded bombastic and self-congratulatory to Mark. That evening, they watched the story break.

Jody Wolfe, the anchor proclaimed, had died a saint's death, and the image of her that hung on the screen was the same photo the press had used when announcing her as a traitor. The tactical lack of a smile in her photo had, first time around, been seen as proof of her duplicity and untrustworthiness, but now it spoke of cool intelligence and counterplotting. It was retconning of a Machiavellian nature, rewriting the previous story of her deception as part of her meticulous cover. She was a twenty-first-century 'super spy', helping to foil a top-secret Taliban plot, potentially saving many lives in Kabul, including US military personnel. Even if Mark had been pumped full of father's pride at this news, he would still have considered this praise over the top. It was as though the media felt the need to make amends for their previous demonisation of her.

Yusuf watched the news broadcast with impassivity. How he'd got mixed up in any of this madness, his weary expression seemed to yell, was far beyond his comprehension.

The news was the final item before the weather, like an afterthought. This airbrushing of Jody's legacy to allow for the public repainting of SIS after her original scandal would have been the absolute *most* the US would have signed off on and exact details of her mission were 'understandably classified'. But, behind the scenes, Mark knew the US President was pedalling like mad to allay any fears the rumours of stolen munitions might have generated, probably pointing his fingers at Turkey and condemning their lax guardianship of weaponry stored at Incirlik Air Base. American and British culpability was being scrubbed from the record books as generously as Jody's betrayal.

It must have hurt the chiefs of the Western intelligence services to be building up a woman who was part of the very reason a bomb needed to be stolen back in the first place, why a detachment of armoured defusion experts had to risk their lives in a shadowy labyrinth against unpaid resistance fighters, but the appeal of a neat, nationalistic full stop was more palatable than the meandering sentences of the secret world's reality.

'You should go back to bed,' Mark was told by the nurse at his elbow. The small blood pressure monitor he wore on his index finger showed a systolic reading of nearly one hundred and seventy.

'Can't you switch that off? Who the hell put a television in a recovery ward anyway?'

'Other patients always seem to enjoy it. You don't mind, do you, Yusuf?'

The little man looked blankly at them both.

'It's all propaganda,' Mark muttered.

The television was switched off and Mark's blood pressure dropped almost instantly.

Their hospital was quiet again, but Mark knew the world outside was far from it. The truth was, the recent attack on the Taliban base – one of, intelligence suggested, dozens of such systems – didn't exactly herald a tidy end to the war, rather the start of a new bloody animosity. The news hadn't shown a single drive-by or market bomb since he and Yusuf had been hospitalised and, in the build up to the Americans' operation, it had been oddly peaceful out there in Kabul, but in much the same way birds vacate an area before a volcano's eruption. Nuclear peace had been only temporarily brokered.

Outside, the sun was beginning to set, the colourful strata of evening sliding behind the mountains and adding dusky solidity and shade to the ruts and creases that draped the sides of the lonely Hindu Kush.

Mark took a deep, surprisingly painless breath and brought his mobile phone to his mouth.

He'd been practising the speech.

'Alessia ... I'm sorry I wasn't the one to break the news. I know you must hate me, and you've every reason, but I need you to know ... I've been strung between two truths for a long time, but my life with you was never a lie. My past doesn't mean I've loved you less, nor did I groom Jody to be a spy, not intentionally. She ...' He wiped his eyes. The strain of mixing lies with facts had become second nature but his monologue, so far, had been an honest one. That was all about to change. 'Our daughter was a hero. I know that doesn't matter right now, to a mother who just wants to hold her baby girl in her arms, but you should be proud. She sacrificed herself so *millions* could live. She will never be forgotten, and died serving the country ... she ... loved.'

The silence on the end of the line became impossible to ignore.

Again, he hadn't had the nerve to ring home. No forgiveness filtered through from the void, but no blame either.

Mark dropped the dead phone. Maybe one day he'd deliver the well-practised message for real.

Yusuf looked away as Mark, for what he resolved to be the last time, wept.

His mission had been to save Jody; yet he'd been the one who'd taken her life. In time, he might look back on her short existence on this planet and find a degree of acceptance for who she'd become, perhaps even smile again at some of her childhood antics and foibles, but Mark certainly had no intention, while the free world lionised his daughter in front of the flashbulbs of a hungry global press, of manufacturing a false pride that might kickstart the process of lying to himself about who she was all over again.

Still the secrets. Still the lies. But the truth about Jody was one that would have to die with him — his heart felt like someone else's; her betrayal his to bear alone — and he wondered how long before the knowledge of what he'd done to her ate him completely.

Mark stood and reached for Yusuf's hand, then kissed him lightly on both cheeks, indicating goodbye. 'Thank you,' he said.

Yusuf understood. '*Khahesh mikonam.*'

The Hazara watched Mark with a sad smile as he strode across sterile air and vinyl floor to his own bed and slid open his bedside drawer. He slipped on his trousers with the ghost of a familiar protest from his left-hand side.

A voice fired from the nurse's workstation. 'Going somewhere?'

'Decompression's over,' announced the former Head of Recruitment and Asset Validation as he reached for his jacket. 'I can't rot here, watching traitorous TV reports hour after empty hour.'

The nurse threw him a quizzical look. 'I sure don't think you're ready to leave, sir.'

'I'm going anyway. I don't have a home to go to anymore, not really, but my mission's over.' He thrust on his ruined shoes.

'I can't tell you where I'm heading, because I'm not certain myself, but I guarantee your physiotherapists would agree with me that I need to keep moving.'

As his nurse watched in disbelief, Mark Wolfe ignored the protests from his own bruised body and strode as fast as he could from the bone-white ward.

Acknowledgements

Writing a novel, it'll be no surprise to hear, can be a lonely job. Unlike the life of a professional musician, for example, where collaboration with actual human beings is often essential to the art, so much of the life of a novelist depends upon dragging yourself to the laptop when many other more sociable pursuits exist to distract you. Even the long walks that generate story ideas are necessarily undertaken alone. But the most joyful part of the process, and often the most terrifying, is when drafts are shared and the job, after months of isolation, allows for a brief moment of harmonising. I have been blessed to have had assistance throughout this book's journey from some fine voices indeed.

Huge thanks go to Matthew Strawson, always my first reader, who gently pointed out embarrassing errors before they became dangerously embedded and provided much-needed early encouragement. Likewise, Louise Greenberg, who was there for me with structuring suggestions, and knew exactly which words needed to stay and which had to go in the bin.

The contributions of my literary agent, James Wills, have been phenomenal and I must publicly thank him for his patience and diligence, and especially for his advice with the end of this book. Thank you also to Hannah Weatherill at Watson Little for shouting the novel's praises as widely as possible. Massive thanks to my editor at Bonnier Zaffre, Ben Willis, whose meticulous notes helped stick the landing, and also to Jon and Rianna and the rest of the team for help fine-tuning.

Lastly, heartfelt love and gratitude to Patricia, Ben and Lorelei. I don't have the words to express what your invaluable support means to me, but this book wouldn't have been possible without you.

Keep reading for an exclusive extract of the next
Mark Wolfe thriller

A Funeral for a Spy

Coming soon

1

THE HUMID MAY AFTERNOON FADED on Capri. A dagger of light was all that remained of the direct sunlight in the private courtyard, and it hung against the whitewashed wall above the elderly spy's head like a cartoon arrow pointing out the man beneath the legend. At least, that's what his guest thought at the time, for the longer he spent in the older man's company, the more he was inclined to think in metaphors. It was the geopolitically explosive final year of the eighties, though neither man could have predicted just how explosive it would soon turn out to be.

The younger man, recalling the green placard bearing the word *Vendesi* outside the compact property, said, 'I noticed your For Sale sign.'

A chuckle at this. 'Perhaps I always have been.' The elderly gentleman's voice was a soft, well-educated lisp, but his eyes were as sharp as the English slate he'd left behind. 'A man is his home. And yet, inevitably, decor will fall out of favour and once-valued guests move on.' He swept a languid arm across the canopy of clear sky behind the curtain of serpentine vines. 'It is the way of things. I don't have much longer within these walls. Are you sure you won't take a drink?'

Mark Wolfe refused and the old man nodded, pleased with the novice's professionalism. Perhaps it had been more of a test than a genuine offer.

'You don't mind if I ...?'

'Go ahead.'

Mark watched him pour himself a shot of *grappa* from the slender bottle on the table between them.

'The doctors say I shouldn't,' the older man admitted, 'but it's a habit one can't shake off. Much like the sacraments, I dare say.'

On light feet, Mark rose and trod to the high wall adjacent to the alleyway, checking for eavesdroppers. A slice of the Tyrrhenian sparkled behind the pines, her boats insectoid and luxuriant. The warm breeze still rustled the new shoots on the fig tree at the perimeter of the patio.

'I detect *la forza* within you, Mark. You move like a handsome tomcat but there is a wild attitude beneath the surface. You haven't been long out of the military, have you?'

Mark studied the blue landscape the way a hawk watches a burrow. 'You've owned this home a while?'

'Forty years. Visit twice a year. In four weeks, I complete the work of six months elsewhere but, between you and me, I don't consider myself overly talented. It's simply a matter of putting in the hours. Are you ... gifted in your field?'

'I'm still standing.' Mark's voice was as tight as the Fairbairn-Sykes knife strapped to his left calf muscle.

'Young men all feel immortal, especially once they've looked death in the face. I'm not prying. I know you can't tell, not even an old man who'll soon be taking his sordid tales to the ground.'

He stood, his glass already empty, then shuffled inside. There was something noble and haunted about him, Mark thought. Like a man whose years had crept up on him by mistake. At that moment, Mark knew with unshakeable conviction he himself would never make it to old age.

He followed him indoors.

Like the outside of the property, the interior was whitewashed, bare. This was a utilitarian idyll, devoid of unnecessary personality, where the old man came to avoid distractions, nothing more. Even the bougainvillaea spilling across the front windows was somehow less ostentatious than the neighbours'.

'Have the Camorra always been here?' Mark asked, sensing it was now safer to ask the questions he needed to.

'Of course. I've never been able to abide bullies. I had a similar experience with the mafia in the Côte d'Azur. My pamphlet about it didn't come to much.' He creaked towards his armchair. 'I wanted to see the man they'd sent. Forgive my curiosity; I'm interested in people.'

'It's no problem.'

'You're at the beginning of your intelligence career. I'm at the end. Though I never got my hands too dirty. Traded knowledge for half a century. That's me. A simple peddler of stories.'

'I read one of your books,' Mark said, surprising himself.

'Trifles,' the older man announced. 'Was it an entertainment or one of my literary follies?'

Mark kept his eyes on the vast view out of the window. It was almost time. In two hours, if all went well, he'd be wearing another man's blood on his hands. 'The one about the vacuum salesman.'

'Ah, an *entertainment*.' The delight was controlled, and as the eyes sparkled Mark saw a glimpse of the attractive face he must have worn when younger. The jowls were doughy now, and the eyes hooded, and the overall demeanour was not dissimilar to a politician who'd fallen into disgrace, or perhaps a member of the clergy – an image prompted by the crucifix upon the wall – caught with his trousers down. A handkerchief was flourished from his pocket and he coughed violently into it. 'This is my last summer here. I wanted this matter dealt with before I departed for good.'

'Of course.'

'We English are experts at sticking our noses into other people's business, aren't we? But not everything can be left to Uncle Sam, especially in Europe. There are rumours of Germany's reunification, the Cold War seems to be thawing, but money still makes men mad, and there is evil at work where there is profiteering. Did I already ask whether you wanted a drink?'

Mark glanced at his watch. 'I should go.'

'How do you plan to get off the island afterwards?'

'I have a route. The *carabinieri* won't trouble me.'

The man's eyes flashed, as though remembering a past life. 'They might come here. To see if I've heard anything.'

Mark was strangely touched by the old spy's fantasy. This man was a long way past his days of field work, the hungry traveller frequenting the fleshpots of Cuba, the Congo, Nicaragua, but he still dared to think he might enjoy one last adventure.

Mark remembered the wire hidden beneath his jacket and asked, 'Have you really retired? Do spies ever?'

'Not really.'

'And if someone asked you to cross the river one last time?'

When he finally spoke it was as though he did so for the direct benefit of the tape machine Mark would listen back to, thirty years later. 'I'm crossing it now, aren't I?'

'This is hardly Indochina.'

'It is for the families who can't escape the iron grip of the Camorra. For those who pay with their lives if protection money is beyond their budget. This is a rich part of Italy they operate from, but across the bay there' – he gesticulated towards unseen Naples – 'poverty fights to raise its head with dignity. The river you speak of cannot be rowed back on. Like Macbeth, I am too steeped in blood: "*Should I wade no more, returning were as tedious as go o'er.*"'

A sharp noise – maybe a bird taking flight – slanted Mark's head towards the outside world.

'There you go again: acting like an animal only marginally at ease with his feral instincts. I think, if we weren't playing for the same team, you'd scare me just a little, Mark.'

'Why did you get in touch with London after all this time? You must have suspected these men a while.'

'The exact nature of the power behind them was lost on me until … Last month, a minister was butchered in his bed for daring to speak against "the family". This group of criminal thugs influencing government policy at the highest level are a threat to the very diplomatic security of the Union. It's simply not how the rest of us play cricket.'

Mark grunted in agreement. But his government wasn't averse to the occasional spot of ball-tampering, he knew.

'By the "power behind them", you mean Russia?'

'Where a blind eye's turned towards corruption, you'll always find Moscow. This is a wealthy island. The men here are more than a *sottosezione* of the Camorra, they're practically their own rogue mafia, and they don't answer exclusively to their Neapolitan heads any longer. Believe me, they're in the pockets of the Soviet Union. I'd like to think I've put the Communist rumours surrounding me to bed, but I can understand why MI6 remain concerned; they do so insist on thinking in black and white.'

Mark took a decisive step towards the door. 'They're meeting in an hour.'

The elderly gentleman scrutinised Mark as if the next move in a chess game needed playing. 'They'll be late. They're Italian. Would it seem odd if I were to be present at our little accident?'

'Yes.'

He crept from the living room nevertheless, slowly unfolding himself as he did so, then out through the short hallway, sweeping his cream-coloured coat around his shoulders like a bullfighter. Only when the man's back was halfway up the short pathway outside his property, fiddling with the bolt on his wrought-iron gate, did Mark relent and follow.

'Being seen together is operationally unwise,' he said as he overtook the old man.

The laugh behind him was deadpan. 'I'd have died of boredom in Berkhamsted if I thought running into danger unwise. You're about to start a war, and I'd like to be there for its first strike.'

*

Mark waited in Piazza Umberto, where chattering tourists now sat in almost total shade. The view of the sea to the east side of the square was drowned in a human tide of photographers, as were the smoothed, grey steps leading to the church of Santa Stefano. A flower-seller ran the gauntlet between tired tourists, but Mark never saw him make a sale. More often than not, his advances encouraged the sightseers farther into winding streets which turned back on themselves, swallowing the travellers in their cool, steep stone, where the smells of diesel and sunscreen and limoncello were equally strong and the expensive sandal shops and perfumeries jostled for filthy lire from yachters and royalty alike. The contrast to Anacapri, where the old novelist had made his second home, was stark.

Couples wandered in and out of the square as he sipped water at his cafe table, ignoring the sound of the chittering cameras being wound on, the keening gulls, the praying bells. He focused on his target five tables away.

Andrea Angellotti, a suspected *caporegime* for the key Caprese family, lit a cigarette and awaited his aperitivo, which arrived in lightning-fast time, ahead of everyone who'd ordered before him. He was dressed in pale, pastel colours, pristine ice-white deck shoes. Aviator sunglasses were as dark as his hair, his teeth whiter than the cardigan draped around broad shoulders. His flirting with the waitress was like that of a spoiled child; he pulled at her apron, sized her up, and generally acted like he owned the place in that way aggressive tomcats do when marking their territories.

Through the square, another well-dressed man – if not an *over*dressed one; the red carnation upon a black suit came off as showy in the dwindling heat – sharked towards Andrea, but the intended target didn't stand, simply gestured to the seat opposite, offered the small bowl of olives.

This new man was Roberto Esposito, a *consigliere*, or advisor, within the Neapolitan crime family. The summer seemed to have visited him before anybody else; his skin was as dark as teak.

There would have been several members of both families planted within the diners, Mark knew, to ensure no one got too heated and he'd identified a few of them already. That large, black-eyed man who sat on his own without a drink. The pair who didn't speak to one another, yet both faced the same direction at their single table.

Mark had known about this meeting for a couple of days. It was the last piece of information his mole had passed on before being dropped off the side of a two-masted schooner with his throat cut by – according to a member of the Italian secret police – Signore Esposito himself. This Caprese family, in the eyes of the Neapolitans, were having ideas above their station and the levels of *pizzo*, or protection money, coming across the bay to the Camorra had dwindled in recent years despite a tourist boom.

Mark felt the gun in his armpit, as ever-present as a tumour. Simple as his mission was, Mark knew it would be difficult to get Esposito alone.

The conversation between the two Italians started off quiet, but soon grew animated, with the newcomer's expression turning darker as the shadows lengthened. Mark didn't understand much Italian, but from this distance it hardly mattered. The heavies stationed around the square watched the pair with impassivity, but hands were ready at jacket pockets and belts. The gunfight would quickly turn into a massacre if even one of those trigger-happy soldiers misread a signal.

Finally, after maybe ten minutes, the conversation seemed to calm and, shortly after, the Neapolitan *consigliere* stood. His body language within his sharp black suit didn't reveal whether he'd been forced to relent or had scored whatever deal or compromise he'd wanted with this allegedly renegade mafia faction. While Andrea finished off his aperitivo, Roberto Esposito strode past the sightseers to the funicular and three men stationed throughout the square peeled from their positions at separate tables, then threw down money for their drinks and followed.

Mark waited a moment, observed two further men leave, probably members of the Caprese family checking the Neapolitans were departing their island, then stood too, strolling with languid, tourist insouciance to the same queue Roberto and his own watchers now stood in. The funicular door clattered open and they all entered.

Heavily, the carriage descended, the sound of her giant chain straining every link as the smell of mildew commingled with the sweat of weary sightseers. The Camorra wore tight, indurate expressions and were clearly family, so similar were their sun-baked features.

Re-emerging into dying daylight, Mark followed the Neapolitans across the breezy port towards moored boats bobbing on the crystal waters. He watched them stop for *croquette* from a vendor along the coast, and the men ate from napkins as they crossed the harbour while the tourists swarmed, thronging to the restaurants before their last ferries home. Across the water, Vesuvius slept.

Mark spotted the elderly novelist in the first cafe, a copy of *la Repubblica* half concealing his face, empty espresso cup on the tablecloth.

Behind them all, the next funicular disembowelled itself of passengers, including members of the Caprese gang, minus their *caporegime*, and the group began to wander the *lungomare* like alley cats keeping a wary distance.

Quickly identifying the boat that belonged to the Neapolitans, gleaming chrome and dark wood, the most expensive docked on the shimmering green, Mark jogged past a further three boats before climbing aboard a fragile-looking sloop and pressing himself flat on the deck. The sky still wore streaks of light from the fading sun, claw marks of some heavenly beast desperately trying to scratch its way into the Sorrentine peninsula.

Unhurried, arrogant, Roberto Esposito and his men finally boarded their vessel, their Caprese rivals watching carefully.

The moment came.

When their boat started up – a guttural, throaty expulsion of toxins – Mark fired, the gunshot drowned beneath the roar of the engine.

The *consigliere* span with the impact then crashed, limp, to the deck.

Keeping low, Mark jumped into the neighbouring yacht, then the sailboat beyond, a smaller vessel which rocked a seismic shudder beneath him and almost disgorged him into the shallow harbour waters. The key was in the ignition, as his man within the Italian secret service promised it would be, and he hastily switched on the engine and thrust the control handle into forward before hopping off the boat, as casually as though arriving for a date on the island, and down the gangplank leading to the Naples' ferry.

The shouts grew as the Esposito family became aware of what had happened. Mark stopped to watch them; walking away was the obvious play, but this was no time for amateur dramatics so he reacted the way everyone else was. Some tourists on the dock scrambled towards the commotion but when guns were drawn from the Esposito boat the onlookers dispersed in haste. Bullets drummed into the stern of Mark's weaving decoy vessel as the public babbled in fitful prayer and the human klaxon of confusion and panic rang out.

The spies for Andrea Angellotti, alert to the trouble, turned and, with a false guilt that couldn't have been bought, hurried up a set of tight steps behind one of many gift shops. An incensed Esposito charged towards them, right hand on the gun poorly concealed in his jacket pocket, the crowd tearing itself in two to allow him through. Tables and chairs scattered in their hurried wake.

A sole member of the Neapolitan Camorra remained on his boat with his fallen *consigliere*, steady eyes still scanning the harbour. As his gaze settled on Mark, the young agent felt an electrical charge pass through him, like the premonition of a life spent in fear. For two, three seconds, they seemed to look into each other's souls, then Mark shrugged and walked on.

Across the quay, silhouetted like some pre-Raphaelite masterpiece beneath the swelling sunset, the driverless decoy crunched its bow into the timber causeway as smoke coughed from its stunned engine.

And at his table, baristas flapping around him, the retired spy watched the chaos with stoic eyes like camera-shutters, hungrily recording events for whatever posterity he had left.